# Every Season under Heaven

## Harold Neufeld

ISBN: 978-1-990827-14-3



As a work of historical fiction, *Every Season Under Heaven* uses the actual names of the principal characters. Although key events in each chapter are based on source material and historical research, many aspects of the narrative, the memoir sections in chapter 2, and dialogue are the author's own extrapolations.

The publication of this manuscript has received financial support from the Gerhard Lohrenz Publication Fund, administered by Canadian Mennonite University.

The *Kroeger* represented on the cover is the author's original reproduction and both the background cover and author photos are by Tobia Neufeld.

The photo preceding Chapter 1, depicting the factory workers in Sergejewka, appears courtesy of the Centre for Mennonite Brethren Studies, Winnipeg.

Scripture translations of Ecclesiastes 3:1 are taken from the King James Version, Luther (1912), and also rendered in Plattdeutsch.

*For Tobia and Andrew, Bennett and Russell,*

*and in loving memory of Stefan*

To every thing
there is a season,
and a time to every purpose
under heaven.

Aules haft siene Jeläajenheit;
doa es eene Tiet fe jieda Sach oppe Ieed.

*Ein jegliches hat seine Zeit, und alles Vornehmen
unter dem Himmel hat seine Stunde.*

You can not libel the dead, I think,

you can only console them.

— Anne Enright, The Gathering (2007)

# CONTENTS

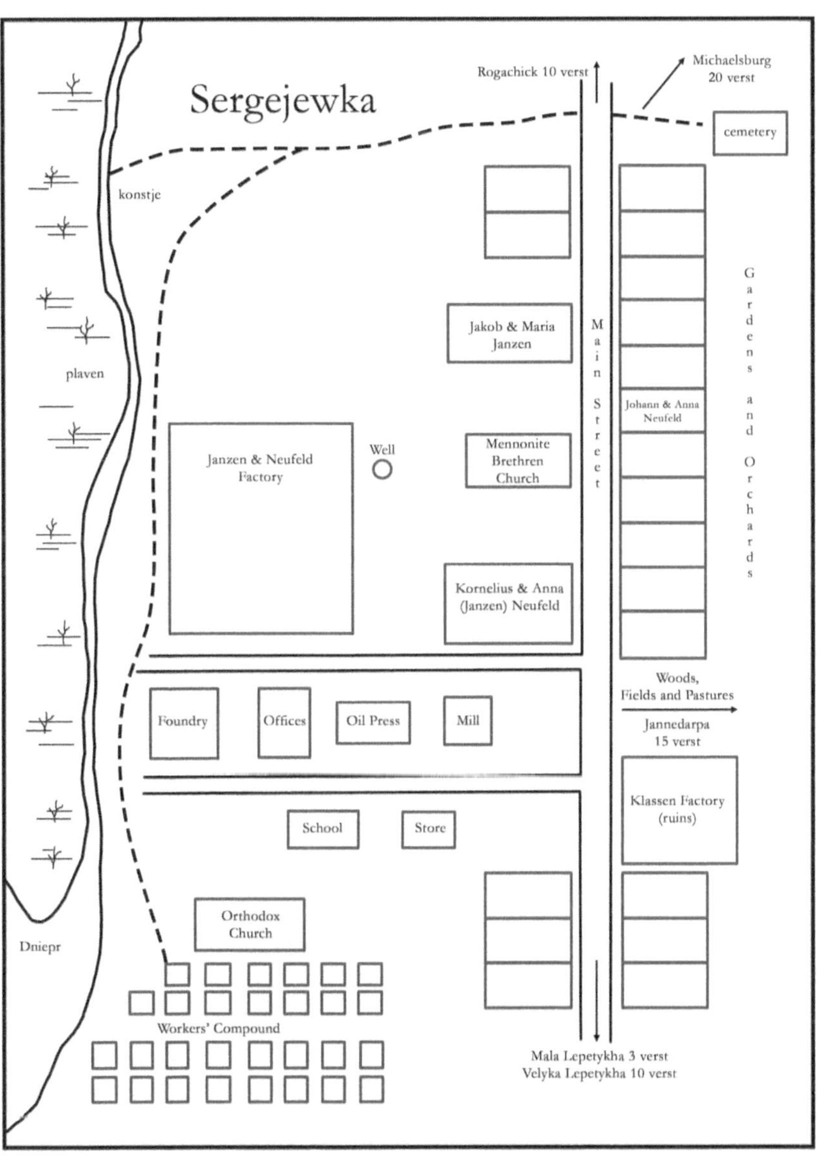

Sergejewka
Rogachick 10 verst
Michaelsburg 20 verst
cemetery
konstje
plaven
Jakob & Maria Janzen
Main Street
Johann & Anna Neufeld
Gardens and Orchards
Well
Janzen & Neufeld Factory
Mennonite Brethren Church
Kornelius & Anna (Janzen) Neufeld
Woods, Fields and Pastures
Jannedarpa 15 verst
Foundry
Offices
Oil Press
Mill
Klassen Factory (ruins)
School
Store
Orthodox Church
Dniepr
Workers' Compound
Mala Lepetykha 3 verst
Velyka Lepetykha 10 verst

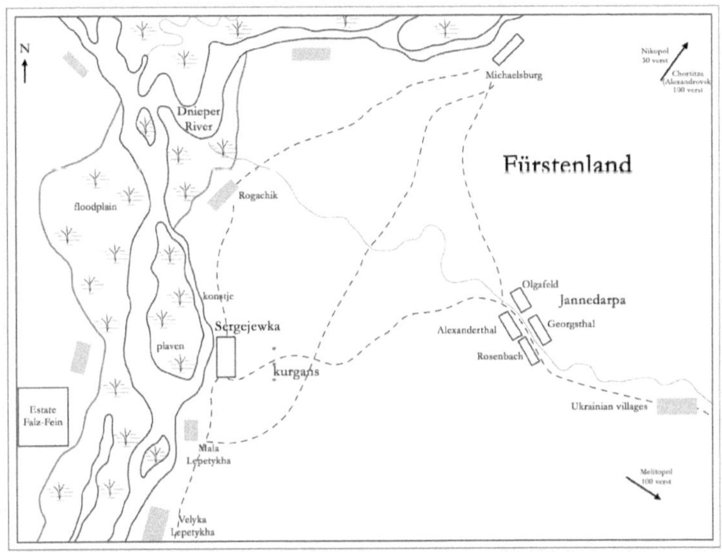


N
Dnieper River
floodplain
Rogachik
konstje
Sergejewka
plaven
kurgans
Estate Falz-Fein
Mala Lepetykha
Velyka Lepetykha
Michaelsburg
Fürstenland
Olgafeld
Jannedarpa
Alexanderthal
Georgsthal
Rosenbach
Ukrainian villages
Nikopol 30 verst
Chortitza Alexandrovsk 100 verst
Melitopol 100 verst

# 1. February 1928

Johann stands in the falling dark and hunches his shoulders against the gale. Snow and wind overwhelm his senses, and he chills quickly after his labour in the warmth of the cattle stalls. He knows he must soon enter the house, but a sudden surge of hopelessness overwhelms him, and he doesn't want to show himself there before it passes. The oldest sons have known for some time. He knows they read his moods, though, of course, they will not expose him by speaking openly. Sixteen-year-old Jasch, especially, who works with his father every day, remembers the well-ordered fields on the banks of the Dniepr, and how, as long as the rains came, labour was translated there into prompt and visible reward. For Jasch, the contrast is obvious. The oldest daughter Annie — *Njuta* — knows too. At eighteen, short and wiry, she has returned from the city and works as hard as anyone. She can see how little has been achieved in this first year.

And his dear Anna? She is both pragmatic and optimistic, and she tries to encourage him. "We promised — how did they say at the English wedding? - *for better or for worse*," she said this morning as she cracked the ice in the water bucket.

"*Ja*," he had replied, "*ja, ja*. Already I can see a bit of butter, but so far not much *Wurst*." He loves that she laughs at his quips. She is strong and lovely but so very thin, and she cannot conceal her fatigue and the terrible headaches that attack her almost daily. And now, with another child on the way, how will it be? He knows she scans his face at mealtimes while he is occupied with one child or another and that she registers his restlessness at night after he turns from her. And he knows, too, that she shares none of his regret at leaving Sergejewka on Dniepr.

Above him, denser clouds swirl in from the northwest and the wind increases, driving the heavy snowfall across the yard. He sighs and trudges toward the house along the passage he had the boys cut through the snowbanks after school that afternoon. By morning it will have filled in, and if the drifts are firm enough to walk on after another cold night, perhaps it need not be cleared again.

The farmyard lies in the dead centre of a square mile section of mostly scrubland, three-quarters of which Johann purchased just before Christmas a year ago after a hurried inspection with the land agent from Winnipeg. The owners, a family of the earlier *Kanadier* Mennonite immigrants, had signed on with a conservative group leaving for Mexico after the Canadian government renewed its insistence on compulsory education in the English language. They had been scheduled to leave Canada in February, and the agent gave his word that the farmhouse would be vacated and ready for occupancy by the 1st of March. But Sawatzky had died on New Year's Day, and alone with five children, his widow had no prospects. All her relatives had already emigrated, and unless they were prepared to take her in once they were settled in Mexico, she was destitute.

Johann and Anna had been cautioned about the risks of moving onto the bald prairie in the middle of winter. When they knocked to give notice, their landlady on Dufferin Avenue gasped in astonishment.

"Now? In this terrible winter?" She offered reduced rates, should they decide to stay, if she could count on an hour or two of housekeeping assistance from Anna. The land agent, too, had prevailed upon Johann and his two oldest sons to keep their jobs in the dairies of *Weidman &* *Fehr* for a few more months. Njuta had found secure employment as a housemaid with a Jewish family in Winnipeg's North End, and she was promised full room and board in addition to her wages if she could stay on for the winter. She would be frugal, she said, and her earnings could go to paying off the *Reiseschuld* the railway company had advanced for travel from Russia to Canada.

Eventually, Johann had agreed to a month's delay. But he had scrimped to make the earliest possible deposit on the farm, and was determined to settle his family and organize their affairs well before seeding time. Njuta could stay with the Bronsteins for now, but he could not do without the boys. He would take possession of the land at the end of March, and the widow Sawatzky would have to see to her accommodation one way or another.

Upon arrival on the first day of April, most of their plans had fallen to shreds. Still grieving the loss of her husband, Greta Sawatzky had made no effort to move out. A letter from in-laws in Chihuahua promised grudging support, but not until the emigrants had established themselves sufficiently to take her in, likely not until the summer. In the farmhouse, only the kitchen and the adjoining bedroom where she slept with her youngest two children had any heat. Clearly, she could not be thrown out into the snow.

Opposite the house, at the edge of the garden, was a small summer kitchen. Five paces by six, it would be home to Johann and Anna and six children for the next ten weeks until the snow receded and God's good earth emerged. The cookstove would provide enough heat, and a few planks thrown across the table at night, and covered with sacking stuffed with straw, made a bed large enough for the youngest children. Jasch and Hans slept underneath, and Johann and Anna filled the slot behind the low wall of firewood with more straw for themselves. The cattle cars they had ridden out of Russia in November of '26 had been even less comfortable, but the journey from Sergejewka to Riga had taken only seven days; it would be seventy, before the widow Sawatzky abandoned her plans for Mexico and moved in with relatives in Niverville.

Inside the house, Jasch and Hans are engaged in horseplay near the wash basin, laughing and slapping towels at each other. Mariechen is fourteen, and she passes dishes down to Peter, who is helping to set the table. At five o'clock it is already dark, and the kerosene lamp flecks the tablecloth with dancing shadows. Anna sweeps aside the burlap that curtains the kitchen window, but she can see nothing through the rime crusting the single pane of glass between her and the blizzard. Johann usually comes in with the boys, but tonight he is delayed. She slides the pot of soup back over the heat and begins ladling water from the bucket into the kettle.

She is about to ask the boys about their father when she hears his step on the veranda.

Johann shuffles in, stamping snow off his boots and cupping his hands around his breath. Removing his cap and taking in the room, he leans over for little Helene, who toddles over to him expectantly. He scratches her cheek with his chin stubble, which sets her squirming and giggling for more. Then he tousles Abram's hair while looking over at Peter, who is frail and quiet, calling over to him. "*Na*, Peterchen, what are you up to?"

The boy looks up but does not answer. He had been hospitalized with meningitis immediately upon arrival in Winnipeg and has not fully recovered.

Anna sets a platter of potatoes in the centre of the table, and when all are seated, the chatter subsides as they wait for Johann. The grace he says this evening is extempore and longer than usual. He prays for the wellbeing of his mother, and Anna's, back in Russia. He names sisters and brothers, uncles and aunts, and prays for the safety of their families. He prays especially for his younger brother Peter, who has recently returned to Sergejewka after months of imprisonment on charges no one understands. In the only letter they have received since leaving Russia, Peter's wife, Neta, writes ... '*he hardly speaks. He is broken in body and spirit. He cannot work and I fear for his mind.*'

Finally, Johann expresses thanks for the health of his own family and for the food they are about to receive. But tonight Anna notices the omission of the gratitude, standard among Mennonite émigrés, *'for freedom and release from the oppression of Russia.*'

Johann's first full survey of the yard and buildings in April of 1927 had revealed an enterprise in advanced stages of neglect. The door of the cattle shed dangled on a single rusted hinge, and most of the windows were cracked or broken. When the snowmelt began, the great mounds next to the barn that Johann had assumed were hay turned out to be cattle manure amassed over many years. Of the four cows and a calf Johann had seen in December, and which were included in the purchase contract, only one cow remained. Emaciated and mangey, it had long since stopped producing milk, and stood motionless between two thin horses. What had become of its calf, Johann could not discover. The entire barn floor was covered in compacted manure so thick that the horses could not raise their heads without meeting the ceiling. A dozen scraggly chickens wandered about the premises, fending for themselves as they dodged the hooves of the larger animals. The additional livestock granted him by the *Canadian Pacific Railway* (CPR) — a sturdy horse and a Jersey heifer — arrived in May, but both beasts shied from the closeness of the accommodations, and Johann decided to keep them in an adjacent lean-to until the barn could be cleaned.

The outbuildings had been similarly neglected. In the granary, a scurry of field mice sounded as Johann opened the door. The small heap of grain in one of the compartments was mostly chaff and black wild oats. The other two bins were empty. When Johann went to the house to inquire as to the whereabouts of last year's crop, Mrs. Sawatzky nodded in the direction of the fields. Her husband had been too ill to harvest, she said, and in any case, the stand of wheat had been too poor to warrant the expense of a threshing crew. What of her two oldest sons, sturdy boys of fourteen and seventeen, Johann asked. Surely they could at least have kept the barn clean and the cattle fed. The poor woman did not meet his eyes. She shook her head, sighing her mute despair as she turned away, leaving Johann at the door.

Spring came early that year. Well before the move from the summer kitchen to the house, most of the snow was gone, and everywhere the sun coaxed swirls of vapour from the blackening fields. Four hundred eighty acres — ten times the size of his farm in Ukraine. He had wanted to buy only the quarter section with the house and yard, but there was no room for negotiation. '*Alles oder nix,*' the agent had said. Johann had opted for *alles*, knowing that nothing would come of *nix*. He also knew that most of the land had never been cultivated and that years of hard work faced him and his children if they were to clear and plant enough to live on, let alone sell sufficient produce to pay off the mortgage and the travel debt. He was not afraid of hard work, and neither were his sons and daughters, but it puzzled him mightily that two previous generations of *Kanadier* Mennonites had not managed to clear more than fifty acres in as many years and that, overall, the farm was in such appalling condition.

Perhaps, Johann thought, the cluster of graves the children had discovered a quarter mile from the house was a clue. Without a family of robust sons and daughters, farming, here as in the old country, was not viable. Only one stone still stood partially erect, the only one professionally cut.

It marked the grave of a young woman — *Margaretha Penner (1890-1919)*. Around it were scattered the graves of children, their crude markers of wood and stone fallen and thatched with dead weeds and grasses. The few dates still legible linked them to the flu epidemic of a decade earlier.

When the spring melt did not flow obediently off the land, the puzzle was clarified further. This soil was quite unlike the sandy fields on the banks of the Dniepr. The upper layer quickly became waterlogged, while the heavy clay underneath remained frozen long after warm weather roused the farmer's urge to plant. Equally troublesome was the overall contour of the land. Everywhere, dense stands of poplar and willow thrived, shielding the shallow sloughs from the force of the sun. The agent had boasted about drainage canals running west to the Red River, but as Johann soon learned from his neighbours, the canals often flooded due to their inadequate size and the tendency for their steep sides to collapse or else to become choked with weeds and scrub. On the scattered acres that had been cleared and cultivated, every depression became a shallow lake. The largest of these provided nocturnal roosts for returning waterfowl, and they would not dry until well after it was too late to plant. Wild geese were a welcome addition to the family diet, surely, but bread flour would be scarce until more acres could be cleared and drained.

While waiting for the fields to dry, Johann had set the boys to rehabilitating the farmyard. The livestock were tethered outdoors to browse the early grass and dandelions, and the boys began clearing the barn. With pitchfork, pick, and shovel, they peeled back layer upon layer of manure and loaded it onto the wooden sledge. The task was made more ghastly by periodic discoveries of putrefying carcasses of newborn calves and a colt. Late one evening, Jasch, working alone in the gloom, bolted when an otherworldly squawk burst from the bloated lungs of a dead chicken underfoot.

Johann was an expert horseman, and his first act upon arrival on the farm, almost before the luggage was fully unpacked, had been to purchase hay and oats from old Mr. Muir, one of the *Änglische* neighbours who also lent him a wagon to haul it the half mile home. By the time their labour was required, the horses had been well fed and groomed for a month, and could be persuaded to haul the endless loads of manure to enrich the gardens and the nearby fields. When the barn was clean and repaired, Johann arranged for additional credit to buy a dozen milk cows and a team of young workhorses. On the day he and the boys drove them overland from the railroad station in Niverville and corralled them in the meadow, he summoned Anna and the children to the centre of the yard, and under the vast canopy of sky and sun, they joined hands and sang a hymn of thanksgiving to celebrate the beginning of their lives as Canadian farmers.

At the table, there is usually much talk and laughter. The toddlers clamour for the attention of their older siblings whom they have missed during the school day. Njuta and Jasch, whose labours are required at home, do not attend school but they and their mother quiz the young scholars and try to absorb the English words and phrases they bring home. Sometimes Johann joins in, mocking explosively the bizarre consonant clusters and confusing diphthongs of '*Eng-Glitsch*!' to the delight of Anna. For Hans and Mariechen, and especially for shy little Peter, school is an ordeal. Each of them is a head taller than anyone else in their grades, and they are humiliated by the smirks of their *Kanadier* seatmates as they struggle with the rudiments of the language. Only Abram is the right age for first grade, and he seems singularly untroubled. Fortunately, the teacher is *onsa-eena* — 'one of ours' — and unless the school inspector is present, a significant number of each day's lessons are conducted in German — stories and poems, Bible lessons, rehearsal of the catechism and, at the end of the day, the singing of familiar folk songs and hymns. Herr Fast is fifty, stern but understanding. He pays kind attention to Hans, who will soon be fourteen and will likely not attend next year, drilling him in English pronunciation and providing reading materials to take home for practice. Although the children mimic Fast's failure to sing in tune, and joke about his immense eyebrows and moustache, they respect him, as indeed they are regularly admonished to do.

Tonight, the banter around the supper table is more subdued. In mid-afternoon, while Johann was hauling a sledge-load of firewood from Kleefeld, the weather had turned quickly. Anna sent Jasch early to guide the schoolchildren through the storm, and they had arrived home exhausted. Now, with the heavy round of chores behind them — milking and feeding the cattle, splitting firewood and bringing water from the well — they quickly succumb to the warmth of the kitchen and the pleasures of the meal. There are moments when the only sounds are the ticking of the *Kroeger* clock on the wall and the irregular crescendos of the blizzard.

After the meal, Hans pulls out his harmonica, but he quickly tires of it and wanders upstairs to find Jasch. Little Abram is busy teasing his sisters, snatching at their dolls or tugging their braids until they squeal. His energy is undiminished; he rode on Jasch's shoulders most of the way home from school and is still too young for farm chores. On a stool near the stove, ten-year-old Peter is occupied with the collection of arrowheads he and his brothers found near the ancient Crow Wing trail during the summer. He arranges them in the cigar box where he also keeps his sling-shot. When he is done, he calls Abram and they follow their older brothers upstairs.

Njuta and Mariechen finish cleaning the dishes and take Lena away to prepare her for bed, leaving Johann and Anna alone at the table. They reread the letter from Johann's brother in Sergejewka and ponder steps they might take to help him and Neta emigrate. Anna is tired, and Johann asks how she is feeling at this stage of her pregnancy. She thinks she is fine, she says. It's only the cold and her fatigue that trouble her. They agree to keep the children home from school if the weather does not clear. There will be tasks to keep them busy around the house and barn.

The house trembles as the wind intensifies. Rising from his chair, Johann wraps an arm around his wife's shoulders and kisses the top of her head. Then he dresses and goes out for a final inspection of the barn. When he returns he picks up the edition of the *Mennonitische Rundschau* Brother Wieler passed to him after church yesterday and stands with it while he warms himself at the stove. He ignores Canadian news, scanning for reports from Russia. His cousin Herman is the editor now, and he regularly prints correspondence from Mennonites around the world. But there is no news from Fürstenland. Johann returns the paper to the kitchen table. He trims the wick of the lamp and draws it closer to where Anna sits, knitting a pair of mittens. Once more he touches her shoulder and whispers '*Gute Nacht.*'

When Anna hears the bedroom door close, she rises. She draws the rocking chair nearer the stove and picks up her needles again. She listens to the sound of the wind, the voice she has come to know as the primary force in this vast and open land on which they have settled. She has seen it rip the soil from fields, hurl rain and hail against the walls and windows of the house, and bend the garden corn to breaking. But tonight she finds it strangely comforting. She is inside, and there is the warmth of the fire. Johann is home, sleeping in the next room, and there are no soldiers in the yard. She sets aside her knitting and settles back in the chair, letting her thoughts pass back through the intervening years.

> *Ach, what a time that was! Johann, conscripted, far away in the military hospital ... and I so alone with the children while armies swept through the village again and again — the Germans and Austrians, the Reds, the Whites, the Nationalist Greens, and Makhno's Blacks. Ja, a veritable* Regenbogen *it was! From horizon to horizon, for seven years, an angry rainbow of murder and mayhem ... in Sergejewka, the workers rose up after Onkel Kornelius died in 1917 ... the oldest of his sons-in-law took over and made a real mess of things. Herman Herman was his name, and the workers, even the Mennonites, mocked his incompetence ... Ha-Ha they called him beside his back ... the factory failed, and when the Germans retreated in '18 the entire family fled with them ... the workers murdered the managers, Goertzen, Klassen and Fast ... they couldn't find Onkel Gerhard so they killed his son instead.*

The memories are stark and vivid, and Anna finds she is whispering.

> *We had to be so careful ... 'Don't let them catch you speaking German! Whisper your hymns, and only at night. If you pray, do it alone' ... accusations of betrayal, and certainly there were informants among our people! You could not trust, nor were you trusted. And then, when Johann finally came home from the war, he was elected Schulze! So now it was always Johann who had to deal with every threat and complaint! How is it possible that he can even think of going back?*

It is past eleven, and Anna's mind is drifting. Johann's snoring stops, and she hears the creak of bedsprings as he turns on his side. She rises from the rocking chair, stokes the stove one last time and quenches the lamp. The stove snaps and flairs, a plucky but ineffectual challenge to the cold that seeps in from the rage outside. She slips in beside Johann as softly as she can. His dreams are always of Russia, and sometimes she hears him whisper the names of horses or friends. Once or twice he has reared up in bed after troubled visions of the war. She smiles wryly as she listens for his breathing. Tonight he is dreaming in Ukrainian, and he murmurs the name of the village ... *Serhiivka ... Serhiivka ...*

It is well past midnight when Johann wakes to the sound of the veranda door slamming in the wind. He lights a lamp in the kitchen and finds a length of twine. Pulling on his coat, he steps into the weather and knots one end of the twine around the latch and the other to the leg of the bench beside the door. He lays a shovel across the twine to keep the tension. In the pitch darkness it is hard to gauge the snowfall, but he judges that the strength of the wind has doubled in the hours since he went to bed. Re-entering the house, he considers that his family and the cattle will be safe enough, but the enormous accumulation of snow bodes ill for the day when it will all turn to water and delay the spring seeding.

Drafts from poorly fitted windows, and from cracks in the clapboard shrouding of the walls, converge in the centre of the room. Johann stokes the stove with as much wood as it will hold and sets the water pail near enough to prevent it from freezing. Silently, he carries his armchair from its place at the table and sets it next to Anna's rocker. He sits in his great Russian fleece with his feet underneath the stove. In the flickering lamp-light, the *Kroeger* tells him it is nearly three o'clock. In two hours he will have to wake Njuta and Jasch for the milking if he is to get the cream separated and hauled the half mile to the road in time for the collection. But in this storm, he wonders if Kehler's team will be able to get through the drifts. What will be will be, he thinks, and for some time he dozes fitfully in his chair.

He is roused by the racketing of the veranda door. Surely, he thinks, the twine cannot have failed. As he rises the sound is repeated, but now he recognizes an urgent knocking. He hurries out to the veranda and fumbles to free the knots. A horse whinnies in the dark, and a figure steps quickly inside and begins to speak. It takes a moment for Johann to recognize Anton Doerksen, with his hood and beard so shagged with snow and ice. Johann draws him to the stove and pulls up another chair. But Doerksen will not sit.

"Johann," he gasps. "Teacher Fast is out in this. His wife came to us with the children. I came as fast as I could. He did not come home last night. He went to Niverville in the afternoon with Friesen to check on his parents. Friesen said he would wait for him, but Fast said no, he would walk back. It wasn't snowing yet, but the wind was rising. He was warned, but you know how he is."

Anna has heard the disturbance and enters the kitchen, alarmed and fumbling with her glasses. "*Was ist, Johann*? What has happened?" Then she sees Doerksen and retreats a few steps, securing her nightgown around her waist.

"Anna, you must wake Jasch and Hans. Tell them to dress and come to the barn. And we will need hot water and blankets." She leaves the room to find her clothes, and Johann re-stokes the fire. Leaving the cover aside, he slides the bucket over the open flame.

"Come," he says, snatching mitts and scarves from the closet near the door. Doerksen follows him to the barn and tethers his horse in an empty stall. He helps saddle two of Johann's horses and stays in the barn while Johann returns to the house. The boys are rubbing sleep from their eyes. They are nearly dressed, and Johann urges them to hurry.

"I don't know how long we will be gone," he says to Anna. "You should wake Njuta soon to start the milking." He looks at her for a moment, considering her condition. "Perhaps you could help her? If you are able?"

Back at the barn, Doerksen is stamping his feet and shuddering with cold, and Johann sends him home to tell Mrs. Fast that a search has begun. When Jasch and Hans arrive he instructs them to ride directly west until they find the ridge running between the town and the school, Fast's most likely line of travel. There they must turn south towards the school, carefully searching the ground a hundred yards or so on either side. Once at the school, they are to circle the schoolyard in expanding spirals until he can meet them there. The storm will have obliterated all trails, so they must remain within sight and hearing of each other.

After his sons have gone, Johann leads his fastest horse out of the barn and harnesses it to the sledge. By the time Anna arrives with crocks of hot water wrapped in blankets, he is ready. With a slap of the reins he is off to rouse the neighbours.

Hans and his brother know the terrain well. The first portion of the ride is through their own fields, and stands of willow, dimly visible against the greying horizon, are familiar landmarks. It is bitterly cold, but the wind has slackened and the snow has nearly stopped. By the time they reach the ridgeline, they can see and hear well enough to separate from each other by fifty yards or so. Hunched deeply in their winter wear, they begin their search. For an hour they progress slowly south in the direction of the school, weaving back and forth in broad double arcs that crisscross the median line. After a half-dozen of these, it is Hans who spies the black post that marks the corner of the fence enclosing the community pasture. Only the top strand of barbed wire is exposed above the drifts. From here, still a quarter mile away, the boys can see the dim shape of the cottage where the teacher's family lives, and just beyond it, the blur of the school building itself. They ride more quickly, and Hans says, "If Fast found the fence, perhaps he followed it home after all."

But Jasch dismisses the idea. "Then we would know by now."

When they reach the schoolyard Jasch dismounts to check the cottage. Hans does not go with him. His horse is fidgeting in the cold and needs to keep moving. He decides to follow the fence line beyond the far edge of the schoolyard. A dead calm has filled the last moments before sunrise, and Hans is alone. He rides slowly, waiting for his brother to reappear. In the distance, he can see the faint outline of the bulky gate structure, and as he comes closer, another shadow, thick and oblique, that does not belong there. He stops the horse and squints into the middle distance. His senses quicken, and something deep inside him knows what he has found.

The teacher sits leaning against the gatepost, one knee drawn up against his chest. Snow has drifted across his lap, and his feet are submerged. His left arm rests on a knee, and the other, extended beside him, sags from the wire, the coat sleeve snagged on a single barb. His face is towards the sky and tilted to one side. One eye is crusted with snow, the other half-open. Something between a grin and a grimace lies on his lips. He has found the fence he has been looking for since losing the ridge in the whiteout. But he has gone too far. The zone of safety is already behind him. Hand over hand, he has followed his false pilot ever further from refuge until, overwhelmed by exhaustion and the cold, he has rested for a while.

For an endless minute Hans stares down at the corpse. Then his horse snorts and stamps a hoof. He turns quickly, and a brief trot brings him back to the teacher's cottage, where his brother is just emerging. The house is empty, but Jasch has taken time to shake off the cold.

"There is no one … ," Jasch begins, but he is silenced by his brother's vigorous gestures to mount and follow. They tether their horses to a post some distance from the corpse and approach on foot. There are distant voices, now, from other searchers converging on the school grounds. And silhouetted against the eastern horizon is their father, standing upright on the heaving sledge, snapping the reins and bellowing for speed.

When Johann arrives, he covers Fast's face and upper body with one of the blankets. He throws the others around the boys' shoulders and passes them a crock of water. Its heat cannot help the teacher, but the boys drink deeply and then pour out the rest so it will not crack the vessel when it freezes. Johann puts an arm around each of his sons and draws them to himself. There are no words until the other riders arrive and assist in transferring the body to the sledge. Then Johann sends the boys home to get warmed before they help with the milking. He and the other men will take the body into the schoolhouse. Someone will alert the authorities in town while Johann crosses the field to the Doerksens to tend to the widow.

Late that night Johann goes out to the barn to check on the livestock. He notes that there is a breeze again, this time from the south. A good sign, he thinks. It will be warmer soon. He hangs the lamp from a nail on the centre beam and warms his hands on the glass chimney. He upends a nail keg and sits. He extends his legs into the aisle and leans against one of the uprights. It is always a few degrees warmer here among the cattle, and he feels the tensions begin to ebb. He reviews the events of the day: the search, the trauma of discovery — especially for young Hans, who has spoken hardly a word since returning home, the loss of a good teacher, and the terrible grief of the young widow.

Johann's thoughts shift to practical matters. Kehler did not collect the milk today after all. Anna and Njuta had worked mightily to get it to the roadside on time, but the boys retrieved it and brought it into the house after their return from the search, or it would have frozen. In the morning, he will have to sledge it the four miles to Kronstal and bring back enough empties for tomorrow's milk. Surely, Kehler will collect again now that the storm is over.

He scans the low ceiling of this miserable cowshed. Hardly a barn at all, he thinks. Nothing like the showpiece he built in Sergejewka, his pride, and the envy of his neighbours, with its hayloft and grain bin under the slope of a thickly thatched roof and the covered walkway connecting it to the house. He sees the frost nipples glittering in the lamplight on every exposed nail and reaches to scratch one with his fingernail. Yes, they had thought they knew winter! There had been deep snow, certainly, and ice on the Dniepr thick enough for teams to cross with a ton of firewood. And there were winter storms. But it was always either cold or windy, never both at once. This blizzard began and ended with twenty degrees of frost. The wind has ripped shingles from the house and granary, and in Russia snowdrifts such as these would have been unimaginable.

Johann is not accustomed to self-pity, nor does he feel it now. He can work, suffer, and go without, and not feel personally diminished thereby. But there are his children to consider. What are their prospects? Njuta will likely leave soon — there have been overtures — but she says she will not marry until the others are old enough to take over more of the work.

The younger girls will not shirk house and garden work, and he knows his sons will labour as hard as he does. But what is this land capable of producing, even if he can manage to clear a few more acres each year?

The first wheat crop has been a disaster; planted late on the debris of Sawatzky's final failure and drowned in a deluge of rain just as the secondary leaves emerged. Even with relentless labour and the best of luck, what can he hope for? The garden, the livestock, and the milk will suffice to feed his family. He is sure of that. But the year of reprieve from repayment of the *Reiseschuld* ended in December. He has begun payments in kind — a third of all eggs and poultry, with pork and beef to follow, once they are mature enough to slaughter. The representative from the Mennonite board has said it will satisfy the CPR for now. But the mortgage will have to be paid in dollars, and the first payment is due before the next harvest. In spring, if the cows remain healthy, there will be calves. He can perhaps sell one or two, but he needs to build his own herd. And he will need to find enough pasture for them, even if it means renting from the neighbours until he can clear and drain more of his own land.

Johann retrieves the lantern from its place on the beam and walks the length of the barn for a final survey of the stalls. All seems well. The sow is swelling and will likely give birth within a week, he thinks. The cows lie on their bedding, chewing the cud. The horses never lie down, even in sleep, but tonight they seem restless. He calls each one by name and pats them firmly on the rump. He scoops oats for each one and a little extra for Mishka, his favourite. She rests her muzzle on his shoulder for a moment and reminds him of the only time during all the troubles in the Old Country when his life was directly threatened. Resting his horses after the steep climb out of the Rohachyk ravine, he'd been tightening their girth straps when he felt the cold steel of a pistol barrel on the back of his neck. The bandit demanded to know which of the two was the better riding horse. Knowing he would be suspected of lying, Johann opted for the truth. He pointed to the gentle three-year-old he had raised from birth, and was ordered to unhitch the other. Johann complied and handed over the reins. The stranger was in no hurry and stood smoking while Johann reconfigured the harness, climbed to his seat on the wagon, and resumed his journey. At the first bend, he turned to watch. The gunman mounted and was instantly thrown to the ground. A vicious kick to the ribs flung him into the weeds, where he lay writhing while the horse — a nasty beast only Johann could handle — made a beeline for home. Johann had considered going back to attend to the man, but there was the matter of the gun.

Johann tightens the collar of his coat around his neck and steps outside. The largest snowdrift runs square across the yard, blocking his view of the house. Hard as iron, it squeals under his boots as he ascends to the top. The wind is steady, and the night sky is cloudless and strewn with a million stars. He stands gazing upwards, wondering if his brothers and sisters in Russia see the same stars, whether night after night they, too, look up and wonder. And his mother; what is she thinking now about her resolve to stay?

A pang of nostalgia for the village on the Dniepr courses through him as, for the hundredth time, he doubts their decision to emigrate. There had been seasons of desperation, it was true. The Great War, the revolution and the civil war. And Anna alone so much. Then there were the wrenching adjustments to the new regime, with its ambiguous demands and the constant flux in regulations.

Difficult times, certainly. But Russia was more than misery and fear. He had always known how to manage. Even during the terrible famines of 1921/22 and again in '25, his family had survived. The forced requisitions of grain had ended with Lenin's New Economic Policy, and he had been able to sell a small surplus for hard currency. The German language was permitted again, and as community life revived, a cautious optimism had allowed him to hope that life could return, if not to the old normal, at least to a level of stability that would sustain more than mere survival.

He had managed to keep most of his land during the Redistribution, partly because of his large family but also, perhaps, because as *Schulze*, he had been useful in mediating some of the tensions that arose as the *Komitee* insinuated itself into village affairs and disrupted traditional Mennonite ways. When neighbours suffered greater losses than Johann, whispered suspicions circulated, which caused him some grief. But that had come to nothing. He had always kept good relations with the Ukrainian villagers, including those in Sergejewka itself. He was fluent in the language, and his skills as an animal healer were known throughout the region. Some of these neighbours had spoken up for him, and their word had been good enough for the *Komitee*.

The factory was another matter. He had warned the owners and managers—all relatives of his—that under the new regime they could not expect to remain in control. He told them that if the deteriorating economy led to violence, the factory and its assets would be prime targets. His Tante Anna was furious and had denounced him to the church as siding with the revolutionaries. He felt he had given a good account of himself before the elders. They heard him respectfully, and he thought that would be the end of the matter. But ill feelings had persisted, and it pained him to have discovered recently that the rumours had emigrated with his accusers to haunt him here in Manitoba. *Schwitke*, 'the quick one,' was his Ukrainian nickname.

"Yes," muttered some who had known him in Sergejewka. "Oh yes. *Schwitke* indeed; fast and loose!"

How long he has been standing at the top of the snow bank, he does not know. His lamp has died, and in the house only the kitchen window is still aglow. Anna will be writing a letter or reading the Bible, he thinks. Or perhaps nursing one of the headaches for which the only relief is intense heat, as near to the stove as she can tolerate. On the lee side of the great drift, the gale has swept the snow clear to the frozen mud beneath. Johann crosses the yard quickly, and enters the house. He whispers a greeting as he pulls off his coat. But the kitchen is empty. Anna has gone to bed, leaving the lamp burning for him on the washstand next to the kettle of warm water. Johann washes and dries his hands and face. Then he blows out the lamp, and in the instant darkness, he gropes his way to the bedroom. He undresses and edges in beside Anna, who shifts in her sleep. The bed is warm, and within minutes he is asleep.

# 2. A Patriarch Remembers

## Beginnings

From its headwaters near Smolensk, southwest of Moscow, the Dniepr River flows through Belarus and Ukraine, emptying into the Black Sea near Odessa some two thousand *verst* from its source. Herodotus travelled its southern reaches and declared it second only to the Nile among the great navigable rivers of the world, its waters rich in fish and its flood plains lush with grass. Greek colonists along the north shore of the Black Sea knew it as *Borysthenes*, and the tribes that thrived on either side they called Scythians. For half a millennium, these horsemen of the steppes flourished, excelling in metallurgy and developing a highly organized culture and economy, which they fiercely defended against incursions, repulsing even the armies of Alexander the Great. After their decline in the third century BCE, various Celtic and Slavic nomads vied with each other for access to grazing land. And beginning in the sixteenth century, they also contested with the Zaporozhian Cossacks for territorial control. By 1788, the last Cossack fortress (*sich*) had been destroyed by Catherine the Great, and the bands driven from the region. Catherine's program of settling the vast grasslands of southern Russia proceeded apace, and over the next decades, at her invitation, two million Western European agriculturalists would pour into Little Russia, helping to secure the region against the recently defeated Ottomans. Among them were a few hundred Mennonites, and they established their first settlement on the right bank of the Dniepr at the foot of the great rapids near the island of Chortitza. During the next century, their numbers increased to more than a hundred thousand, and their colonies proliferated across the steppes on either side of the great river.


Among the descendants of these settlers is the industrialist Jakob Wilhelm Janzen, grandson of one of the first Mennonite families to emigrate from Prussia in the 1780s, and himself a founding pioneer of Sergejewka, the last of six villages to be established (1868) in the Fürstenland colony on the left bank of the Dniepr, a hundred *verst* downstream from Chortitza.

Janzen is only vaguely aware of the broad sweep of history. For most of his life, he has been preoccupied with his own times: the welfare of his family, the prosperity of his factory, and the nurturing of *die Brüdergemeinde* – the Mennonite Brethren congregation, which he serves as senior minister and regional elder.

Janzen is sixty-eight years old and ailing. He sprawls deep in his chair in the shade of the pear trees lining the garden path. Below him the sunlight glitters on the lazy *konstje*, a small, natural diversion of the Dniepr that breaks away from the main channel of the river several *verst* upstream and re-enters it again after passing through the village. Thirty *verst* to the north, on the opposite shore and invisible around the great bend of the river, is the city of Nikopol.

Next to Janzen's chair a sheaf of papers lies strewn across a wooden bench, a few fist-sized stones securing them against the breeze. In recent years, Janzen has begun collecting materials and jotting notes for a *Lebensgeschichte*. But he has always set them aside again, impatient and dissuaded by his clumsiness as a writer, by the relentless demands of the factory, and by his doubts that anyone will value an account of his life.

Then, just a few weeks ago, after a Sunday dinner animated by good-natured disagreements about family lore, his granddaughter Anna came to him with her husband Johann. It would be a gift to the family, she said, if he were to write his memoirs. He'd had an eventful life, and no one was better placed to write a history of the village. Jakob had listened in silence, chuckled modestly, and nodded his thanks for their interest. But he did not commit himself. Privately, he was humbled that the request should have come from this pair, for he knew they still bore the hurt of recent events in which he had played a crucial role. Perhaps this was an overture that could lead to reconciliation. Sometime soon, he vowed, he would meet with them again, and they would talk.

Kornelius Neufeld, Jakob's son-in-law and business partner, has also encouraged him and offered his support. Kornelius is an astute businessman and an excellent manager, and from time to time he has tried to persuade Janzen to relax his oversight of the shop floor. No one will say it, but the older man's judgment in business affairs is no longer reliable. Janzen doesn't quite know this, but he finds himself increasingly on the periphery during consultations with upper management, and there are awkward silences now after some of his pronouncements.

Following one such incident a few months ago, Kornelius took Janzen aside and addressed the matter as tactfully as he knew how. He assured his father-in-law that his wisdom and experience were highly valued — indispensable, in fact. But the department foremen were highly trained and competent, and especially now, since the merger with the Klassen factory, there was an oversupply of qualified men. Day-to-day matters were best left to them. Perhaps it was time for Janzen to consider whether it might not be best to pull back a little and put his mind to other things.

In principle, Janzen agreed. He would spend a few morning hours in the shop and devote his afternoons to pastoral duties. But the mental adjustment had been difficult, so accustomed was he to invigilating all stages of production — the foundry, machine shop, assembly rooms, paint shop, and front desk. Absence from the factory made him anxious, doubly so when news of blunders reached his ears, errors he would have helped to avoid had he been present. Gradually, he had come to realize that half-measures would not do. A clean break was called for. He would retain his financial share in *Janzen & Neufeld Kompanie* but leave his son-in-law in sole charge of operations. When he announced his decision Kornelius warmly approved. He smiled wryly and added, "Perhaps now, Papa, you can finally get beyond your endless procrastination and write your memoirs?" It was a gentle rebuke, and the old man took it kindly.

Shifting in his chair, Jakob reaches for his papers and begins fingering through them. There are his old diaries, most of them coverless now, with pages torn or lost; tenancy documents dating from his arrival in the village forty years ago; a few product photos tucked into the slender sales catalogue of the defunct Klassen factory; and the recent portrait of himself and Kornelius, front and centre, with the supervisory personnel of *Janzen & Neufeld Ko.* In a sheath of heavy stock, folded in quarters, is the genealogical chart he has painstakingly compiled of his lines of descent. And, in a bulky carton under the bench, a miscellany of scribblings on the backs of envelopes and old letters, factory documents, and calendar sheets – the ghostly silt of a half-century, recovered from remote closet corners and dusty cabinet drawers.

For an hour, Jakob peruses the documents at random, gauging their value for his present purposes. He sighs and winces at ancient joys and sorrows, and once or twice he tilts his head and gazes at length towards some distant place beyond the river, consolidating a memory or settling an ache of regret. Though he struggles these days to remember yesterday's weather, his recollections of long ago are sharp. He marvels: *How fleeting the time in which so much of my life has passed.* A lifetime of action and industry has engendered in him a deep-rooted sense of the future as a steady ascent, and he is aware of a profound disinclination for the downslope.

The late afternoon breeze teases a few papers from Janzen's lap and sifts them to the ground. Then it subsides entirely, and the papers lie undisturbed. Janzen nods in his chair, and neither birdsong, nor the hum of insects, nor the happiness of children at play are enough to rouse him. Only when the factory whistle signals the shift change, and his wife Maria comes down to the garden to summon him for *Faspa* does he wake. Together, they collect his things, and she helps him through the gate and into the house. When they are gone, the garden above the Dniepr is motionless and empty in the heat of the afternoon.

## From *The Memoirs of Jakob Wilhelm Janzen*

### VORWORT

*Dear friends have prevailed upon me from time to time to leave a record not only of my own life but also to document the story of our beloved Sergejewka and the good people who have lived and toiled here. If I have so far resisted, it is not because I do not think it important that it should be done. Rather, I have felt inadequate to the task, having so little education and never having developed much skill in writing. But now even my grand-children insist that it is no less than my obligation to do so. I cannot doubt their sincerity, and since they refuse to stop plying me with questions, I have agreed that I should make the attempt, after all, to set down the essential events of my life and times as far as I am able. Perhaps only in this way I may be able to earn for myself a little peace.*

Jakob Janzen, 1913
Sergejewka, Grossfürstenland, South Russia

My father was Wilhelm Wilhelm Janzen, and when his father died he inherited the farm in Alt-Kronsweide. It was at about the same time that he married my mother, Anna Heinrichs, also of Alt-Kronsweide. The village was not far from the Dniepr in the northern part of the Chortitza colony. The land was rather sandy, and the water was poor. When most of the farmers relocated to lower ground beside a small tributary of the Dniepr, my father decided to stay. He had good buildings and not much money, so to him it seemed better to remain. Six or eight other families also stayed in Alt-Kronsweide, and everyone managed for some years. But one spring the wells dried up, and water for the house and barn had to be brought from the river, and that was too much. My parents found a farm in the new village and joined their former neighbours. My father told me how he and his friend Elias spent most of one winter pulling down the barn and rebuilding it in the new place.

I was born shortly after that move in 1845, and my sister was born five years later. Our poor mother suffered terribly both times, and after Lise's birth our mother could not recover. She became very ill and died a few weeks later. I can say that I remember being cared for and loved. I sometimes think I remember her face and maybe even the sound of her voice, but in those days we did not make photographs, so there is nothing that can stir other memories. I do recall my father's grief. It frightened me to discover that grown men could also weep, although I have learned that since.

Father was a hardworking man, and with two young children to care for, he soon found another wife, my stepmother Mika. She was also from a Kronsweide family, but from one of those who had not moved to the new location. She was much younger than my mother, and as I think of her now, maybe she wasn't quite prepared to be our mother. But she was kind, and she provided well for us. In time, my two half-brothers were added to our family.

My childhood was a happy one. Like all Mennonite villages, Kronsweide had many children, and I was never alone unless I wanted to be, and that was seldom. I was thirteen when my father said he needed me to help on the farm. I could stop going to school and begin learning to work. Some of my friends went on to the Zentralschule in Rosenthal, but our friendships continued. Even later, with the hostilities about matters of faith, I kept those friends. They did not agree with me about our new direction, and truthfully, in those early years I was not always sure about everything either, but we did not stop talking. Really, I could say we loved each other as friends. None of them came to live here in Fürstenland, but when I go back to the Old Colony I still make time to visit one or two of them.

When I was twelve years old I became aware that something was changing in the way my father and stepmother spoke about the church. From time to time, visiting preachers from Germany passed through our villages, and they expressed concern about the spiritual conditions among our people. They invited several men in Chortitza, from Einlage and Kronsweide, to a conference in Berlin, and when these men returned they spoke passionately about the need for renewal. Most of these men were not ordained ministers, and they were forbidden from preaching in our churches, but they held meetings in homes. They said that we Mennonites had fallen asleep in our sins and needed a thorough waking up, an *Erweckung*. Being born into a religious community was not enough, they said. Without genuine repentance and a personal commitment to a life of faithfulness to the gospel, church attendance and baptism were just empty forms. They distributed pamphlets and books and urged us to join together with others of like mind. The Spirit was already at work in the Molotschna colony, they said. People there wanted to be re-baptized, and by full immersion, in order to mark this new and joyful turning back to God. They hoped for the eventual trans-formation of the whole Russian Mennonite world.

At first, my stepmother was more enthusiastic than my father, but it didn't take long until he became quite bold in his support of the movement. Although he was not very talkative, he was a deep-thinking man. He spoke to me about these matters so carefully that I thought he must be worried about encumbering me unnecessarily at my age. Eventually, he approached me more directly, and we talked at some length. I don't remember exactly what he said; these ideas were quite new to him, and I think he was uncertain how to express them. Mostly, he emphasized the need for confession of sin and a personal acceptance of God's forgiveness. The signs of true believers, he said, were a joyous confidence in their salvation, and a commitment to following the example of Jesus in moral living and peaceful relations with their neighbours.

Certainly, not all of this was new. In catechism classes at school, we learned about the love of God, and many of the ministers were devout men who preached morality and confession. But many of our people rarely attended church, except for weddings and funerals, and baptism for them was just a requirement if they wished to get married. Also, it was not hard to think of examples of immorality among us. There was often talk about improper relations between men and women, and to address this matter there were special meetings after church when I and other unbaptized were asked to leave.

Alcohol was another serious problem in our colony. The larger villages all had taverns, and I was often shocked by the rough talk I overheard. In summer, men would gather at outdoor tables in the evenings, smoking and drinking, and making lewd jokes when women passed by. At wedding celebrations, when the service ended and the ministers had left, there was much drinking. More than once, there was a scandal. In Einlage, the Russian police had to be called when fights broke out among the young men. My own uncle was one of those arrested. What must the Russians have thought about us, who claimed to be the quiet in the land? News of these and other incidents reached the government, and these reports were thrown in our faces in later years when our exemption from military service was challenged. How could we claim to be non-violent when our people did indeed fight — among each other, no less?

Two or three of my older friends were already caught up in questionable activities, and they tried to draw me in as well. It was difficult to resist, and I confess that I did not always do so. But the guilt that followed was hard to live with, and the more involved my parents became in the new movement, the more I felt that perhaps I did not need to travel the same road as these friends. It was very awkward with them. I didn't want to present myself as better than they were, but I couldn't easily explain. I knew they were annoyed when I did not go along with them. When I was fifteen, my father and stepmother began to have meetings in our own home. At first, there were only five or six people, but as it became known that my father was becoming a voice for the renewal movement, others joined in. My parents did not press me, but they made it clear that I was welcome. One of the men who had travelled to Germany also attended when he was able. I remember his prayers. They were different from any I had heard before, loud and very emotional, as though he was pleading with someone who was actually in the room. He taught us new hymns he had brought back from the conference. *Ich weiß einen Strom* was one we sang regularly. For me, it is particularly memorable because we sang of that beautiful stream on the banks of the Dniepr at our first baptism a few years later.

It was not long before we began to experience resistance. Our *Schulze* was a good-natured, peace-loving man and not personally opposed to our meetings. But it was his responsibility as supervisor of the village to deal with complaints from others. When he spoke to my father the first time he only asked us to keep our meetings private and to keep the windows closed if we were singing.

But the leading minister of our church was strongly opposed. Some in our group had openly talked about ours as an alternative – even superior – form of worship. This would not be tolerated, he said. We were threatening the unity of the church and creating division in the community as a whole.

Well, there had never been complete unity among Mennonites. In Prussia, and long before that, in *die Niederlande*, the Flemish and Frisian Mennonites held to quite different teachings and practices. I won't explain here all the ways in which they differed, but each group had its own protocols for the ordination of ministers and elders, as well as different requirements for baptism and church membership. Each group insisted that their practices were the right ones, exclusively so, to the extent that intermarriage between Flemish and Frisians was strongly discouraged. When

Mennonites from both groups emigrated to Russia it was hoped that they would blend and establish a single body. But almost immediately, the Frisians (and this included my grandparents) banded together in Einlage and Kronsweide, leaving the Flemish to settle in the other villages. Each group established their own church and kept to their own practices. Neither one expected to convince the other, and each was satisfied to let the other do things their own way. Perhaps for the times, that was as good a solution as any.

But our group was different. We were perceived as a threat by both the Flemish and the Frisians. My father quietly explained to our minister that we had no intention of starting a new church. We faithfully attended Sunday services, and we meant no disrespect to the leadership. Our fervent desire was for personal renewal, and the purpose of our meetings was to feed that hunger by studying and praying together. If we spoke to our neighbours about our new-found life, it was only because it was a joyous thing that we wished for others as well.

But the minister was not satisfied. As my father spoke, he got more and more angry. He had seen firsthand how quickly the 'infection' had spread in Einlage, he said, and he condemned the claim of assurance of personal salvation as sheer arrogance.

This man was my stepmother's cousin. She tried to calm him, but he ignored her and shouted at my father. "You are already a baptized member of our Mennonite church! From what, then, do you claim to be converted? Are you, perhaps, after nineteen centuries, a new prophet or apostle!?"

Such hostility from local authorities, from neighbours, and even from members of our own families, was most unpleasant. On the street of our village, we were mocked, and *Pietist!* was spat at us as a term of derision, as though piety were an abomination. As the movement grew, so did the opposition, and I think it was in early January of 1862 that members of the ministerial council brought a formal petition to the *Oberschulze* in Chortitza-Rosenthal demanding that the authority of the central office be directed to this matter.

We could not have predicted the vehemence with which the chief administrator of the colony condemned us. In a circular distributed to each village, we were vilified as "fanatics ... wicked ... dangerous ... delusional." A number of prohibitions were outlined, with orders for strict enforcement by the local *Schulze*. Our house meetings were forbidden; all villages were placed under a ten o'clock curfew, with watchmen ordered to evict anyone not in their home village; "sectarians" who persisted would be arrested and handed over to Russian authorities for imprisonment or exile; any foreigners belonging to our "pernicious sect" were to be escorted out of the colony as soon as travel became possible in spring.

Shortly afterwards, we heard about the first baptism in the Molotschna colony, where equally severe edicts had been published. Believing that baptism should be a public witness, several courageous men had determined to baptize each other in the River Tokmak one morning, only to be driven off by furious residents. They had returned the next day to a more concealed location and succeeded, witnessed only by their wives and children. Now Heinrich Neufeld and Abraham Unger, our neighbours from Einlage, travelled there to be baptized by the Molotschna brethren, who also ordained them and authorized them to conduct baptisms in our own colony. Word spread that as soon as the ice was off the Dniepr, Unger would baptize any who were willing. Suddenly, each of us faced a difficult test of our faith.

This was the winter of 1862. My father and stepmother and I spoke earnestly about the consequences we might face. For both of them this would be a second baptism, something that would be deeply offensive to the elders. Since I had not yet been baptized, perhaps I would be exempted from punishment, although the new mode of our baptism, by immersion, would doubtless be condemned. I was certainly afraid. I felt like one whose commitment to a hazardous venture is firm but who nevertheless relies on the courage of another to carry me through deep waters. For me, that was my father. I clearly recall a swelling of my own resolve when I heard his voice ring out as he declared his intention to proceed.

"No step of obedience is without costs," he said. "The light of God has illumined my soul. Should I smother it now?"

News of our plans leaked out, and for the authorities, this was the sheaf that tipped the wagon. The wrath of the chief colony administrator and his deputies descended on us. The authorities rooted out the leaders of our group and called them to account. I no longer remember the exact order of events, and in any case, so much was happening that it is impossible to write about it all. I will write only of things I saw with my own eyes or that I heard from the mouth of my father. In his own case, the consequences were terrible.

All the men who had led house meetings in the villages were rounded up. Einlage and Kronsweide were especially targeted because it was there that the stirrings of our movement had begun. By now, our village had a new *Schulze*, and he was a very different man than the previous one. He called a meeting of the whole *Gemeinde* and made my father stand before the assembly. The *Schulze* also stood and glared directly into my father's face. He demanded that our meetings cease immediately and ordered my father confined to our home. My father replied that his obedience was to a power higher than the law of men, and he would not promise. The *Schulze* fell into a rage and was prepared to beat him, but on that day he was restrained by others. He ordered my father locked up for the night. My stepmother was allowed to see him that evening, and she said that he was quite calm and confident.

The next day he was again brought before the council. Again he stood firm, and this time there would be no reprieve. The *Schulze* ordered his assistants to drag my father out of the building. They flung him onto a heap of straw and tore most of his clothes off. Then he was mercilessly flogged with heavy stakes, ten lashes in all. There would likely have been more, but one of the blows struck him on the side of the head, and he lost consciousness, so the beating was stopped. As the *Schulze* was leaving, he berated my father once more.

"There you have it, Janzen! Perhaps that will knock the Pietism out of you!"

Someone came to where I was working in our barn and told me what was happening. I rushed to the place to see my father being led off under arrest. He had his clothing under his arm, and he could not easily walk, so badly beaten was he. For two days and nights he was confined in a summer kitchen. It was cold, and there was no heat in the room and no bed or blanket. He was given a block of wood to sit on, but his bruises would not allow him to sit for long. Nor would his clothes fit over his swollen limbs. None of us were allowed to see him or bring him food.

On the third day, he was handed over to one of our neighbours, who had to agree to keep him confined. As it turned out, this man took compassion on him and treated him with great kindness. He fed him well, dressed his injuries and gave him warm clothes. Then father was taken away to a cell in the administration offices in Chortitza, and from there he was finally allowed to return home. He had been gone for nine days altogether, and I remember that it was Friday when he returned to us. I clearly remember this because the baptism was just two days away on Sunday, and we were sure it would be too much for him, so weak was he, and still in pain. But his spirit was unbroken, and he was determined that nothing should keep him from this act of obedience.

And so it was; a day I will never forget. The Dniepr had broken up, and great chunks of ice were churning in the middle of the stream. But there was a small cove protected by an outcrop of rock. In summer the water here was shallow and warm, and we liked to fish among the reeds and water grasses. Now the water was higher and it twisted around in slow eddies that had taken out the heavy winter ice. In this place, we gathered just before dawn on the morning of March 18. We were about a dozen from Kronsweide, and also a few who came from Einlage; among them, though I did not know it, were my future wife and her parents. It was cold and blustery as we stood in a close circle while Abraham Unger read the scriptures. He had written a sermon, but the wind took his notes, so he spoke from the heart. He prayed a blessing on us, and we sang.

> Ich weiss einen Strom, dessen herrliche Flut
> Fliesst wunderbar stille durchs Land,
> Doch strahlet und glänzt er wie feurige Flut,
> Wem ist dieses Wässer bekannt?

Then he and Heinrich Neufeld broke up the skin of ice that had formed overnight, and Unger stepped into the waters. He motioned to us to follow him one at a time. Neufeld stood nearby to ward off the panes of fresh ice that kept floating too close. He could see that Unger was shaking with the cold, so much so that his speech was affected. He quickly stepped in to assist, so then the entire rite took less than ten minutes. Two-by-two, we threw off our coats and waded chest-deep into the stream. When each of us reached one or the other of the ministers, he clasped both our hands together in one of his and asked us to affirm the statement of faith. Then we were lowered backward and fully immersed in the frigid Dniepr with nothing but the brother's hand on our back for support.

Never before or after have I been so cold. The shock was immense. But I was young and strong, and my greatest concern was for my poor parents. They had been among the first, and as soon as I emerged from the river I hurried after them. One of the brothers had prepared shelter for us in a herdsman's cottage nearby, and I found them there. It was a large single room with a stove near the middle. Along one wall, a curtain had been hung, and behind it the women were changing into dry clothes. I was sure my stepmother would be fine, but it was clear that my father was not. I saw that he was being attended to by other men near the stove. They were helping him take off his clothes, and I could see how his legs and back were swollen and dark with bruises. One of the men was kneading his feet to relieve cramping. Father smiled weakly and tried to extend a hand to me, but he was shaking uncontrollably. When he was dressed, I threw a blanket around him and drew him as close to the stove as I could. By the time the women emerged, and the men were finally able to dress, I thought the shivering would crack my ribs. When we were all assembled again, Unger started on the remaining verses of *Ich weiss einen Strom*, and we all joined in as well as we could. I already loved that hymn dearly, but I could not help considering how that beautiful stream with its waters so free had also been full of ice, and how it had nearly claimed us for eternity that morning!

There were more baptisms in the weeks and months ahead, until we were almost a hundred souls. There was much rejoicing among us, and we did not hesitate to share the peace we had found with others. As we had feared, the authorities stepped up their opposition and Neufeld and Unger were especially singled out. In May they were arrested and sent to the regional chief of police. They gave a good account of themselves there, but the Mennonite church and the colony administration did not relent. For a number of years, we suffered persecution of every kind, even the very real threat of being

officially declared to be not Mennonites at all and exiled from
the colony.

I will not prolong this account of the beginnings of our
*Mennonitische Brüdergemeinde*. It is a difficult and complicated
story, and many of the details are vague to me now, almost fifty
years later. We continued to meet outside the established church
buildings, usually in our homes. And I will say that our parting
from the main body of *Kirchliche Mennoniten* was painful on all
sides. I must acknowledge, also, that within our new and struggling *Gemeinde*, there was not always peace. Too often, the joyous
fellowship we celebrated in those first tumultuous years was
broken by dissension. In their enthusiasm, some brothers and
sisters went to great excess, dancing wildly, shouting, and even
kissing each other during the services. Others, who were alarmed
at this, tried to institute rules that were far too strict. Some of our
leaders were no longer on speaking terms and tried to excommu-
nicate each other from the Brotherhood. To this day, I am
saddened by my memory of these affairs. So many errors of judgment! My good friend Peter Martin Friesen is writing our history,
and he has promised to tell the whole story just as it happened,
the good with the bad. He has written to me, and I have shared
with him all that I have said above.

As for my parents, they remained joyful in the Lord always! as the
scripture encourages us to be. But my father's health was broken.
Whether his ill-treatment at the hand of the *Schulze* or his
suffering at the baptism was the greater cause, I do not know. No
doubt, together, they inflicted a heavy toll. Within a year, his
speech and his memory began to fail, and by the spring of '64 he
was gone. He was 46.

The period after my father's death was extremely difficult. My
sister Lise was twelve, and she helped Mika with the housework
and the care of our two step-brothers while I gave myself whole-
heartedly to the farm work. My father had been a good teacher,
and there was little I did not know about running our farm. But
it was a great deal of work for just one man. We soon experienced, also, the economic consequences of our persecution. New
regulations forbade anyone from conducting business with us as

long as we persisted in our ways. I could no longer sell eggs to my
neighbours or milk to the cheese factory. Our grain had to be
taken to Russian brokers outside the colony or sold to the Jewish
dealers who came by during harvest time when the prices
were low.

One exception to the prohibitions was the payment of our debts.
It was clear that if our beleaguered farms were to fail, our creditors would not be repaid. So, there were calls for prompt repayment of loans. My father had left moderate debts that we could
have managed under normal conditions. But the sudden
demands from all sides could not be met. The end came when
our stepmother took Lise and me aside and announced that she
planned to remarry. Her new husband, Herr Klassen, was not a
member of the Brethren, but neither was he opposed. He was a
widower with children of his own, and his house was large
enough for us all. He assured me there would be work for me on
his farm. I felt my heart crack, for I had dearly hoped that my
parents' farm would one day be my own. Now it was not to be. In
hindsight, I realize that in the long run I could not have managed
the affairs of a full farm on my own, but at the time it was a heavy
blow.

There could not be an auction sale because of the prohibitions, so
our creditors simply confiscated those things of value that they
considered would cancel our debts. They did very well, I think,
and it was hard to watch the fruits of my parents' labour vanish
into other hands. Klassen could not afford to take over the land
himself, but he arranged to lease portions of it to others in the
short term in the hope that the restrictions would eventually be
relaxed and it could be sold. And that is what happened some
years later. Klassen was a fair and honest man, and he gave me my
full portion of the proceeds when we most needed it in
Fürstenland.

Much as I had come to love my stepmother, I felt disinclined to
adapt myself to a step-father and yet another set of step-brothers
and sisters. Besides, Klassen did not really need me on his farm, as
his oldest children were already of age. I had entered my twenties
and I felt it was time for me to strike out on my own. I soon

found work on the Unruh farm in Neuenburg some five *verst* from Kronsweide.

I entered as fully into the labours on the Unruh farm as I had on our own, and I enjoyed my life there. I soon learned that the Unruhs and their oldest daughter Maria had been part of our group, baptized into the *Brüdergemeinde* on that unforgettable March morning a few years back. Unruh told me that it was the example of my father's courage before the *Oberschulze* that had persuaded them. It gave me joy to know that my father was not forgotten.

The family was large, and as I became aware of how engaged the oldest children were in regular duties in both house and barn, I began to wonder how long my services would be needed.

I was also aware, during my second winter on the farm, of a certain alertness on the Unruhs' part whenever their oldest daughter, Maria, and I crossed paths. I suspect we gave them good reason, since we had indeed begun exchanging shy smiles and glances. Sometimes we spoke for a few minutes, and afterwards I always felt certain possibilities blossom in my heart and mind. Maria was not yet eighteen, almost four years younger than I was, and I had no doubt it would be judged unseemly to approach her with any serious intent. But eventually there came a day when Maria and I dared to speak about 'us.'

'The lame will leap like a deer!' says the Bible, and indeed, my heart did leap to learn that she would have me if I would have her. I knew I should first have spoken to her parents, but this blessèd moment had come upon us so unexpectedly. Maria went to her parents the next day, and we all talked together. It humbled me to hear them say that they had come to know me as a decent man, and it seemed to me that Mrs. Unruh, at least, had perhaps hoped a little that we might find each other. We agreed that we would wait for a year, and they gave us their blessing. I remember that afterwards Maria came to me and said, "How do you feel, Jakob?"

"I feel great happiness," I said, "but also a good measure of *Unruhe*!"

She laughed at my joke, much more loudly than I would have expected. "Restlessness! Yes, indeed," she said. "I feel it too. And impatience. A year is a long time!"

Her father came to see me that evening and told me as kindly as he could that it would be wise to 'create a little space' in the interim. With his help, I quickly found work on the large Koop estate. Unfortunately, this was some distance away from Neuenburg, but it was closer to Einlage so that I could still see Maria and her family on Sundays when they joined our worship services.

With my hopes now so high for the future I was filled with great energy, and I was pleased when Koop recognized my skills and appointed me supervisor over the three other *Knechte*. My new master was an ambitious man and not easy-going. What had pleased Unruh did not always satisfy Koop. If he saw one of us unoccupied even for a moment, he said he would need to know why he was paying us full wages. Not content with just running a farm, he bought and sold grain, and in winter, when he sent me across the river to Alexandrovsk with a wagonload of wheat or barley, I would bring back coal and iron for his blacksmith shop. One of the workers was being trained in that work, and I liked to assist him when I was able, especially in the winter when the shop was the warmest place on the farm. We made nails, garden tools, hinges and kitchen implements for our own use but also to sell. It was one of several skills I learned that winter, making it much easier for me to find work in my first year in Fürstenland.

I vividly recall the one occasion when Koop took me to Ekaterinoslav. It was a three-day outing, and we took two wagons to bring back equipment for the smithy, and timber and window glass for an extension to the cattle barn. It was the first time I had travelled beyond the boundaries of the Chortitza colony. It was thrilling to see the great mills and factories our Mennonite people had built in that city, far beyond anything in Chortitza. But the grand houses of the wealthy owners left me wondering, I must say, how this fit with our teachings about modesty and humility. That is something that worries me to this day, even as I now have to include myself among those who have achieved much success.

At the end of our year of waiting, Maria and I held our wedding on the Unruh farm. As was the custom, I was not allowed to see her or speak to her for a day before the ceremony, and I have never forgotten the shock of joy I felt when she emerged from the house gloriously adorned with lace and flowers, with her sisters on either side. We received warm congratulations from all who attended, especially from my sister who had come from Kronsweide for the occasion.

For a year we lived with Maria's parents in a small room that was no longer needed as maids' quarters. Again I worked with my father-in-law, and during that winter Maria and I spent many an hour discussing our future. Our first child was soon on the way, and we wished to establish ourselves independently before too long. We knew that the prospects of finding a farm nearby were poor. Besides the sanctions still in place against us as members of the *Brüdergemeinde*, there were already hundreds of Landlose in the villages of Chortitza. And those families that did have land usually had a son who would inherit it. The government refused to allow the expansion of our colony, and at this time, even the division of large farms into half-farms was strictly prohibited. Eventually, the landless would petition the government with enough force so that it relented, but for us that came too late. The best opportunity for us, it seemed, was Fürstenland, a new settlement that was opening about a hundred *verst* south, near Nikopol. We applied to the authorities and were pleased some weeks later to receive permission to transfer. We wrote to the *Oberschulze* of Fürstenland, who replied with a commitment to finding temporary accommodation for us. Plans for a new village were underway, and the surveyors would begin their work as soon as the snow was gone. He wrote that it would be a year before we could count on getting our own farm, but there was a great need for labourers and tradesmen in the five villages already established.

Maria's parents were saddened to hear of us leaving, but they did not withhold their blessing. My stepmother and her husband came to see us off. Klassen had finally found a buyer for our old farm, and true to his word, he brought a bank certificate confirming that half the proceeds of the sale had been deposited for us at the bank in Rosenthal. You can imagine how welcome that was at this stage.

We also had an unexpected visit from our dear *Ältester* Abraham Unger. He was the leader of the Einlage *Brüdergemeinde*, the same elder that had baptized us. Now he came to say farewell with a gift of a beautiful new spring-mount wagon from his famous factory. These comfortable wagons were his own invention and the envy of all who could not afford them.

"A belated wedding gift," he said.

I was deeply moved, since he knew I had not always agreed with him in matters of the faith. His rigid insistence on immersion as the only true form of baptism and as a precondition for communion had alienated many, including some of our other ministers. I had close friends who were baptized in the old way and whose faith I could not doubt. But they were not allowed to worship or receive communion with us. Unger knew I had been hurt by this. It grieved him, too, that we could not agree, but he would not bend. However, he was not without a heart, and he had told me more than once of his horror when he heard how my father had been treated by the *Schulze*. I well remember how he broke down several times when he preached at the funeral. Now, here he was with this most generous gift! We embraced each other that morning. In later years he had much sadness — in the church, certainly, but also in his own family. I have heard that one of his grandsons, a certain Jakob Penner, is now a communist in Canada.

Maria's father gave us a matched pair of mares, which we hitched to the heavily loaded Ungerwagen. We travelled first to the colony office in Rosenthal to collect the papers authorizing our emigration to Fürstenland, and to the bank to arrange for the transfer of funds. Then through the hills and the southern villages of Chortitza to the track on the right bank of the Dniepr that would take us to Nikopol.

The journey was not difficult, though the roads were muddy with snowmelt and the swaying of the wagon made the baby restless. The air was warm, and for the most part, the skies were clear, so we were not uncomfortable. We even managed to sleep a little in the afternoons when we stopped for an hour to let the horses graze. Only at night, if we could not find a village to take us in and we had to sleep under the wagon, did we feel uneasy. The nights were cool, and we were anxious about the risk from bandits. But God protected us, and we arrived in Nikopol safely in only three days.

The next morning we crossed the river to village #3, Michaelsburg. Here we met the *Oberschulze* Dueck, to whom we submitted our papers. We were greatly relieved to learn that a house was waiting for us in #4, Rosenbach, one of the cluster of four villages we now call the *Jannedarpa*, fifteen *verst* to the south. Isaak Elias, the owner, had returned to Chortitza on short notice to manage the farm of his ailing parents and was looking for a tenant. He had leased out his cropland, so farming was not an option for us in the short term. But the barn and gardens were free for our use as we wished.

The fruit trees were already in blossom when we arrived, and we lost no time planting potatoes and other vegetables. Our new neighbours sold us a cow and a half dozen piglets, and we adopted a few old hens we found wandering about in the yard that seemed to have no owners. We set a dozen eggs under them, and in a few weeks we had our first flock of chicks. We could buy grain and hay to feed our animals and flour for our bread from one of the local treadmills. All in all, we were satisfied that we would not go hungry while we waited for our place in village #6.

## The Village

The Emancipation Edict of 1861 freed some twenty million serfs throughout Russia, among them the many thousands indentured to the vast private estates of the Grand Duke Michael Nikolaevich. He was the youngest brother of Tsar Alexander II, and the collapse in the supply of bonded labour brought about by his brother's reforms resulted in a significant reduction in income. To compensate for his losses he authorized the sale or lease of a number of tracts of his less profitable lands.

The Grand Duke's agent, Moritz Schumacher, travelled regularly between the estates under his management. Having passed several times through the villages of Chortitza, he was well aware of the chronic land shortage among the Mennonites. By the early 1860s, more than half the population of Chortitza was landless and disenfranchised, relegated to wage labour, and with no influence in community affairs beyond their remittance of the compulsory head tax. The issue had reached crisis proportions and threatened to escalate into an open revolt of the poor.

In 1863, Schumacher met representatives of the colony with a proposal for the rental of twelve thousand dessiatine of land on the left bank of the Dniepr near his base opposite the city of Nikopol. Negotiations were amiable, agreement swift, and mutual trust sufficiently high so that no legal contract was deemed necessary. The terms: 1.25 rubles per dessiatine annually for the first fifteen years; one dessiatine per household rent-free for buildings and gardens; and rents to be collected by the *Schulze* of each village and forwarded to the office of agent Schumacher on the anniversary date of the founding of the settlement.

The new colony was called Grossfürstenland, Land of the Grand Duke. Between 1864 and 1868, six villages were established, with room for some 200 families in all. The villages were numbered in the order of their founding and only later named after the Grand Duke's children. Among the flood of applicants from all parts of the Old Colony were members of the newly established *Brüdergemeinde*, and survivors of the Great Fire of Osterwick, which had destroyed much of the village and left sixty families homeless, many of them from the landless class. Peter Dueck, who had led the negotiations in Chortitza, transferred to the new settlement to serve as its *Oberschulze*, and he established his headquarters in #3, Michaelsburg. For Jakob and Maria Janzen, #4, Rosenbach, would be no more than a transit point. Their home for the next fifty years would be #6, the last village to be built and the last to receive a name, when in October of 1869 the Grand Duke christened his infant son *Serge*.

### From *The Memoirs of Jakob Wilhelm Janzen*

For a year I worked in the blacksmith shop of Heinrich Esau in the neighbouring village of #1, Georgsthal. It was good and wholesome work, and I earned enough to support our growing family. More than once it occurred to me that farming was much more difficult and financially uncertain than the work I was doing in the blacksmith shop. My wages were not high, but they were stable. Farming, I well knew, had few guarantees, and to start afresh on unknown land would be a great challenge. But my whole life had been spent on one farm or another, and I had come to love that life. I do not think I ever doubted in those days that I would follow the same course that my parents and grand-parents had taken. But for now I was more than content with my labour as a blacksmith.

Esau was a generous master. He gave me free use of his shop to make the tools and implements I would need in Sergejewka, and

for the raw iron he would accept only what he had paid for it. I
also taught myself how to build the simple furniture we would
need. This labour on my own behalf gave me much pleasure, and
it took up several evenings each week after the regular work of the
shop was done. The other evenings, as well as my early morning
hours, I spent seeing to our livestock and gardens and doing what
I could to help Maria with the household and our growing family,
which, before the end of our first year in the colony, included a
second daughter.

As often as I could, I travelled with several other men the fifteen
*verst* to the site of the new village. I clearly remember how my
anticipation grew each time we mounted the last rise until we
could finally see the Dniepr stretching far into the distance on
either side. We usually came down through a stand of large trees
just above where our cemetery is now. From there we could look
down to the left and see the place where the village would be. The
cemetery is still a beautiful place, where I go to remember the
many people of our village who have been laid to rest there. I
especially remember those who were here at our beginnings and
how, in those early days, it seemed there was only life and endless
time before us.

As soon as the surveyors had completed their work, we began
clearing rocks and trees from our assigned lots and plotting out
gardens and orchards. Each of us built a *Semlin* on the edge of
the village site where we could stay for a few days while we
worked. These were the crude shelters whose ruins you can still
see in a few places in Sergejewka; just low sod walls around a
square hole dug in the ground, waist deep, with a roof of poles
and more sods, peaked just high enough so we could stand up
inside. Later, the *Semlin* was home to four of us when Maria and
the children joined me there, before I had completed our first
proper house.

That day finally came in early April of 1868. Maria had not been
to Sergejewka at all, and her first impressions were confused. She
was delighted to be close to the Dniepr again, but she was more
than a little set back by the primitive conditions we would live in
while we established ourselves. She knew about the *Semlin*, but
perhaps I had somewhat exaggerated its glories. When I took her
to the edge of our allotment and showed her the swelling in the
ground where we were to live for the time being, there was a

silence quite long enough to make me nervous. Perhaps, I thought, she was praying for strength and endurance. She looked up at me after some time, and her lips formed a tight little smile. But her eyes said nothing, nor did she speak. Finally she nodded her head, solemnly, as one does when taking in news that changes everything. She took little Mariechen by the hand and led her inside, and when they emerged again she began to unload the wagon.

Since then, Maria has said many times that, in her opinion — which agrees exactly with mine — the placement of our Sergejewka is by far the most beautiful of the Fürstenland villages. Perhaps something should be said of this for those of my readers who have not been blessed to see it for themselves.

In the old days, a traveller approaching from the east would cross great stretches of open steppe with little to see until he arrived at the three *kurgans,* where the ancient peoples buried their dead. They have stood there for centuries, like sentries guarding access to the Dniepr, and the traveller would have to pass between them to the band of dense forest that follows the top of the river valley. The old trail continued through the trees to where the ground falls away in a gentle slope. Only then did the village come into view, and beyond it and far below, the Dniepr, threading its way south along a narrow course at the bottom of its immense valley. Today, of course, most of the trees are gone. The old trail has vanished under the plough, and roads lead south to Lepetykha, northeast to Michaelsburg, and east to the other four villages, the *Jannedarpa*.

Our village rests on a plateau that interrupts the drop from the steppe. On the other side of this terrace the ground falls steeply to the flood plain below, where a small stream that has broken away from the Dniepr ten or twelve *verst* to the north passes by the village before emptying into the main current again. This stream is our beloved *konstje,* where we bathe in summer and the children learn to swim. After the spring floods have subsided, there is a *plaven* between the two streams — a floodplain island dotted with willow thickets and lush grass for our cattle. Driftwood snags on the willows and helps trap the rich silts that remain when the water recedes. This is our most fertile soil, and it is always on the *plaven* that we plant our famous watermelons, the best and biggest in the land. In spring, when the *konstje* runs high and clear, it is the preferred place for baptisms, not only for our congregation in Sergejewka but for the *Brüdergemeinde* of all of Fürstenland.

Much has changed in the last forty years, but the original Sergejewka was like Mennonite villages everywhere in Russia: one long street down the middle, with thirty farmyards spaced equally on either side. There was no expectation in those first years that industry would develop here. All of that was in the future; in the beginning there were only farms.

In any new settlement there are worries about its potential for survival, and Sergejewka was no exception. Our first concern arose when we planted our first crop and discovered that here, so near the river, the soil was much sandier than elsewhere in Fürstenland. It held moisture poorly, and we knew that on these southern steppes we could expect only moderate rainfall. Would this land produce the surplus, beyond our own food require-ments, that we would need to pay the annual rent? There would be no other source of money.

There was another, related concern, one we shared with the other Fürstenland villages. How reliable were the arrangements with the Grand Duke? Could we risk investing in permanent houses and barns? Bricks would have to be brought overland from Molotschna and timber by river barge from the forests near Chortitza. Both were expensive, and if the *Fürst* chose not to renew the lease when it expired in fifteen years, we would have to leave everything behind. These were some of the doubts that troubled us in the first years, and as later events would prove, they were not unjustified.

For these reasons, most of us decided to build very simple homes, much in the style of those one sees in many Russian villages, with walls of rammed clay from the river bank and a pitched roof of local wood, roughly hewn and thatched with rushes. Before winter, I also built a cattle shed of sturdy poles set in the ground and wattled with willows from the plaven. Its roof was thatched, like the house, but almost flat. With a blanket of snow it was as warm as any proper barn. Better buildings would come a few years later when we had learned to trust our situation more fully. And so we began our life in Sergejewka. Each of us was assigned sixty-five dessiatines, which we planted with wheat and barley. In some places our fields overlapped with the small private plots previously cultivated by the serfs that had belonged to the *Fürst*. The serfs had been removed to other locations, and that first spring our planting was delayed while we dismantled their huts and removed other obstructions. There was much labour, and the days were long. We counted it a blessing, that first year, that the terms of our lease required a portion of the land to be left fallow. With so many other demands, we could hardly have planted it all.

As soon as our homes were completed and our first crops were in the ground, we formed a village council and elected our first *Schulze* to order and supervise our mutual affairs. The council designated land for a community pasture and hired a herdsman from Rohachyk. We dug a deep well in the centre of the village, and enclosed it to prevent contamination from cattle and other animals. We laboured together on these tasks, and the bonds that developed between us were strong. The *Fürst* had made a donation of wood for the construction of a school building in each village, and for a few years, until we could build our first small *Versammlungshaus*, it was used also for Sunday services. Our neighbours were not all of the *Brüdergemeinde*, but in the beginning we all joined together for worship, first in our homes and later in the school. That was an intimacy that I have often missed in the years since.

It did not take long before all thirty farms were occupied. There was much optimism as we settled into the familiar routines of Mennonite village life. There was good pasture for our cattle, the first crops were better than expected, and we made the necessary connections with merchants in Velyka Lepetykha for the sale of our produce and the supply of things we could not produce for ourselves. We found a teacher for our children, and our village council was strong and forward-looking. In our own family, Mariechen and Annchen were healthy, and soon we were awaiting the birth of a third child.

The only cloud that darkened our skies was a rumour that the government was threatening to cancel certain privileges that had been guaranteed when our people first came to this land almost a hundred years earlier. One of these concerned our language. We had always used the German language in the schools; it was the language of our people, and of our Bible, which we used to bring our children to the knowledge of God. Now the language of instruction was to be Russian, and if our own teachers could not speak it, we would be required to hire Russians.

Much more threatening to us, however, was the warning that by a certain date all exemptions from military service would be cancelled, which would require us to betray a teaching more dear to us than almost any other. Our leaders from Molotschna and Chortitza went to St. Petersburg to defend our principles, but they did not succeed in obtaining a meeting with anyone with decision-making power. By 1872, the whole Russian Mennonite world was churning with emigration fever. The first families left for America the next year, and hundreds of others were preparing to do so as soon as they could obtain exit visas. Eventually, in an effort to staunch the flow of some of the country's best agriculturalists, the government offered concessions in the form of alternate service in the forestry department or the medical corps. To some, this compromise was acceptable, and they decided to remain. Others rejected the concessions on the grounds that conscripts would still be members of the military and would be required to wear the uniform, even in the *Forestei*.

These details of what was happening elsewhere in Russia I first learned from a stranger, Peter Stoesz, who was passing through our village. He had recently returned to his home in Bergthal Colony after six months at the pedagogical seminary in Chortitza, only to be told that his 'higher education' had over-qualified him to teach there. To him this was laughable, and he was angry and deeply disappointed with what he considered the backwardness of the Bergthal leadership. The *Ältester* had dismissed him as arrogant and warned him not to contaminate the colony with his attitudes.

Stoesz was about my own age, and we talked one evening as we walked on the bank of the Dniepr. He was bitter about many aspects of Mennonite life and culture, and he declared himself strongly in favour of the termination of our privileged status, which had always been unrealistic. "It is high time," he said, "that Mennonites recognize how blind we are to the millions all around us who toil in the squalor of poverty while we soar above them like eagles over mice."

I remember that those were his words. He would not return to Bergthal. Neither would he emigrate with the rest of his family. His destination was St. Petersburg, where he would study the Russian language in order to qualify to teach in any school in Russia, and he was quite sure it would not be a Mennonite school. Already he used the Russian form of his name, although we both understood that between us, it was something of a joke. I met Pyotr Jakovitch Stess again many years later when I travelled to Nikopol on factory business. He had found work there as a civil servant in the land tax office.

I will give only the briefest account of the next three years. Across the entire Russian Mennonite world everything was in turmoil. The first group of *Bergthaler* left in 1874, and within three years their entire colony had been abandoned. From the six villages of Fürstenland, more than a thousand persons left the next year. Our own *Schulze* took twelve Sergejewka families with him. Those who emigrated before they could find new tenants left that task to the village council. For a time, this proved to be a severe hardship for us. On a *Pachtkolonie* like ours, each village is collectively responsible for rent on all the land assigned to it, no matter how much of it is actually in use. Until new tenants could be found, our individual levies would be doubled. Maria and I still had funds from the sale of the farm in Kronsweide, but there were poor families who had already been landless in the old colony, or who had lost everything in the Osterwick fire. They were now in difficult straits, and I know of at least three families for whom this tipped the scales. With the promise of cheap land in America, they decided to emigrate just to escape this unsupportable burden. Soon more than half the farms in Sergejewka were abandoned, and our village would have failed entirely less than ten years after its founding, had it not been for an entirely new and unexpected development.

## THE FACTORY

Maria Janzen enters her husband's study mid-afternoon and, as so often in recent days, she finds him slumped over his desk, asleep. His pen has fallen from his hand and bled onto his papers. She blots the stain as well as she can, then touches his shoulder and whispers his name. "Jakob, I have made coffee."

He rouses and looks about him, struggling to discern his whereabouts. He rubs his left arm, then remembers that the numbness there is permanent. He stares at the pages laid out on the desk.

"*Ach* Maria," he says. "Look at this mess." He gestures dismissively at the disarray and turns to look up at her. He shakes his head. "You know, Maria, the older I get, the better I was."

Jakob laughs at his joke, but Maria is not amused.

He fumbles with the sheet he's been working on. "So clumsy I am with words. I sometimes feel I am scribbling with my elbows."

Maria cannot reassure him. "*Na ja*, Jakob," she sighs. "We have grown old." She helps him to his feet and guides him through the door and into the kitchen, where the maid brings coffee and a plate of the sweet *Röllchen* that are his favourite.

Each evening, after he is asleep, Maria recopies what her husband has written that day. In the two years since he began his memoirs, a vagueness has descended upon Jakob's mental life, and the writing has, indeed, become awkward. Some days Maria finds only brief notes on a page or two and she is left to her own devices, deciphering his scrawl as best she can and evoking her own memories of the past to supply missing information. He is writing about the factory now, and she finds she must soften his criticisms of partners and associates. To her great dismay, she finds expletives and sudden fierce invectives, underlined and circled, against former business rivals, creditors and factory personnel — even members of his own family. These she strikes altogether, and she wonders how it can be that this pious man, whom she has known and loved for almost fifty years, can allow himself to write what he would never dream of speaking aloud. In the mornings she reads back to Jakob what she has written, and he does not remember what is not there. He thanks her and is satisfied. "It is very good ... I think? Is there more I must write?"

She helps him pick up the narrative and leaves him at his desk again.


On the day Jakob finishes his account of the takeover of the Klassen factory, Maria finds him at the window of his study, looking across the street to the offices of *Janzen & Neufeld Ko.* The noon whistle has sounded, and the voices of workers on their way home for lunch reach them from the street. Clouds have banished the morning sun and a light rain glistens on the black chimney of the factory. Jakob is leaning precariously on the back of a chair. Maria sees how frail he has become, and she frets over him.

"Jakob. What are you doing? You will fall, Jakob!"

He laughs weakly and turns to face her. "My dear Maria Unruh. Always so *unruh-ig!*"

She does not recognize his lucidity, nor the happiness in his eyes. She sees only that he is very tired and she goes to help settle him in the chair. He is quiet for a moment. Then, with a sudden motion, he raises his head and looks up at her.

"Maria." He points to a sheaf of papers on the chair beside the desk. "Maria. I can tell you it is finished. Nothing new has happened in these last years. I will write no more. I am finished!"

Later that evening Maria adds a few summative paragraphs before taking the final instalment across the street to their granddaughter Anna, who is making a fair copy of the memoir. Her husband Johann will post it to the printers in Nikopol the next time he travels to Lepetykha.

### From *The Memoirs of Jakob Wilhelm Janzen*

In 1876, when the outflow of emigrants had almost stopped, Maria and I were wonderfully surprised by a visit from Kornelius Klassen from Kronsweide. He and his wife Hannah were especially dear to us, as all four of us were baptized together on that bitter morning in March of '62. Klassen built farm machinery in a small factory near Chortitza, but competition from larger firms was making it difficult for him, and he was looking for a fresh start. He had disembarked from the steamer at Velyka Lepetykha, where he had been impressed by the harbour. If there was space for a small factory, he said, Sergejewka would suit him well. Klassen wound up his affairs in the Old Colony and established a workshop on the edge of our village. Before winter he had set up a small foundry and an assembly room, and ordered enough pig iron and coal to see him through the winter. Among our farming families he found ten young sons, and production began as soon as their training was complete. This marked the beginning, not only of our first industry but of the transformation of our village from a simple farming community into the factory town it is today.

It will be impossible for me, gazing back through the milky waters of memory, to give a full account of all that has transpired in the thirty-five years since the first of Klassen's reaping machines left the assembly room. I wish I could say all has been sunshine and birdsong. As is true of all of man's endeavours, successes were mingled with trials and tribulations, and we have laboured under all weathers. I will set down only what seems to me most consequential.

When Klassen learned of my experience in the Esau ironworks, he asked whether farming was so much in my blood that I would not consider working with him in the factory. He was in urgent need of supervision for his unskilled recruits. If I could oversee the assembly process, he would attend to the more technical work of the foundry. I agreed to help him during the winter and whenever I was free from farm work during the rest of the year. Klassen was a master of his craft, and more often than not, the agents who came to inspect our products placed orders. I well remember the day Klassen showed me a sizeable order from the Old Colony. He pointed to the name inscribed on the letterhead and winked at me. The same man who had refused his wares in Chortitza as too expensive now recognized their superior quality and was willing to pay the additional freight from Sergejewka. When the original foundry proved inadequate, Klassen invited his nephew Abraham to build a larger one and run it as his own enterprise. Our workforce grew, and I soon found it a hardship to supervise the factory and run my farm at the same time. When Klassen proposed that we should become partners, I was glad to accept. I had no difficulty finding tenants for my land since, by then, new families were moving in to replace those who had emigrated. I invested the funds remaining from the sale of my parents' farm in Kronsweide, and Klassen and I shared equally in all costs and profits until 1882 when Klassen announced his intention to retire to a farm in the new Mennonite Brethren settlement in the Kuban district.

This was the beginning of a chapter that still brings me sadness and regret. Klassen sold his interest in the firm to his nephew Abraham, who thus became my new partner. Factory and foundry were merged, with Abraham retaining the greater share of sixty percent since my partnership with his uncle had not included the new foundry. Abraham and I were the same age and had been on good terms from the first day we met. From the start of our new partnership, however, there were matters on which we did not agree. For the most part, these were minor creases which were easily ironed out, and we did not allow arguments to hinder our good relations.

But there was one issue that plagued us and nearly drove us to bankruptcy in less than five years. Abraham and I had greatly underestimated the safeguards his uncle had kept in place. Experience had taught him how quickly a business could sink under the weight of debt, and he had been scrupulous in matching production as closely as possible to demand. "Surplus inventory," he said, "is a millstone around the neck." Each winter, he wrote to our distributors requesting their sales projections, and throughout the growing season he paid close attention to the progress of crops in all the regions where we sold our machines. At first, such cautions seemed unnecessary to us. The quality of our products gave us an advantage, Abraham said, and if need be, we could afford to reduce our prices a little without greatly affecting the bottom line in the ledger. I realized somewhat earlier than he that we were taking dangerous risks, and I tried not to think that it might be his majority share that allowed him to ignore my concerns. Even in poor years, when farmers had little money, Klassen resisted reducing the second shift, even when unsold ploughs and mowers were already rusting in the factory yard. When we shipped some of these on credit, dealers we had always trusted failed to make good, and I regret to say that some of these were our own people in Crimea and Molotschna. It was a grievous miscalculation on our part. Our accounts receivable mounted as fast as the heap of invoices from our suppliers. Appeals to the banks in Nikopol and Kherson for credit fell on deaf ears, with the result that we were forced to apply for receivership.

In Nikopol we found a financier willing to consider our situation. Jakov Anton Tenno was Estonian and one of the strangest men I have known. He spoke fluent Yiddish, German and Russian, and his speech was eloquent, though hardly more so than his long and ominous silences. I remember how, as he listened to our plight, he nodded impatiently, as one might who was all too familiar with failed enterprises and knew our story even before we spoke. He agreed to come to Sergejewka to inspect our factory and examine our affairs. We opened our books to him, and for a full hour Tenno spoke not a single word while Klassen and I stood by on one leg each. He stood hunched over the figures, slapping the pages vigorously back and forth and nicking them harshly with his pencil before skimming each ledger off to the end of the counter while reaching for the next. He asked no questions until he was done, and then only to inquire as to the name of our bookkeeper, Wohlgemuth, to whom he paid the highest compliments.

We brought coffee then, and he consented to the offer of a chair. After a minute or two of terse small talk, Tenno pushed his cup aside and stated his verdict and his terms. The firm was salvage-able. Shipments on credit were prohibited. Production must be strictly matched to demand, and our workforce reduced accord-ingly. He would advance funds to our creditors to ensure that supplies would not be cut off. He would visit twice a year to examine the books and collect his fee. If after five years the firm had recovered, full ownership would be restored to us. If we failed, the factory and contents would be sold at auction. Now, if he was to meet the ship at Lepetykha, he would soon need to leave. Could we let him know within the hour or should he expect the pleasure of our attendance at his offices in Nikopol within the week?

Klassen and I walked the length of the village and conferred together. All other options were found wanting. We returned to the factory, where Tenno was making a final survey of our equip-ment and supplies. We confirmed the arrangements, shook hands, and he went on his way.

That was in 1886. The next few years were meagre, but Tenno's regime proved sound. With his approval, we sold off older inven-tory at cost and made improvements to our new models. We learned that the factory in Olgafeld was beyond capacity, and we signed a contract with Niebuhr to cast gears and structural members for his machines, which allowed us to keep most of our workers. During this period we had good rains, which meant that landowners and district *zemstvos* were able to buy from us again. After five years, Tenno declared our affairs in good order, and we were released from receivership.

It was on my initiative that the Klassen-Janzen partnership dissolved shortly after we regained full control in 1891, and I wish to emphasize that this had nothing whatsoever to do with any conflict between us. In fact, when we parted ways, Abraham insisted that after so many years in partnership, first with his uncle and then with him, I was entitled to half the value of the firm, and that was the price he pressed me to accept. He and I remained friends, and I might add that he was more than generous in minimizing my share of responsibility for the misjudgments of the early years. The explanation for my decision to leave the firm will require a step back in time, and a treatment of events that touch directly upon my family.

It was in 1889, while we were still awaiting our release from receivership, that Abraham's twenty-year-old cousin Kornelius Neufeld arrived in Sergejewka looking for work. He learned quickly, and it became evident early on that his enterprising soul could never be satisfied with life as a shop labourer. He discovered design flaws in our machines and inefficiencies in our methods, and he was able to propose solutions to these problems. Within a short time, he had acquainted himself thoroughly with every division of the factory, from foundry to sales floor and removed any doubt there might have been about his value to our firm. Nor did his keen eye fail him when he passed through the factory gates at day's end, as we discovered when he approached Maria and me to ask for the hand of our daughter Anna.

Shortly before their wedding, Kornelius discussed with me the possibility of building our own shop. I went to Klassen for his opinion on how this might affect his business, and he had no concerns. His casting contract with Niebuhr was on a sound footing, he said, and he was operating at capacity. The small shop my son-in-law and I had in mind would hardly offer much competition. Klassen went so far as to suggest that we merge our supply requisitions as a saving to us both. He asked only that

Kornelius remain with him for a time in order to train a new supervisor to replace him.

We opened our shop in the fall of 1892, and *Janzen & Neufeld Ko.* was born. We expanded slowly, both of us working closely with our hired workers on the shop floor, and for the first three years all went well. Our reputation for quality and reliability spread quickly, yielding contracts with *zemstvos* on both sides of the Dniepr, as far away as Kherson.

Then came the unprecedented drought of 1895/96. Again, our warehouses and the factory yard were choked with inventory. Refusing to deliver on credit was an empty threat. Even the *zemstvos* did not reply to our appeals for payment for machines we had delivered in good faith. The earlier fat years were devoured by the lean, and we sorely regretted our aggressive repayment of the loans we had taken for the expansion of the factory. It was difficult, at the end of some months, to meet the eyes of our workers when we had to defer a portion of their wages.

Of course, we were not alone in our plight. On one occasion, I met Abraham Klassen on the wharf in Lepetykha, and we commiserated. He was physically ill with anxiety. His workforce was larger than ours, and Niebuhr had cancelled his contract with the foundry. The banks in Odessa and Kherson had turned him down, and he was on his way to the mother colony, Chortitza, for emergency relief. With tears in his eyes, he described his exhaustion from the burdens of ownership. He would gladly trade his lot for that of a farmhand, he said.

The crisis passed, and abundant rains in the next three years produced the largest harvests South Russia had ever known. And, like the sudden bursting of a dam, orders poured in. The *zemstvos* were able to clear their accounts with us, and new customers from Berdyansk and the new Mennonite settlement near Orenburg requested our brochures.

But it seemed Sergejewka was always between the hammer and the anvil. With the land lease renewal of 1900 came yet another steep increase in rent. Again, talk of emigration buzzed in the villages of Fürstenland, and this time the destination was Siberia. The outflow was so great that visitors returning to Chortitza and

Molotschna predicted the collapse of our entire colony. Every village fell into arrears, and the authorities issued a prohibition of all further emigration until our collective debt was cleared. Sergejewka was by far the hardest hit, and we were warned that if we did not comply by the spring we would be forbidden to plant our fields.

Again, half of the village lay empty, and we found ourselves desperately short of workers. Unskilled labourers like our *Zuschläger* — the young hammermen who assisted the black-smiths at the hearth — as well as the assembly crews, painters, and carpenters' assistants, were mostly younger sons of farmers, and they left with their families. We were forced to beg patience from both customers and creditors in the hope that matters would improve. But to no avail. The factory and its contents were appraised, down to the last lump of hard coal strewn in the yard. The assessment was registered in Velyka Lepetykha as surety against our debts, and the spectre of bankruptcy once more mocked us in our dreams.

As the crisis deepened, my son-in-law questioned me about my earlier dealings with Johann Anton Tenno. I was most reluctant to go a second time to that strange man, but when Kornelius returned empty-handed from the banks in Rostov and Odessa, I relented, and we went to see him in Nikopol. As before, Tenno spoke very little, and again his terms were sharp and non-nego-tiable. This time, he ordered that everything not absolutely essen-tial must be sold at auction to reduce our debt. We would continue production at our current reduced capacity, increasing it only as revenue and demand permitted.

To us, the goods identified for auction were worth at least ten thousand rubles, but under the hard conditions of those days we were fearful that there would be few bidders willing to offer more than a fraction of their value. In this we were not mistaken. However, if we had thought Tenno an odd man, he was to prove stranger still on that day. He outbid everyone on every item, and when the auction concluded, he directed us to reinstall the equip-ment he had bought. He placed the proceeds of the sale — his money — in our hands and told us, "Put this to good use. You will reimburse me when you recover." It was an act of generosity and goodwill for which we had no explanation other than that he recalled the successful recovery of *Klassen & Janzen Ko.* years earlier.

After this calamity, Kornelius was determined to secure a workforce independent of the farming community. He recruited professional foundrymen from Molotschna who committed to a three-year term. In the Russian and ethnic German villages in our region he announced free housing for single men and families quartered on our premises. Schooling would be provided for the children of married workers, and he would cover the cost of a second classroom if it became necessary to hire a Russian teacher. The strategy was successful, with the result that factory operations soon returned to full capacity.

Under the duress of these difficult days I had become quite ill, so much so that I was forced to beg Kornelius to release me long enough so that I could recover my strength. I took up farming some of my land again, and I must say that this return to God's good earth restored my spirit more than any medicine could have done. During this period, I was also able to attend more closely to the affairs of our church, where I had recently been elected to the leadership.

After a year of rest, I returned to the factory much restored. With our labour supply assured, the firm was well on its way to recovery. Alas, the same could not be said for our friend Abraham Klassen. The travails of the last years had left him despondent. He had mistakenly counted on the resumption of his contract with the Olgafeld factory and had not pursued other markets to make up the deficit. When Tenno released *Janzen & Neufeld Ko.* from receivership, Klassen was still deep in debt.

There came a day in July of 1906 when he called us both aside after the Sunday service. He said plainly, "I can go no further." Bankruptcy was imminent, and rather than losing everything to auction and leaving seventy employees without work, he asked us to consider taking over his factory. If we could clear his most pressing debts, he said, the balance could be paid over an eight-year period.

For us this was a complex matter. We had just opened a new section for the manufacture of furniture, and our own workforce had risen to more than one hundred. I could feel the years piling up upon my shoulders and could not promise to remain engaged with the firm much longer. The weight of this decision would rest with Kornelius. He undertook the negotiations and came to an agreement with Klassen that was acceptable to us all. It was in this way that the two factories became one.

The years since the merger have gone well. We employ one hundred forty workers in Sergejewka with additional staff in Taganrog and in Orenburg in the Urals, where we have our own sales outlets. Our success has recently become a matter of public record. The government directory of Mennonite industry in Russia names us as the eighth-largest producer of agricultural equipment in the land. Particularly satisfying have been the testimonials from the Secretariat of Agriculture praising the quality and reliability of our products.

Looking back to 1876, when the older Klassen opened his little shop and hired ten or twelve workers, we could not have imagined the transformation that our village has since undergone. Each person we have lost through emigration to America or Siberia has been replaced threefold, so that Sergejewka is now the largest of the Fürstenland villages. No longer does it mirror the typical Mennonite *Strassendorf,* with its single street lined with houses and yards on either side. Nor can we truthfully say that Sergejewka is still a *Mennonite* village, since fewer than half of our inhabitants are Mennonites, and most of these no longer rely on farming for their livelihood. The rest of our people are the Russians and ethnic *Volksdeutsche* who occupy the more than forty workers' cottages on *Janzen & Neufeld Ko.* property at the south end of the village.

Much, indeed, has changed. That early traveller who stood at the edge of the steppe and gazed down upon the empty terrace where the nameless village #6 was yet to be built would most certainly not recognize the place today, though the slopes that rise behind Sergejewka still dazzle with blossoms each spring while the ancient *kurgans* keep watch above the great river as it flows, silent and strong, on its way to the sea.

# 3. Jascha's Flight

Jascha began fidgeting soon after the second sermon began. He stifled a yawn, and Isaak, his neighbour, noticed and elbowed him sharply in the ribs. Jascha retaliated and was startled by the rap of a knuckle on the back of his head. Onkel Gerhard Enns, his mother's uncle. Why did Onkel Gerhard always sit behind him? It seemed that wherever Jascha and his friends chose to sit from week to week, Onkel Gerhard was always there. Jascha straightened his back and resolved to ignore his friends and become as quiet as possible. The church was stifling hot, and as the voice of the preacher faded, Jascha's head began to nod. Once or twice he roused briefly, and from the corner of his eye he saw his friend Isaak grinning at him. Again, fatigue overcame him and his head lurched sideways against Isaak's shoulder. He started upwards again, just in time for a double rap from behind. Fully awake now, he sat frozen until the final hymn was announced and everyone stood to sing.

When Jascha and his friends emerged from the meetinghouse into the heat of the August sun, Onkel Gerhard was waiting for him at the hitching post. He took one of Jascha's ears between thumb and forefinger.

"Jasch! Do you think that just because your father is away you can do what you like?" Jascha stood on tip-toe to relieve the upward thrust of Onkel's grip. He whimpered a mild protest, but Onkel would not permit interruption.

"I tell you, Jasch, if this behaviour doesn't stop, you will get one you will remember long after your father comes home from the war. Look at me! Do you hear? I'll thrash you thoroughly!" With a final glare he relaxed his grip and strode off across the church yard.

Jascha rubbed his ear as the other boys came over to him. He was in pain, and his eyes were shining, though he did not cry. Isaak, who had been partly responsible for Jascha's misery, touched his arm and tried to cheer him. Little Albert Wohlgemuth, Jascha's bench-mate in school, had kept a safe distance until Onkel Gerhard was well away, and he came over now to comfort him. All of the boys were wary of Onkel Gerhard. They had never seen him smile, and whenever he read the Scripture at the beginning of the service he always chose passages that seemed to catch the loving God unhappy or angry. "For I am a jealous God, punishing the children for the sins of their fathers!" he would declaim, and his eyes would pierce the congregation right and left. This morning, he had finished with one of his favourites: "Be ye perfect, even as your Father in heaven is perfect!" He read loudly in his high tenor voice, with sharply separated syllables, and Jasch always looked for the spray of exclamation in the shaft of sunlight angling across the podium from the windows.

Little Albert said he had overheard stories from workers in the factory where Onkel Gerhard was the manager of the foundry. Albert's father worked in the office, so he didn't know firsthand, but some of the men said they didn't like working for Onkel Gerhard. They shook their heads and clicked their tongues as they described his mistreatment of the apprentices and how the Russians would swear under their breath whenever Onkel Gerhard walked through their workspace.

Huddled around Jascha, the boys took turns mocking the Onkel in whispered voices, each trying to outdo the other.

"Be Ye Per-fikt! Eeffenn Asss Yourr Vaterrr im Him-melll iss Perrr-fikt!" They snickered at each fresh attempt and kept a careful eye out for Onkel Gerhard and other adults who would surely take offence at such blasphemy.

The congregation began to disperse, and the boys separated to join their own families for the walk home. Jascha's brother and sister had gone ahead, and his mother called him to join her. She had observed the incident in church, and she wondered privately whether it was her son or her uncle who had created the greater disturbance during the service. But she had not seen the aftermath in the churchyard. She placed her hand on Jascha's shoulder.

"It is difficult to sit so long in church, *ja*?"

Jascha hesitated. If she had seen, why was her voice so soft, so kind?

"Mama, why do we have two sermons?" he asked, reassured.

"*Na ja*. That's just how it always has been. But I wonder too, sometimes. I like to think about what the first brother has said, and then the thinking has to stop because I have to listen to the second one too." She chuckled, and Jascha grinned up at her.

"Mama, why does Onkel Gerhard always look at me so angry? He makes me think of roosters and sauerkraut."

Anna laughed at her son's wit and squeezed his shoulder.

"What? You don't like sauerkraut?" She leaned over and murmured in his ear. "But this morning, Jascha, it wasn't just looking, was it? I saw what happened in church. You know, Papa asked Onkel to look after his family while he is away and not to let you stray. He is very strict, I know, but Papa will be coming home for a few weeks, and Onkel Gerhard will not think about you then."

Their farmyard was almost directly across the street from the meeting house, and the kettle was already on the stove when mother and son arrived at the door. Jascha went to his room to change out of his Sunday clothes. His mind was crowded with contradictions. Onkel Gerhard conducted the choir masterfully and with beautiful results, yet there did not seem to be a song in his heart. He was one of the Brethren, yet did not always behave in ways that were pious. Some of the boys said they had seen him with a cigarette on the road to Lepetykha one day. They had clearly seen the smoke, and his exaggerated motions to clear his beard and wipe his nose hadn't fooled anyone. Jascha wondered, now, if maybe Onkel Gerhard even drank brandy. That would be even worse, as it was strictly forbidden in the *Brüdergemeinde*. Maybe he wasn't really a believer. Maybe he had been baptized just so he could marry *Ältester* Janzen's daughter. It was frightening to think about. If it was true, then what? How many others were like Onkel Gerhard, who spoke holy words and sang beautiful songs in the church but exhaled anger and darkness in the village? Not all adults were like that, certainly not Mama, who prayed so earnestly, sometimes with tears in her eyes. Adults were a mystery he could not untangle.

Sunday afternoons were quiet and lazy, and the adults liked to open the windows and nap in their front rooms or in the cooling breezes of their summer kitchens. Loud play was discouraged on the Lord's Day, and if he was alone, Jasch found these hours heavy on the heart. After he had helped to clear the dishes, he left the house and joined a group of boys passing by on the road that led out of the village. If no one suggested a game, there would at least be a few hours of companionship.

The sun was hot, and when they had skirted the last yard, the one where Onkel Gerhard lived, the boys took the steep cart trail down to the edge of the slow waters of the *konstje*. Shoes and stockings were heaped on the bank, and they waded out into the centre of the pebbled streambed, and for an hour they followed it at leisure to where it emptied into the depths of the Dniepr. Then they turned around and began to make their way upstream again. There was splashing and pushing and banter, and Jascha took some gentle teasing about the redness of his ear and Onkel Gerhard. But these were his schoolmates, and he understood that they empathized with his humiliation. By the time they returned to their entry point on the bank of the stream they were all joking and laughing about other matters.

Retrieving their footwear, the boys left the creek and made their way back up the trail. A small breeze had sprung up, and after the cooling waters of the creek, there was sudden energy for stone-throwing. The posts supporting the rail fences around each of the neat farmyards and gardens made convenient targets. Isaak, the oldest and tallest of the boys, called a halt at an impossible distance and announced a try. He missed, and the group advanced a step at a time until another boy called out the next challenge. He, too, missed, as did the next three. Eventually, after several more advances, Isaak's stone struck a post, and he dropped a pebble in his pocket as a counter.

The competition intensified then, and no one had noticed their encroachment on the boundaries of Onkel Gerhard's property when Jascha called his first challenge. He stood on the edge of the stony ditch, checked his stance, and made several practice feints as he had seen Isaak do. Then he let fly with such force that he lost his footing. He fell forward into the drainage channel and landed heavily on his side. His stone flew the full distance, but instead of hitting the post, it ricocheted sharply off the uppermost rail and hurtled with barely diminished speed directly towards Onkel Gerhard's summer kitchen. There was a collective gasp as the boys took in the trajectory of the rock and its awful implications. Then came the crash of breaking glass, and before the echoes of the last shards had vanished the boys were running as fast as they could towards the road that led back to the village.

Jascha regained his feet as quickly as he could, but he was slowed by pains in his hip and side.When Onkel Gerhard raged from the summer kitchen where he had been taking his Sunday nap, Jascha was the only culprit still in view. Flourishing a stick of kindling from his woodpile, he ran after the boy, shouting terrible threats of thrashing and maiming such as the boy had never heard before.

In Jascha's mind, Onkel Gerhard was a very old man, so he was dismayed at the increasing volume of the footsteps behind him as he ran limping up the path. He knew the other boys had taken the main road. But he calculated that if he crossed it and continued on the footpath to the cemetery, the steep incline would slow the old man down. At the crossing he veered upwards, and as he had hoped, the sound of Onkel's footsteps receded quickly and then stopped. Near the top of the rise he stepped off the trail and crouched to look back through the underbrush. A hundred meters away the old man stood on the open trail, stooped over now, hands on his knees and gasping for breath. He was no longer carrying the stick. After a minute, he straightened slowly and stood staring upwards toward the cemetery. Jascha crouched deeper in the scrub. Onkel Gerhard seated himself on a stump at the side of the trail, still breathing heavily. He wiped his face with his handkerchief. Then he rose again, and without looking back he began trudging slowly down the slope until Jascha lost sight of him in the row of acacias that lined the main road.

Small gnats swarmed in the shrubbery, and Jascha stepped back into the sun and continued upwards. There was a wooden bench just inside the cemetery gates, and Jascha sat for a time. He opened his shirt and trousers to examine his bruises. There was little to be seen, but there was a steady throbbing in his right leg, and his side ached so that he winced whenever he took a full breath. Gradually his breathing slowed, and when the drumming of his heart subsided he scanned his surroundings. He felt uneasy here alone, though he knew the place well from funerals and from visits to tend the family graves.

From where he sat he could see the gravestones. He had been four when both of his grandfathers died within two months of each other. Grandfather Neufeld was very old and had been sick for a long time, but Opa Enns had died suddenly during a fit of the sleeping sickness. He was forty-nine, and Mama thought that was young. Onkel Gerhard was his brother, and he was already forty-eight, so maybe ... ah, but no, he should not have such thoughts.

Jascha watched a field mouse scramble up and across a row of tiny graves. Wilted bouquets of flowers lay sprawled across black earth still neatly mounded and bare of weeds. The whole church had attended the funerals of these children, three in less than a week during the typhoid terror in spring. He recalled the long processions from the meeting house, how the weeping of the families was the only sound as the congregation encircled the awful holes in the ground. He vividly recalled the inert faces in the open caskets, and how Onkel Kornelius had rejoiced in his sermon that these souls could not be lost since they were too young to be 'answerable.' To the grieving parents he recommended the example of the ancient Job who, despite the loss of ten children, hundreds of camels and his own health, remained a model of faithfulness and piety, so that Satan lost his wager with the Lord. Jascha's teacher told the story often and with high drama, and Jascha always felt great puzzlement at the idea of the good Lord making wagers with the devil.

Onkel Kornelius always concluded his graveside sermons with dreadful warnings to those old enough to be 'accountable' who were still unconverted, and this had put Jascha in a whirlwind of confusion over sin and the last judgment. He knew he was not righteous like Job. He had many sins that would surely count against him. At home, he was often angry with his brothers when they annoyed him with their childishness, and he sometimes struck them and made them cry. At school, when old Herr Kasper turned to the slate board and the other boys made mocking gestures, Jascha joined in, even though he knew it was disrespectful. Then, just a week ago, he and Isaac had hidden on the *plaven* and spied on the women and girls on their bath night in the *konstje*. He was sure he would not do a deed like that again, but now it lay there like a great inkblot on his conscience, along with many other sins that he would need to repent before ... before what? What was that critical age? There were older graves in the same row, weedy and without flowers now, and he wondered about his cousin, who had been almost fifteen when he died of scarlet fever a few years ago.

Far away on the other side of the great river the sun was slipping toward the horizon. Jascha knew he would have to start for home. But if he returned along the footpath he would have to pass Onkel Gerhard's house again, and he dared not risk that. He decided to push on through the cemetery to the top of the slope. From there he could skirt the fields on the upper flats, and once he connected with the Lepetykha road he would know how to find his way home. It would be a long walk, but the alternative was too hazardous.

Jascha rose from the bench and tested his limbs. The soreness had increased, but he would be alright. He noted the lengthening shadows of gravestones across his path, and he did not stop again until he reached the top of the cemetery. Crouching to pass between the rails of the enclosure, he found himself on a grassy buffer between the band of ancient trees that followed the course of the valley, and the fields of wheat on the steppe land above. He had never been here alone before, but the lay of the land was self-evident. As long as he kept to the edge of the fields he must come to the road.

Jascha made good progress, but he was thirsty and hot. When he stopped to rest at the end of the first field he was startled to notice through a gap in the trees that the sun was already touching the forest on the other side of the Dniepr. He started up again promptly, but after a hundred metres his way was blocked by a great gash in the landscape, a ravine that opened somewhere far to his left and widened and deepened as the slope increased towards the river. It was thick with debris and mud after recent rains, and he saw that it could not be crossed. He began tracking alongside it upwards into the fields. He could not know how far he would have to go before the ravine tapered out, and he felt the first signs of panic. He had come too far to go back to the cemetery, and he ran along the edge of the ravine, checking every minute for a crossing place.

In the distance ahead of him, silhouetted against the eastern sky, Jascha could see the three great *kurgans* the legends said held the tombs of ancient kings. The thought that he might have to go near them filled him with dread. The older youths of the village often took picnics there, but he had never been allowed to go. Jascha's father had told him how thieves had cut great trenches through the middle of each mound, looking for gold and bones. And the Ukrainian boys at school claimed that during thunderstorms and winter blizzards you could see the ghosts of Scythian warriors swirling their swords as they battled to defend their graves against the tomb robbers. They said you could even hear their cries and the clash of armour.

Jascha did not think these stories were true, but on the steppe, alone at night, all certainties vanish, and fear is its own truth. He knew it *was* true that professors in Nikopol had discovered something awful inside an enormous *kurgan* very close to Michaelsburg, where Papa's cousin lived. A queen had been buried there, covered in gold and jewels. That was not so bad; the truly horrible part was that her servants and a hundred horses had been killed and buried with her so she would not have to be dead alone. The professors had removed the skeletons, and the weapons and daggers had been taken away and studied. He knew this because Papa's Onkel Kornelius, who was rich and owned the factory, had visited the museums in Nikopol and Kiev and had seen these things for himself.

Jascha's pace had slowed, and he became aware that the floor of the ravine had risen nearly to the level of the fields. He looked up to study the ground ahead of him and was startled to see the first of the *kurgans* towering directly before him, near enough that he could make out the great gash in its side. Here the fields were poorly drained and muddy, and the grassy depressions between them lay in shallow water so that his shoes were wet and heavy. To follow the other side of the ravine now, back towards the blackness of the forest, was daunting. There might well be more ravines in the way, and there were wolves and other night creatures among the trees. Papa had taken him outside one moonlit night to hear them howl. Somewhere still ahead of him, Jascha knew, a well-worn cart trail led back to the village from the more distant fields. It would be out in the open and drier, he thought, and he decided to find it, though it would force him to pass between the tombs.

By the time he came alongside the first *kurgan,* Jascha was exhausted. The throbbing in his hip hobbled him, and the pain in his ribs diminished only when he held his breath. In his misery, he began to doubt that he could get home at all, even if he could find the track.

A great heap of boulders the villagers had cleared from the fields and thrown up against the southern slope of the *kurgan* gave him a place to sit and rest. He took off his wet shoes and wrung out his stockings. The heat of the day still radiated from the stones, and he lay on his uninjured side for a time, his legs folded up against his chest. Clouds swept in to cover the moon and stars, and looking back towards the great river, he saw, like a final exhalation of the dying day, a vast fog rolling upwards toward the open steppe. There would be a heavy dew, but his clothes were already soaked through, and he was cold. Night congealed around him, and in the dark his misery expanded.

Thoughts of Mama and the kitchen stove drew him like the pole of a powerful magnet. His fear of Onkel Gerhard dissipated, eclipsed by his current plight. He felt the emptiness that surrounded him, his smallness in the immensity of the universe, and he had the uncanny feeling that the universe was watching, and that the universe was God. It seemed to him that a great eye had opened, an eye that would not close, that roamed the inner chambers of his soul and whispered what it found there: a bleakness he did not understand, a darkness deeper than anything around him in the night world. Onkel Kornelius's gigantic voice echoed in his soul, and his great finger swept down and across the front benches where Johann sat with his friends during the funerals. *'All have sinned and come short of the Glory of God!'* Somewhere, he knew, as part of the overall scheme, there was also Love, but Jascha could not feel it. Was this the awakening of his own accountability? God and Lucifer wrestling for his soul? The boy was not equipped to doubt the teachings of his elders, and he was overwhelmed in a surge of horror at the cosmic arrangements and in terror for his own soul. All else fell away. There was only this, the truest thing he had ever known. This, surely, was the wrath of God.

Utterly depleted in body, mind and spirit, he slept. And there, among the stones of the place, little Jakob dreamed a dream. Onkel Gerhard stood at the top of a vast translucent *kurgan* whose flame-blue light radiated in all directions and filled the world. His face glowed, and his long hair streamed and sparkled miles behind him in a roaring gale. At his right hand stood the holy Lord, and together they looked down at the sleeping Jakob, gesturing at him amusedly and singing a strange and ragged melody. 'Be ye perfect!' was the refrain they chanted again and again. Then they nodded to each other and strode off in opposite directions, their laughter echoing across the firmament. Camels and horses fled before a mighty wind, and somewhere an old man sat on a heap of ashes, while in the distance, amid the sounds of singing and dancing, a great multitude sat feasting.

The dreamlight dimmed, and when Jascha awoke it was to a sharp awareness of his situation. He was lying on the bones of ancient warriors in the black of night, far from home. He was shivering uncontrollably in the wind that had sprung up while he slept. His hip throbbed severely, and he knew he was unable to proceed in the dark. He drew up the collar of his shirt as high as it would go around his neck, and for the first time he began to cry.

Chaim Dachenblecher was exhausted after a long day on the road. Trade had been good, but he had overtaxed himself and his horse, canvassing all four of the *Jannedarpa* as well as one or two of the smaller peasant villages along the way. It was past midnight, and he was still a half hour from Mala Lepetykha, where he would have to stop for the night. Travelling in the dark always made him nervous, and in these lawless days local bandits were bolder than ever, making it even more dangerous, especially for the Jews of the region. He had stuffed the harness bells with rags, and he did not sing or whistle. That was why he was able to hear the muffled sounds of sobbing as he passed near the first *kurgan*. He thought at first of nocturnal creatures, a night owl perhaps, or wolf cubs. But he stopped his horse and peered into the darkness, listening intently until he recognized the voice of a child. This was more than passing strange. So close to Sergejewka? Surely this was not a trick bandits would play. They would have no need, at this time of night, to lure a traveller off an empty track.

The pedlar led his rig into the weeds that ringed the *kurgan*, keeping the reins wrapped around his hand until his feet found a boulder and he was able to tether the horse. Feeling his way across the uneven ground, he began to call out softly. *"Ver iz es? Ver iz dort in der nakht?"*

There was no answer, and the sobbing continued. He rounded the curve of the *kurgan* and repeated his call more loudly.

"Who is it? Who is out here in the night?" The crying ceased abruptly, and for a few moments there was only the sound of two souls breathing. Gently, he called once more, and this time Jascha whispered from a few paces away.

*"Hier ... hier bin ich. Ich bin hier!"*

Dachenblecher knelt among the stones and lifted Jascha in his arms. The boy was trembling violently and could hardly speak. The pedlar wrapped him in his coat and carried him to the cart.

"*Aber meyn kind! Vas tustu da alle aleyn in der nakht?*" But Jascha only begged for water. Dachenblecher gave him a few of the small pears he had plucked from the trees lining the village streets he had travelled that day. He tried again.

"But my child, what are you doing here all alone in the night?" Jascha bit hungrily into the fruit and settled more deeply into his wraps.

Returning to the trail, the pedlar quickened his pace, and it was not long before he saw the glimmer of lanterns in the distance. He called out once or twice, but his voice was lost in the breeze and the hiss of ripening wheat on either side of the trail. Approaching the village shortly thereafter, he was met by a group of riders who confirmed the boy's identity before galloping back to signal the end of the search with blasts of the factory whistle. Jascha's home was just a stone's throw from the factory, and when horse and wagon arrived, the villagers accompanied the pedlar to the door where Anna and her children were just emerging to discover the news. Anna let Dachenblecher cradle the boy inside and carry him to the sleeping bench beside the stove. While Anna tended to Jascha, neighbours crowded in to hear the pedlar's account of events. Astonishment and expressions of gratitude followed, and after answering a question or two, Dachenblecher lifted his cap to the assembly and made for the door. But Anna followed him, enquiring where he would go at this late hour and pressing him at least to eat something if he would not stay the night. He said if she could give him a little oats and water for his horse, he would go on to Mala Lepetykha, where his friend, the merchant, would surely give him a place to rest until the morning. Anna took his hand and held it for a time in both of hers. Her eyes were wet, and she could not speak. She motioned to one of the men to accompany the pedlar to the stables and told him to supply whatever was needed. And with that, Dachenblecher bowed faintly, touched his cap once more and was gone.

# 4. Onkel Gerhard

The foundry of *Janzen & Neufeld Ko.* was a hazardous workplace. Thirty-five men milled about its sweltering confines, one team weighing out pig iron while another prepared the caustic blend of manganese, phosphorus and sulphur that would transform it into steel. Crew chiefs shouted to make way as their men bore crucibles of incandescent metal through the exits to the casting moulds waiting on the ground outside. At the furnace, one man raked ash and clinkers from below the grate while apprentices replenished the anthracite above. A foreman bawled instructions above the clash of the blacksmiths' hammers and the roar of the bellows while bewildered novices tried vainly to keep out of the way. The rhythmic throb of pistons and the clatter of valves and couplings penetrated all sectors of the factory from the adjacent engine room. Timing and coordination were paramount, and amid the din and frenzy, Gerhard Enns, master of the foundry, governed with a critical eye.

Enns was a nervous man, rarely at rest, and not a patient master. Apprentices were never quick enough chipping off the slag, and always too late quenching the castings in barrels of water. Workers regularly felt his ire, not only for minor infractions but for accidents entirely unforeseeable, such as the recent damage to supplies when a sudden windstorm ripped a corner from the roof of a storage shed. Rain had entered during the too many minutes it had taken to secure shrouding.

On that occasion he had raged, but it was the day-to-day scoldings, the accusations of laziness or incompetence, and the occasional threats of violence that rankled more. The Mennonite workers who saw him in other walks of life knew how to take Onkel Gerhard and were merely bemused by his antics. This shop floor martinet was, after all, the tender custodian of the finest rose garden in Sergejewka and the mellifluous tenor who sang along heartily as he conducted the church choir.

"*Ja ja*, Enns, *ja ja*," they murmured, winking at each other behind his back.

The Russians and ethnic Germans, however, deeply resented his temper. Amongst themselves they groused, and to Enns they steadfastly refused to speak.

Until one day Enns flung a three-pound hammer at an apprentice who had sloshed molten slag on the clay floor and caused a flareup of coal dust and debris. The flames were easily doused, and the boy was not hurt, but Enns chased him off the premises, spewing after him the vilest maledictions. Four Russians dropped their tools then and moved in on him — older, experienced men who had borne his abuse for years. For a moment Enns stared at them, confused. Then, recognizing a credible threat, he backed into the factory yard. When the men followed, Enns retreated to the office. But they entered there as well, and Enns slid behind the counter, feigning interest in the order board on the opposite side of the room. Wohlgemuth, the firm's accountant and paymaster, looked up from his desk, sensed an urgency, and quietly approached the counter. The Russians removed their caps and calmly requested to speak to the owner.

But Kornelius Neufeld was on an extended leave of absence, far advanced in his final illness. His sons-in-law were in charge now, with young Herman, the most senior of the three, occupying the executive office. Summoned from a consultation in the paint shop, Herman was annoyed, first by the interruption, and more so at the incursion of labourers into the firm's holy-of-holies. But he read the severity in the faces of the four men and enquired as to their business. When they declined to speak in the presence of the office staff, he motioned them into the inner office and closed the door. He greeted each man tersely by name while his chin gestured at chairs. He did not offer them tea. Rotating his armchair to face the delegation, he dropped himself into it carelessly and asked which of them wished to speak for the group. Three of the men turned to the fourth, a senior man named Kyrylenko, who cleared his throat and began.

The foundry master Gerhard Enns, he said, showed nothing but disdain for Ukrainian workers — for all non-Mennonites, in fact, but Ukrainians especially. He treated them with uniform harshness, making no allowances for inexperience or accident. New apprentices were instantly fearful of him and veteran employees learned to be constantly on their guard. His corrosive presence dominated the workplace, robbing the men of their concentration and damping all enthusiasm for the work.

Herman interrupted once or twice, remonstrating against exaggeration. But then Kyrylenko described the incident with the apprentice. This may have been the most dangerous incident to date, he said, but it was not the first. He concluded with an emphatic demand: if Enns were not removed from the foundry the workers would request reassignment to other divisions of the factory. Failing that, they were prepared to leave altogether and without further notice.

When Kyrylenko finished speaking, the men picked up their caps and did not wait for a reply. At the office door Herman promised no more than that he would speak to Enns. He nodded them out briskly, speaking each man's name, silently noting to himself — and to them — that the names would not be forgotten. Enns was no longer in the office, so Herman closed the inner door, returned to his chair and sat in silence. The audacity of the men had taken him aback, and he was flustered and angry. In the past, a man might have approached him in the yard, cap in hand, with a respectful request for a transfer or to register a concern of some sort. But an ultimatum? Even in the political turmoil of the times, this was a startling precedent.

The threat was an empty one; Herman was confident of that, and in his mind this only heightened the insult to his intelligence and his dignity. August 1914 had caught Russia unprepared, and in the panic of mobilization every industry suited to the task had been ordered to retool for the production of materiel, with the commitment that their workers would be exempt from the draft. Herman knew there was not one man among the hundred twenty who did not understand that employment in the factory was his only surety against the carnage of the Eastern Front. Herman's cousin, Johann Neufeld, had visited the factory while on furlough from his military duties as an orderly in Kherson, and he recognized several of his patients among the workers, men who had slipped from the military hospital to avoid being sent back to the war. These deserters, especially, were vulnerable should they be found at large and would not be likely to leave the asylum of the factory.

Herman turned to the *samovar* and poured himself a glass of tea. This matter would pass, he thought, as he settled more deeply in his chair. Oh, he would speak with his Onkel Gerhard, and perhaps he could even bring the two men together for a chat. Kyrylenko was a reasonable man, reliable and experienced, and an excellent crew leader who had rarely missed a day in his many years with the firm. He was angry, no doubt, but in these troubled times he had no other prospects. He would not leave.

Troubled times indeed. Herman thought of all the changes the firm had undergone since the beginning of the war. He remembered the cavalier dismissal with which the partners of *Janzen & Neufeld Ko.* had greeted the first order from Petrograd. They'd had no doubt the letter had been sent in error and that the exemptions from military involvements Mennonites had enjoyed since the age of Catherine the Great would prevail. A second letter had also been ignored. But then a third letter arrived in the spring of 1915.

Herman had walked into the inner office to find his father-in-law Kornelius standing next to the window with his body angled so the last evening light illuminated the letter in his right hand. Except for the slight trembling of the paper, he was utterly motionless. With his other hand he held the empty envelope and braced himself against the back of his chair. He looked up as Herman closed the door and wordlessly passed the document over to him. The letter bore the official letterhead of the Supreme Council of Tsar Nicholas II and was stamped with the insignia of both the Ministry of War and the Ministry of Commerce and Industry. Herman parsed the letter carefully, wrestling with the complex grammar of the high imperial style. Twice he reread the long paragraph, hoping that his poor command of the language was misleading him. Scanning it one final time, he was forced to concede that there was no mistake.

*To the honourable proprietors of the firm Janzen & Neufeld Ko. of Sergejewka, Taurida Gubernia: Having ignored earlier directives for the manufacture of supplies for the prosecution of the current war, you are hereby informed that requisitions by said firm for resupply of coal, steel, and hardwoods are refused as of June 1, 1915. Should the respected gentlemen find in the intervening time that consideration of their duty to the Motherland allows them to alter their position, they are requested to confirm in writing their consent to the manufacture and delivery of specified materiel as per the enclosed documents. In that event, local representatives are empowered to authorize the resumption of shipments of supplies.*

*Supreme Council to His Imperial Majesty…*

Affixed to the letter was a requisition for five thousand shell casings to be delivered to the military depot in Kherson by a specified date. A third document detailed the technical specifications for ordnance of three different calibres.

Herman had participated in anguished meetings of senior staff. News of the ultimatum spread through the workforce and the village. Consternation ran particularly high among church leaders, some of whom came from elsewhere in Fürstenland to consult with the partners. To some, the principles of pacifism were sacrosanct. Other more cautious voices emphasized the anti-German sentiment that had escalated in Russia since the beginning of the war. Already, military detachments were combing German-speaking settlements, seizing pistols and hunting rifles. Government agents, vigilant for signs of collusion with the *Fritzi*, interrogated young men, pressured them to enlist, and mocked them for cowardice when they refused. Then there were the land liquidation decrees, which specifically targeted Russian subjects of German extraction. How these would apply in a tenured colony like Fürstenland no one knew, but an outright refusal to cooperate in the matter of munitions manufacture might well bring reprisals more dire than the shutting down of the factory, serious as that would be in and of itself.

Both partners were ministers in the *Brüdergemeinde* with Jakob Janzen serving, also, as the regional *Ältester* in Fürstenland. Both men had unfailingly upheld the principles of pacifism, but neither had faced a test as agonizing as this. When the two men met alone, Janzen argued from scripture.

"There is a time for every purpose under heaven," he said. "We have had our seasons of building up. Perhaps this is the time for tearing down."

But his son-in-law, ever the pragmatist, had rationalized. Without resupply, the factory would be forced to close within a month. One hundred twenty men would be unemployed, and most would be sent to the front, where they would become killers and likely be killed themselves. Keeping the factory open would prevent this — a peaceable act, surely. Besides, the orders, after all, were for empty shells. Where, by whom, and for what purpose they would be armed and deployed would be entirely on the consciences of others.

The impasse between them lasted for a week, until Janzen came to his decision. He would not stand in the way if Kornelius wished to acquiesce in this matter. His only request was that, before Neufeld wrote to confirm the government contract, *Janzen* be struck from the company letterhead. He would withdraw from the firm entirely, and *Neufeld Ko.* would stand alone.

In Herman's office, ten minutes passed ... twenty ... a half-hour, while he reviewed the events of two years ago. Since then, Jakob Janzen had gone to his eternal rest, and lay buried on the slopes above the village. And Kornelius Neufeld remained in hospital in Odessa after a disastrous surgery, unlikely ever to return to the factory. The next generation was taking over. The firm's entire management and supervisory staff was a tangle of uncles and in-laws, brothers and cousins and nephews. And Onkel Gerhard Enns was among them. It would fall to young Herman to speak to the much older man about this morning's debacle. Yes, he would keep his word to Kyrylenko and the others who had called on him this morning, much as it galled him to have had the promise extracted from him under duress. He rose to his feet just as the factory whistle signalled the noon break. The *Kroeger* on the wall behind him chimed in accord, and Herman left the building to find Onkel Enns.

When Kyrylenko and his men entered young Herman's office, Gerhard Enns waited until the door was closed before moving from the window towards the exit. Wohlgemuth's smirking queries annoyed him, and he scowled at him, mumbling something about *'verdammte Russen!'* as he slammed the door behind him and strode off the factory compound. He decided it would be wise to avoid the foundry for now. He would walk north along the centre street and out of the village altogether, to find the solitude he needed to settle his soul. Katharina and the children would not miss him, as he often took his lunch at the factory.

At the end of the village he took the narrow track that led down to the *konstje*. He sat on a rock at the edge of the stream and leaned back against a tree. He pulled out his tobacco and fumbled for his pipe. It was frowned upon, yes, but there was no one here, and it would be alright, he thought. A pipe would calm him. But then he looked across to the *plaven* on the other side of the stream and thought better of it. The island had emerged early from the spring inundation and was already dry. Women were collecting the driftwood snagged in the willows and piling it for burning, while others spaded up the freshly deposited silts in preparation for planting. One of the women recognized him and called out in greeting. He lifted his cap but did not speak.

Gerhard came often to this place by the stream. Whenever possible, he liked to come alone. Here, above the valley floor, in the cool of the trees, he felt some measure of release from the pressures of daily living — the foundry, the village, church, the choir, home. After the spring surge the stream had slowed, and in a few translucent pools fingerlings glinted in the sun. He watched them panic as, with thumb and forefinger, he flicked a pebble into the water. They calmed quickly and returned to the centre of the pool. Twice more he troubled the waters before he gave up the game and leaned back once more against the tree.

In his heart of hearts Gerhard deeply regretted his temper; again and again he had regretted it. He had never understood himself in this regard, how his impatience in the smallest matters would rise in a splintered instant and overwhelm him in an unreasoning rage against which he felt utterly powerless. In his earliest memories there had already been something of this. Recalling the awfulness of incontinence after his mother died when he was eight, he recognized that even then he had felt more than embarrassment. There had been dismay at his own failure, certainly, but also the keenest rage focused upon the aunt who had taken him in so reluctantly and then cruelly stabled him with the cattle at night when he wet the bed. He had cried himself to sleep there, as any child would, but never without clenched fists.

In his youth Gerhard had displayed a fierce independence of spirit, rather than overt anger. He was bored to numbness in school and frequently punished for his rebellions. His first apprenticeship to a locksmith in Halbstadt had ended abruptly when materials were ruined due to his petulant disregard for the shop steward's guidance. Neither had he completed probation at the clockworks in Chortitza, the master citing a careless disregard for the finer details of the craft. At twenty-two, Gerhard was left still craving an anchorage of one kind or another from which he might deploy his powers. Then, in 1890, when Jakob Janzen came looking to train a new foundry man, he had signed on. His brother was the miller in Sergejewka, and he would take him in until Gerhard could settle on his own.

When *Klassen & Janzen Ko.* disbanded less than a year later, Janzen took Enns with him to the new shop he and his son-in-law were building at the other end of the village. Here the workforce was small, and Enns had risen quickly — "to the top of the slag," he said, in wry disparagement of his crew. This rough work suited him, drawing on his great physical strength and boundless energy. As he became more proficient, it provided him with something else as well: a measure of aesthetic satisfaction and personal accomplishment. He had always taken pleasure in drawing and sketching, and the elaborate designs he created for gearing and spokework caught the attention of buyers and merited a small increase in prices for products listed in the illustrated catalogues of *Janzen & Neufeld Ko.* In 1895, when Enns married Janzen's daughter Katharina, his position was secured.

The new firm expanded quickly, and Gerhard's work as manager of the foundry became more demanding. In the forge where the blacksmiths and their assistants laboured there were ten hearths now, all centred around a great central stack. The capacity of the smelting furnace had been doubled, and a steam hammer installed in one wing. Enns was able to delegate certain tasks to an assistant, but he nevertheless found himself near the limit of his own abilities. As long as Jakob Janzen and Kornelius Neufeld were in place they had seen to it that only reliable men were sent to him, even if it meant prying them from more pleasant assignments. But the sons-in-law of Kornelius — The Three Wisemen, he called them privately — who were now in charge, appreciated neither the technical nature of the work nor the hazardous conditions that prevailed in the foundry. Of late, Herman had begun sending untested recruits — "to be trained," he said. When Enns reminded his nephew of the risks, and requested that he be consulted before such assignments were made, Herman had been irked, referring testily to the difficulty of finding workers at all in these troubled days.

Matters became worse when, despite government commitments to the contrary, conscription brigades took several 'non-essentials' from the factory floor. After that, Herman made sure that workers engaged in non-military manufacture — furniture, farm equipment, household implements — were men whom age or infirmity would disqualify from military service. Those eligible for call-up he sent to the foundry or to the finishing floor, where the shells were machined after rough-casting. Enns had fumed when Herman spoke of closing the joinery shop altogether until the war was over and assigning the carpenters and their helpers to supply a second shift in the foundry. The armaments contract was proving lucrative, and the first shipment, ahead of schedule and praised for its quality, had been followed immediately by a second requisition, with promises of more to come.

The women cross over from the *plaven*, and Gerhard helps them tie up their skiff. They exchange a few pleasantries before moving on to their homes in the village. When they are out of sight he pulls out his pipe and smokes. After a time, he leaves his stony seat for a grassy hummock in the sun. He lies back in the grass and watches the pillowy clouds traverse the sky. It is warm and there is no wind.

When Herman finds him, Gerhard is asleep. His pipe is cold and has fallen from his hand. Herman drags a boot in the grass and clears his throat to wake him gently.

"I thought I might find you here, Onkel Gerhard." He crouches beside him in the grass. The older man rubs the sleep from his face and raises himself on his elbows.

"*Na ja*, so be it." There is awkwardness on both sides. "So, Herman. How did my good men speak of me?"

Herman thinks for a moment. "What happened this morning, Onkel Gerhard, cannot happen again." He describes the complaints of the

Russians, minimizing their ultimatum for the moment but stressing the morale of the crew.

Gerhard tries a bit of humour. "*Ach*, Herman. You send me these young scamps who know nothing. I will not ... "

But Herman interrupts. "Onkel Gerhard, it is the older men who are angry. It is Valentin Kyrylenko who came. He is our top man, the best. These are the ones who say they cannot work with you any longer."

Gerhard scoffs as he rises awkwardly and faces his nephew. He raises his voice.

"They cannot. Ah ha! They cannot? And where will they go?"

Herman turns and walks a few paces to the edge of the stream and looks across at the *plaven*. When he returns his tone has changed. Both men know that Herman's present authority derives solely from the absence of others. He is not a naturally courageous man, nor is he particularly competent in management. When he stands stock still before his uncle and presents his proposal, neither man fails to detect a debilitating blend of fear and pretentiousness. It is a rehearsed speech, short and tactless.

"Onkel Gerhard, is there another place in the factory where you could work?"

Enns freezes in place. His eyes narrow, and his jaw sets. He stands like a statue, staring incredulously into the face of his nephew. Finally his lips part, and he drops his words evenly, one short phrase at a time, into the void between them.

"You know, Herman? You are one of them. A young scamp who knows nothing. Your wife's late grandfather Jakob Janzen, and her father Kornelius. From them I could hear this. From you? Never!"

He straightens his cap, fumbles his pipe out of the turf and strides off in the direction of home, leaving Herman to gaze after him. And far beyond him, to where thick black smoke rises from the factory chimney.

Herman arrived at work three days later to find Kyrylenko standing in the sun near the factory gate. Kyrylenko removed his cap and waited for the

*Chef* to speak. He nodded when he learned that Herman had kept his promise and had spoken to Enns; he nodded again, more slowly, when he heard that Enns would not be replaced. Then he looked up at Herman to say that he was going home to Mala Lepetykha and would not be returning. Might he be permitted to enter the office to see the paymaster? Kyrylenko had come alone, but were there others, Herman wondered? He asked him to step into his private office, and this time he pointed to the *samovar*. Kyrylenko accepted, and for a few moments the two men sipped their tea.

"Look, Valentin. I ask you, is this necessary? Enns is a hard man; I know this. He knows this too. We have spoken, and he has promised."

It was a lie, and he held his breath while Kyrylenko put down his glass. When he spoke, he was bolder, less formal, and he was not afraid to look Herman in the eye.

"I know Enns very, very well. Almost twenty years I know him. Many times he promises, and it is worse now. For me it is finished. I will not stay."

Herman sighed. He began to speak, but then he paused, and in the long silence only the clock on the wall was audible. Then Herman rose from his chair and motioned for Kyrylenko to remain while he stepped out to speak to Wohlgemuth. When he returned to tell Kyrylenko that his pay would be ready in a few minutes the man was already standing. He declined to name others who might also leave. But at the door he stopped and extended his hand to Herman.

"Twenty-six years," he said. "And for a long time it was very good. For this, I would thank Janzen if he were living. I ask you to thank Neufeld for me when you see him next."

They moved into the main office then, and Wohlgemuth came to the counter with the envelope. Herman placed it in Kyrylenko's hand. Outside, they shook hands once more before parting. When Herman returned, the office staff were curious, but he passed through without a word and quietly shut the door.

At the end of the month, six more workers collected their pay and left, all seasoned workers above enlistment age. Herman made himself more visible on the foundry floor. He brought Koslowsky or Wedel with him on daily visits, and between them they tapped the men one-on-one for brief infusions of support and encouragement. Enns was resentful and humiliated at their invigilation of him on his own turf, but privately relieved at the likelihood that this would mollify the rest of the crew and prevent further loss of manpower. Occasionally, when one of The Three were on the floor, he left his assistant in charge while he walked the village streets. On the hottest days he went home to his summer kitchen for an afternoon nap.

That is where Katharina found him on the last Friday of June, frantic with the news that Kornelius Neufeld had died in hospital in Odessa.

"Appendix ... gruesome ... perforated bowel ... egress via surgical wounds ... zinc casket welded shut because ... "

"Enough! Enough! The children must not hear!"


Gerhard hurried to the home of the widow and found her surrounded by family and half the office staff. He embraced his sister-in-law, spoke words of comfort, and then made his way over to where The Three stood in conference. They dispatched him to announce the owner's death and to shut down the factory until Monday, the workers to be sent home with the full day's pay. He went to the foundry to oversee a final pour. Then he ordered the fires damped and sent a boy to alert the night watchman to come early.

In the months after the abdication of the Tsar in March of 1917, worker unrest radiated across Russia from its origins in the cities of the north. Unlike official expropriations during the last years of the empire, which had been rare and for which owners had been at least partially compensated, less orderly takeovers were now commonplace. Factory owners and millers were driven off and replaced by worker committees. Firms engaged in the manufacture of materiel were still under the nominal protection of the state, but that had not suppressed internal unrest. As inflation soared and the value of the pay packet plummeted, grievances with working and living conditions, and long seething disgust at the obscene wealth of the owners, had merged with the revolutionary spirit of the day to create an atmosphere of unease and unpredictability. At *Neufeld Ko.* tardiness and absenteeism became common, and formal requests for pay increases soon morphed into strident demands. Deference to the bosses dissipated, and when someone discovered that Herman's first name also doubled as his second, *Ha! Ha!* began to circulate as a nickname. More ominously, and apart from the general turmoil, there was heightened personal risk for supervisors who had made enemies. Gerhard Enns knew he was one of these.

The first time they came for him Enns was not at home. Mild January weather had extended the shipping season, and he was on a river freighter with a final delivery of shell casings before freeze-up. From Kherson he would proceed overland to the *Neufeld Ko.* outlet in Taganrog on the Sea of Azov, where he was to conduct an inventory of company stock and check the accounts. If the trains were running, Herman had asked him to continue on to Orenburg to inspect the warehouse there. In all, Enns expected to be gone for some three weeks.

Of the eight men who appeared at the factory gate near the end of the workday, four were former employees. Valentin Kyrylenko was not among them, but eighteen-year-old Pavel, the apprentice who had dodged Enns's hammer, was their leader. They had come looking for work, he said and demanded to be taken to the master of the foundry. When Heinrich Braun, the elderly watchman, informed them that Enns was not there, they shoved him aside and advanced on the foundry entrance. Several of the men were far short of sober, and one of them stumbled on the threshold, causing much mirth among the others, who slapped the sides of his head and berated him as disqualified since he would surely fall into the smelting pots.

Once inside, they milled about the workstations, greeting everyone boisterously and interrupting the work of those they recognized. Crew chiefs, most of them Mennonites, ordered them to leave and were roundly mocked for their efforts. Pavel mimicked their accents and tipped the cap from one man's head. But on this day it was only Gerhard Enns they were looking for, and when it became clear that they would not find him, they gravitated towards the exit. Several of the staff converged on them at a distance to encourage their departure, and there were no further incidents. At the door, Pavel turned once more and, with a great shout, called for the men to throw down their tools and join the revolution. Then he made a show of scanning the workplace as though mapping it in his brain. He stared into the face of the nearest Mennonite.

"We will find him," he growled. "You can be sure. Tell him we will find him." Then he turned and left with his comrades.

Koslowsky, one of the managerial triumvirate, had witnessed the incursion from the fringe of the foundry floor but had not intervened. Herman listened to his account and shrugged off the whole affair as a drunken caper. But he agreed that Onkel Gerhard would have been incensed and might well have sparked a more violent clash had he been present. Clearly, Pavel was a hothead. He lived only a bowshot away in Mala Lepetykha, and if revenge was in his blood, he might well return. They would add a second man at the gatehouse and provide the night watchman with an assistant. And Herman decided to send Gerhard a precautionary telegram in Kherson.

The rider dispatched to the telegraph office returned from Lepetykha to report a large crowd in the central square, delirious with revolutionary fervour. From the bandstand a woman from Nikopol had raged for an hour, calling for the takeover of factories and the liquidation of their owners. The rider had gone to the home of Heinrich Rempel and found him preparing to escape with his family. His flour mill had been seized, and his life threatened. Also fleeing *en masse* were the Jews of the town, among them the courier Dachenblecher, who carried the mail and was Sergejewka's ear in Lepetykha and the surrounding regions. He was in a panic and said he would stay awhile with his elderly parents in one of the Judenplan villages where he had been raised.

Gerhard Enns did not receive Herman's warning because non-military use of the telegraph office in Kherson had been suspended. Neither did the news reach him in Taganrog, despite his being delayed there for more than a week due to railroad disruptions. As a result, Gerhard was blithely unaware during his sixty-hour journey eastward to Orenburg that Sergejewka was in peril.

Enns strongly suspected that his travel assignment was Herman's tactic for diffusing tensions with the workers. But from the outset he had recast it in his mind as a gift. He had rarely travelled beyond the mother colonies, had never seen the Urals, and he meant to make the most of a rare opportunity. He need not worry about his family; they were in the capable hands of his in-laws. If he was not delayed too long in Orenburg, he might even make a dash to Omsk and Chelyabinsk to visit old friends who had abandoned Sergejewka during the rental crisis at the turn of the century. With the railroads extending ever deeper into the Asian sectors, there might well be sales opportunities to explore in these newer settlements. No doubt the adventure would refresh his spirits and improve his capacity for patience in the workplace.

The journey was not without its trials. The army had priority on the rails, and his carriage was shunted to sidings for hours at a time during splicing operations, or while Red Cross trains were flagged through on their way to hospitals in urban centres. Food and water were not always available during stops, and the stations were no less crowded and filthy than the carriages. More than once, he was accosted by hungry troops returning from the war, or reviled as a German by those still heading to the front.

Despite the dearth of creature comforts, Gerhard found the journey stimulating, though the exhilaration any traveller experiences in new territory was only part of what he felt. This was a Russia impossible to imagine from within the insular world of a Mennonite village. Views from the grimy carriage window — the filth of the towns and the gaunt faces of the workers, the hovels in dilapidated villages, the ragged peasants and their barefoot children toiling in their tiny plots, the mess and shambles everywhere — these did not in the least soften the disdain he felt for the backwardness of the Russian people and their perennial incapacity for self-betterment. But for the first time in his life, Gerhard was struck by the sheer scope of the misery he saw, and it rattled him.

Upon his arrival in Orenburg, Gerhard made his way directly to the warehouse, where the manager greeted him warmly. After a brief exchange of pleasantries he placed a thick bundle of letters in Gerhard's hand and showed him into his private office. Gerhard closed the door and found a chair. For a minute or two he sat in silence, stretching his limbs and observing his surroundings. A narrow shaft of morning sun entered through a puncture in the curtain and pencilled the wall at his side. Slowly he untied the string holding the packet together and noted the postmarks on the envelopes. There were letters from Katharina, one from his oldest son, and from Herman a detailed account of events in the factory. Opening them in sequence, he began to read. What he learned was deeply discomfiting, and it confounded all his plans.

There had been skepticism and dismay when Herman stood before the men on the first Friday of January to apologize for a shortfall in their pay. He asked for patience, and promised to make good in subsequent months. But then he had stepped off the precipice. Surely they must know, he went on, how diligently he had laboured to keep them all in work at a time when, due to the war, the market for seed ploughs and reaping machines had fallen so precipitously. The manufacture of war materiel had kept the factory open these three years, but it had failed to compensate for the decline in other revenues. It would be necessary to make difficult adjustments.

Gradually, as the import of his words emerged, the murmur grew louder and Herman faltered. *More information to follow ... beg you to understand ... coming days ... simply not possible ... regrettable reductions ...* He tried once more to apologize, but he was overwhelmed by a roar of rage and defiance. The loudest voices bayed for a work stoppage. "If Ha! Ha! can so easily dispense with some of his workers, we will see how he manages without any of us!"

The three-day strike that followed was but a prelude to the complete takeover of the factory a day later. Representatives from Alexandrovsk, two students and a factory labourer, arrived unannounced and declared the factory under the control of the workers. Russians occupied the head office and most of the supervisory positions. Valentin Kyrylenko was summoned back from Lepetykha and installed as head of the foundry, his decades of warm relations with both Janzen and Neufeld overlooked by the workers, for now, in deference to his competence. The Three were retained on base wages as 'consultants' essential in the interim for their overall grasp of the firm's affairs. On paper, ownership and liability remained firmly in the name of the widow Anna Janzen Neufeld, with son-in-law Herman responsible for payroll.

Herman pleaded with the workers' committee not to replace men lost through attrition or enlistment. But they bawled him out of the office, threatening him with dispossession of the family's assets. He made a desperate round of the Fürstenland villages, begging to borrow, but there was little to be found. His friend Niebuhr in Olgafeld had long since given up his factory and fled, and smaller enterprises were all on the point of collapse.

Although it was not safe to travel far afield, Herman made one perilous venture to banks in Nikopol and Kherson where he was granted some small relief — contingent, it was made clear, on his continued commitment to the war as long as it lasted, and with no grounds for optimism thereafter. Even as he looked for funds, therefore, Herman was on an urgent quest for a buyer.

While he was away, members of the new workers' *Komitee*, three men and a woman, presented themselves on the doorstep of the finest residence in Sergejewka. They had brought a bailiff with them, and for several hours they traversed the house, the barns, and the outbuildings, making a detailed inventory and assigning exorbitant values to each item. At first, Anna Janzen Neufeld naively considered that the accounting was intended as surety against the thievery that had become endemic in the village. However, the bailiff brusquely explained that the inventory would be registered in Lepetykha against shortfalls when the workers were paid at the end of each month. Before leaving, he asked Anna to review the document and apply her signature. Aghast at the vastly inflated figures, she refused to sign. But the bailiff was a patient man, and his synopsis of her position was concise. He reminded her that there was little to stop the workers from evicting her entirely, and that it was in her best interests to cooperate. Below her signature he added his own, as witness. Finally, he informed her of the option to repurchase her possessions at any time for an 'easement fee' equivalent to the assessment, to be paid in gold rubles.

By the time Enns finished reading it was long past noon. His eyes ached, and he was stiff and sore from sitting immobilized for so long. The shaft of sunlight had fallen from the wall and lay at his feet on the floor, and no one had called him to lunch. While he read, he had heard nothing. But now, from the other side of the closed door, there came the voices of the agent and his customers, the ambient sounds of commerce. For a long time he sat silent and unmoving. The relative peace of mind he had nurtured during his travels had collapsed. In the time he had been away, the Sergejewka he knew had been irrevocably altered. He called to mind the grassy banks of the *konstje*, those few hours last summer before

Herman had found him asleep in the sun, the voices from the *plaven*, the placid pools, the fingerlings. Then he thought of the factory and the workers, of Pavel, and of Katharina and the risks to his family, and he felt his spirit drop like a stone into the sea.

Gerhard concluded his business in Orenburg within two days and left for home via Nikopol. There he made enquiries among friends and business associates, and when he could discover no compelling reason for delay, he hired a team and driver to take him across the frozen Dniepr to Michaelsburg, where he rested for a few hours in the home of a friend. Then he walked the last twenty *verst* to Sergejewka, arriving before dawn to find his household in an uproar. Neighbours were repairing his front door and boarding up the shattered windows of the house. Inside, his wife was trembling uncontrollably as young Herman tried to extract from her a description of the invaders. His oldest son was being attended to in the bedroom. He had been beaten, and his arm was broken. He raised a bloodied face and spoke through clenched teeth.

"They came for you again, Papa. They have just left. They come every few nights now. And they will be back."

That morning, Gerhard Enns became a fugitive. He hid a rowboat in the willows of the *plaven* and gave his family the names of contacts across the river. His son, recently married, pleaded with his father to let him take his wife, and his mother and sisters, to relatives in the villages of Molotschna. Reluctantly, Gerhard agreed. But he was a wily man, accustomed to trusting his instincts, and he refused to accompany them. In the days after they were gone, he slept for a few hours at a time during the day and joined the patrols at night, leaving the village altogether for a day or two only when rumours reached him of imminent danger.

# 5. Anna

Anna Enns had begun singing in the choir at age nine when her sparkling soprano caught the ear of her uncle Gerhard, the director, one winter morning as she passed him on her way to school. He took her to the next practice and brought an apple box for her to stand on beside the women in the front row. A decade later her voice had ripened to a rich alto, and in sessions at home and in the women's group that occasionally sang in the evening services, she supplied the bass line raised an octave.

Much as she enjoyed singing in the choir, that, and attendance at the Sunday *Versammlungen* were the limits of Anna's engagement in religious life. It was true she had made a spiritual commitment of sorts at one point during that desperate year in the wastes of Siberia, where her family had fled to escape the escalating rents of the Fürstenland settlement. But the initial joy of her conversion had soon flagged. Her prayers rebounded as echoes of her own voice, and she found herself adrift in absent-spirited complacency. She was sixteen when her family returned to Sergejewka, and soon all of her closest friends requested baptism. Yet, each spring, when her Opa Janzen, the *Ältester*, issued the invitation for baptismal candidates to declare themselves, Anna demurred. She kept to her place in the choir and sang from the river bank as thirty or more candidates from the six villages of Furstenland stepped forward to be immersed in the waters of the *konstje* and welcomed into membership in the *Brüdergemeinde*.

Then, when she was nineteen, a gruesome fatality in the factory had persuaded her. The great belt that ran from the steam plant to the machines on the shop floor had been relaxed during the replacement of a link in the drive shaft. While the repair was being tested, David Unger, responding to a call for assistance, had stepped over the spinning shaft into a loop in the slackened belt, instantly tensing it against the friction of the drive pulley. Poor David had managed just one shout before his body was spun at a hundred revolutions per minute and dashed to the floor and against the steam pipes overhead. Every bone was broken, they said, and a cousin whispered that the head was empty. At the funeral the young man's brother had wept as he spoke of seeing David on his knees in prayer on the morning of his death, and of the great comfort this brought to the family.

Horror had penetrated Anna's heart and crushed her defences.

*He was my own age*, she thought. *We were in school together. He had begun speaking to me recently whenever we met in the street. Could this come to me too, so suddenly?*

For the first time in her life she felt an overwhelming urgency regarding the salvation of her soul. She confessed her sinfulness and prayed fervently for forgiveness. A week after the funeral she approached Opa Janzen and declared her desire for baptism. Her grandfather blessed her intentions but expressed bewilderment that she had not come forward in spring along with the others. He reminded her that baptisms were formal, colony-wide affairs and to conduct one for a single candidate would be highly unusual. He counselled her to hold off until the spring when there would again be a large group of candidates, and she agreed. *Finally!* she thought. *I have asked, and I am committed. Now I can be content to wait.*

On a Friday night shortly after her interview with her grandfather, Anna was about to leave for choir rehearsal when her mother stopped her at the door. She was strangely animated, twisting her fingers and retracting a furtive smile before allowing it to return. Then she calmed herself and reached for Anna's hand. She whispered that Johann Neufeld had arrived from Steinau across the river and was staying with his Onkel Kornelius and Tante Anna. He had asked permission to speak with her. When Anna simply stared and did not reply, her mother cleared her throat.

"My dear Anna, if you wish, I can tell him no. He can, perhaps . . ." Anna shrugged. "Well! If he wants to talk, we can talk. But first, I'm off to choir practice." She edged past her mother, took the path through the garden and strode along the street towards the meeting house. The import of her mother's announcement thrilled and unsettled her, and she found she had to focus intently in order to sustain her usual confident gait. The street seemed narrower than she remembered; every window was watching, and the trees that lined the road leaned in to listen to her beating heart.

Like most of the girls in Sergejewka, Anna hoped for marriage. But she had come to doubt her prospects in that regard. She did not consider herself attractive. The family portrait taken a year earlier showed her leaning forward from the back row, severe, half a head taller than anyone, and gangly as a sapling. Since her early teens, her father had called her *Jalmäa*, carrot, until she persuaded him that it no longer amused her. The photograph embarrassed her, and she set it off to one side of the mantlepiece whenever she tidied the great room.

So was it now to be, after all? Anna remembered seeing Johann Neufeld only once before when he visited his sister and his Onkel Kornelius and Tante Anna during leave from his service in the *Forestei*. He was twenty-two years old, and though he was not overly tall, there was a singular robustness in his movements, and he seemed exceptionally alert to everything around him. From the village youth she heard rumours of his prodigious physical strength and his prowess as a wrestler. She also heard how he had been converted to faith through the preaching of itinerant ministers in the forestry service and that he had undergone baptism there. She had taken mental note, and thoughts of him had occupied her from time to time in the days that followed. She said nothing to anyone, and to ask his sister or uncle about him could never have crossed her mind.

Anticipation of the imminent appointment distracted her during the rehearsal, and she fumbled her entries and forgot words of songs she had known for years. She felt immobilized by a keen sense of crisis flavoured equally by exhilaration and trepidation, so that the rehearsal seemed both endless and ephemeral. When it ended, she spoke briefly with a friend but declined an invitation for tea. When she got home she went to her room and tried to steady herself. She whispered a prayer for guidance, and she was still standing bent towards the mirror with her fingers tensed around the edges of the bureau when her father knocked softly and entered. He closed the door behind him, and when she turned to face him he was smiling.

"Johann Neufeld is here, Anna," he said softly. "Onkel Kornelius brought him to us, and he has asked permission to speak with you." He paused when she turned to face him. Her face was tense and expressionless.

"This is very sudden, I know. And you surely need not hurry to give an answer. But your mother and I know something of his character. We would not stand in your way should you decide to accept him."

Anna's cheeks had reddened while her father spoke. She looked down at the floor, then over her father's shoulder towards the door.

"Come. We will bring you together and stay for a while. Then we will leave you to talk with him alone until the tea is ready. We have sent the children away for an hour so they will not trouble you."

Anna ran a comb through her hair. She met her father's eyes and forced a thin smile.

"*Na ja*," she sighed. "So be it. Let us go."

When Anna entered the room, Johann was standing at the window speaking with her mother. He stepped forward and nodded, greeting Anna by name. They took the chairs her parents offered. Peter and Maria welcomed Johann and formally introduced Anna as their eldest daughter. Anna was relieved to discover that Johann seemed more nervous than she was. He leaned forward with his elbows on his knees, rubbing his hands together, all the while glancing alternately down at the floor, then up at her and at her parents. She noted the directness of the eyes below his thick, reddish hair. Her parents inquired about affairs in the Nepluyevka settlement where Johann and his parents lived, and after a few more minutes of quiet conversation Peter and Maria Enns rose and went to the kitchen, leaving the young couple to navigate the perils of courtship on their own.

Johann began with an apology for the abruptness of his visit, explaining that he had only just completed his service in the *Forestei* and had arrived home to discover his family's farm in disarray. His oldest brothers were already married and had left the settlement to establish their own farms elsewhere. He described how his father's long illness had finally left him entirely incapacitated. His younger siblings would not be able to manage alone, so the farm would be sold as soon as possible. Then he would be free. With the current harvest at its peak he had not had a moment's reprieve until just now, when rain had slowed things somewhat.

He told Anna, then, that he had seen her in the village during earlier visits and had heard her strong alto during Sunday services. He had made discreet enquiries in letters to his Uncle Kornelius, who spoke well of her and encouraged him to persevere. He had thought of writing to her as well — had, in fact, written, but had not found the courage to post the letter.

"But I am here now," he said, "and I don't like mumbling through the wool." He looked up at her and paused for a moment. "Anna, I have come to ask whether you might find it in your heart to consider me as a husband."

He reached over and touched the back of Anna's hand, patted it once or twice, and then retreated.

"You did not expect this today, I know," he said. "And it is too much for me to ask for an immediate answer."

During Johann's monologue they had remained seated under the window facing each other and Anna had hardly moved. Now she looked up at him, and though she did not speak, in her eyes he thought he saw a glimmer of the answer he was seeking. Once more he reached over, and with a firm grip this time, he pressed both of her hands together in his.

"I am staying with my Tante Anna and Onkel Kornelius. I must leave at first light to catch the ferry for Nikopol. You may write to me, and if you agree, I will arrange to visit again soon." He straightened in his chair as the voices of Anna's parents intruded. They brought in the tea and cakes, and there was an awkward silence as cups and saucers were passed.

When everyone was served, Anna spoke.

"Mama, Papa. Johann has asked me to marry him, and I have given him my word."

Johann looked up, startled. "But ... you have not spoken a single word!" A jovial spark lit his eyes, and his face cracked in a grin as she replied.

"Ah, but it was not necessary to speak many words. You have persuaded me."

They all rose from their chairs then and joined hands and embraced. Peter Enns reached for Johann's shoulder and drew him aside for a private exchange. They spoke for a few minutes about Johann's prospects and explored the possibility of sharing the Enns farm between them once Johann's affairs in Steinau were settled.

The sound of the younger children returning reached them, and Maria Enns opened the doors of the room to let them hear the news. Johann asked each of them their names, tousled the heads of the youngest ones, and hinted at gifts when he returned. Then the children left for bed, and Johann said his farewells to Anna's parents.

Johann and Anna walked the long street of the village and down the path to the *konstje*. The night was clear and moonless, and a chilly air rose from the vast valley and met them as they descended to the water's edge. Johann stopped and turned to face Anna. He drew her to himself and murmured his joy and his gratitude.

"We will learn to love each other. I promise you," he whispered. He would come again as soon as his labours on the farm allowed. They would announce their betrothal then and determine a wedding date. Once more he embraced her and touched his lips to her forehead before taking her back to her parents. In the morning he was gone.

When he returned in early October, Johann was optimistic and impatient. The crop had been better than expected, and he had found a buyer for the farm who wished to occupy it before the snow was gone in spring. He announced that he wanted to be married and settled in Sergejewka by early in the new year. When Anna reminded him that the church would not consent to the marriage before she was baptized, he dismissed her concerns. Things would be worked out, he said. He would speak with his Onkel Kornelius, who was her Opa Janzen's son-in-law and a lay preacher in the church.

They settled on the first of February as a wedding date, and when Johann came back in November they went to see Grandfather Janzen. Johann explained the situation in Steinau and the arrangements he had made to work with his future father-in-law in Sergejewka. He and Anna would live with her parents until he could find land of his own. This would not be possible if the wedding had to be delayed until after the next baptism.

Occasionally, while Johann spoke, Janzen nodded his head or rumbled softly to indicate that he understood, but he did not interrupt. When Johann finished, Janzen roused in his chair and looked up at Anna. It had been wrong of him, he said, to place practical concerns in the way of her call to baptism. It could have been managed. He apologized and declared that if it were not so late in the season he would perform the rite even now. But by this time of year, what little water was left in the *konstje* was already crusting over each night. Then he turned to Johann and expressed sympathy with his situation. But, as leader of the congregation, he would not contravene the ordinances of the *Gemeinde* in these matters. Johann protested. Surely, he said, Anna's firm commitment to baptism, before she had any inkling of marriage, had integrity. Clearly, it met the spirit of the ordinance. But Janzen was inflexible. He promised to conduct the earliest possible baptismal service in the spring, after which the wedding could take place immediately. If the couple insisted on an earlier wedding, he could have no part in it.

Anna never forgot how incensed Johann had been. He had written immediately to ask his old Onkel Herman to officiate at the wedding. As a senior itinerant charged with the wide-ranging oversight of much of the Mennonite Brethren world, Onkel Herman was regularly called upon to adjudicate unconventional situations. In his own village, a young man, unbaptized, had compromised a female member of the church, and when they married to minimize scandal, Onkel Herman had officiated. He had then excommunicated the woman for fornication and, two weeks later, reinstated her upon her confession and a plea for forgiveness. He had elicited the young husband's own public confession and, after an appropriate delay, baptized him and received him into the church. Elsewhere on his travels, he had united Mennonites and Orthodox, Mennonites and Catholics, once even a Roma woman and one of his own nephews – all of them marriages that local ministers had refused to perform. Onkel Herman always found a way. He would not disdain the union of a pure and pious young woman to a man already baptized and in good standing within the *Brüdergemeinde*.

The response was slow in coming. Onkel Herman was a friend and confidant of Jakob Janzen and was reluctant to give offence. While Johann and Anna waited, the two men exchanged letters of their own. Positions were clarified and certain obstacles removed, and early in the new year, letters of confirmation and congratulations arrived, one for Anna and the other for Johann in Steinau. A month after Christmas, Johann crossed the river in a cutter and team of four, bringing with him a trove of wedding gifts from his sisters and his friends. The wedding was held a few days later after the Sunday service, with Onkel Herman officiating.

When guests began leaving near the end of the reception, Onkel Herman took the couple aside. After formal congratulations and a warm embrace for each of them, he stepped back and cleared his throat. It was felt by the Brotherhood of Sergejewka, he said, that Johann's impatience in the matter of marriage to Anna and his disregard for the wishes of the leadership warranted a disciplinary response. He would be welcome to attend Sunday services, of course, but he was to abstain from communion and from participation in congregational meetings — a ban that would be lifted the instant Anna emerged from the waters of baptism in the spring. Johann was stunned. He had received no hint of difficulties, and he had taken Janzen's acceptance of Onkel Herman as officiant as tacit permission. Anna learned, then, that Johann could be sudden in anger and slow to forget, a facet of his character that surprised her and made her wary of crossing him.

Anna sighs at her memories of these events of nearly a decade ago. It is late, and she sits alone in the silence of the kitchen. The children are finally asleep and she is exhausted from the day's labours. The tea Katya, the maid, placed before her when she left for home in the workers' barracks has gone cold. In this hour of solitude Anna reads a psalm, then she bends over her Bible and gives thanks for the blessings of the day. She prays fervently for her family, and tonight especially for the safety of Johann, who is long overdue.

In the next room a child whimpers, and Anna rises from her chair. She finds a shawl and covers the infant Peter, who settles again. She lights a lantern and enters the frosty passageway that joins the house to the barn. The door grates on its hinges, and the dog rises from her bed in the straw, stretches, and wags her tail in hopes of attention. The lantern merely glazes the darkness, and she raises it as high as she can. The chickens have roosted, tightly crowded for warmth and well away from the goose and gander who rouse with Anna's approach and hiss softly to reassure their own nervous brood. The cattle rustle in their stanchions, tonguing the last strands of hay in their mangers. Some have settled for the night and are chewing the cud. Anna strokes the flank of a heifer and judges that it may calve before Johann returns. She counts the week-old piglets snuffling the teats of the sleeping sow and sees that all have survived. She shuffles to the far corner of the barn and draws up the milking stool. She sits, leaning against the wall while she scans the neatly-stacked blocks of dried manure she uses to fuel the kitchen stove. Nothing has been disturbed, and except for herself and Johann's brother Peter, no one knows that gold rubles are concealed there.

From where she sits, she sees the row of empty horse stalls. She shakes her head wearily.

"Johann, Johann," she sighs. "What have you done?"

Two months ago, just before freeze-up, Johann had managed a short leave from his duties in the military hospital in Kherson. Stepping off the steamer in Velyka Lepetykha, he met Slyanko, the overseer of the opulent Falz-Fein estate on the other side of the Dniepr. Slyanko had crossed on a desperate search for horses. He recognized Johann from previous dealings and knew of his reputation as a horseman. He took him aside. The baron was in a panic to escape to the West, he said. Most of his own herd had been requisitioned early in the war, and after the October Revolution the farm hands had run off with the rest and burned the stables. With ships and railways commandeered by the army, and fighting all along the river, Odessa was out of reach. The baron's best prospect was a nocturnal sprint out of the region, hopefully to safety behind German lines. Slyanko was authorized to pay generously in hard currency. Johann brought the overseer home with him, and after a brief inspection, his prized team of four matched beauties changed hands. After midnight he helped Slyanko lead them across the river flats and swim them to the opposite shore.

Anna glances again at the empty stalls and thinks how Johann must have agonized over that decision. This was a team he had assembled over a number of years, buying a colt at the Lepetykha fair, a yearling mare from a neighbour, and breeding his own stock to produce a pair of young stallions. But Slyanko was generous, and Johann had not deliberated long. *Schwitke,* they called him, 'the fast one.' He was decisive, and he rarely allowed himself to regret decisions once taken.

"It's for the best," he had said to Anna. "The war is endless. That we have so far kept our horses is a mystery. Now, if the revolution is not put down, it will spread across the whole country and we will surely lose them, and with no compensation. There will be more oats and hay for the cows now to keep them strong and give us healthy calves. And there is money to see you through another year if I cannot be released before then."

The next day he returned to Kherson, and Anna was alone again.

And then, just six weeks later, Johann had appeared on the doorstep, free at last after nearly four years of service. Preparations for planting would soon be underway in Sergejewka, and Johann scoured the Fürstenland villages to find horses. But the venture failed. Making a circuit through the neighbouring Ukrainian villages, he found much suffering and destitution. These people, too, had lost most of their horses to the war. They knew him well and were glad to see him. Over the years, he had often treated their ailing animals and advised them on the quality of stock when they met him at the auctions. He never asked for payment beyond the bare cost of the various flasks and ointments he provided, and he was well-liked for his generosity and goodwill. Now they were amazed to find he had sold his prize team and was looking to buy.

Soldiers returning to their villages from the front reported that deserting cavalry units had been turning their horses loose or shooting them rather than allowing them to be confiscated by their despised officers to be sold for profit. Now, with Ukraine's negotiation of a separate peace with the Central Powers, the supply of horses was sure to increase. There were the occupying Germans, of course. As they advanced across the region they would take what they needed for themselves. But the newly independent nation was no longer at war, and if one were willing to risk a week's journey to the railheads further west, one would certainly find horses not too battle-scarred or shell-shocked for farm labour.

Anna remembers her astonishment when Johann announced his intention to travel with the Ukrainians. Her incredulity had quickly collapsed into tearful dismay and helpless anger.

"Four years you have been away!" she had cried. "In the hospital, at least you were safe. Now you want to go travelling? Now? With bandits everywhere and Bolsheviks swarming like field rats? Workers throwing off their masters, stealing what they can and destroying everything else! And like a Cossack you want to race off across the steppes!"

"Only as far as Krivoy Rog, Anna. Four or five days each way. It is not that far."

"Krivoy—! Johann, you will be killed! Five children, Johann! Think of us
. . ."

But her supplications would not move him, and she knew it. His mind
was fixed, and he would do what he would do. She remembers how she
drew aside the curtains the following morning and watched as Johann
stepped out to greet the riders from Rohachyk and the two Lepetykhas.
She saw how the others deferred to him as leader. There were four of
them, and Johann brought them in for breakfast. When he went to the
back room to collect his things Anna followed him, and he turned to her.
Of Slyanko's rubles, he said, he would need less than half. The rest should
remain untouched, if possible, since gold would attract unwelcome attention in the village. But if need be, she should go to cousin Herman at the
factory. He would know how to be discreet.

She remembers his tight embrace, and how he had turned to the children
who had gathered around.

"A week or two," he said, "and we'll have the finest horses!" He grinned at
them. "I promise. In time for the seeding. And maybe a pony for you!"

He kissed them and lifted his pack to his shoulder. Once outside, he
untied the reins of the mare he had borrowed from the stable of Onkel
Gerhard, who was still in hiding. He led the men across the street to the
factory grounds. Before they mounted, Johann turned once more and
waved a jaunty farewell. But Anna had stood inert, her expression fixed.
She tilted her head in his direction only once, refusing to bless the
venture, yet fighting the impulse to run to him. But the instant the riders
were out of sight, the perils of their journey had filled her imagination,
and she was filled with regret. She recalls that moment now, as she rises
from the milking stool. "If he does not return," she thinks, "his last
memory of me will be my sullen withholding."


Anna leaves the barn and secures the door of the passageway. The tinkling
of the prayer bell of the Orthodox chapel reaches her from the edge of the
village. Then the single iteration of the midnight gong marks the beginning of a new day.

"It is Friday," she whispers. "They will rehearse tonight." Perhaps she will
rejoin the choir, at least for rehearsals. During her illness after little Peter
was born, she lost her voice and has not sung since. But her strength is

returning, and Njuta is nine and responsible enough to mind the children for an hour. One must keep singing, she thinks. Perhaps she will go. She closes the Bible and stands to her feet. She thinks about taking the tea to the slop bucket and wiping up the spilled cream that has run almost to the edge of the table. But weariness overwhelms her, and she leaves it for the morning. She secures the front door and blows out the lamp.

# 6. Johann

Though he had minimized them to Anna, Johann was keenly aware of the many hazards that faced him and his accomplices on their quest for horses, and he wondered which of them he should fear most. The entire country was seething in chaos. After the October Revolution, Ukraine's aspirations for independence had spawned numerous nationalist movements centred in Kharkiv, Kiev and elsewhere, all vying for supremacy and often in active conflict with each other. The 'Red' Bolsheviks and reactionary 'White' armies were deep in civil strife, and both were opposed by rural peasant militias, the 'Greens,' that sprang up everywhere in defence of their villages against confiscations and reprisals. And following Ukraine's signing of a separate peace with the Central Powers in early February, hundreds of thousands of Austrian and German troops were sweeping in to implement an occupation deeply resented by all parties and offering a new target to the anarchist Nestor Makhno, under whose Black flag tens of thousands were rallying.

The five men followed the track beside the factory grounds and down the slope toward the *konstje*. The winter had been severe, and deep drifts choked the narrow channel of the frozen stream where the men crossed over to the *plaven*. At this time of year, with the Dniepr at its lowest, the island extended many *verst* to the north, and they would ride its full length to get as near as possible to the broad river flats at the great bend below Nikopol. There the river divided into a web of smaller streams that would be easy to cross even if the ice was no longer strong.

This was Johann's home turf, and he led the way. The snow was deepest near the steep bank of the valley, so he crossed to the other side of the island and followed its shoreline. At first there was little speech, but as the group made progress, light banter began to flow between some of the men. The two peasant sons from Nyzhnii Rohachyk, Ihor and Vasyl, were young and energetic. Ihor had been released from the army short days ago. He had served only a few months and had seen no action. He congratulated himself now that he was set to marry his sweetheart and start his own farm. His friend Vasyl had volunteered early in the war, but myopia had disqualified him. Their village was not far from Michaelsburg, and as they engaged Johann in conversation, it emerged that they knew some of his Mennonite acquaintances there.

Nineteen-year-old Stepan came from a large family in Velyka Lepetykha whose livestock Johann had treated on occasion. Johann was surprised to find him in place of his father, an excellent horseman who had declared his own firm intention to travel with the group. When the war broke out, Stepan had desperately wanted to enlist, but as a youngest son, he had been charged with maintaining the farm and supporting his parents and sisters. He chafed at his lot and had more than once threatened to abscond. Johann seriously doubted Stepan's competence and was more than a little annoyed at the substitution. The lad appeared to have little enthusiasm for the enterprise, keeping to himself and exhibiting a sullen disregard for the others.

The fourth man was Valentin Kyrylenko, the same quiet crew chief in the foundry who had left his post shortly after Onkel Kornelius's death the previous summer. The *Komitee* had recalled him after Gerhard Enns left, but due to ongoing tensions with young Herman, and indeed, with the *Komitee* itself, he had lost no time training an assistant, which allowed him to absent himself from the factory for extended periods of time. Over the years, Johann had met him in the street occasionally and was vaguely aware that tensions with Onkel Gerhard had led to his departure from the factory. The half-smile on Kyrylenko's lips whenever the two men happened to catch each other's glances said that he knew of Johann's family connections. Kyrylenko had been employed in the factory in one role or another since he was fourteen and had risen to successive positions of responsibility there. Now in his middle age, he had taken over his aging parents's farm. But he had little appetite for the task, and Johann judged privately that it would be rough going for him if he could not solicit the help of his neighbours.

By mid-afternoon the riders had cleared the *plaven*, and after navigating the maze of frozen channels and islets on the flood plain, they mounted the steep west bank of the river. They avoided the major thoroughfares near the city, keeping instead to the cartways that threaded their way through the quilt-work of snow-covered fields surrounding the peasant villages.

Once Nikopol was well behind them they took the high road, and their progress quickened. Several smaller rail towns lay on their projected route, and Johann had thought perhaps fortune would strike early. But it was not to be. In Kostromka and again in Apostolowo, local residents scoffed at any suggestion that farm horses were to be found in the markets.

"Believe me, I have tried," said one of their overnight hosts. "By the time the trains get this far from the front, only the poorest are left." He jerked his thumb over his shoulder at the wheezing creature behind him, its head hanging low to the ground. He laughed contemptuously.

"Look at this one. It was the best I could do, and believe me or not, my neighbours are jealous. They have not even this!"

On the fourth morning, a column of black smoke appeared on the horizon, issuing from the stacks of the great ironworks of Krivoy Rog. All day long, like the biblical pillar of cloud, it led the travellers onward. They arrived late in a village not far from the city and entered the gates of a substantial farmyard. The house was a large, low building with a roof of steeply peaked thatch. Next to it stood a well-built stable. The fences seemed in good repair, but there was clutter everywhere, hinting at recent neglect.

Kyrylenko knocked at the door, and it opened to reveal the face of a very old man. He peered at Johann and his companions in the dim light of his lamp, and for a time only his eyes moved, toggling left and right, scanning each man's face repeatedly. Then he stepped outside, and Johann could see a woman peering around the man's right shoulder. Kyrylenko spoke for the group. After brief negotiations and the transfer of a few rubles, the old man reached back inside the house for his cap and coat and led the men and their horses to the stable. He untwisted the length of wire that secured the door, and when it creaked open he took a step back, bowed slightly, and gestured for the men to lead their horses into the dark interior. A cow near the door shied briefly as the horses passed by. The man followed them in and pointed to a row of empty stalls where the horses could be tethered. He raised the lamp and pointed to a small tub of barley, thoroughly contaminated with insects, weed seeds and other detritus.

"You are welcome to it," he said. "The oats are reserved for the cow."

He hung the lamp on a nail near the entrance and adjusted the wick. There would be breakfast after sunrise, he said. Before leaving, he pointed to the heap of straw they could use for their bedding.


In the morning the men rose early. From their own meagre supplies they opened a sack of oats for the horses. Then they led the animals out to graze at the edge of the yard where the sun had exposed last year's grasses. When they saw smoke rising from the chimney, they knocked and were admitted for breakfast. There was black bread and a little butter, an astringent gooseberry compote, and a bitter brew of roasted barley. Their hosts stood by while the men ate, and only when the travellers rose to take their leave did the old man enquire as to their intentions. When Kyrylenko finished explaining their mission, the old man said he knew nothing that might help them. For himself and his wife, he said, he could only hope that their son, a junior cavalry officer, would be allowed to keep his horse when he returned from the front. But they had received no letters in more than three months, and by now they had grown wary of the postman.


Entering Krivoy Rog some hours later, the men made their way to a hostelry in the western sector of the city not far from the railway yards. They paid to stable their horses and went to find the station and arrange for lodgings. And just as they approached the row of food vendors inside the crowded terminal, their fortunes turned. A great booming voice rang out above the din.

"Yvan?!"

Johann turned to see the astonished face of Dr. Kozlov, the surgeon under whom he had served for more than three years in the military hospital.

"Yvan! I can't believe it is you! But what in the name of all the powers that be are you doing here?"

Johann introduced his companions and described their quest. "And you, good doctor? How is it we find you so far from Kherson?"

"Ah, you see, it's fine to say our war is over, but there are still so many wounded near the front lines, and we want to get them home as quickly as possible. I am now chief surgeon in charge of one of these hospital trains."

He gestured at the train and the medical personnel boarding to assist with the patients. One of the orderlies drew the doctor aside for advice on the care of a particular case, and the two men conferred for a moment. When he returned, the doctor announced that he was hungry and invited Johann and his accomplices to join him, not at the noisy kiosks but at a finer restaurant nearby.

Dr. Kozlov was full of news. Affairs at the hospital in Kherson were busy as usual, he said, and his excellent assistants were in charge. Many of the convalescents had been sent home to make room for the latest casualties, but Johann would surely remember the wounded German prisoners for whom he had been called upon to translate. One or two were still there. Kozlov also remembered Johann's uncle, who had spent some months in his hospital after a risky appendectomy in 1916. He laughed at the memory of a particular encounter between Onkel Kornelius and one of the prisoners. Always jovial and gregarious, Kornelius had met a German officer shuffling down the hallway of the ward and greeted him with a robust, "*Guten Morgen, Herr Leutnant!*" The officer had scowled malignantly.

"*Bin kein Leutnant. Nur Korporal!*"

Without so much as a blink of an eye, Kornelius had slapped both hands to the sides of his vast belly.

"*Und ich? Nicht mal Korporal. Nur korpulent! Hah hah hah!*"

Kornelius had no idea, said Kozlov, how close he had come to a thorough drubbing with the officer's crutch. He was deeply sorry to hear of Kornelius's death in Odessa.

The others listened as Johann and Kozlov shared their memories. They heard about the first meeting between Johann and the doctor. A friend of

Johann's, a Mennonite orderly assigned to the surgical ward, had fainted dead away while assisting the doctor with a messy amputation. Kozlov had kicked him out, and Johann was seconded from the kitchens where he had been working as a butcher. The gore had not fazed him, and he had been reassigned to the surgery.

Then there was the time Johann's reputation as a wrestler had drawn an order from the commander of his unit to disarm a drunken sailor on shore leave, who was threatening all and sundry with a knife. Kozlov's eyes gleamed as he described how he had witnessed Johann climbing the wall behind the man. Then the great leap that followed, and how the sailor had still been mocking the 'yellow infantry' when the knife was kicked out of his hands, and he found himself helpless, with Johann lifting him off the ground with one arm under the crotch, and the other arm slung tightly around the man's face. The doctor shook with laughter and slapped Johann's shoulder.

"You should have seen how the scoundrel kicked and cursed the whole time as this man carried him some fifty paces to the guard room and waited for someone to come with the key. He threw him inside and slammed the door. And not once did he let the sailor see his face!"

It was late, and the discussion turned to the matter at hand. Kozlov was skeptical. Technically, yes, Ukraine's war was over, but local factions in the region were still at loggerheads, not to mention regular insurgent attacks against the Germans.

"Besides," he said, looking around at the faces at the table, "if you are looking to the army for horses, you have surely not seen how the poor beasts have suffered. Even among those that have escaped the bullets and the gas, you will not find many without broken minds. Like so many of the men, they live now in terror and cannot be calmed. The best reserves, those who have not seen battle, are taken by the Germans, or by our own officers who sell them for prices you cannot afford. I'm afraid you will have to go far to find what you are looking for. I have heard of horses in the Volhynia villages near the Polish border, but ... "

Johann interrupted the doctor, grimacing at the idea. "Impossible. It would take a month. And on our poor horses?"

The doctor turned to face Johann squarely. There was a pause before he spoke.

"Look, Johann, my good man. I am in charge of this train. We are returning to the front at noon tomorrow. Coming east, as you have seen, our trains are full of wounded, but there is plenty of room for you going west. The most direct route is not open to us as the Germans have narrowed the rails to accommodate the gauge of their trains, but by tomorrow night, if all goes well, we will pass through Lutsk on a secondary line. I can arrange to stop there. There are no cattle cars, so you must leave your horses here. If you are lucky, you will find better ones near Lutsk. A day's travel will tell you. As to arrangements for their transport back to Nikopol, I cannot say."

The doctor reached for the chain at his waist and pulled out his watch. If they decided to travel with him, he said, he would clear the way. He shook each man's hand and asked them to meet him again, in any case, for breakfast. Then he walked briskly out of the restaurant and back to his duties.

The men ordered coffee, and for the next hour they considered their prospects. Kyrylenko and Johann favoured accepting Kozlov's offer, but leaving their horses in Krivoy Rog was a gamble. Various routes connected Lutsk and Nikopol, and there was no guarantee they would pass this way on the return journey. If they failed in Volhynia it might be impossible to retrieve their own mounts. Johann's horse did not belong to him, but Onkel Gerhard would not reject compensation in the form of a better one. The two Rohachyks did not trust their poor beasts, even to see them home. If they could not sell them in the morning, they would abandon them to the stablemen. Stepan's two-year-old was far and away the best of the lot, and the young man was adamant.

"I will go no further. I leave in the morning," he said.

Johann and Kyrylenko pressed him to take their horses back with him, and reluctantly he agreed. "Provided that, if you have success in Volhynia, you bring two back for me. I will leave you the money."

Johann offered no guarantees. With a man short, it would be difficult to manage. But he agreed to try.

Emptied of its patients, and with a new cadre of nurses and attendants, the train left promptly at noon. The men had a Red Cross carriage almost entirely to themselves. It had received a rudimentary cleaning during the night, but there were no other concessions to passenger comfort. Hospital beds, on two levels for the severely injured, lined one side of the car. On the other side, intended for the walking wounded, were the slatted wooden benches familiar to travellers in third class. The men stashed their gear under the seats and settled themselves as well as they could. Vasyl and Ihor busied themselves in the rear of the carriage with a game of cards, inviting the orderlies to join in as their duties permitted.

Johann and Kyrylenko sat near the front of the carriage, and during the next few hours there developed between them a level of intimacy neither man would have anticipated. For the first time the former foundryman spoke of his work at *Janzen & Neufeld Ko*. Both owners had treated him well, he said, and he expressed sincere regret at the deaths of both men during the past year. Jakob Janzen had taken him under his wing and taught him his trade and, in time, had placed him in charge of one of the foundry crews. Under Kornelius, his advance had continued until he was assigned to the training and deployment of new apprentices. More than once, Kornelius had offered him one of the cottages on the factory premises. But Kyrylenko preferred to walk the half-hour to and from Sergejewka rather than detach himself from the life of his own village. He had never married and needed only the single room in his parents' home that had always been his.

When Johann broached the subject of Kyrylenko's departure from the firm, there was a long silence, and Johann thought perhaps there might be no reply. He began to shift to another topic, but Kyrylenko interrupted. He leaned forward and looked down at his knees.

"Yvan," he said quietly. "I wish no hurt to you or your family, so you must forgive me if you wish for an answer to your question. Kornelius Neufeld was your uncle. His son-in-law Herman Herman Neufeld, your cousin, is now the manager of the factory."

He paused for a moment before continuing. "I know also that Gerhard Enns, the overlord of the foundry, is your wife's uncle. Enns is an angry boss in a dangerous environment. It was his treatment of Ukrainian workers that finally made it impossible for me to continue in the factory, and young Herman refuses to address the problem. As long as Janzen and Neufeld were alive, I enjoyed my work and it was a very good life. But no longer."

He straightened and leaned against the back of the seat. His jaw was set, and he fidgeted awkwardly. He seemed embarrassed. Johann put a hand to Kyrylenko's knee.

"Valentin, my friend. I did not know the details, but I have heard rumours. Be assured, you have not offended or surprised me."

Kyrylenko looked up at him then and accepted the hand extended to him.

The train rolled at moderate speed across the steppe, stopping at intervals to allow the passage of eastbound trains. In the evening the men asked the orderlies for hot water. They made tea and ate the bread and cheese they had purchased in Krivoy Rog. Some time after sunset there was a delay as supplies were brought on board. Then they were underway again, and the men prepared to sleep. The hospital beds were strictly out of bounds, so they stretched out on the seats and covered themselves as well as they could with their coats.

Johann and Kyrylenko faced each other on opposing benches, and, linked by their common interest in the affairs of Sergejewka and its environs, they continued talking long after the sound of snoring reached them from the back of the carriage. Quietly, Kyrylenko confided that he did not trust young Stepan, that he was a capricious malcontent who consorted with the low-lifes of Lepetykha.

"He was kept back against his will to work on the farm. Now that his brothers are returning from the war, he is as likely as not to run off to one or other of the militias. I doubt we'll see our horses again. He'll sell them at the first chance and take his own black stallion to the Makhnovshchina if he's not too brainless to find them."

Johann spoke of his responsibilities as the elected *Schulze* of Sergejewka. He confessed his anxiety about navigating the tensions arising from the demands of the newly installed *Komitee*. Although the majority of villagers worked in the factory, he said, there were still a dozen families, including his own, whose livelihood depended entirely on their fields and livestock. They faced dire prospects if the plans he had seen for land distribution were implemented.

"But about the factory, Valentin." Johann asked. "You know the complaints. There are more than a hundred workers. What should we expect from them?"

Kyrylenko thought for a moment.

"So far, it's mostly talk. Bravado, stirred up by news from elsewhere. But I think you know, Yvan, that many of their grievances are justified. Frankly, the managers behave as though nothing has changed. I think they have no conception of the power of the workers movement, which is still very young and is now restrained only by uncertainty about what will happen with the Germans."

While the men spoke, the train slowed and slipped into a siding. The carriage shook as an eastbound train hurtled by, and for a minute their conversation was quashed by the rush of noise and the sudden draft that forced its way through the carriage. Peering out into the darkness, Johann caught sight of German insignia partially obscuring the Russian logo underneath. "Look, Valentin. The Germans have commandeered one of our trains."

He straightened in his seat and looked at Kyrylenko. "Surely the workers must fear this. The recriminations that will follow if the German occupation succeeds and restores the factories to their owners."

"Yes, Yvan, I know it. Certainly, they do fear it. But the news is that Germany will be weaker now that so many of their troops are needed to hold the new Ukraine against the Bolsheviks. And fighting on their western front is fierce. The Americans have joined in, and that will make the difference. If the Germans fall in France, the game is over for them. They will be driven out of our land as well, and they will go home with their tails between their legs. This is what I think."

Kyrylenko adjusted himself on the bench. The car was cold, and he drew his coat around his shoulders. When he turned to Johann again, his voice deepened.

"And Yvan, I must ask you. What will happen then to those who have hoped for the Germans to win? You must know, Yvan, do you not, that there are many among your people who wish this? When the workers need no longer fear the Germans, when they are free to exercise their new freedoms without restraint. What will happen then to the great landholders and the high and mighty owners and managers of factories? Who will be afraid then?"

Johann was silent. Scenes from his last meeting with Tante Anna passed through his mind. As the widow of Onkel Kornelius, she was the sole owner of the factory and the only truly wealthy person in Sergejewka. He had explained to her that the *Komitee* would not tolerate, for long, her insensitivity to the demands of the workers for a pay increase to meet inflation. He had begged her to consider her own peril under the circumstances. But Tante Anna gave no quarter. When he rose and took his hat in hand, she had abruptly stood and faced him, her back ramrod straight and her head held high.

"What the Lord has entrusted to us, we will cherish and preserve! And, yes, I do pray fervently for the arrival of the Germans! They will restore *Ordnung*!" She had ushered him to the door and closed it behind him.

Eventually, fatigue overcame the two men. Sleep came quickly, and the train rolled on in the darkness. There were few stops during the night, and the sun had not yet made its appearance when Dr. Kozlov entered the carriage and shook the travellers awake. They were entering Lutsk. There would be a one-hour stop, and he wouldn't hear of seeing them off without a hearty breakfast at his expense.

North of Lutsk, a two-hour walk beyond city limits, lay a cluster of villages — Ukrainian, Polish, Mennonite, Jewish, Prussian. Each had several names, a circumstance reflecting the transience of peoples and boundaries over the centuries. It was to two of these that Johann and his companions were directed by a vendor in a market near the outskirts of the city. They came first to Trochenbrod (Zofiowka/Sofiovka), once a prosperous Jewish town which, from early beginnings as an agricultural venture, had morphed into a regional service centre with workshops, general stores, a bank and law office, and a half-dozen synagogues. It still boasted a vibrant open bazaar where ethnic German and Prussian Mennonite settlers from nearby farming villages came to sell their produce.

It was late on a Friday afternoon, not a market day, and commerce was coming to a close when the four men passed through the town. There was just enough time for Johann to send a telegram from the post office before the last shutters closed for Shabbat. Anna had a right to know where he was, and she would receive his message when Dachenblecher brought the mail.

Leaving the village, the men crossed a narrow bridge over the River Styr and found themselves at the gates of the first farmyard of Jozefin (Josefin/Yuzefin). Here it was Johann's German tongue that opened doors, and within the hour, he and Kyrylenko were billeted in the largest home in the village. Vasyl and Ihor discovered the tavern at the opposite end of the street and took a room there.

For the first time in a week, the two older men enjoyed a full dinner. There was fresh bread, coffee, and good beer, and their gregarious host, Klaus Klauber, plied them with questions. He was an elderly widower, a *Volksdeutscher*, and a Lutheran. He was himself a horse breeder, and he was confident he could find a dozen worthy beasts within the nearby villages.

Kyrylenko asked how it was that local livestock had remained untouched during the war, given that Lutsk itself had been attacked repeatedly.

"Untouched? Oh no, my friend," said Klauber. "Far from it. We were not spared."

He spoke rapidly, shuffling at random through his recollections of the four years of the war. "Already in the first weeks the Tsar ordered all our young German men deported east. Or, if they could, some fled to Germany. It was only us old ones that kept things going here. The Austrians were in Lutsk for more than a year, and they were beasts. But we had our spies, and if we knew they were coming we hid our livestock in forests and valleys that have no roads. We have always been breeders of horses, and throughout the war we did not stop. When the Russians took the city back, we thought we were free, but the Bolsheviks … "

He hesitated, unsure of his audience. He passed around the pitcher of beer before continuing.

"As you can see, our village got knocked about when the armies came through. Now the Germans are in charge. They trust no one, and things are still tense, but we are not molested. They are well supplied here, so close to their own borders, and they don't trouble us. Besides, we are just far enough from the city."

To Johann's concern about rail transport, he replied, "It is much easier now than it has been for some time. Germany is hungry. There are forty trains a week taking cattle, sheep and wheat back to the West. Eastbound, the cattle cars are empty. The Germans try to ingratiate themselves, now, with the people. There should be no difficulty."

In the morning, Klauber took Johann and Kyrylenko on a round of the village and by noon, when the two Rohachyks finally emerged from the tavern, hungover and sheepish, Johann had approved of five horses. In the afternoon, neighbouring villages yielded six more. For himself, Johann selected a pair of Polish Sztumskis from Klauber's own stable. None of the animals were in prime condition, but they were reasonably well-muscled and trained to both saddle and harness. To Johann's canny eye it appeared that two of the mares were in early stages of pregnancy. If he was right, that would make thirteen, and it would do.

Riding through Trochenbrod with their small herd the next day, Johann asked Klauber to stop at the law office. He had requested bills of sale from each of the sellers, and with Klauber as witness, he had these notarized in both German and Russian in order to forestall any difficulties they might encounter on the home stretch.

Several hours later, during the interview with the German attache assigned to oversee the station in Lutsk, it was again Johann who spoke for the group. After examining and stamping their papers, the official dismissed the three Ukrainians and, with a comradely gesture, indicated a chair for Johann. He was a junior officer, not half Johann's age, whose chin had only recently met the razor. He reached nonchalantly for the box of matches on his desk, lit a cigarette, and leaned back in his chair. He billowed a vast cloud of smoke before introducing himself as Lance-Corporal Eugen Mann.

"So, Herr Neufeld. We will find a carriage for you and your horses. But I must say I am intrigued. I would like to know why you, *ein Deutscher*, are travelling with these Ukrainians."

Johann described the depravations that had come to the south Dniepr region due to the war. His companions were trusted neighbours from peasant communities near his own home.

The officer asked about Johann's village, his family, and life in southern Ukraine. He had not heard of *Mennoniten* and was surprised to learn of their large numbers in Russia. He was expecting to accompany the army's advance across Ukraine, he said, and if he found himself on the east bank of the Dniepr, he would like to visit Sergejewka. Johann assured him that he would be welcome.

The two men talked at some length about their very different experiences of military service, about prospects for an independent Ukraine, and for a lasting peace in Europe.

"The Bolsheviks, of course, are the sticking point," said Mann. "They must be dealt with, and what happens in that regard remains to be seen." He stood to indicate an end to the interview, but as Johann reached for his cap and stepped to the door, the officer addressed him once more.

"Herr Neufeld. Since arriving in Lutsk, I have met Russians, Poles and Ukrainians, and even some Jews and Gypsies, who claim they are really Germans. Yet you, with your *richtiges Deutsch*, are the only German I have met who insists he is *not* a German but Dutch. This I do not understand. But let it be. If ever I come to Sergejewka I will find you, and then we can talk further."

He led the way out of the office, and when they rejoined the others, he issued instructions.

"The train leaves for Nikopol in two hours. Our man will meet you on the freight platform and help you load your horses. They will be in the car immediately behind yours. Oats and water are provided. There is no charge."

He shook each man's hand briskly as he wished them well. For Johann there was a tighter grip and a formal *Auf Wiedersehn!* Then he turned and strode back to his office.

The weather had warmed somewhat during the men's stay in Jozefin, and as they sped homewards on the main line late in the afternoon, Johann could see open patches of black earth here and there, and tints of early green on the steepest hillsides. Krivoy Rog would be a twelve-hour leg, then Nikopol three hours later. The carriage was crowded with German infantry, some of whom showed an interest in the four interlopers. But after the intensity of the past days, Johann felt little inclination for talk. Towards evening, the train stopped at a water tower to replenish its boilers, and Johann stepped out to check on the horses. When he returned a few minutes later, Kyrylenko and the two younger men had fallen asleep. This was a German day coach. It was warm, the seats were wide and upholstered, and before the light failed entirely, Johann, too, was asleep.

Many hours later, the squeal of brakes and a sudden deceleration roused Johann instantly. Lifting the window blind, he saw the shadow of low hills against the slate of the pre-dawn sky. Around him, he heard the murmur of drowsy soldiers. The door at the front of the car was thrown open, and an officer strode into the carriage and doused the night lights. There was partisan activity in the area, he announced. Shots had been fired at the train, and signals indicated a disruption of the track not far ahead. A second officer entered, and the two men conferred briefly. While one of them addressed the soldiers, the other approached Johann and his companions. They were on the outskirts of Krivoy Rog, he said. The train would be reversing direction immediately. It was regrettable, but Herr Neufeld and his companions would have to leave the train and continue on horseback.

A night frost had silvered the steppe, and the wind was from the north as the four men began their final trek. The animals gave every sign of relief at their release from confinement in the cattle car. They had been well fed and watered on the train and were impatient to begin. Johann and the two Rohachyks each saddled a horse and led a pair of others using light lines and halters. Kyrylenko rode in the rear, leading the eleventh horse, which also served as the pack animal for supplies they had purchased in Lutsk. As the day brightened, evidence of partisan activity appeared. Crudely drawn caricatures of a mutilated Kaiser nailed to road signs; a fingerpost with the Russian *Krivoy Rog* blacked out and in its place *Kryvyi Rih* in bold Ukrainian Cyrillics.

They had rounded the southern edge of the city and were following the old salt road through a forest of birch and poplar when a dozen men stepped deftly out of the woods and quickly encircled them. With pistols drawn, they motioned for the riders to dismount and ordered them to open their coats. When no weapons were found, the leader motioned for his men to lower their guns. He spoke calmly in Ukrainian.

"You were travelling with the Germans. You were observed leaving their train. Why?"

Kyrylenko replied with equal composure. Each man in the group was a farmer, he said, a peasant whose livestock had been taken during the war. It was spring, and there was an urgent need for horsepower to till the soil and put in the new crop. "We have travelled far to find these animals. They were honestly purchased. We have the papers."

He reached into his coat and produced the Russian copies of the documents notarized in Volhynia. "The freight trains are all controlled by the Germans now. We had no other choice. Our only wish is to cross the river to rejoin our families who are waiting for us on the other side."

While Kyrylenko spoke, the other man examined the papers closely. He refolded them and handed them back to Kyrylenko.

"Your horses are very fine," he said. "Another time we would be tempted. But we must work on foot. On horseback we are too exposed, and the Germans would smell us a mile away."

He motioned for Kyrylenko and the others to remount.

"If I was still a believer, I would say, *s Bogom,* 'Go with God.' "

He signalled to his men, and they retreated to their enclave in the forest.

By late afternoon a fierce wind was roaring in the birches, raising dust devils in the narrow roadway, spooking the horses and driving ice pellets from the shrubbery into the men's faces. Kyrylenko, riding at the rear, called out to say he needed to halt to secure the ties on the packs his animal was carrying. The others had just slowed to wait for him when a farm wagon drawn by a team of four came careening around a sharp bend in the road ahead. It was full of men, a dozen or more, drinking and flinging bottles, the driver cursing and whipping the horses into a frenzy. Johann and the Rohachyks veered to the side of the road and shouted, but Kyrylenko was preoccupied with his task and did not heed the warning until it was too late. The leading corner of the wagon caught him in the shoulder and knocked him sprawling to the side of the roadway.

The driver bellowed in an attempt to halt his team, but panicked by the collision and the relentless whip, the team would not stop. Johann threw the lines of the horses he was leading to the Rohachyks and yelled for them to go on while he rode back to attend to Kyrylenko. He drew the injured man to his knees, grasped his belt and his good arm and hoisted him into his saddle. With a smack to the horse's flank he sent him on his way at a sprint before remounting and galloping to join the rest. At the bend, he glanced back. The wagon had slowed, and Johann caught the glint of rifle barrels swinging around towards him. But by then he had reached the turn, and the barrage of bullets sprayed the forest behind him. Sporadic gunfire continued for a time, but the cursing and laughter receded steadily into the distance. Not soldiers, thought Johann. Nor partisans. Just one of those gangs of reprobates ravaging the countryside and seeding terror wherever they roamed. They would not follow, he was sure of that, and if they tried, their clumsy wagon would hold them back.

Kyrylenko was in agony. His collarbone was broken, and his right shoulder deeply bruised. Johann bound him as well as he could, but after an hour he could no longer support himself in the saddle and had to be assisted by another man riding alongside. Attempting the river crossing with him in such a state was unthinkable, even if the ice was still sound.

The road passed near the Falz-Fein estate, whose superintendent had purchased Johann's horses a few months ago, and it was to this now derelict site that he led the way. Slyanko, the manager, had fled with the baron, but an old caretaker and his wife still occupied a cottage amid the ruins. Kyrylenko was given a cot and blankets while the others watered the horses and prepared to sleep in one of the few stables that had not been destroyed.

Rummaging among the ruins the next morning, the men found a small sledge, repaired it, and lined it with enough mouldy hay to make a bed for the injured man's transport. In the evening, when Kyrylenko declared himself willing to attempt the crossing, they harnessed the most docile of the mares to the sledge. Vasyl would see Kyrylenko home and then cross back over to assist with the rest of the horses.

When Vasyl returned three hours later, the others were ready. There was no moon, and except for the creak of leather saddles, the night was utterly still. As they crossed the *plaven*, the single peal of the midnight bell rang out from the Orthodox chapel, and shortly thereafter, they entered the quiet street of Sergejewka. Old Heinrich Braun stepped from his watchman's booth at the factory gate and raised his lantern in their faces. When he recognized Johann, he murmured a greeting and waved them on. At Johann's gate, the Rohachyks dismounted to help with the animals. Johann propped open the stable doors, and together they led the horses inside one by one. There were his Sztumskis and the two mares, and until they came to claim them, he would keep Stepan's and Kyrylenko's horses as well. Back outside, Vasyl and Ihor shook Johann's hand and thanked him before taking their own animals home to Rohachyk.

For the first time in more than a fortnight, Johann is alone. He is lightheaded and weak in the knees, and he braces himself against the barn wall. For a long minute he stands there motionless with his face to the heavens. He opens his bleary eyes and a cascade of stars descends upon him like a benediction. After a time, he steps into the barn and secures the door. He lights a lantern, and opens the grain bin. He pours generous oats for the horses, and from the loft he pitches down an abundance of hay. When he is done he turns up the flame of his lamp and surveys his surroundings. There is a new litter of piglets. The geese have fattened, and the heifer looks about to calve. The stack of fuel bricks has not been disturbed. He stands in the centre of the barn and inhales deeply. For a half-minute he holds his breath, and the great sigh that follows is an exhalation of gratitude and relief.

Johann makes his way through the passageway and into the kitchen. It is still warm, and he can see the glow of embers through the vent in the stove door. He hangs his coat on its hook beside the door and removes his boots, and as he places them in the warmth to dry he is aware of a great weariness. Passing by the kitchen table on the way to the bedroom he sees a teacup, nearly full and standing in a rivulet of spilt cream. He touches the back of his finger to the cup and finds it is cold. It will not do to wake Anna, he thinks. He will sleep on the daybed beside the stove.

# 7. LENA

When Russia rejected the terms of peace dictated by the Central Powers in February of 1918, Germany and its allies unleashed Operation *Faustschlag* (The Fist), eleven days of relentless attack against a Russian army already in advanced stages of disintegration. Lenin, fearing annihilation on the battlefield and the complete collapse of Bolshevik power, overcame resistance within his executive committee and ordered the unconditional acceptance of terms that included ceding vast tracts of Russian territory, of which Ukraine was the most extensive. The Treaty of Brest-Litovsk was signed on March 3.

But the winds of peace blew no less fiercely than the blasts of war had done. Germany threw its support behind the newly declared Ukrainian People's Republic, and in rapid succession the Bolsheviks were driven out of Zaporizhzhia, Dnipro and Odessa. Before mid-March, a force of 9000 Austro-Hungarians overwhelmed the regional Bolshevik headquarters in Kherson, a day's journey downstream from Sergejewka. And in the next two weeks the German army, nearly a million strong, swept across the Dniepr, through Molotschna and the Mariupol-Donetsk region, and five hundred *verst* further east to Rostov on the Don.

The first three Germans appeared in Sergejewka at midnight on March 15. They had crossed the main channel of the Dniepr in a rowboat and trekked the two *verst* across the river flats guided by the silhouette of the factory chimney against the eastern sky. Their orders were to aid an airman who would touch down at first light in the fields near the *kurgans* above the village. In addition to fuel, he would need assistance in turning his machine into the wind before takeoff. The men were billeted in the home of Johann Janzen, the personnel manager of the factory, who provided the required benzine from the supply kept for the factory's water pump. In the morning, when Janzen rose early to prepare breakfast for the Germans, they were already gone. He heard the plane land while he was dressing, and a quarter hour later, take off again. The three soldiers did not return, and by noon Janzen was under arrest by authority of the Sergejewka Workers' *Komitee*. He was charged with harbouring and abetting the enemy, an offence for which the prescribed remedy was a bullet to the back of the head.

It was Johann Neufeld, in his capacity as *Schulze*, who brought his Tante Anna the news, and it put her in a frenzy. Janzen was the husband of her late sister, and the father of five children. She bolted from Neufeld and ran across the family compound to the factory offices, where she found her three sons-in-law already in deep conference. Herman had sent for Rudenko, the chairman of the *Komitee*, who was employed in the assembly hall. For an endless hour they waited, and when Rudenko breezed through the door of the head office, it was clear that he relished the powers newly invested in him — powers, in this case, over the life and death of one of the petty lords of industry who had for so long governed the conditions of his working life. In mock deference to his employers, he had taken time to wash and shed his shop uniform in exchange for a clean shirt and jacket. His ebony hair was freshly slicked with oil, and he was smoking a cigarette in defiance of strict regulations to the contrary. All three men stood to greet him, but he ignored their extended hands. He shook his head when Herman pointed to the *samovar* and seated himself on the divan before they could offer a chair.

Herman cleared his throat. "Rudenko, I thank you for coming. As you know, Johann Janzen was arrested at his home this morning. We wish to know what you intend."

Rudenko raised his eyebrows quizzically as though only just now discerning the purpose of the meeting. "Janzen? Ah yes. Johann Janzen. A great pity, I'm afraid."

He had thrown one arm across the back of the sofa, and now he thrust his legs forward casually. Anna, who had been pacing the floor and had not taken a chair, stepped forward to face him. In a stern and steady voice, she addressed him.

"You will know that he is a widower with children."

Rudenko belched a cloud of cigarette smoke.

"Five I believe, yes? And exactly what is that to me? The *Komitee* will meet in a day or two to discuss the matter. Until then, Janzen will be safe in the guardhouse in Velyka Lepetykha. You may see him there if you wish."

There was a short pause during which no one spoke. Rudenko's eyes flicked back and forth at the faces of the others.

"Is that all then?" He raised his eyebrows in feigned surprise. "Well. I'm shirking my duties. Janzen would not approve," he smirked. "I should be getting back."

He rose abruptly and reached up to give his cap a twist. Again, no one spoke as Herman followed Rudenko to the door. Outside the office, he addressed the *Komitee* Chairman once more.

"Rudenko. I must beg you ... "

But the other man raised his hand to silence him. His face darkened as he considered what to say.

"It cannot be that Janzen did not know what he was doing. The German is our sworn enemy. It does not matter what was decided in Petrograd or Brest. To invite enemy soldiers into his house, to feed them and house them and, worst of all, to supply them with materiel for their war against us. What is that? I ask you, what is the name for that?!" He spat contemptuously and glared into Herman's eyes.

Herman coughed nervously and nodded.

"But I must ask you to consider, please. It was midnight when they came to his door, and Janzen did not invite ... He has children. Surely there is a chance for mercy? I can promise you it will not happen again."

But Rudenko had already turned, and without further reply he strode back to his work, leaving the young director staring helplessly after him.

That evening, Anna Janzen Neufeld sat for hours at the great oak desk in Kornelius's study. She tried, intermittently, to enter a few lines in her journal, but her mind reeled, and after a time, the pen fell from her hand. The memories of the losses of the past eighteen months were raw and vivid, and this latest grief threatened to overwhelm her. As though parcelled out by Providence in quarterly increments, she had lost four dear ones in the space of a year — her father in January, her sister Helena in early spring. Her beloved Kornelius had agonized for months in an Odessa hospital before succumbing in June. Then in September, while Anna was away settling her youngest children in the boarding school in Ignatievo, a telegram had announced the sudden death of her mother. And were her poor sister's children to be orphaned, now, at the whim of Rudenko and his *Komitee* of scoundrels? It was all too much. Her shoulders shook with sobs, and she thrust herself back in the chair and clasped both hands to her temples.

Darkness fell, and she reached for the switch on the wall. But the silence from the factory reminded her that the late shift had been cancelled, and the steam plant and generator had been shut down for the night. She struck a match and lit the oil lamp beside her on the desk Kornelius had brought from Odessa. Her hands caressed the smooth oak surface and the elegant carvings on the drawer fronts. A surge of grief and longing overwhelmed her, and for a time she wept silently. Kornelius was the only person from whom she had truly felt love, and her life had seemed to end when he died. In his last moments of consciousness he had gripped her hand and whispered for her assurance that *'there remains nothing between us requiring forgiveness?'* She had given him that, and then, like a guttering candle, his life had flickered and died. On the day of his funeral, the *Kroeger* on the wall had run down, and she had forbidden the servants from rewinding it. She could see the shape of its weight and chain lying on the floor in the dark.

The village held its breath. Delegations to the prison in Lepetykha left food and clothing for Janzen, but the emissaries were refused admittance and were turned away without information. On the fourth day Anna decided to go herself. She took Janzen's oldest son with her, and when she announced herself at the gate, a uniformed guard came out to speak with her. Janzen was being educated, he said, and would be released when he had mastered his lessons. He took her parcel and promised that the prisoner would receive it after it was inspected. With a dirty finger, he tousled the hair of the twelve-year-old and asked if he had a word for his father. Cowed by the sinister attention, the boy could only say that he hoped his father would be home soon.

Late on the sixth day, Janzen returned to the village, the marks of his education visible on his swollen cheek and in his limping gait. He had walked the ten *verst* from Velyka Lepetykha, and an early spring rain had soaked him through and through. He was brought inside and a blanket was thrown around his shoulders. While his shivering abated, he described his ordeal. Harsh interrogations had been the order of each day, and a thorough drubbing with boots and fists the night before his release had made him expect the worst. In the end, he had not fared as badly as some of the others, he said, but he had been sent home with a message from his captors: let there be no doubt that he would be the last traitor to escape execution.

Walking from the prison through the streets of Velyka Lepetykha, Janzen had witnessed scenes of uproar and confusion. News of the rapid advance of the Central Powers had clearly unnerved the workers and their organizers. The local militia had doubled in size overnight, and surrounding territories were being swept for weapons and ammunition. In the villages of Mennonites and ethnic Germans, warnings against collusion were posted, and all firearms, down to the smallest rat gun, were confiscated, along with butchering knives and axes.

In Sergejewka, too, the factory workers were nervous. News that the Bolsheviks were in retreat undermined their confidence in the future of the revolution. Doubtless, under the Germans, the powers of the owners would be reinstated, and no one could predict what reprisals might follow against the *Komitee* and its leaders. There was talk of pulling down the factory altogether and selling off the machinery — a threat that was placed firmly before Herman when, at the end of the month, he once again failed to meet payroll. He pleaded with the new department managers — all Russians and Ukrainians now — to reduce the workforce. No one was buying farm machinery, the warehouses in Sergejewka and its retail outlets in Taganrog, Chelyabinsk, and Orenburg were glutted with unsold machines, and accounts receivable for goods delivered on credit were ignored. Nor would the demand for ordinance be sustained for long, now that the guns had fallen silent on the Eastern Front. Despite the workers' seizure of the factory in February, Herman was still, nominally, the managing director, and he pleaded with the *Komitee*.

"At the very least," he begged again. "Let attrition take its course, and do not hire new workers to replace those who leave."

But there was no reasoning with the leaders of an agitated mob fearful of the future and determined to hold on to the control they had so recently wrested from the *Kapitalisty*.

Anna called her three sons-in-law to an emergency meeting in her home and was horrified to learn that Herman had submitted his resignation. He had been laughed out of the office, his gambit dismissed as a traitorous attempt to evade his duties as chief financial officer. He explained to his mother-in-law that he was the *de facto* prisoner of the new management, and it had been strongly hinted that his personal safety, along with that of his family, was closely tied to the solvency of the firm.

In the weeks following, Herman was home only sporadically. He made repeated excursions up and down the great river from Kherson to Dnipro and once, at great personal risk, to the international financiers in Odessa. Except for a moderate downpayment from a *zemstvo* near Kherson for an order of ploughs and harvesting machines, these excursions proved fruitless. Nearer home, the bankers in Lepetykha and Nikopol, with whom the company had a long and cordial history, expressed sympathy. But, caught as they were in the enormous instabilities brought about by the war, the best they could offer were short-term loans at extortionist rates, with nothing less than the factory itself as collateral.

At one point, ten days passed without word from Herman. Then, on a Sunday when Anna, too distraught and absent-spirited to attend the service, had lain all morning on the sofa, her daughter Annika rushed to her side. Dachenblecher, the courier, had delivered an enigmatic telegram from Herman, her husband.

***Urgent STOP Roubles STOP Papers STOP Kakhovka STOP***

Despite Anna's tearful pleading, her daughter packed immediately, taking her passport and the factory Deed of Ownership. She crossed the street to the office to collect copies of the firm's most recent government contracts. From Wohlgemuth, she requested and received a sum she hoped would suffice for whatever purposes Herman had in mind. When she returned to the house, her cousin Peter was waiting to take her to the harbour in Lepetykha. Leaving her infant in Anna's arms, she stepped into the carriage and was gone.

Anna imagined the worst. In Chortitza, factory owners had been tortured and held for ransom. What if Annika could not find Herman in Kakhovka? What if neither of them returned? Lamentations and prayers cascaded from her tormented heart onto page after page of her diaries, overflowing finally in a flood of longing for death and for reunion with her beloved Kornelius. For him, the sufferings of this world had ended in heavenly bliss, and thinking of him now, she imagined him watching from above and weeping in pity for her. She opened her journal at the great desk in the study. *How long, O Lord?* she wrote — words from the Apocalypse of St John the Apostle, the book of the Bible that had terrified her as a child but which now triggered a longing for the Second Coming of the Lord. Then, all sorrows would cease, and believers would be swept up into heaven to be reunited with the blessed dead. At Christmas, old Brother Arndt, ever alert to signs of the times, had announced the blessed event for the 18th of March, and with a mixture of fear and expectation, she had half believed him. That date had come and gone, and Arndt was busy recalculating.

But Anna knew she could not die; it was pure self-indulgence to imagine such a thing. She had children to nurture and protect. Her oldest daughters were married to the three men who ran the factory now, and they would take care of themselves. But Liese and Jakob were at school hundreds of *verst* away in Ignatievo, where she had delivered them into the relative safety of their uncle's boarding school when the workers began to stir. Their letters were desperate with homesickness and fear of abandonment lest the family were forced to flee Sergejewka. She sorely rued the decision to send them away, but by now, travel to retrieve them was out of the question, with daily reports of rail lines and stations blown up and passengers looted and arrested. She would have to entrust their safety to Kornelius's brother, Herman Sr., a man she trusted and respected but did not love. She could not warm to his chronic severity and his astringent criticisms of the elevated lifestyle that had come to her family with the success of the factory. More than once, her Kornelius had flinched during his older brother's diatribes on the subject. She hoped the rumours were true, that he was more temperate with the children in his care.

Then there was Lena, just turned seventeen, whom she had fetched home from the girls' school in Halbstadt when violence erupted there. Lena loved the *Mädchenschule* and she excelled in her studies. Released from the strictures of life in Sergejewka, she had blossomed into an effervescent and gregarious young woman. But she had returned home sullen and morose, with her grief at the loss of her father rising again to the surface after being submerged under the excitement of life in Halbstadt. Apart from her enthusiasm for learning, there had been the exhilaration of her first real friendships with other girls of her age, not to mention the delicate awakenings she felt at the attention of boys from the *Zentralschule* on the rare occasions when the two groups were allowed to meet. Back in little Sergejewka, isolated and bored, she kept to herself, standing for hours at an upstairs window overlooking the factory and the river beyond, sleeping away much of the daylight, and reading or pacing through the night. Her mother tried to speak to her, but Anna, too, was tense and irritable, and the two did not get along.

A particularly unsavoury clash erupted between mother and daughter over breakfast one morning a week or two after Lena's return home. She had risen late, and she was glum. When once again she expressed her disgust with the tedium of life in the village, her mother exploded in sudden anger.

"*Tu was!*" she shouted. "Do something! Anything! Go help in the garden. Go visit your aunts and cousins. Just go! Stop feeling sorry for yourself, and don't weigh me down with your misery! I miss your father too, much more than anyone, and I am alone with that."

She softened then and reached for her daughter's shoulder, but Lena pulled away angrily, nearly upsetting a chair, and in the clamour of her escape, she did not hear her mother's sighs.

Lena left the house and walked briskly along the main street that led to the Leperykha road. Here on the fringes of the village stood the cluster of forty or fifty huts that made up the workers' barracks, and in one of these lived her cousins. They were the children of her father's older brother, who had worked in the factory until his death during the first year of the war. She had liked his quiet humour and easy-going ways, but from over-heard conversations she understood that her father had considered him an embarrassment — a complainer and malingerer, unreliable and in perpetual debt to his brother and to the factory for advances on his pay. After his death, Kornelius was named guardian of the children. He had arranged for a small annuity for the widow and granted her the use, in perpetuity, of the hut and a garden plot. And he had given the oldest boy work in his fields and barns. Once a week, he had stopped at the cottage to see how his sister-in-law was making out, and on occasion, he invited the family for Sunday dinners. But now Kornelius was gone, and there were no more dinners. And since the day Anna had lost most of her land and livestock to the local Soviet, there was also no longer any work for the boy. It had been made clear to him and his mother that his pay would be stopped at the end of the month.

Lena found Tante Herta and her children at work in their tiny vegetable patch. All were shabbily dressed and barefoot, and the youngest was crying unattended near the garden gate. The widow looked up when she heard Lena comforting the child but turned back to finish weeding her row of cabbages before she came over to her. The older children gave her a polite good morning and stood around awkwardly while their mother spoke with Lena.

"So, you're home? How do you like your new school?"

Lena sensed the tension. "I enjoy my studies very much. Halbstadt is a large and busy place. And you? Are you all well?"

After a moment more of small talk, there was little left to say. At the garden gate, Lena stooped once more to comfort the little one. She straightened his cap, and when his crying subsided, she tickled him till he began to laugh. She stroked the locks from his forehead and rose to her feet to wave goodbye to the others. But they were already bent over their hoes and did not see her leave.

Lena walked slowly back into the village. The morning was fine, and she was in no hurry. The sun had vanquished the last snows of winter, and she saw blades of new grass bursting through tufts of the old. The mulberry groves were in leaf and straining to bloom, releasing their fragrances and attracting a chorus of birdsong. A pair of storks, returned from their winter habitat, were refurbishing the monstrous nest on the peak of the old windmill. The Dniepr was free of ice and in full flood, allowing the little *konstje* to discharge its own winter burden and to take up its task of draining meltwater from the steppe above the village. In a few weeks, when the *plaven* emerged from the waters, the villagers would clear it of flotsam and begin planting the community gardens. Lena resolved that she would assist. It would be good to join in the work and to renew acquaintance with some of her old schoolmates. If the war was prolonged and she could not resume her studies in the fall, she would enjoy all the more the prolific harvest of melons, cucumbers, and root vegetables that each year attracted buyers from the autumn markets in the two Lepetykhas and Rohachyk.

As she drew nearer to the centre of Sergejewka, Lena stopped to look back. The barracks were lost beyond a bend in the road, but she saw ribbons of smoke rising in the still air. The workers' families were preparing their noon meal. She imagined her weary aunt putting down her hoe and feeding her children. The thought discomfited her, and she turned again to face the village. From where she stood, she could see the factory her father and grandfather had built, its gigantic chimney splitting the horizon. She could hear the rhythmic palpitations of the steam engine and then the triple shriek of the whistle marking high noon. On the lot adjacent to the factory stood her family's residence, grand and eloquent of wealth, dwarfing even the fine home that had belonged to her late Opa Janzen. Only the factory itself stood taller. With a crystal clarity that was strangely unsettling, Lena suddenly comprehended that her family was very rich.

Long after the midnight bell on a night in early April, Lena stood gazing out of her open bedroom window at the moonlight skimming from the waters of the *konstje,* when she became aware of movement in the cherry orchard. She watched as shadowy figures, stooped and silent, passed between the trees until they were concealed in the gloom next to the house. For half a minute, there was nothing more. No dogs had barked, and she wondered if perhaps she had imagined it. Then the silence was broken by the sound of a sharp rapping on wood. The sound came not from the house but from the cattle barn thirty paces away across the yard. She looked up to see the glint of moonlight on a rifle barrel extended from the open window of the hayloft. To the left, in the black shadow of the flour mill across the street, there was the sudden flare of a match.

Then darkness again, and a voice she recognized. It was her cousin Peter, and his voice was not loud but hard and clear.

"It will go hard with you should you proceed with this business."

Then another light, this time from the grating in the topmost window of the factory, and another voice.

"As you value your life, it will go hard with you. We are not alone."

From below her window, Lena heard muttered curses above the sudden rustle of clothing and the scuffle of feet in dry grass. Then the sounds of flight down the gravelly road that led out of the village. Lena looked across to the barn. She saw the window close again. Then there was silence, and she lay back on her bed. She did not undress, nor did she sleep. She had not known about the night watch nor of the perils it signified, and the discovery startled her. It did not feel like fear, only an ambiguous confusion that stirred in her mind until first light swept away the darkness.

An early morning survey of the town revealed numerous incursions that had not been thwarted by the night patrol. A dozen dogs were found dead by poison. A healthy calf and a clutch of hens were missing from the Martens farm. From the supply stores behind the factory, quantities of coal and hardwoods had been pilfered. And in the north sector of the village, the thieves had taken two horses and a saddle. Hoof prints led up the path to the cemetery and onto the steppe in the direction of Rohachyk.

Lena and her mother were still at breakfast when cousin Johann came to report that their house, too, had been approached and to ask that they check for missing articles and evidence of vandalism.

Anna became enraged. "So it has come to this!"

There followed a storm of invective against Russians, Ukrainians, Gypsies, Jews, and Bolsheviks, not exempting "even our young Mennonites that lounge about all day and are up to no good at night!"

Johann was not a patient man, but he could find no reply. Dazed, he waited until she finished and collapsed in her chair. Then he reached for his hat and rose from the table.

"Tante Anna," he said quietly, "please calm yourself. We will do what we can."

She looked up at him, breathing heavily.

"*Na ja*," she said with an air of resignation, pitching her napkin to the centre of the table and rising from her chair. "Who knows what the Lord still has in store for us. Of course it's all in His will, but I, for one, cannot imagine what He gets out of it." She turned abruptly and sailed from the room, her silks billowing in her wake. Only then did Lena turn to look into her cousin's face.

"They were right under my window, Johann. I saw them. And they weren't all Russians. Some of the swearing was *Plattdeutsch*." She got up silently and went up to her room, and she did not come down again until the evening.

Alone in her room, Lena thought about her mother's emotional austerity, wondering about its sources. She was forced to admit to herself that, although in some deep well of her being she loved her mother, she did not much like her. At school, Baladin, the science teacher, had drawn a diagram to show how the earth and sun orbited around a common centre of mass at some distance from either of them, and Lena thought of that now. She and her mother seemed to be in perpetual rotation, circling each other warily, without ever a meeting of minds and hearts.

She heard one of the housemaids passing in the corridor and stepped out to say she was not hungry and would not be coming down for lunch. She waited until the girl descended to the ground floor. Then she turned to the portrait of her father that hung near the window at the top of the stairway. It was a likeness that her mother hated.

"Nikkel should stick to crows and cows," she said whenever the subject arose.

Lena knew the painting was technically poor, but she preferred it to the photographs in the rooms downstairs. It captured something of her father's joviality and the spirit of goodwill that permeated all her memories of him. She had felt drawn to her father as metal to a magnet. As a child, she had loved being near him in the factory, had admired his easy relations with the crew captains, and seen how he joked with the men on the shop floor. On Sunday mornings, he was by far the most engaging of the preachers, though his broad gesticulations and the colourful anecdotes with which he illustrated his sermons occasionally gave offence to the other preacher brethren. And he could be too loud, a failing for which he sometimes apologized when he caught himself mid-sermon.

For a long time Lena remained standing before the portrait. In the silence of the deserted hallway, she heard again how her father had whispered her awake before dawn and taken her fishing beyond the *konstje* on the great river itself. Drifting under the silvery moon, they had listened to the howl of wolves in the woods. Barely visible above the rise behind the village were the shadows of the great *kurgans*, and her father had explained their ancient and mysterious origins. And in the eastern sky, rising above the tops of the oaks, he had pointed to the great sweep of the comet whose reappearance, he said, had been prophesied long before he was born by an Englishman named Haley. They had returned to the house before anyone was awake, and her father had cleaned the fish and fried them up for everyone's breakfast.

Lena's thoughts were interrupted by the double blast of a ship's horn, and she stepped to the window to look. The packet from Nikopol was making its way downstream, and the signal meant that passengers for Sergejewka would disembark shortly in Velyka Lepetykha and would need to be met at the dock. She wondered momentarily if perhaps her sister Annika had found Herman and they were finally home. But that could not be; they would be arriving from Kakhovka in the south. She returned to the portrait of her father, glowing now in the golden light of the afternoon.

Once, when she was ten, he had taken her with him to Michaelsburg. They left the main road to see the excavations at Solokha, the greatest *kurgan* of all, where the Scythian queen had been buried. He told her about the gold artifacts that had been found there. He had seen them in the museum in Kiev, and he promised to take her there when she was older. How attentive he had been to her questions and how careful and comprehensive his replies. He seemed to know everything. After she learned to read, he had shown her how to use the great *Brockhaus Enzyklopädie* with its red leather covers. He had brought it from Odessa, and on a Christmas holiday in that grand city, he had taken her to the bookshop at the top of the Giant Staircase where he had purchased it. He had taken the family to the opera house to see *The Nutcracker,* and she had been mesmerized. The dazzling lights, the music, the beauty of the costumes and the grace of the dancers had pierced her young heart, and tears of painful joy and bewilderment had coursed down her cheeks. She thought of that experience now as a marker of the contrast between the world she longed for and the asphyxiating boredom of this stodgy little hamlet where nothing ever happened and from which she saw no means of escape.

It was nearing the supper hour when Lena ended her seclusion and came downstairs to find a crowded dining room. No meal was set, but all sixteen chairs were taken, their occupants hushed and pressing forward on the plush upholstery, elbows on the table. A dozen others stood around the circumference of the room, and all eyes were on Herman and Annika. Lena found a place between the china cabinet and sideboard and listened as Herman described how he had narrowly escaped capture by concealing himself under an overturned lifeboat on the steamer from Kherson.

" ... had just sent Annika to the captain's quarters for safety. They came alongside us in the dark and boarded us before anyone knew they were there. They were looking for Germans. I knew they would look under the boat, and they did!" He scanned his audience for effect and lowered his voice, gathering himself for the punchline.

"But they didn't see me! They saw nothing at all, because I had crawled up and stretched myself high above the undersides of the seats!"

He laughed heartily and slapped the table with his open hand.

"After that, the captain was too terrified to stop anywhere until we reached Nikopol."

Several in the audience joined in the merriment, but it was a hollow mirth. Wedel and Koslowsky, Herman's chief associates in the factory, smiled weakly, glanced sidelong at each other, and both began to speak at once. But their mother-in-law, impatient and terse, waved them off.

"Herman, that's all fine and good. We're glad, of course, that you're home in one piece. Now, what are the prospects for the factory? And the Germans who have promised to restore order, why have we not seen them?"

Herman summarized. The German occupation was consolidating in all major centres, but there were pockets of resistance everywhere, which made progress in any specific locality unpredictable. It was a month since the signing of the treaty at Brest-Litovsk, and the Germans, relatively certain now of their hold on Ukraine, were transferring entire divisions to support their forces in France and Belgium. In the meantime, they were taking drastic measures to secure the land against a return of the Reds. He had just come through Kherson, where there had been a roundup of Bolsheviks and a mass execution of their officers.

Someone brought Herman a glass of tea from the *samovar*. He sipped for a moment, stifled an extended yawn, and cleared his throat before continuing.

"As for the factory, I can tell you that I was able to collect on a few outstanding accounts, enough to keep us going for a few weeks. But there are no new orders. The retailers and the managers of the *zemstvos* are not naive; they know that our warehouses are at capacity. They can buy on short notice, and they seem determined to wait until we are forced to drop our prices below sea level. We have small orders from our people in Omsk and Ignatievo, but we can't risk shipping there because the railways are in shambles."

When Herman finished, he looked around the table expecting questions. But it was clear that he was exhausted from his travels, and no one pressed him. There was a murmur of thanks and then the low buzz of conversation as the company pushed back their chairs and moved toward the doors. Lena greeted a few of her aunts and in-laws but did not leave the room with them. When the maids finished collecting the cups and saucers, she was alone again.

# 8. Occupation

Johann was working in the stifling heat of the barn loft when he heard the growl of an approaching engine. A minute later a German military staff car entered the village. Johann watched as it slowed at the turn in the road and came to a stop near the factory gates. The car was rather worse for wear — not surprising, he thought, since, judging by the direction from which it had arrived, the Germans had taken the track from the crossing at Kamianka, a cart road at best and a squelching bog after the recent rains. The driver stepped out briskly, opened the rear door, and stood at attention as his superior emerged, the epaulettes of an *Oberleutnant* glistening in the brilliance of the day. The officer adjusted his cap, unbuttoned his coat and stood surveying his surroundings. The third and fourth men took up stations at opposite ends of the vehicle, sidearms at the ready, alert for activity among the buildings on either side of the street.

Johann set his pitchfork against the wall and wiped the sweat from his forehead. He slapped his dust-caked cap against his thigh and began descending the ladder. The Germans had long been expected, and as *Schulze* of the village, he had obligations. He hurried through the passage that linked the barn to the house. In the kitchen he bent over the basin and splashed water on his face and arms. Glancing through the window as he reached for the towel, he saw that a crowd was already gathering around the car. Johann ran his hands through his hair and repositioned his cap before leaving the house. He angled across the street and edged his way into the growing ring of bystanders.

The First Lieutenant was finishing a set piece declaring the peaceful intentions of the German army and its firm resolve to defend the independence of the Ukrainian People's Republic against the Bolshevik enemy. When he had finished, he handed his papers to the driver and, discarding formalities, began shaking hands with those nearest him. Hearing their words of welcome, he expressed delight at finding himself among friends and astonishment at their proficiency in his mother tongue.

Johann decided to wait until the crowd thinned before putting himself forward. Then he saw the factory doors open and young Herman emerge with his two brothers-in-law. From the Janzen-Neufeld residence, Tante Anna was also approaching, straightening her hair with one hand and clutching her handbag with the other.

"Yes," he thought, "they will certainly want to be among the first."

For a minute or two, Johann watched as the various members of the factory hierarchy merged and approached the lieutenant. He wondered if perhaps he might be allowed to remain permanently in the background. Personally, it would suit him just fine not to be called upon. After all, his role in the village was modest and domestic, while the Germans' primary concern would be to keep industry and agriculture alive, with grain and manufactured products flowing back to the homeland.

While he was thus preoccupied with considering his own response to this new reality, Johann suddenly became aware of snatches of a phrase repeated in a pure German voice somewhere close behind him, slow and rhythmic and just above a murmur, and he realized it had already sounded a half dozen times or more.

" *... und die Pferde? ... haben Sie sicher nach Hause gebracht?*"

Only when he heard his own name spoken did he associate the voice with the subject, and he knew the speaker even before he turned and looked into the boyish face of Officer Eugen Mann.

As soon as it became evident that the inhabitants of Sergejewka posed no dangers to the Kaiser's army, the young officer had relaxed his vigilance at the rear of the staff car and begun scanning the crowd for Johann Neufeld, whom he remembered from their meeting in Lutsk back in February, and who had told him about this village and its peculiar people. He wondered if Johann remembered him, and he had stood behind him for some time murmuring quietly, " ... and the horses? ... you brought them safely home?" before resorting to "Herr Neufeld," which had finally caught Johann's attention. The officer laughed at his ruse as he shook Johann's hand and took his elbow to lead him out of the crowd. The two men stood in the shade of a mulberry tree and began to talk.

Mann explained that he was serving as temporary adjutant to *Oberleutnant* Albrecht. He had just been promoted to Second Lieutenant, and his assignment was to lead a detachment of sixteen men being stationed in Fürstenland in order to police the region. The rest would be arriving when they had completed a reconnaissance of the other German villages — or did Johann still insist on Dutch? Sergejewka had been selected as their headquarters. The unit would set up its own field kitchen, but they would need billeting. The *Oberleutnant* would make the arrangements, and the army would reimburse their hosts. But if Johann could help make the necessary contacts, it would facilitate matters.

As they spoke, Anna and Herman were engaged in animated conversation with the First Lieutenant. Anna gestured as she spoke, nodding frequently and deeply enough to simulate a bow. Herman, too, displayed an uncharacteristic buoyancy. With a broad sweep of his arms, he indicated the extent of the factory and the attached flour mill. He pointed to the front gates of the compound, evidently offering a tour of the premises. The discussion ended on a high note, and the lieutenant gestured for his adjutant. Mann excused himself, and Johann left the shade of the tree and crossed the street to resume his work.

Anna Janzen Neufeld was breathless as she left the lieutenant and made her way home. Finally! The Germans would guarantee safety in the village and the salvation of the factory. She noted with grim pleasure that not a single Russian worker had come out of the shop, nor had any of their families come from the barracks. The Germans would restore order — the famous German *Ordnung!* — and the workers knew it. Let Rudenko and his *Komitee* sneer at her and her family now! No, there would be no more of that! As she rounded the corner of the meeting house, she breathed her gratitude and praise. The sun poured down in blessing, and the waters of the Dniepr glowed with a deeper blue than she remembered.

In her mind, Anna was already formulating plans for the accommodation of the soldiers. There was the Janzen residence, the home of her deceased parents. Second in size and quality only to her own home, it stood empty except for the one room she allowed her cook Anastasia, on condition that she keep the house in order. She felt entirely vindicated now in her decision last winter to wrest sole ownership of the house from her siblings. The fury she had felt at the time embarrassed her still, but really! They had no right to proceed with the settlement of the estate while she was detained for weeks with her children in Ignatievo. They had notarized a bizarre joint ownership, intending to rent rooms to factory workers and strangers. She had wept before them all and refused to sign the document, declaring it an insult to the memory of their parents and a personal slight she would not forgive. It had taken days of forceful persuasion and seven thousand of her own rubles, but she had bought them out. Now she owned the entire compound with both houses and the factory. And since her father, in his time, had donated a corner of the property for the *Brüdergemeinde* church building, it too was in her name. Shortly after the repossession, Kornelius's older brother, the itinerant *Ältester*, had passed through the village and preached another of his *wealth-and-the-eye-of-a-needle* sermons, though he did not raise the subject with Anna directly – perhaps, she thought wryly, because he himself had moved yet again into a larger house of his own in Ignatievo after acquiring a partnership in a flour mill.

The Janzen house would accommodate most of the Germans. The rest, she decided, she could billet in her own home. There would be room even if, as she still hoped, Jakob and Liese were able to get through from Ignatievo for the school holiday.

First Lieutenant Albrecht remained in the village until his entire contingent had arrived and been assigned their duties. Reconnaissance of the area had convinced him to dispatch some of his men to the four *Jannedarpa* – the villages clustered twenty *verst* to the east, where night raids and home invasions were causing panic, and where, just a few days ago, the Jewish apothecary and his wife had been murdered, and their jewellery stripped from severed fingers. This left only twelve men in Sergejewka, but, as Albrecht emphasized in his address to the sullen assembly of factory workers on the morning of his departure, the choice of Sergejewka as a base had not been an accident: with the harbour at Lepetykha close at hand, reinforcements from German garrisons at Kakhovka or Kherson could be summoned on short notice.

The soldiers spent their first day laying out wire for a field telephone to Velyka Lepetykha. In the evening they set up their kitchen in a lean-to shed Herman had ordered cleared on the factory grounds. Then they were assigned their billets. Johann took Eugen Mann on a walk through the village and introduced him to Anna. She gladly took him in, along with his friend August Harger.

The arrival of the occupying army ushered in a period of relative stability, and had it not been for the distant thump of artillery from the direction of Nikopol to the north, one might have forgotten that conflict was still raging in the wider world. In the factory, labour unrest was suppressed under the fear of reprisal, and the voice of the Workers' *Komitee* was muted. The village street, all secondary tracks and footpaths, the banks of the Dniepr and its little tributary, the *konstje*, were under regular surveillance. Once daily, a pair of uniformed servicemen visited the factory offices or strolled across the foundry yard. And each evening at dusk, when Mennonite men formed their night patrols, they were joined by an armed member of the Kaiser's Imperial German Army.

Now the only sounds Lena heard when she stood at her window at midnight were the scufflings of night creatures and the restlessness of horses in the paddock. Occasionally, the low voices of the patrols drifted up from the street. If Eugen or August were on duty, she might waken when they returned to their room before dawn. Sometimes the other man would wake as well, and she would hear muffled speech or the lilt of stifled laughter. Once, having risen early to catch the sunrise, she passed by their door and imagined she heard her name.

Sunday, the 25th of June, was the first anniversary of the death of Lena's father. Immediately after the morning service, the extended family met in the Neufeld home to share a meal of remembrance. And since, for the first time, Eugen Mann and August Harger had attended the service they too were invited to the table, and Lena found herself seated between them.

Though she had become accustomed to their presence in her world, Lena and the two soldiers had rarely exchanged more than a greeting in passing. In the formal setting around the table, however, she felt obliged to open a conversation of some sort. After a covert glance at each of the men, she turned to Eugen on her right.

"You must find our services somewhat different from yours, is it not so?"

The officer smiled as he put down his water glass and cleared his throat. "*Na ja,*" he said. "In religion, as in all matters, every *Volk* has differences. I suppose it cannot be otherwise."

"And?" Lena waited. "What did you think?"

"I liked the choir very much, but they sing with no organ or conductor. For me, this is strange."

Lena informed him that her Onkel Gerhard normally conducted and explained why in recent months he had been absent from the village. But the choir was well trained, she said, and they did not easily forget his instruction.

"I did not recognize the hymns, except the one at the very end, which we sing also in the Lutheran church. *Entrust your ways to God.* It is by Paul Gerhardt, I think. A very old hymn."

Lena was startled. Somehow, she had not expected this from a soldier.

"Yes," she said. "So you know it? It was my father's favourite hymn. In his last hours, he could no longer sing, but Mother says she heard him whisper '*befiehl du deine Wege.*' They were almost the last words he spoke."

August Harger leaned in from the left. "Is it the custom always to have two sermons? I must say I found them somewhat long."

Lena gave a wry smile. "Yes, there are always two. My father was one of the preachers, and if my sisters and I could catch his eye, we would pretend to yawn. Then he would look at his watch and hurry to the end. 'Again too long?' he would say on our way home. But his eyes were shining, and we knew it was all good fun. Fortunately, today Brother Teichroeb at least was brief."

Their conversation was interrupted by repeated bursts of laughter. Johann Neufeld was recalling the Model T Ford he had helped his Onkel

Kornelius ferry over from Nikopol, and how it wheezed and died in all weathers. How the muck and mire of the steppe overcame its twenty-two horsepower engine on nearly every excursion, requiring only two of Johann's *real* horses to tow it home. And how finally, in exasperation, Kornelius had sold it for fifty Nicholas rubles to one of his machinists, but only on condition that it never be seen in Sergejewka again.

Eugen had caught the last part of the story, and he smiled at the narrator's wit. Then he became pensive and turned again to face Lena.

"The people in the congregation who prayed at the beginning of the service. Are they appointed to do this? For me, this is very new. I have not heard praying like that."

"No, no one is appointed or compelled; it is entirely *freiwillig,* though, of course, not everyone is comfortable doing so."

The kitchen staff brought in tea and sweets, and conversation flourished around the table as well as in the living room, to which some of the young couples retired and from which the sounds of the *Klavier* and gramophone soon emanated. In mid-afternoon, parents collected their children and left for home, and when Officer Harger excused himself to prepare for duty on the evening patrol, Lena was left alone with Eugen Mann. The afternoon's discussion had traversed a wide range of subjects, and Lena was feeling the strain of interrogation. Eugen seemed genuinely interested in her descriptions of life in the village, but she was keenly aware of her inexperience in conversation with men. She sensed a subliminal simmering of something she could not name, something enticing but at the same time vaguely disquieting.

The room had nearly emptied when Eugen also stood to leave.

"*Fräulein,* I must thank you for a most illuminating conversation. And I hope you will not refuse me similar pleasures in the future."

Passing behind Lena's chair, he brushed her shoulder, and she felt the weight of his hand as he let it rest there for a moment. From where she sat, she could see him approach her mother through the archway, and she heard him express his gratitude for the honour of inclusion in this family event.

Lena's sister Maria had been speaking with their mother, and after Eugen had passed them in the corridor, she came over to Lena and stood silent before her with an enigmatic grin on her face.

"*Na? Was denn?*" said Lena. Maria winked at her younger sister.

"That was a rather long chat with a handsome young soldier. You think we didn't notice? So, don't give me your 'Well, what is it?' "

She smiled broadly and extended both hands to coax Lena from the chair. Lena blushed deeply and shook her head in disavowal.

"Maria! Really! He merely wants to know who we are and how we live. And all about the factory and the farms."

Maria's vigorous nods were a mockery. She chuckled.

"And your eyes, Lena? You couldn't stop looking at him. What questions do you suppose those big eyes might have raised for *him*?"

"*Ach*, enough! Such ideas, Maria!" And she stepped around her sister and strode off, shaking her head and leaving Maria laughing behind her.

The sister's wink blossomed quickly into village gossip, and although Lena and Eugen were rarely seen together, and then only in the company of others, everyone knew. Alone among the members of his detachment, Eugen became a regular attender at Sunday services, where he sang with energy and apparent conviction. When the fruit trees along the street sagged with pears and apples, and companies of youth gathered to harvest them, Eugen would be there if he was not on duty. On Sunday afternoons, there were leisurely strolls along the river or crossings to the plaven to wander among the willows and the maturing garden plots. On calm evenings Herman would launch the pleasure barge that had belonged to Lena's father, and young couples and their unmarried peers would float out on the *konstje* and row to the centre of the Dniepr to enjoy sunsets and the early stars. Someone would bring a fishing line, and there might be a guitar or two and singing. On such occasions, the lovers' paths would cross, and there would be feigned accidents of touch and exchanges of furtive smiles. And within the wider fellowship of friends, nods and nudges all around.

# 9. MOTHER & DAUGHTER

Under the German occupation, passenger service became more reliable, and in early August Jakob and Liese were finally able to return home from school in Ignatievo. They were accompanied by their older cousin Kornelius. A recent graduate of the Moscow Institute of Commerce, he had been contracted to tutor a group of Sergejewka's youth in preparation for entry to the *Halbstadt Kommerzschule*. He would teach in the mornings, and in the afternoons he would join his brother Herman in the factory, where his training as a technical engineer would be an asset. The Germans, Eugen Mann and August Harger, transferred to the old Janzen home to allow Ka Ha, as everyone called him, to set up a classroom in the large room they had shared.

As the heat of summer began to abate, the routines of life in the village returned to near normal. With the influence of the *Komitee* diminished, land redistributions were rescinded, and villagers were able to reap what they had sowed in the spring. Accompanied by their German guardians, crews progressed from field to field, their long ladder wagons and reaping machines drawn by teams of horses. On the communal threshing floor, men and women worked together, aligning the sheaves of wheat or barley in two concentric rings with heads overlapping. Threshing stones drawn by a pair of horses rolled over the sheaves, shattering the husks and releasing the kernels, which were then taken up and removed for winnowing. Lofts were cleaned and readied to receive the bounty, and alongside the stacks of hay cut earlier in the summer, mountains of straw grew as the harvest progressed.

That summer, the gardens on the *plaven* were fruitful beyond expectation. And in the autumn, her favourite season, Lena took pleasure in helping to load the barge with watermelons for transport across the *konstje*. From the landing they were carted to cauldrons in the village to be boiled down to the thick syrup for which the village was known.

Towards evening on one of the last days of the harvest Lena waited alone on the bank of the *konstje*. Her coworkers had returned to the *plaven* for the last of the melons, and the cart she had helped load was on its way back to the village. She was weary and glad to be left alone. There was a large, flat rock on the edge of the stream. It lay tightly flanked by two trees that leaned over the water, and it had long been a cherished seat for solitary souls. Lena rested there now and remembered walks with her Opa Janzen, who had told her of his first visits to this place before there was a village, when he and the other men had built their *Semlins,* the pit-and-sod shelters whose ruins could still be seen on the fringes of the village. He had shown her exactly how, long ago, he had leaned back against one of the trees and rested his feet against the other while sitting on this very rock. She smiled wistfully, recalling how the dear old man had strained to squeeze himself into the space.

As Lena waited, the light began to fail. It was the time of day she loved best, and to be alone at just this time in this lovely place filled her with rare joy and tranquility. Even her anxieties regarding her future with Eugen subsided as she surveyed her surroundings. To the west lay the great valley where the dark waters of the Dniepr slid southward on their way to the Black Sea. Above her, the cobalt canopy of early evening. And all around, a vast silence marred only by the intermittent murmur of voices from the *plaven*. The factory engine had ceased, and in the distance she could see the last of the workers retreating down the Lepetykha road, where evening fires in the workers' cottages were being lit.

As she watched, a single figure emerged from the near edge of the village and turned down the cart path toward her. It was Eugen Mann in uniform, and he was in a great hurry. Several times he looked back over his shoulder, evidently keen not to be followed. He was nearly out of breath when he reached her.

"Lena," he said. "My dear Lena. Finally, I find you alone. We must speak."

She motioned for him to sit, but he remained standing. "Eugen, please! Do not stand in the open. You know we cannot be seen here alone together. My mother ... "

He glanced over her shoulder to the cart path. It was empty. "It is alright. If someone should come, I am only here waiting for August when he crosses from the *plaven*. We are both on duty tonight." But he took Lena's hand and led her away from the stone bench to a grassy seat below the lip of the creek bank. He turned to her.

"Lena, between us it is no longer a secret. I want very much that we should be together. And I think it is so with you also, is it not?"

Lena looked up into his face, hesitating as the import of his words settled in her mind. "*Ach*, Eugen. You know it. But Eugen, how can this be? My mother ... "

He interrupted her gently. "Lena, I would like to speak to your mother. Oh, I am quite sure I know what she will say. She will speak about the uncertainties of the war. She will say that you do not know me well enough. She will insist you consider what it means for you to marry a non-Mennonite. And she will surely say you are too young. I do not believe that is true, but I am willing to wait, and I will tell her so."

He looked into her eyes as he spoke. When she did not answer, he looked away for a long moment. Then he continued in a voice that had lost its ardour.

"Lena, listen. The news from Berlin is not good. We are losing important battles In the West, and it is no longer only a rumour that our forces will have to leave Ukraine. If we are to have a future together, it cannot be here in Sergejewka."

The voices from the *plaven* became louder, and Eugen rose quickly.

"My dear Lena. Let me speak with her. Better still, perhaps you too ... " He broke off as the clatter of the returning cart intruded from the turn in the road. He reached for her hand and bent to press his lips to the top of her head. "My dear Lena," he breathed.

A moment later he emerged at the top of the creek bank, the quintessential German soldier. With head held high and one arm tucked behind his back, he strode to the landing where the cart and barge were about to converge. He and Harger helped transfer the last of the produce to the cart before leaving to join the night patrol.

"Oh, for goodness sake, my child! What can you be thinking!?"

When Lena announced her intention of marrying Eugen, Anna's expressions of shock, strong and unmistakable though they were, struck notes that rang vaguely false, both to herself and to her daughter. And in actual fact it could not have been otherwise, since she had long been aware that the tense deference the pair had shown each other early on had been replaced by a friendly ease. At first, she had put it down to the familiarity that sets in whenever people live for a time on the same premises. But once or twice she had risen late and found them still at the table long after the maids had cleared away the breakfast things. Eugen's *Guten Morgen* had been awkward, and he had soon left the room.

Lena's overall demeanour had changed as well. There were fewer complaints, and she had reengaged with the household and its routines. Occasionally, she was heard whistling as she went about her tasks, a new and welcome cheerfulness that, within limits, she displayed also in her relations with her mother. Anna had taken note, and it raised her suspicions. She became more watchful, and when Eugen moved out of her home it had relieved her mind.

Now, in a daze, as though she had not heard herself the first time, Anna repeated, *"Du liebe Zeit, mein Kind! Was denkst du!?"*

Lena smiled weakly at a flaw in the carpet. She could not face her mother directly.

*"Mutti.* I am in love with Eugen, and he loves me. He will come to see you, but we thought it best that I speak to you first."

Anna's shoulders sagged. She lifted her eyes to the ceiling. Finding no witness there, she dropped them again to meet her daughter's, all the while shaking her head slowly, disbelieving. *"Mein Kind, mein Kind,"* she murmured again.

There followed an enumeration, in precisely the sequence Eugen had predicted, of the reasons why this marriage was impossible. With conflict raging all over Europe, who could tell where Eugen would be a month from now? Or, for that matter, where Lena's own family would be if protections were withdrawn. She was only seventeen. What could she know of love? She barely knew the man, nothing of his past, nothing of his motives. Anna hinted darkly at the reasons for her cook's distress the morning she had come to say she could no longer stay with the soldiers in the Janzen home. Eugen was a soldier. Why did she think he was any different than the others? Then there was the matter of Eugen's faith — the church of Luther, despiser of Anabaptists, including Mennonites, for their rejection of infant baptism. Surely she could not make peace with that?

Anna waited for a reply. She bent to grasp her daughter's arm. Lena flinched, but she kept her silence. Her mother's voice grew hard.

"Lena, you know not what you are doing. You are a child. I will not permit it. And I ask you, do not ask Eugen to speak to me about this. Tell him I forbid it."

In the lengthening nights that followed, Anna's distress filled page after page in her journal. Verses from The Book of Lamentations and from the deprecatory Psalms were followed by vivid expressions of anger, pain and hopelessness. Occasionally, upon re-reading an entry, she was shocked by her own excesses and tore whole pages out of the book and burned them in the fireplace. Then she would weep silently, longing for Kornelius and sighing his name in the darkness of his study.

After Eugen's removal to the old Janzen residence, meetings were more easily arranged and the lovers' trysts became more and more frequent. On the pretext of checking on her aunt and cousins, Lena could leave the house in broad daylight and find Eugen on the Lepetykha road, where she knew he would be on patrol. On her way to the cemetery with Jakob and Liese to tidy their father's grave, she might pass by the field kitchen at mealtime and leave a message for Eugen. Whereas in the past she had stood all night at an open window, now she would sometimes slip past cousin Ka Ha's bedroom door and steal down the back stairs. Once outside, she would make her way to the bank of the *konstje* and wait, hoping that Eugen had received her note. Often he surprised her by being already there, and under a lustrous harvest moon they would sit on the bank of the stream, or on the stone between the two oaks. He would wrap an arm around her shoulder and draw her to him, and together they would watch the last of the season's glow worms etch the darkness with their mysterious flares. She would ask him about himself and about life in East Prussia. He told her he had been enrolled in a business school and had been on the cusp of graduating with a diploma in accounting when he was drafted; that his father had been killed early in the war, and his mother, still grieving, had seen him, her only son, off to the eastern front; that his mother would embrace Lena as her own daughter should it be possible for him to take her there. Their talk, though intimate, was sombre; her mother's inflexibility, the intractable war, and the unthinkable — that the Germans would retreat and Eugen would be forced to leave without Lena.

During one such assignation, the two lovers sat in the grass on the bank of the *konstje*. Low shrubs on the *plaven* loomed over the water like a night watch. The air was brisk, though winter was late, and there was no snow. Eugen had brought a sheepskin robe, which he drew across Lena's shoulders, and for a time they spoke of love and sorrow. Then, speech lapsed and a tender silence prevailed between them. The bell in the Orthodox chapel had long ago tolled the midnight hour. The moon sank and slept in the forest on the other side of the valley. Above them, a blaze of shooting stars signalled the planet's annual passage through the dust of the great comet of 1910. The fleece was large and warm, and Lena raised its border to bid Eugen join her. Their shoulders touched, and she felt his arm circle her waist. She turned to him and felt the warmth of his breath on her cheek. Her pulse quickened as his hand found the back of her neck, and she felt the first gentle press of his lips on her own. It was only a brief touch, but she knew, suddenly and beyond all doubt, that she would marry this man. Despite all the objections of her fierce mother, she would marry Eugen. And she told him so.

# 10. November 1918

Lieutenant Mann began visiting the factory offices almost daily. The staff were cordial and answered his many questions about the organization and workings of the firm. Wohlgemuth, in particular, enjoyed the officer's company, and he indulged the officer's curiosity about the firm's accounting practices, showing him the order papers, the accounts receivable and the estimates of future sales — at which Herman raised an eyebrow. The Germans were soldiers, he said to the bookkeeper, not business partners.

But it was Herman's attention the young officer sought most often. One morning, shortly after Lena's declaration, he asked for a comprehensive tour of the compound, and Herman was happy to oblige. He led the way to the foundry, where they watched the rough-casting of artillery shells. Amid the smoke and flare of slag and the clang of iron, he shouted into Eugen's ear: Did the officer understand that he was witnessing the manufacture of armaments intended for deployment against his own army? It was the final consignment, he said, in a contract issued more than a year ago, before the October revolution. Invoices for recent shipments had not been honoured, and it was not likely that the firm would collect on this one. Nevertheless, Herman explained, the workforce must be kept busy at all costs, or simmering discontent would come to a boil again.

In the machine shop it was the massive lathes that interested Eugen. *"Deutschland,"* he noted wryly, pointing to the faceplate. Next to one of the machines stood a cart stacked with finished casings. The officer picked up a shell, turned it over and held it up to the light. He studied the figures embossed on its base and whistled softly.

"75 millimetres. These are shrapnel shells, Herman – made, as you say, for use against the German army. But these of the middle calibre, they will fit our guns too if we have to take on the Bolsheviks."

They passed through the warehouses where row upon row of unsold ploughs, mowers and reaping machines filled every available space. Then the assembly rooms, the paint shop, the carpentry floor, and finally, the separate building that served as the headquarters of the firm, where the designers and draftsmen also had their tables. Eugen began to thank his guide for the tour, but Herman led him to his private room and pointed silently to a chair. The *samovar* was cold, and he called for tea to be brought from the main office.

The sudden formality made Eugen uneasy. Evidently, pleasantries had ended, and consequential matters were at hand, matters he could well guess at. After the tea was brought and they were alone again, Herman rolled his own chair out from behind his desk and sat almost knee-to-knee with the young soldier. He lowered his voice and began.

"Eugen — and I hope that by now we may use first names — I am aware that you have an interest in my wife's sister, Lena. I understand that the feeling is mutual between you, and I'm sure you know that Lena's mother is deeply distressed over the matter."

Eugen began to reply, but he was interrupted.

"You feel, perhaps," Herman continued, "that this is none of my concern. Under normal circumstances that would be so. But her father is dead, and in his place I am obliged to tell you, first off, that Lena, at seventeen, will not be separated from her family. Her mother and her sisters, and I myself, will see to that. Secondly, it is almost certain now that Germany is finished. In France, the front has collapsed, and no doubt your armies will be withdrawn from this new Ukraine as well.'

Herman leaned in closer to the officer, and his voice was cool and hard.

"Should you elect to remain here when your army withdraws, you will not last a week. You will be hunted down and murdered, if not by our own workers or the nationalist militias, then by the anarchists, or more likely the Bolsheviks, who have been waiting in the wings for affairs to turn in their favour."

Eugen opened his mouth to speak, but Herman was not done.

"So, my dear man. You see how matters stand. I sympathize with your situation, but you must release Lena. You must break off with her. There is no other way."

For a long moment, the two men stared steadily into each other's eyes. Eugen was seething, and he struggled for calm. His voice shook, but he had twice been interrupted, and now he would have his say. He began quietly.

"And you, Herman? Your family? The factory? Have you thought it through? What will become of you when our protections are removed? Surely, you know your workers despise you. Believe me, I hear every day how they speak about you and your family, and I saw their black looks as we passed through the factory just now. Oh, they will not dispose of you just yet, but only because they do not know how to run the shop on their own. I ask you, Herman. Where will *you* go when the factory fails altogether and you are suddenly dispensable? You say the German army will be withdrawn, and I will have to leave. Perhaps that is so. I have received no such orders. But if that should happen, where will *you* go? I ask you again, have you thought it through!?"

Eugen's voice had risen to a crescendo, and he ended in a near taunt. Herman sighed and sat back in his chair, his vulnerability and desperation exposed by the officer's repartee.

"You can be sure," he said quietly, "that I think of little else these days, *mein Freund.*"

The commotion of the clerical staff leaving for the evening penetrated the paper-thin walls of the office. Wohlgemuth knocked twice and entered to place the day's accounts on Herman's desk. When he had gone, Herman rose and rolled his chair back behind the desk. He turned to the soldier and smiled wanly.

"Herr Mann. We owe you and your men a great debt for your presence in our village this half year. Let us not, at this late date, become enemies. We shall speak again."

Eugen took the proffered handshake with grace, but he was not ready to leave.

"Listen, Herman. Please, hear me. I am not a dishonourable man. Lena and I are firmly pledged. To each other and before God. I sincerely desire her mother's approval, and I have told Lena that I am willing to wait as long as necessary for marriage. But I beg you, should worse come to worst, let me take her to safety. Surely that is not in my interest alone. I must ask you to let me speak with Lena's mother."

Herman put his hand on the officer's shoulder and guided him to the door. He thought for a long moment before answering.

"It is not my decision, but I will have a word with her. You have my promise."

The officer stepped past Herman to the walkway. He put on his gloves and raised the collar of his coat against the rising wind, before turning once more to face Herman.

"Perhaps one night you might join me on patrol? It is a good time to talk."

"We shall see. But first, let me speak to Lena and her mother."

Word of the abdication of the German Kaiser arrived in Sergejewka before dawn on the 10th of November, not via the field telephone, which had once again been sabotaged, but from a cavalryman who rode at top speed from Lepetykha. Breathless, he leaped from the saddle and knocked at the door of the Janzen residence. Lamplight appeared in one of the windows, and a moment later, a soldier, still half asleep, undid the lock. The courier stated his business and waited for the appearance of Lieutenant Mann himself, whom he saluted, before wordlessly passing him the telegram. Eugen read it twice, and when he had signed the receipt, the courier remounted, and with a final salute he sped from the village.

A few hours later, as the men were assembling for their noon meal, a Daimler Marienfelder, its canvas covers flapping in the wind, pulled into the factory compound and stopped at the field kitchen. The truck's cargo had shifted during the rough drive from Kamianka, and everything was pocked with mud. Several of the men stepped forward to assist with repairs while the officer in charge emerged from the passenger seat and found Eugen. His message was concise: An end to hostilities was under consideration in Europe, all troops to remain in place while the field command awaited instructions from Berlin. Lieutenant Mann should expect the return of the men assigned to the Alexanderthal villages. When they arrived, he was to redeploy half of them to Lepetykha to assist in securing the harbour. Finally, he was to plan for a disciplined evacuation to the railhead in Nikopol if and when the order came. That was all.

News of the armistice arrived in Sergejewka on the 12th, the day after the signing, and this time the messenger was Chaim Dachenblecher. Cut off by the perils of the times from his customary routes through the villages on the open steppe, the pedlar had been forced to restrict his trade to the half dozen settlements on the left bank of the Dniepr between Velyka Lepetykha and Michaelsburg, which he served also as carrier of the mail.

Dachenblecher was well known to the patrols, so when they stopped his cart at the edge of Sergejewka at six in the morning, it was only to grill him for the latest intelligence. He handed them the German papers that had arrived during the night. Under massive headlines, the front page of the *Odessaer Zeitung* proclaimed the end of the war and listed the key terms agreed to at Le Francport. These included the immediate abrogation of the Treaty of Brest-Litovsk. The Germans would have to go.

Within days, the occupation, which had taken two months and a million men to accomplish, was in full reverse. Eugen received orders to abandon surveillance of the roads, which would, in any case, soon be crowded with German armoured divisions retreating westward to the river crossings. His sole priority now was the protection of Russia's German citizens, and to that end, he was ordered to postpone the withdrawal of his detachment from Sergejewka for as long as possible. During the latter stages of the evacuation, his men were to be released in pairs to join the retreat at intervals of several days. He himself was to be the last to leave.

A week after the armistice, Herman watched from an office window as a column of military vehicles passed through the village on their way to the harbour at Lepetykha. As the din of a hundred engines filled the air, workers threw down their tools and milled about outside the factory, chanting curses at the departing Germans and vowing to chase them all the way back to Berlin. Herman was incensed. He strode out of the office to order the men back to work, only to be mocked in turn. Rudenko elbowed his way through the crowd, shaking his head and grinning maliciously. "Remember who you are, Neufeld," he said, tapping Herman's chest with his forefinger. "We give the orders now, and yours are simple.

Keep your mouth shut and the pay packets stuffed." He swaggered off, and his mates grinned over their shoulders at Herman as they reentered the shop.

That evening, Eugen and Herman took their first joint patrol. The night was clear, and a bitter wind rattled the iron gate of the Janzen residence where they had agreed to meet. The lieutenant, armed and uniformed, wore his military greatcoat tightly belted against the weather. Herman drew the sheepskin robe he had inherited from his father-in-law high around his neck and waited while Eugen cupped a match to light a cigarette. Then the two men began their walk, finding their pace as they headed down the empty street towards the cart road that led down to the *konstje*.

They were silent and on high alert, the escalating discord in the village very much on their minds. The events of the morning coursed through Herman's mind. Clearly, the sight of the Germans homeward bound had emboldened the workers. They had jeered the two soldiers Eugen had released that day and pelted them with refuse as they hauled their packs after themselves into the back of a truck. Their insolence towards his own person had unnerved and angered him. It confirmed for him that any semblance of control was no longer in his hands. After all, he had not even been permitted to resign! The irony left a bitter taste in his mouth. He was a hostage who would never be released because he held the key to the only hope of the firm's survival. And if even that vanishingly small hope evaporated? If, in the next seven days, he could not beg, borrow, or collect on outstanding accounts sufficient to satisfy the workers? What then? He tried not to consider the consequences of failure.

The men stopped to catch their breath, and Herman pointed across the street to a large, well-ordered yard. No smoke rose from the chimney, and there was no light in the windows. This was the home of the widow Elias, Herman explained. Her locks had been forced while she was putting her children to bed a few nights ago. When she could not provide the strong drink the intruders demanded, they ransacked the house and sabred her mattresses and pillows in search of money. Among them she recognized a coworker of her late husband. Now, too terrified to remain in her own home, she had taken to sheltering with other families for protection at night.

The Elias home was near the junction with the cart road, and a few minutes later the men stood on the dock. The wind had risen to near gale force, and they could hear the chafing of twig on twig in the undergrowth on the opposite side of the *konstje*. Herman waved off Eugen's offer of a cigarette, and the officer moved into the lee of a thicket to light one for himself. When he returned, Herman spoke.

"Well, Herr Mann. I must congratulate you on your patience tonight. I can tell you that I have had a long discussion with Lena's mother, as promised. When I take you to meet with her, you may find her somewhat changed."

He glanced up at Eugen, but in the dark he could not gauge his reaction.

"I have spoken also with Lena, and they have asked that you come to the house tomorrow afternoon. Will that be possible? Lena's mother suggests four o'clock."

"Yes, Herman, of course! I will come. But Herman, surely you can tell me ..."

Light laughter interrupted him.

"No, Eugen. I can tell you only that we spoke of many things. I will say no more until we can all meet together."

Once more, Eugen protested, but Herman clapped him on the shoulder and stepped off the dock.

They resumed their walk on the narrow trail that followed the bank of the *konstje* to where it merged with the Dniepr just beyond the factory. They were approaching the pump shelter at water's edge when a sudden movement twenty paces ahead halted them. Some dark enterprise was underway, and the muffled chink of steel on steel reached them through the howling of the wind. Eugen cocked his revolver and motioned for Herman to stay in place. As he stepped forward, there was a sudden scramble, and two shadows sprang into a rowboat moored next to the pump. Then, a flurry of rowing, and as the men watched, the boat slid out of the *konstje* into the wind-whipped chop of the main stream of the Dniepr.

Within the pump enclosure lay an assortment of wrenches and a hacksaw. Eugen stood watch while Herman knelt to assess the damage. The pump had been carefully unbolted from its mounts and was not harmed. But the intake conduit had been cut free and pushed aside so that most of its length lay beneath the water. Herman stood with hands on hips and stared downstream.

"Whoever it was, they were from elsewhere," he said. "The workers would not steal the pump. Their livelihood depends on it, and they know it."

Herman concealed the tools under the floor of the shack, and for two more hours the men tramped Sergejewka's streets and lanes, kneading their gloved hands and stamping their feet when the cold invaded. They tested gates and doorways, peered through fences into gardens and barnyards, and twice made the rounds of the factory premises. Once, their passing raised one of cousin Johann's dogs and its sudden bark startled them. Herman spoke its name, and the dog recognized his voice and settled again.

They returned to the Janzen residence at dawn, where the morning patrol was about to set out. The stove was hot, and there was tea. Eugen hung up his coat and poured two glasses. He placed one on the table for Herman and stood warming his hands around the other. Herman had loosened the top buttons of his robe, but he was weary, and as soon as his glass was empty, he reached for his gloves. The lieutenant looked up.

"So, four o'clock, then?"

"Yes. At Anna's. Don't be late."

At the door, Herman turned. "And best you get some rest before then, *mein Freund.*"

He closed the door behind him, leaving the officer alone to decipher his parting wink.

# 11. Peril

On the street outside Anna's house that afternoon, Herman was stopped by Johann Neufeld. Although the cousins had not always been on the best of terms, Herman had come to understand something of Johann's predicament, wedged as he was between his obligations to the people who had elected him *Schulze*, on the one hand, and the demands of the *Komitee* on the other. On most matters not directly concerned with the factory, Johann was the go-to man in the village, arbitrating neighbourly conflicts and overseeing local projects. More recently, however, as the *Komitee* insinuated itself more and more broadly into community affairs, he had found himself increasingly drawn into uncharted waters.

The men exchanged greetings, and Johann came promptly to the point. The foundry man, Kyrylenko, had crossed over from the factory at noon to see him on the pretext of consultation about an ailing horse. There was nothing amiss with the animal, but he made a great show of having Johann examine each hoof, all the while speaking in low and urgent tones of matters entirely unrelated. Then he had slipped a note into Johann's hand. Johann outlined the essence of Kyrylenko's message.

"The details are in the note," he said. "You will understand that he could not risk delivering it to you personally at the factory."

He waited while Herman read it for himself. It was a handwritten scrawl, Ukrainian, and Herman struggled to decipher it. Then he raised his eyes, and there was a long silence as he turned to gaze at the factory gates on the other side of the street.

"So it has come to this," Herman said softly. "Kyrylenko and I no longer speak. But he is a good man."

"We travelled to Volhynia together for horses," said Johann. "He warned me then that this day would come if Germany lost the war. Yes, you are right. He is a good man. He does not love us, but he wishes no one harm." He made as though to leave. "What will you do?"

Herman glanced once more at the note before folding it and putting it in his coat pocket.

"I will, of course, speak to Anna and the family. It is not only myself now. It appears we are all under sentence."


At four o'clock, Eugen passed through the arched gates of the Neufeld residence. He walked briskly up the walk, flicking imaginary dust from a fresh uniform. Herman was waiting for him on the steps, and the men stood in the cold as Herman conveyed Kyrylenko's warning. After a brief conference that ended with much head-nodding, the men entered without knocking. They were met by Lena's youngest sister, who led them along the corridor to the living room where Lena and her mother were setting out refreshments on a side table. Tante Anna shook Eugen's hand formally and indicated chairs for the two men. She sank into the cushions at one end of a long sofa facing the men, and after serving the tea, Lena took her place at the opposite end. There was a tense moment while cream and sugar were passed around. Then Anna began.

"Herr Mann, I thank you for coming. You have asked to speak with me regarding your proposal of marriage to my daughter. Lena and I have had many talks in the last month, and no doubt she has told you of my concerns."

Herman suppressed a smile.

*Talks? Yes,* he thought to himself. *But also a great deal of wailing and gnashing of teeth, the daughter pleading for understanding, and the mother demanding obedience and respect — both women at one point hurling beatitudes at each other: 'Blessed are the meek, and the pure in heart, my child!' And Lena's livid response, 'And you, mother? You, who*

*revile my deepest wishes and destroy all my hopes! Oh, I won't take turpen-
tine like the Giesbrecht girl, but mein Gott, Mutter! Blessed also are the
merciful!'*

Anna continued.

"Herman speaks of you as an honourable man and vouches for your
sincerity. I have seen nothing to contradict this, so I count nothing
against you in that regard."

Eugen acknowledged the affirmation with a polite nod as Anna
proceeded with what was clearly a carefully prepared speech.

"There is the serious matter of our faith and our beliefs regarding
baptism. For us, the only true baptism is one that is chosen freely, by a
believer who comprehends the meaning of the act. Should you have children, I must have your word that you will not forbid them this."

The officer had given this question some thought, and he was prepared to
answer.

"Frau Neufeld, I have attended your services for the past six months, and
I assure you I have the greatest respect for the teachings of your people. I
know neither Greek nor Latin, but if I have understood correctly,
Anabaptist means *Wiedertäufer* — those who rebaptize. I will gladly
commit to allowing our children to choose baptism for themselves when
they are old enough to do so."

A faint smile flashed across his face as he continued.

"And should our children wish this, I only ask this in return. Let me
guarantee for them an authentic *re*-baptism by having them christened as
infants. I ask this for the sake of my poor mother, whose heart will other-
wise break."

The cleverness amused Herman, and even Anna could not suppress a
smile. Lena, blushing since the first mention of children, was silent as she
waited for her mother's response.

"Herr Mann. Let us not trifle with sacred matters. You have promised
what I asked. Let us leave the matter there."

Herman had been impatient for an opportune moment to break into the
conversation. Now he took Kyrylenko's note from his pocket and
unfolded it.

"Mama," he said, "there is another matter of great urgency, not only for Lena's future with Eugen but for all of us in the immediate present. Friendly ears in the factory have reported to cousin Johann that we are in great danger. There is a scheme among the workers to make away with us the moment the German presence ends. Rudenko and his crew may be behind it, though Johann thinks not. It need not be him; there are others who blame me for everything."

He waited for the import of his words to take effect.

"I already know I cannot pay the men what they are owed this week. If I am still here on Friday, with or without German protection, it appears that my life will not be worth a Kerensky kopek. And if I flee alone, the danger to you would only be increased. They may well do to you what was done to Rempel's family in Lepetykha when he would not betray his brother."

Anna was indignant, and she half rose from her seat.

"*Mein Gott*, Herman! What are you thinking? To abandon the factory! All that the good Lord has entrusted to us, everything left behind for the filthy Russians to destroy? What can you be saying, Herman!?"

Herman's reply was quiet and distinct.

"I am saying, Mama, that tonight, under the shroud of darkness, we must begin to pack. All of us, the Koslowskys and Wedels too. We will leave in a day or two, as soon as we can be ready. We will return when it is safe."

Eugen had waited until Herman completed his announcement. Now he followed with compassion, but with no loss of urgency.

"Frau Neufeld, Herman and I can see no other way. Officer Harger and I are the last two soldiers left in Sergejewka. My commander has left it to my discretion to determine when we make our final withdrawal. If today's warning is accurate, there is little Harger and I can do to protect you any longer. It is the signal for us as well as for you. At present, with partisans and the Red Army already pressing at all the river crossings from Kherson to Yekaterinoslav, it is no longer safe to cross at Nikopol. Instead, it will be best to travel southeast to the railhead in Melitopol, where our army is still in full control. We will find room for you on a military transport. And Harger and I will, of course, accompany you to Germany."

Outside, the laughter of children returning home from school mingled with the voices of workers leaving the factory. Each person in the room presided over a private silence in which reason and emotion vied for supremacy. Lena had said little, and the abrupt deflection from the subject of her marriage to the imminent threats to her family had left her disoriented. Herman and Eugen had had their say, and now they turned expectantly to the matriarch for a response.

Anna's mind was whirling. The possibility of flight had been in the air ever since the workers' rising a year ago. But overt threats had subsided during the occupation, and in the interim she had become somewhat accustomed to the vandalism, the petty thefts, and the knocking at night with never anyone there when the door was opened. These things were unnerving, but she had taken them in stride, trusting augmented night patrols and her confidence that the restoration of order was only a matter of time. To abandon the village, the grand home her Kornelius had built for her? And the factory, the source of their wealth and well-being? This was beyond impossible — until now.

"Mama? What are your thoughts?"

For a few moments, Anna stared steadily at her son-in-law. Then she turned away without speaking. It had crossed her mind more than once that Herman's way with the workers was at least partly to blame for the current crisis. His highhanded manner with them, his impulsive, improvised modes of governance, which raised the eyebrows even of his co-directors, and his refusal to delegate authority to those who knew their craft far better than he did. Surely these were in play, shaping the attitudes of the workers toward him and now toward his whole family. Always 'the manager,' he frequently ran ahead of circumstances, often with disastrous results. His younger brother Kornelius had been involved in the factory as well since his arrival in July. How was it that Ka Ha seemed to be on exceptionally good terms with the workers and had never once been threatened? But all that was irrelevant now. The current threat was real and could not be ignored.

Herman leaned forward in his chair and broke the silence once more.

"Mama, we think it best if Eugen and Officer Harger move back into the house. Perhaps the old servants' quarters near the back door? For security until we are able to leave."

Anna nodded. "Yes, that is for the best, no doubt." But her voice was flat, resigned.

The maids entered to remove the tea service, and the interruption allowed for a relaxation of tensions. Herman's wife, the Koslowskys, and the Wedels, were sent for, and Anna called Jakob and Liese, her two youngest, to join them. Together they moved into the dining room and took seats around the table. Eugen excused himself. At the door he spoke briefly with Lena before leaving to join the night patrol.

During the interval, Anna appeared to have accepted the inevitability of flight. Now she took command, describing for the assembled family the perils at hand, the decision to escape, and stressing above all the urgency of discretion as they made their preparations and bid farewell to friends and family. Johann, the *Schulze*, would need to know, of course. His brother Peter was Anna's yard manager, the last male still in her employ. He would arrange for drivers and teams for the wagons that would take the family through dangerous territory. Each household was to pack only the essentials, caching precious valuables with friends, or interring them, until the day when the family would return, hopefully no later than spring.

The family disbanded, leaving Anna and Lena alone at the table. A westerly wind was rising from the valley, sweeping up the slope and through the village. Anna went to the window and drew back the curtain. Scattered flakes were sifting through the air, and ashen clouds hung low above the river, promising a heavy snowfall before long.

"*Mutti*?" Lena hesitated, unsure. Her mother released the curtain and turned to her.

"Mama, do I understand that you no longer stand between Eugen and me in the way of our marriage?"

Her mother's smile was thin and deliberate. The family conference had exhausted her, and her face was colourless. She returned to the table and supported herself with both hands on the back of a chair.

"Lena, Lena," she sighed. "You and Eugen will do what you must do. I can see that. Now that we are all fleeing together, let us first see if our little ship can find a safe harbour somewhere. Then I will not stand in your way."

Lena's breath came in a gasp. She rose quickly and rounded the table. Her mother stood waiting, and for the first time since either of them could remember, Lena embraced her mother, her body convulsing in silent sobs.

In the morning, Herman took his mother-in-law to the bank in Velyka Lepetykha, where a hostile management refused their request to close the family account, limiting their withdrawal to 60,000 roubles. Later in the day, the money, all in paper currency, was sewn into the linings of blankets and winter coats. Anna summoned her man Peter, and with Herman at her side, she gave instructions for the concealment of the rest of the family's wealth. Silverware and household adornments of worth were to be wrapped in oilcloth, silver and gold currency sewn into canvas bags, all to be sealed against the elements and buried between the two largest pear trees. Peter was to see to it personally that the manuring and tilling of the entire orchard would obscure all signs of disturbance. The family strongbox was to be left empty and unlocked in its usual place behind the stairs in the vaulted cellar of the house.

When Peter approached his brother for the loan of his horses, Johann balked at the request. As *Schulze* he was under scrutiny from all sides, and he could hardly allow himself to be seen aiding and abetting the flight of the rich. But he quietly negotiated with sympathetic neighbours for teams, drivers and wagons. If all went well, these would be returned within the week.

After nightfall, neighbours and relatives appeared at the rear entrance of the house, where the wagons were being loaded. They came two or three at a time, whispering their farewells and their longing to follow in the near future. Amid embraces and stifled weeping, Anna's brother sat alone in his wheelchair, wrapped in blankets. Silent and resigned, he watched the loading of provisions. Anna stepped away from the commotion to engage him at the edge of the crowd, assuring him of her determination either to return or to rescue him and his family as soon as she was able. There was a sudden outcry of '*Mutti! Mutti!*' and Liese ran to her with the news that Jakob could not be found. After a frantic search among the homes of his friends proved fruitless, Jakob reappeared, still sobbing, from the cemetery where he had spent an hour at his father's grave.

The moment of departure came just before midnight on the 23rd of November. Anna's two eldest daughters occupied the first wagon with their husbands and children, along with a tearful Fräulein Martens, their nanny, who had overcome her reluctance and agreed to accompany the family. Anna rode in the second wagon with the three youngest children and her recently married third daughter and her husband. Shielded from the cold by beds of hay beneath and heavy blankets above, the fugitives set out in the direction of the *Jannedarpa*, with Officer Harger riding well ahead and Eugen behind. They would avoid the main road and keep to the web of cart paths that meandered between the fields. Under the watchful eye of Providence, three nights' travel should get them to the railhead in Melitopol.

# 12. Escape

They stopped briefly in Alexanderthal, waking a few close acquaintances to give notice of their departure. Passing southeast, they skirted the large town of Verkhnii Rohachyk, near enough to make out the roofless buildings and heaps of charred rubble that bore witness to reprisals against local resistance during early stages of the revolution. Then, into the black night in open fields beneath a patchwork of broken cloud. The track was rough, and each time she woke from rare snatches of sleep Lena became more aware of her general discomfort. Her mother, too, was restless, and from the other wagon came intermittent cries of the little ones protesting the jolting of the wagons. Several times, Eugen rode up from his post at the rear of the convoy to check that all was well, and Lena felt reassured.

Before dawn they drew their wagons into a dense copse on the bank of one of the small streams that cut across the steppe. Under an increasingly ominous sky, they led the horses down to drink and then concealed them in a small clearing and tethered them to graze. They tented the wagons with oilcloth, and after a breakfast of rusks and cheese they climbed back into the wagons to sleep. Officer Harger, on first watch, rode out to study the terrain and to choose a way forward for the next night's travel. Eugen and the two drivers crept underneath the wagons and covered themselves with their coats. The grove shielded them from the wind that arose in the afternoon, and the rain was sparse, settling on the covered wagons in a pleasant patter that encouraged forgetfulness.

Late in the evening, soon after they had set out again, Eugen, who had ridden ahead, returned at a gallop with a warning of trouble.

"We must leave the trail," he said. "There is a band approaching, and they are up to no good. They did not see me, but they are coming this way quickly."

The drivers veered off into fields of winter wheat. The horses shied at first at the uneven footing and the unfamiliar drag of wheels sinking in softer soils. When Eugen judged that enough distance had been achieved, he called a halt. In the darkness they could see little, but they could hear the jangle of harness links and the snorting of weary horses. Twice, a voice cried out in protest and resistance. There was a chorus of angry shouts and a single shot rang out. Then, only the clatter of receding hooves.

Herman and his brothers-in-law left the wagons to confer with Eugen. One of the drivers rose from a crouch to report damage to his rig. In leaving the road, a wheel had struck a boulder, denting the rim and shattering a spoke. He could not see well enough in the dark to check the axle, he said, so they would have to travel slowly until they found the means to repair the wagon.

They returned to the trail, and after four or five hours of slow progress the driver of the first wagon called a halt. Dawn was two hours away, and his horses were exhausted. Herman stepped forward. On business trips between Sergejewka and Melitopol he had often stayed on Mennonite estates, and he thought several must lie nearby. There was just enough light by now for him to scout for landmarks. If Eugen would accompany him, he was sure they could find shelter before the sun was up.

In an hour the two men were back, and with the dawn already gilding the underbellies of the clouds, they led the caravan to shelter for the day.

Lena woke from troubled dreams. Straw was matted in her hair and tangled in the collar of her coat, but she was warm, and the hand on her shoulder was Eugen's.

"Wake up, Lena, my dear. There is food and tea. We want to begin while we still have a little light. We have a chance to reach the city before morning."

Lena opened an eye and saw the blue of Eugen's. She registered his smile and responded sleepily with one of her own. She raised herself on an elbow and looked out of the cave in the straw where she had spent the night. She had been comfortable, and it was an odd sensation to be awakened to the dying of the day. She could see her mother standing with Liese around a small fire in the farmyard where the family had taken shelter. It was the Lenzmann *chutor*, a large estate abandoned by its owners and suitable as a refuge only because its pillaging earlier in the year had removed all enticements to whatever marauding bands remained in the area. Upon their arrival in the early morning hours, they had found the doors of the residence splintered and the windows shattered. Appalling odours met them when they peered in through the broken glass. The house had been utterly defiled, and there could be no thought of sleeping there. But at the edge of the compound, a few stacks of weathered straw remained, and it was into these the family had burrowed against the chill of the morning.

The men stood around the fire warming themselves, speaking in low voices as they calculated the odds of reaching Melitopol by morning. They had fed the horses from the store of hay in the wagons and let them lip the spilled wheat and oats that remained near the ruined granaries. Among the debris, a replacement had been found for the damaged wheel and the wagon had been repaired. Once the sun had set they should make good time. The biggest concern was the increasing density of population as they approached Melitopol. Passing through at least one or two of the towns would be unavoidable. If this happened in the dead of night, the men conjectured, it would at least minimize the likelihood of trouble.

Lena emerged from her place in the straw to find her older sisters tending to the children and brewing roasted barley to go with the rusks and slices of ham. She surprised Liese and her mother with a morning hug and stood with them while they ate. Together they watched as Jakob emerged from behind the ruins of the barn with Eugen's heavy Mauser on his shoulder, laughing with the officer as they marched as if on parade. Eugen had refused his pleading to be allowed to shoot, but he had taught him how to load and aim the gun. Shooting would have to wait for a time when it would not attract attention. He took the rifle from Jakob and went to saddle his horse.

As they drew nearer to Melitopol the narrow trails converged in well-beaten thoroughfares that pointed inevitably to larger villages. Several of these they were able to skirt, but some hours after midnight a large town sprawled before them, and their options narrowed to a single road that led directly through its centre. Although the town was dark and silent, a few solitary souls walked the central street, stopping to stare at the travellers and gesturing rudely at the uniformed officers who rode at the front and back of the procession. In the market square a group of vendors had begun setting out their wares. They gathered to mock the travellers, and the vapour of their breaths rose under the glimmer of the street lamp as they shouted their derision.

"Good riddance to the rich!" they cried. "And to the filthy Germans!"

They shook their fists, and several of the younger men feinted pursuit before retreating in laughter. But there was no violence, and the party was able to pass unhindered.

Soon after passing through the town, the rail yards of Melitopol came into view directly ahead on the city's northern fringes. They could hear the pulse of shunting engines and see their thick plumes of smoke against the sheen of the predawn sky. While still some miles from the city they took the wagons off the main road and prepared a meal. While the family rested, Herman and Eugen rode ahead to make contact with the German authorities. They returned several hours later accompanied by a military escort, and from that point on, progress was swift. The military barracks were adjacent to the rail yards, and once the family was assigned their quarters, Herman was taken to see the *Kommandant* in charge of the city. Before nightfall he had obtained approval for passage to Germany.

Eugen had been confident of a week's journey on an *Urlaubszug,* one of the so-called 'vacation trains' that regularly transported soldiers on leave between Melitopol and Germany, and the family had provisioned themselves accordingly. In these late stages of the German withdrawal, however, schedules had been accelerated, and the last such train had left the day before the family's arrival. Instead, after a delay of several days, the family was assigned space in a freight car spliced between the horse wagons of the Regiment of Mounted Pioneers of Württemberg, who were on their final return to their base in Germany. The three brothers-in-law were supplied with military uniforms and ordered not to leave the train without them. Women and children were to be kept out of sight altogether except with the express permission of the officers. Most of the space in the car was occupied with hay and the kit and gear of the cavalry unit. A small central area was swept clear of combustibles to make room for the small stove assigned to do battle with the draught that blew freely through the car. In the constricted space left to them, the sixteen travellers would have no privacy and little rest during this second stage of their exit.

Sabotage had become endemic during the occupation, and it was a rare train that was not delayed by wreckage of infrastructure, or that failed to draw small arms fire from local militias or nationalist operatives. The most serious episodes involved the well-armed and organized bands of the anarchist Nestor Makhno, whose Revolutionary Insurgent Army had swelled to several tens of thousands of fighters, and whose primary field of operations the train could not avoid passing through. The retreat of the occupying armies had emboldened the insurgents, and the Germans were regularly drawn into fierce rearguard actions. Before the train left Melitopol, a unit of machine gunners filed out of the station and took positions on the runways on either side of the engineer's cabin, on the coal tender behind the locomotive, and on the platforms between the cars. One of the soldiers, assigned to the protection of the family, slid open the car door, startling the sleepers. Seeing two German officers already there, he exchanged a few words with them and left to find another post. If the presence of armed guards was reassuring, thought Lena, it also confirmed the danger.

Once during the night, the train made a comfort stop — men to the left, women to the right in the shrubbery beside the tracks. It was cold and undignified, and for a long time afterwards, Lena heard stifled weeping from her mother's place in the hay. From her perch in a hammock she had slung between two stanchion hooks, Lena could hear snoring and occasional murmurs of conversation. And once, at a station stop when platform lights penetrated gaps in the walls of the car, she was amused to see Fräulein Martens and Officer Harger sitting next to each other in the hay, deeply engrossed in quiet talk. It confirmed suspicions that had arisen in her mind while still in Sergejewka, and she smiled in the dark, secretly thrilled for the lonely Maria, news of whose sudden departure would surely not reach her parents in the Kuban for many weeks. In the close confines of the cattle wagon there could be no open talk of romance. Still, she thought, if the opportunity arose, she would be ready with a wink or two. She drifted into a fitful sleep and woke again only when the train stopped suddenly an hour before dawn.

Two or three adults stood in the flicker of the tiny stove. Others stood farther back in the shadows, vigilant against errant sparks that might ignite the hay. The tea kettle was steaming, and the women were shuffling in the luggage chest for cups and breakfast supplies. Lena could hear Herman declare that they must be very near Alexandrovsk. Nothing untoward had occurred during the night, he said, and he wondered about the delay. He slid the door of the car open far enough for him to drop to the ground. Eugen followed him, and the two men went forward to investigate.

The locomotive stood in darkness. Running lamps had been extinguished, and the engineer had damped the boiler fires. Eugen stopped suddenly in mid-stride and grasped Herman's sleeve. Beneath them, faint vibrations shook the ground. And below the sibilant hiss of escaping steam, a deep throbbing from somewhere in the near distance filled the air. It was a sound both men recognized, a vast multitude of horses in full gallop, and mingled with it, sporadic gunshots and the cries of riders. The corps of guards left their posts and gathered at the front of the train. They crouched in the dark, their weapons at the ready. But the stream of riders was at least a half *verst* away and appeared to be crossing the railway tracks and moving off towards the east. The engineer and fireman stood with the soldiers and spoke in low voices. A single messenger, they said, had come racing towards the train from the station in the village ahead, swinging his lamp in a wild signal for an emergency stop. Coming alongside the engineer's cabin, he had said to wait until he returned.

Gradually the din subsided, and when all was still, the engineer ordered the fires brought up again while he awaited the return of the messenger. Herman and Eugen were talking with the soldiers at the front of the train when German voices came to them out of the night. Two officers walked into their midst, leading exhausted horses, and with them was the station messenger. The track was clear again, they said. The train could proceed. German forces at Alexandrovsk had driven off a surprise attack by the Makhnovshchina, a force of at least five thousand men. Fighting had lasted hours and ended with a rout of the insurgents. The pursuit was ongoing, but Makhno was well away, and Alexandrovsk was the next stop.

The South Terminal in Alexandrovsk, flanked on all sides by a heavy German guard, had incurred only minor damage during the skirmish with Makhno's army. Rifle fire had shattered a few windows and pitted the walls of the terminal, but trackage remained intact. When the door of the car was rolled open, the family looked out on a world of confusion and debris. German officers shouted orders as freight was shuttled in and out of the station, and on the sidings, shunting engines assembled trains and removed damaged rolling stock. For much of the day the train stood in the station while a new locomotive was brought in and first-class passenger cars were added for the comfort of a Field Marshall and his entourage of high-ranking officers.

With the heavy German presence, the family was allowed some hours of respite from its confinement. Officer Harger found a seat in the station for Anna. He brought her a cup of tea and stayed to attend her while her daughters and Fräulein Martens took the children to a small park at the rear of the station grounds.

It was the last day of November, and a brilliant sun blunted the chill. Herman and his brothers-in-law paced the railway platform, watching as a dozen pushcarts heaped with luxury foodstuffs were trundled out to stock the officers' dining car. The talk turned to the state of their own supplies. Six days after leaving Sergejewka they had still not crossed the Dniepr, and already their provisions were severely depleted. With nine-tenths of their three-thousand-*verst* journey still ahead of them, it was clear they would have to buy additional supplies.

"I believe I know what you're thinking."

The three men turned to face Eugen, who had come up behind them.

"Clearly, I was wrong to think this would be a short journey. But I have explained our situation to the commander of the regiment. We are to receive a hot meal from the kitchen car each day, as near noon as our stops allow. It would be wise to purchase whatever else we can before we leave Alexandrovsk since there are no guarantees of regular stops hereafter."

In Melitopol the Germans had advised them to exchange most of their currency for Deutschmarks since the ruble would be worthless on German soil. But with spies everywhere and insurgents eager for reprisal against stragglers of the defeated nation, it would be foolhardy, now, to proffer German currency in the station kiosks, even if vendors might be persuaded to accept them. The three men returned to their car to retrieve their remaining rubles. Then, in full military uniform and accompanied by Mann and Harger, they passed through the terminal to the public market.

They returned an hour later with large sacks of *bublik* — irregular bread rings, boiled and baked — and a few pounds of coffee and one of tea. Meat of dubious provenance had been passed over, and there was no milk. They would try their luck again along the route. In the meantime, the infants would have to subsist on bread softened in water or tea.

The family returned to the train to find much of the hay removed to feed the horses in the adjacent wagons. The additional space allowed for greater safety for the stove, and the women began slicing the *bublik* and stringing the slender rings around the fire to dry. By the time the train left the station, bedding had been reorganized, and for most of the family, rest came more easily than at any time since their departure from Sergejewka.

The train rolled through the city and gathered speed as it approached the great river. It was the middle of the night, but Anna was wide awake, and she knew exactly where she was. She imagined high noon and herself standing in the open door of the car with a broad view of the Dniepr. Just there, still on the east bank and a few *verst* north, was Andreasfeld where, early in their marriage and just after the birth of little Maria, Kornelius had attended a preaching seminar. She had never visited the village, but its name would forever be associated in her mind with the desperate lone-liness that had discovered her then and that had remained an abiding presence throughout the rest of her life. Indelible in her memory was the poignancy with which *'wehrlos und verlassen!'* had rung true in Kornelius's absence. *Defenceless! Forsaken!* While he was away she had tried to sing the words of that hymn, but she had wept them instead, and she had never managed to reach the reassuring refrain. She was less alone now, with grown children and her youngest almost fourteen. But, Oh Kornelius ... !

The train slowed, and its rumbling modulated to a clatter as it passed onto the upper level of the Kitchkas bridge. From this vantage point, if she looked across to the west bank, almost directly below the bridge, she knew she would see the village of Einlage with its beautiful church. Perhaps she could guess the exact location where, on a March morning in 1862, her parents, still unmarried, and all four of her grandparents had been immersed in the the icy waters of the Dniepr in the first baptism of the *Brüdergemeinde* in the Chortitza colony. From the great height of the bridge she would surely also be able to see the remains of Alt Kronsweide, where she and Kornelius had visited the graves of the first families in both their lines to arrive from Prussia in the 1790s.

These scenes unfurled in the inner light of memory and imagination, and it was sufficient; she did not need to see, and she did not wish for daylight. She thought of the river itself, of the water passing under the bridge at that very moment. How long until it reached Sergejewka? Somewhere near Nikopol, a portion of these waters would separate from the main stream and flow through the village in the beloved *konstje*. As it passed, what would it find there? She thought of her poor brother Jakob and his children. She thought of the plight of the factory, of her friend Aron Fast, who had reluctantly agreed to take on the senior management, and of Herman's brother Ka Ha, second in command. Neither of them had come under direct threat, but the world seethed with conflict and danger while she and her family fled to safety in the West. And Gerhard Enns, her brother-in-law, who had brought his family back to Sergejewka during the German presence. Were they still there? And Gerhard himself? Where would he hide now that the workers were again free to pursue their program of vengeance?

The train completed the crossing and resumed its monotonous rumble. Nearby in the hay, Lena moaned in her sleep, and from the other end of the car came the sound of men snoring. Anna turned on her side, and sleep transported her to the cemetery in Sergejewka where she stood alone among the open and empty graves of her parents, her sister Helene, and her beloved Kornelius, all of them exiled, it seemed, even from the realm of the dead.

Leaving the Dniepr, the train crept in a great northwesterly arc through lands ravaged by war and burgeoning civil disorder. For Anna, there would be no more dreaming. The entire countryside was matted with razor wire, pocked with the craters of a million shells, and spidered with an endless maze of trenches and earthworks, some of them still draped with the remains of the dead. Stocks of munitions left by the fleeing Austrians had been seized by insurgent militias who fought the advancing Red Army and executed lightning raids on German trains. Each night the passengers could hear small arms fire, the smack of bullets striking the cars, and return fire from machine guns mounted on the train. During unexplained stops, all speech was stifled, and women and children concealed themselves deep in the hay while the two officers cocked their rifles and stood near the doors. Leaving the train, except in the direst need, was unthinkable, and when desperation for food demanded an excursion, even Herman was barred. The soldiers took his money and brought back what they could.

For fourteen days, from Alexandrovsk through Belarus to Prostken in East Prussia, there was no respite from fear and uncertainty. The misery was shared by the several hundred soldiers on the train, most of whom had been in constant service for nearly a year and had suffered the privations typical of armies in defeat. Finally, in the relative safety of German-controlled Prostken, there was a chance for baths, delousing, and a change of clothing. The Russian train was abandoned, and the family, still accompanied by officers Mann and Harger, completed its journey on a German passenger train, arriving two days before Christmas 1918 in Kornwestheim on the outskirts of Stuttgart, to find Germany on the brink of its own revolution.

# 13. PAVEL

Young Pavel fancies himself a protege of Nestor Makhno, whose successes against the Germans and Austrians have made him famous. But it is his raids on the opulent estates and industries of foreign colonists that inspire Pavel's enthusiasm. Makhno's radius of operations does not encompass either Lepetykha or Sergejewka, and Pavel has never met the man, but he is determined to emulate him within his own narrow sphere.

The anarchist movement in Velyka Lepetykha gains momentum. Pavel is not at its head, but he commands a small militia which roams the territory on both sides of the river. When he and his band return to Sergejewka, it is long past midnight on a cold winter night. Gerhard Enns is less often on Pavel's mind now, and he cannot know that Enns and his family have returned during the German occupation and are asleep in their own beds. At Pavel's side, however, is another disgruntled employee of *Neufeld Ko.* who is looking for Klassen, a foreman in the assembly rooms who, as long as the Germans had his back, lorded it over the workers like a Tsar.

The band has been drinking heavily. They make no secret of their presence in the village, so that when they arrive at Klassen's house he has already been alerted. They beat on a neighbour's door and recognize Aron Fast, the nominal manager of the factory, whom they pistol whip for Klassen's whereabouts. He cannot advise them, but Goertzen, his son-in-law, comes to investigate the disturbance, and under heavy blows, he bleats that Klassen is on the side street near the factory. The two men are seized and forced to accompany Pavel's troops as they follow Klassen's tracks through the snow to the *konstje*. Klassen has heard them coming and he crosses to the *plaven*. But he flounders in the drifts and cannot escape. The three men are forced to their knees and summarily shot.

The clatter of hooves on the icy street and the raucous laughter of Pavel's men as they entered the village have roused Gerhard Enns from sleep. He fingers the curtain aside and sees only soft moonlight on the frosted thatch of the neighbour's barn. Angry shouts of men, sounds of resistance, and the cries of women reach him from further down the street. He dresses quickly and is about to wake Katharina when he hears the pistol shots. Then, the retreat of the bandits at full gallop back through the village, firing at the moon, their curses and laughter resounding between the factory and the church.

Gerhard prepares for a lengthy absence. He sends his family back to Molotschna, while he seeks refuge across the river. Travelling north to the Judenplan villages, he finds sanctuary for the winter with a Mennonite family on one of the demonstration farms. In the spring he purchases a small cottage in Durilov, a sleepy Ukrainian village well away from the river. He summons his family to join him there, and for most of a year he is left in peace.

Although Durilov is spared much of the violence of the civil war, unrelenting requisitions of horses, clothing, and food take a heavy toll. Gerhard's son is pressed into frequent service as a carrier, first for the Whites, then the Reds. On occasion, affiliates of the Lepetykha anarchists also pass through, demanding supplies and transport. Is it perhaps one of these men, riding beside the younger Enns in an open sleigh, sharing a sheepskin rug against the bitter cold on the open steppe west of the river, who ferrets out the boy's parentage and reports to Pavel? This time, when Gerhard eludes his pursuers, they take his son in his stead, and for ten days the family agonizes. Then they learn that he has been imprisoned in Velyka Lepetykha, interrogated, tortured, and shot. It is Christmas Eve, and his pregnant bride runs screaming into the night.

# 14. Drought

The autumn harvest of 1920 had already been poor. Then, shortly after the sowing of winter grains in September, instead of the anticipated showers, a vicious windstorm raged across the region, tearing thatch from roofs and layering every surface with fine grit. For three days and nights the fragile soils of Fürstenland were ripped away and flung into the blackened sky, and when the storm abated, hardly a seed was left in the ground.

Though it was late in the season, a few courageous farmers, Johann among them, wagered precious stocks on a second seeding. They were rewarded with rains sufficient for excellent germination, and before long the fields shimmered green with sturdy stands of wheat and barley. But then came The Winter Of No Snow. The fields lay naked, leaving tender roots exposed to the killing frosts of January. In spring, the mighty Dniepr failed to rise above its primary channel, and the fertile *plaven* was left unwatered.

With the prospect of famine compounding the calamities of civil war, anguished appeals for assistance went out to Mennonite agencies in Canada and the United States. The distances were vast, and logistics under prevailing conditions so daunting that it was not clear what the petitioners felt they could expect. But after successive crop failures, local resources were exhausted, and without help from the outside world, total collapse seemed inevitable.

With postage at a half-million rubles — the price of a loaf of bread — mailings abroad were rare, collective efforts. Johann was one of a dozen joint cosignatories of letters detailing conditions in Sergejewka. These were posted to the *Mennonitische Rundschau* where, after fleeing with the retreating Germans in 1918 and emigrating a year later through Canada to Pennsylvania, cousin Herman was the assistant editor. The letters were published, but apart from editorial breast-beating and a small rise in the number of aid parcels received by individual families, there had not until recently been any sign that aid of the required magnitude was forthcoming. Finally, in the summer of 1921, word came that, under the auspices of the American Relief Administration, the Mennonites of Canada and the United States were poised to come to the rescue.

The drought refused to break, and searing heat in May and April ensured that the autumn harvest would fail as well. Fruit trees lost their blossoms before the bees could tap them. Grape vines died, berry bushes failed to bud, and silkworms perished in the leafless mulberry trees. In the *Jannedarpa* no feed could be found for horses and cattle. Newborn calves could not suckle and were slaughtered with their mothers for their hides and what little meat they could yield. On the floodplain below Sergejewka, clumps of sedge grass and perennial weeds survived here and there, sufficient to support a few sheep or goats, but herdsmen had to be deployed in groups to guard against poaching. Pigs, which even in the worst of times might have scavenged to survive, were annihilated by an epidemic of swine flu. With the live-stock gone and the fields barren, there was neither straw nor manure for fuel. Trees were cut down for firewood and when they were gone, villagers dug out the stumps as well. In the bed of the *konstje*, dead fish lay bloated in brackish pools, and all summer long, only deep-rooted weeds and snaking drifts of yellow dust thrived in the melon plots of the *plaven*.

Desperate to find seed for yet another attempt at a winter crop, Johann travelled to the Zagradowka colony west of the river, which, alone among the Mennonite colonies, had been blessed that year with a modest harvest, though even here, he saw families setting out their meals on window ledges, having sold or bartered all their furniture for food during the privations of the previous years.

For three days he canvassed the settlement, dodging local authorities and pleading with individual farmers for half a sack of wheat in one village, a bucket of barley in another, a few pounds of millet, rapeseed, buckwheat, anything they could spare, until he had managed, at considerable cost, to purchase enough to sow a third of his land.

Arriving on the west bank of the river on his way home, Johann climbed from his seat on the wagon and allowed the horses to drink. Alone and dispirited, he sat in the sere and dusty grass and scanned the horizon beyond the opposite shore where his village lay. A few empty clouds hung suspended above a march of dust devils swirling downslope towards Sergejewka. To the south, only the blanched and endless sky lay between him and Kherson two hundred *verst* away. In the northeast the sky was darker than he remembered, due he was sure, to ramped-up activity in the vast manganese works near Nikopol.

The horses drank their fill and made what they could of the withered sedges nearest them. Harnessed to the wagon, they would not wander, and Johann thought it would be a relief to take some rest before fording the river. Kneeling beside the stream, he removed his hat and opened his shirt. He washed his face and neck, and lay back, covering his eyes with the brim of his hat. He breathed deeply and realized how utterly fatigued he was — not only from the labours of the last few days but from the cumulative stresses of these terrible years. As so often before, he strained to feel the nearness of God. "*Lieber Gott,*" he whispered, "let not your people perish."

He tried not to imagine what yet another crop failure would mean, but the spectre emerged unbidden nonetheless. Then the vision cleared, and the refreshing images that followed — of clean black earth, rain, and sturdy horses — were already the substance of his dreams.

On a barren limb nearby, an eagle preened its feathers after gorging on the carrion that lay strewn upon the famished land. A pair of storks descended to fish at water's edge. The only sound was the hiss of the horses' tails as they swept flies from their flanks. As Johann slept, the bearing of the light breeze shifted, settling finally on due north.

Johann woke when he felt the tug of the first strong gusts on his sleeve. Startled to find the sun already notched by the tips of the nearest trees, he roused himself quickly. The air had cooled markedly, and as he climbed to his seat on the wagon he heard the distant roll of thunder. He turned to face the great bend in the river and saw that a bank of heavy cloud had formed while he slept and was advancing from the north. Pacing his team carefully along the uneven shoreline, Johann studied the surface of the water. With the Dniepr as low as it had ever been, it should be possible to ford almost anywhere, but he chose a place where strong ripples hinted at shallows and a pebbly bed.

On the other side of the main channel, the floodplain was dry and firm, and within the half hour he had crossed the *plaven* and was urging the horses up the bank beside the factory. The wind had strengthened and the heat of the day had vanished. Dark clouds milled about overhead, and the first large drops of rain provoked small explosions of dust in the street as Johann brought his team to a halt in his yard.

When the rig was safely inside the barn, he led the horses to their stalls and filled their water troughs. Both animals looked sickly, their necks outstretched and their heavy panting interspersed with dry heaves. Johann thought it likely that the sedges they had browsed while he slept had done more harm than good. Standing in the open doorway, Johann scanned the street for prying eyes before risking a daylight raid on the stash of oats he kept hidden in the summer kitchen. He added a few handfuls of powdered clay before pouring the mix into the manger. The clay would soothe the beasts' discomfort until the rough fare had passed from their stomachs. He inspected each hoof for injuries incurred on the journey. Finding none, he rubbed the horses down and passed from the barn into the house.

Anna heard him enter and stepped into the kitchen, closing the door of the bedroom carefully behind her. There was enormous relief in her eyes, along with a certain consternation that Johann read immediately but could not interpret. He came to her and put an arm around her waist. "*Johann*," she whispered. "*Vier Tage!*"

"Yes, I know," he replied. "I was sure I would be back in three, but it was not easy to find what I needed. I had a short visit with Onkel Gerhard in Durilov, and he had some oilseed for me. He and Tante Katharina send their greetings. As you can imagine, they are still deep in grief and are looking to emigrate. But, Anna, why are you whispering? Are you ill again?"

She told him then that her mother had arrived with her daughter-in-law and three children. They were all resting in the back room after an eight-day wagon trek from Ignatievo. Cousin Kornelius had accompanied them, but he would be leaving again in a day or two after checking affairs at the factory. Drought and famine were raging there as well, she said, but it was not hunger that had driven them off. Ka Ha spoke vaguely of horrors that he would not relate while children were present.

"I know, Johann. We are already hungry ..."

Her voice trailed off when she saw the set of his jaw and his downcast eyes. For a long moment he stood rigid and silent as he absorbed the impact of the news. Then his face lifted suddenly, and he looked directly up into Anna's eyes. "We will make it work," he said. "Do not worry. There will be a way."

He took her hand in his. "Can you bake bread with feed oats?"

"I do not know," she said. "We have never tried." Johann embraced her, and when he touched his cheek to hers it came away wet.

"Well, we must try," he said. "I'll bring in some oats after dark and grind it for you. We'll sift out the hulls. The horses can do without for a while."

He prepared to return to the barn. At the door to the passage he stopped once more. "Anna?"

She looked up and he winked at her. "*Es wird schon alle werden*. It will be alright."


All that night and well into the morning, a steady rain fell. In the hard-trodden earth of the street, puddles overflowed into the ditches. But on the steppe above the village, the fields drank deeply and held secure every drop that fell. Johann kept Jasch home from school as soon as the surface was dry enough, and together they set to work. With the horses in weakened condition, the customary deep cultivation was not possible. Johann set the plough just low enough to loosen the soil and cut away the weeds that had flourished during more than a year of neglect. Six days of seeding followed, and by the last days of September they had planted wheat, barley and millet on ten of Johann's thirty dessiatines. It was all they could do, as no more seed could be spared from reserves that must see them and their livestock through the winter. Twice more it rained and, as in the previous year, a thick stand of seedlings appeared. October remained warm and sunny, and when Johann probed the soil he found the roots well established.

This time the first frosts of December were accompanied by a heavy snowfall that swaddled the seedlings in its protective blanket. And while the fields slept, Johann, for the first time in a year, allowed himself a surge of hope.

But the harvest was still many months away, and the promised American aid must arrive soon if lives were to be spared. Across all of southern Russia, unspeakable suffering was already the order of the day. Before he left for home, cousin Kornelius spoke of his earlier attempts to reach Sergejewka. Everywhere the railway stations were clogged with citizens, stranded and desperate, as they waited for transport out of the region. Starving orphans wandered the countryside, and in Kharkiv a hundred were found frozen to death in a cattle car on an abandoned siding. Disease invariably accompanied malnutrition, and thousands of all ages were dying. At one stop, Ka Ha had been forced to step over a body on the platform, and thinking he had detected movement, he turned and bent to offer assistance. But it was only the swarming of lice that had created the illusion of life. In towns where no one had the strength to dig graves, the dead were piled like cordwood at the cemetery gates. In the Volga region, where the drought had begun a year earlier, Kornelius had passed through the eerie silence of villages where not a single sheep or cow remained, and no dogs barked. All had been eaten, every horse butchered. Old women hunted rats and mice, and children picked through old cattle dung for undigested grains of oats and barley. Whisperings of cannibalism were no longer merely rumour, Kornelius said. In Ignatievo, where his father was the minister, families of the dead buried their loved ones secretly, at home and in the dead of night, to avoid detection by flesh robbers.

The mail was sporadic, and weeks went by without so much as a newspaper arriving in Sergejewka. Johann was surprised, therefore, to find Chaim Dachenblecher at the door one morning with an official-looking letter addressed to *Johann Neufeld: Schulze, Sergejewka.* He invited the courier inside and showed him to a chair at the kitchen table. The man was much diminished and clearly not well. He was breathing heavily after the simple exertion of stepping from his cart and walking to the door. Johann put the letter down while he brought a glass of water.

"What have you eaten today, Chaim?"

Dachenblecher shook his head but did not speak. Johann unlocked a cupboard and took down a metal canister from behind an empty crock on the top shelf. He removed the lid and brought out a barley rusk and a few acorns and placed them before the pedlar. Then he sat as well, picked up the envelope and turned it over several times. It had been postmarked in Alexandrovsk, the city across from Chortitza on the Dniepr.

"*Na ja*," he said. "What could this be?"

Dachenblecher put down his glass and immersed the rusk to soften it. He pointed a ropey finger at the envelope.

"The Alexanderthal villages each got one," he said. "And Michaelsburg too. I have just come from there. I didn't ask, but there was some excitement."

Johann seated himself across from the courier and opened the envelope. He nudged aside an empty cup and unfolded the single sheet of paper. With the palm of his hand he smoothed its creases on the table and began to read. The letter was typed in German under the letterhead *Das Mennonitische Zentralkomitee*. He read slowly and silently, nodding occasionally and murmuring once or twice in apparent satisfaction.

Dachenblecher had finished the rusk and stood to leave, but Johann motioned for him to sit again. "No, no, Chaim. Stay. You will want to hear this," he said. "A ship has arrived in Constantinople with food and clothing from our people in America. It is only waiting for permission to enter Russia."

He bent over the letter and scanned it once more for essentials. "According to the letter, distributions will begin in Khortitsa, and then wherever the need is greatest."

Johann raised the page so Dachenblecher could see the final paragraph. It was handwritten, and had been signed in a different hand. Johann tapped it with his finger. "Apparently, we are high on the list. The elder from Chortitza passed through Fürstenland not long ago and named Sergejewka the most depressed of our six villages. I am to make preparations and find workers to assist when the Americans arrive."

Dachenblecher struggled to his feet and leaned against the window ledge to find his balance. He put on his cap and reached for his mailbag.

"I suppose it would be too much to hope ... ," he said softly.

Johann looked up.

"What I mean is, if we are not Mennonites ... ?"

His voice trailed off again, but his meaning was clear.

In February, two Americans disembarked in Lepetykha and rode Dachenblecher's cart to Sergejewka. Though they had the strangest names and spoke only a few words of German, they insisted they were Mennonites. The one named Slegel would tour the villages of the settlement to assess local needs, while Yoder would continue on to Alexandrovsk to supervise the off-loading and warehousing. Supplies gathered by Quakers, Jews and Mennonites had been shipped together on the same ship, said Yoder, and the agreement with the Russian government stipulated that relief would not be ethnically targeted. As soon as possible, he said, he would ship foodstuffs back downstream to Fürstenland, and all citizens of the region would benefit. Johann hastened to set up kitchen facilities in his Tante Anna's empty residence and a bakery in the Martens home, and a week later the first lines formed along the central street of the village for once-daily rations of a pint of soup and five ounces of bread.

But for many, relief had come too late. The dying began in Sergejewka long before the arrival of American aid, and it continued throughout the eighteen months that the kitchens operated. Factory workers had never had secret stashes of grain to hide from the brigades. With the millstones silent and the shelves in the little village shop empty, when their patchwork gardens failed the workers starved. Among the first to die was Heinrich Braun, the husband of Johann's sister. After hobbling through the village on grotesquely swollen feet, he collapsed in the snow near Johann and Anna's gate, and it was clear he was beyond saving. Clutching at his distended abdomen, he drank the cup of bone broth Anna held to his lips. When he begged for another, Johann warned him to wait for a few hours before taking more, so he left again. But his organs had already collapsed, and he died later that night. Johann helped the family shroud the body — no wood could be spared for a coffin — and together, they laid it on Johann's wagon.

Shortly thereafter, Heinrich's brother and their father followed him to the grave. All three men had been employed in the factory, the father as watchman, and the brothers as carpenters.

Twenty times more that winter, Johann was called upon for his services. His were the only horses still capable of the trek up the slope to the cemetery on the northern margins of the village. There could be no funeral services, as the building had been shuttered by the authorities for nonpayment of the church tax. Brief graveside ceremonies were permitted, and the first victims had proper graves. But as the winter progressed and the ground froze, no one had the strength to dig graves, and the shrouded bodies were placed side by side in a shallow trench and covered with frozen sods to await proper burial in spring.

The sombre processions became ever more sparsely attended until one morning only Johann and Anna and the old minister Teichroeb accompanied the children of the widow Elias to her grave. Teichroeb was eighty years old and frail, and though the day was fine and Johann had given him a chair, he paused frequently to catch his breath as he read a psalm and offered a few words of comfort. Then he spoke the prayer of committal, and gestured for the children to sprinkle handfuls of earth on their mother's grave. After a few moments of silence, Johann beckoned for them all to ride back on the wagon.

He turned the horses' heads homeward and started towards the village. It was March, and a warm wind blew from the south. Snow melt meandered down the slope and across the cart path on its way to the *konstje*, and the horses strained as the wheels of the wagon sank in the sandy soil. Johann gazed over the roofs of the village to the Dniepr beyond. The river had begun to rise. Surely this year the *plaven* would flood, and the gardens would flourish. The trail levelled, and Johann made the turn into the village. Ahead, he could see the lines forming in front of the soup kitchen. His passengers were also hungry, and he flicked the reins to hurry the horses. Over his left shoulder, he could just make out the top of the nearest *kurgan*. It marked one corner of his field. It would be late June before the grain was ripe, but tomorrow he would take Jasch, and they would walk together to look for signs that the roots had survived the winter.

# 15. Hunger

Johann dressed in the dark and left the bedroom where Anna was asleep. There were still embers in the stove, so he stuffed it with straw, added a brick of dung fuel, and slid the kettle over the flame. He put on his boots and lifted his coat from its hook. The door that separated the kitchen from the barn sagged, so he raised it with the strength of his arm to prevent the screech it would make on the floor. He closed it again behind him and adjusted the flame in his lantern. The light merely mingled with the darkness and did not drive it off. But Johann did not need more light to know that something was amiss. The cows had backed away from the manger and were straining at their halters, their hindquarters nearly in the centre of the aisle. The heifer was lowing mournfully and staring straight ahead — at what, he could not tell.

Johann groped behind him and felt the handle of the pitchfork that leaned there against the wall. He twirled the implement in his hands and spoke into the silence.

"Who is it? Who is there?"

There was laboured breathing and a long, constricted groan like the sound of a soul escaping. Extending the pitchfork before him with one hand, Johann raised the lantern high and advanced a few steps to gain a better view. The vague shape of a body lay sprawled face down in the manger. Johann spoke quietly and sternly.

"Come out, whoever you are, or my pitchfork will find you."

There was anguish and no hint of threat in the plea that followed.

"*Myloserdya, O myloserdya, ya ne mozhu,*" a tiny high-pitched voice pleaded. "Mercy, O mercy. I cannot."

Johann propped the fork against the wall and brought the lantern forward. He set it on the window sill and turned to the manger. The stranger had tried to roll on his side, and one arm was extended upwards in a wordless appeal for help. Johann knelt and put his hand under the man's neck and raised him to a sitting position. There was no weight there, and Johann thought for a moment that a child lay there, wound in the clothes of a grown man.

"*Myloserdya, myloserdya!*"

His breath came in gasps, and he was weeping now. Johann helped him to his feet, but he was too weak to step over the sides of the manger. Johann embraced him from behind and set him down, but his legs would not hold him, and he collapsed into Johann's arms. His heels dragged as Johann drew him across the earthen floor to a milking stool and helped him lean back against the wall.

"Who are you? What is your name?"

The man's chest was heaving, and his voice rasped so that his words were scarcely audible. "*Vody. Vody.* I am so thirsty."

Johann left to bring a dipper of water from the kitchen, and when the man finished drinking, the arm holding the vessel collapsed into his lap. He stared straight ahead and sighed.

"Ahh, *Yvan. Schwitke. Schwitke Yvan.*"

Johann stared at him, perplexed. Who was this stranger who knew his nickname? He brushed the hair from the man's brow and leaned over to study his face. The eyes stared back at him, and there was a delay as the man struggled to speak.

"Yvan. You don't know me?"

Johann straightened and stepped back. "*Mein Gott!* Kozenko! What, in the name of heaven?"

The man's sudden weeping prevented a reply. Johann grasped him under the arms and raised him to his feet. He helped him with his pants, which had fallen to his ankles.

"Come. It is cold here. But we must be quiet. They are all still asleep."

Johann helped him through the passage to a chair next to the chimney. He could hear Anna stirring and went to explain. When they emerged from the bedroom a few minutes later, Kozenko was doubled over, his forearms crossed on his knees and supporting his head. He did not stir when Johann put a hand on his shoulder.

Anna brought out the half-loaf of bread that remained from yesterday's baking. The slices would be paper-thin this morning. With Anna's mother and the children still present, there were twelve mouths to feed. But this man was near death and must be given something.

Johann kept a careful eye on Kozenko, scarcely able to believe this was the same man he had known as a regular visitor to Sergejewka. After his wife died in childbirth he had come more often, and eventually, as a second bride and guardian for his children, he had married the daughter of one of the blacksmiths who lived in the factory barracks. He had requested the use of Johann's carriage and his matched pair of blacks for the wedding procession from Sergejewka to his home in Rohachyk. Johann had agreed to the loan but insisted on himself as driver. He recalled how the young bride's family had garlanded his horses with flowers and brushed their coats with kerosene until they glowed. And how, upon his leaving Rohachyk after the wedding, he had been applauded and given a bouquet for Anna.

That was the spring of 1918, after Johann's return from Volhynia, and in the intervening years he had not seen Kozenko again. The robust, gregarious labourer was no more. Now his clothes hung in tatters from fleshless shoulders. Black veins bulged at his temples above angular cheekbones that threatened to pierce a papery skin that barely concealed the skull beneath. His eyes, bleary and vacant, had retreated into cavernous sockets from which a constant dribble of fluid emanated. It was a wonder the man had not met his death in the manger, and far from certain that he could be saved even now.

Johann stood at the stove, roasting a few tablespoons of barley for the morning *pripps*. He crushed the grains with mortar and pestle and emptied them into the coffee pot. He added boiling water from the kettle, and when it had steeped for a few minutes he brought a cup for Kozenko.

From the other rooms came the sounds of the family waking, and Anna went to dress the youngest. She reappeared ten minutes later with Abram on her hip. Her mother stood behind her with her own two youngest, studying the stranger in the room. Kozenko had come to the table, and Johann was at his side breaking small pieces for him from a crust of bread. With a spoon, he dipped each morsel in the harsh brew and passed it to the other man's lips. At first, Kozenko struggled to swallow, and several times he waved off the offerings until he could regain himself. Then he ate and drank hungrily, and Johann cautioned him of the dangers, for a man in his condition, of haste and excess. When his cup was empty and half of the bread was gone, Johann slid the plate aside.

"No more for now, my friend. The rest will be there for you later. First you must wash and sleep. Then you will eat again."

Johann helped him, first to the washbasin, then to the cot near the stove. For a time, Kozenko lay staring up at the ceiling. Then he turned slowly on his side to face the wall and, as though a vessel filled to the breaking point had finally burst, his grief poured from him. Great sobs shook his body, and he clutched both sides of his head with trembling hands. Johann covered him with a sheet, and with a finger on his lips, he motioned for Anna to bring the children to their places at the table.

Late in the afternoon, Kozenko sat hunched in a chair near the kitchen window with his hands between his knees. Johann brought him the rest of the bread and sat down across from him. The man could hardly sit upright, and his replies to Johann's questions were scarcely above a whisper. Two of his children, he said, contracted typhus during the first months of the famine and had been too weak to recover. When repeated requisitions by the 'tax collectors' stripped his village of the last of its grain, the mill where he worked was forced to close. Since then, he had been unemployed, and with no other source of income, he had bartered everything he owned for food while there was still a chance to save his wife. In the end, hunger took her too. He had sent his one remaining child to relatives across the river in Nikopol, where the boy stood a better chance of survival — fed, perhaps, on bread stolen from his own village. For months now, Kozenko had been reduced to begging from his neighbours. But they were destitute themselves and had driven him off, finally, with threats and imprecations.

"And the barn, Kozenko? Why the barn?"

Kozenko's voice was hoarse and hollow.

"Yvan, I have nothing. I thought perhaps the cows had left a few grains. When I found only straw, it was the end for me. I wanted only death. I thought of the river, but I had not the strength to get there, and I fell asleep."

Kozenko said he was cold. Johann draped his coat over the man's shoulders and brought him a cup of hot water from the kettle. There would be *pripps* again in the morning, he said. When the bread was gone, Johann brought a few acorns. Even after leaching and roasting they were bitter, but there was some protein there, as well as starch and a trace of fat.

That evening, after the children were in bed and Kozenko was asleep in the summer kitchen, Johann sat for an hour with Anna and her twice-widowed mother. Anna was still recovering from her second bout with typhus, contracted after giving birth in the fall, and her voice was weak as she spoke of her growing concerns for the children. The infant had been taken to nurse with other women in the village, and she was a healthy child. But the others were malnourished and chronically hungry. Jascha, especially, who was fourteen and worked outdoors with Johann, was gaunt and short of breath. He could not tolerate barley flour and often had hours of stomach pain after consuming the coarse bread Anna baked with it. And when she had ground tumbleweed and thistle heads to supplement the flour, all the children had sickened.

Johann rose and swept the curtain aside. A full moon was setting beyond the Dniepr, and he stood at the window watching the sheen on the water. His back was to the others, and he spoke only to himself.

"We simply must get through ... we must find a way ... somehow we must get through."

He was whispering, but every syllable was accented. His mother-in-law overheard and echoed his words.

"*Ja, ja, Johann. Irgendwie werden wir's schon durchmachen.* If the Lord wills it," she added.

Johann turned back to the table and saw the world-weariness in his dear Anna's face. It twisted his heart, and he drew her shawl high around her neck and shoulders. He helped her rise from her chair and released her. Anna shuffled to the stove, and with a heavy cloth she picked up a brick that had been warming there.

"*Komm, Mütterchen,* I'll warm your bed for you."

The old woman stood, but before she followed her daughter, she laid her hand on Johann's wrist and looked into his eyes.

"*Gute Nacht, Johann.* You are a good man."

The door closed behind them, and Johann moved to the cot beside the stove. He removed his boots and leaned against the wall with his hands locked behind his head. His mind was clear, and the facts before him, dire and dismal as they were, did not confuse him. His sole purpose, which blazed like a hard blue flame every moment of each day, and to which his very soul was dedicated, was the survival of his loved ones. By now, only four other families were still farming in Sergejewka, and terrible as these years of drought had been, Johann counted himself among the fortunate. Despite unrelenting government levies and the predations of bandits and soldiers of all stripes, his extreme frugality, combined with a good measure of wit and cunning, had so far prevailed as a bulwark against starvation.

But now there was almost nothing left to which frugality might be applied. Under the unblinking eye of the pitiless sun, thirty-five degrees of rainless heat had ravaged the winter crops that had looked so promising in April. The Dniepr had risen only briefly before retreating once again to its main channel. On the *plaven*, cucumbers and melons had vined speculatively and died. Potatoes and beans failed to sprout, and onion shoots wilted and vanished. By June, a dry crust of cracked clay concealed only dust underneath.

Relief from overseas had ended abruptly when the American president discovered that, throughout the famine, the Soviet government had continued to export grain from southern Russia — fifteen thousand tons in 1923. The Mennonites had continued to operate as long as their supplies lasted, but by now their kitchens, too, had gone cold. The only glimmer of hope lay in the success of the next harvest, still some months away. If only they could hold out until then, perhaps the worst was past, and this relentless season of death would end.

One by one, images of events of recent years rose in Johann's mind as he sat in the dying warmth of the stove. He recalled the impact of the sudden withdrawal of the Germans and the return of the Bolsheviks. The policies of War Communism had been immediately extended to include Ukraine, and massive requisitions of farm produce began without warning during the summer harvest that followed.

He had been hard at work on the threshing floor when the first brigades arrived. They came from the Alexanderthal villages and Rohachyk, and their wagons were already nearly full. From the *Schulze* they demanded to see the tally sheet on which each farmer's yield was recorded. Of the sacks of finished grain piled under the canopy, they counted off three of every four and carried them to their own wagons. Johann and the others who gathered to protest were waved off. Their remonstrations and pleadings were futile, and the soldiers accompanying the brigade pushed them back with rifles across their chests.

"The army is hungry! The cities need to eat!" one of the soldiers bellowed.

At first, Johann stood his ground. He addressed the political officer accompanying the brigade and introduced himself.

"Comrade Komissar," he said. "The harvest is already poor, and you are taking food from the mouths of children. We will have no seed for the next crop. If you take the oats as well, our horses ..."

"Comrade!? You call *me* comrade?" the man snarled and prodded Johann's chest with the butt of his rifle. "Fat German kulaks are not my comrades!"

The others laughed and continued with their work. Their wagons were quickly overloaded, and they left, vowing that they would not be long in returning to collect the remainder of the quota.

Johann recalled the frantic haste with which the rest of the harvest of 1919 was concluded. By the time the brigades returned, much of the wheat had been milled, and the bulk of the oats and barley secreted away on each farmer's property. But the brigades were not easily deceived, and when they had taken most of what remained in the communal granary, they began a search of farmhouses and barns.

Sergejewka was their last stop before the harbour in Lepetykha, where they were to deliver their cargo. They were in a celebratory mood, and by the time they scrambled into the gloomy loft of Johann's barn, they were drunk. They probed the mounds of straw, and finding no obstructions, they flung their iron pikes out of the window to the ground below and clattered back down the ladder. In the dim light of the loft, they had failed to notice that the straw had been only minimally threshed, with most of the heads still largely intact. There was good barley there, and oats, enough to sustain Johann's cattle and horses for a month or two.

Requisitions became a regular event, and after each harvest Johann divided what little was left of his crops and secured them in widely separated locations. In a far corner of his fields amid the debris of a collapsed peasant village, he concealed a dozen sacks of wheat in an ancient root cellar. When the first frosts signalled the closing of the summer kitchen, Johann and Jascha scaled its roof with a trowel and a few bricks. On the pretext of repairs to the chimney, they secured an iron shaft and pulley across its opening and looped a length of rope around it, leaving the ends dangling to the hearth below. Johann stitched up eight narrow sacks of oats, and together, he and Jascha hoisted the lot up the chimney.

But surprise searches were common and increasingly thorough, and in midwinter, when the brigades were reported approaching from Rohachyk, Johann had rushed through the snow in the predawn darkness with a pan of embers from the kitchen to set a smudge fire in the summer kitchen. Smoke billowed from the chimney, and when the brigades threw open the door, they found Johann in his undershirt and unbuttoned trousers, rubbing his eyes and straightening the bedding on the cot.

More recently, after the brigades uncovered grain stashed under barnyard muck in the peasant villages, Johann had wrapped precious sacks of barley in oilcloth and buried them in a shallow pit next to the manure pile. The brigades arrived and worked through the steaming mass but found nothing. By the time they were done, they had moved the entire heap precisely over the pit where the grain was concealed. When they were gone, Johann moved the manure back again in anticipation of the next visit.

These ruses had so far been successful, but Johann could take little delight in them, in part because he attributed much of their success to the stupidity of the searchers, but also because he knew the stakes were immense. Incidents of 'hoarding' were severely punished, often in direct proportion to their cleverness.

And government brigades were not the only hazard. Hungry eyes were everywhere in the village, and he did not doubt that his every move was witnessed. Only in the deepest hours of the night could he venture out of the village to the root cellar to retrieve enough wheat for a few loaves of bread. For the horses and cattle, he took no more from the chimney each night than he could conceal in the pockets and inner pouches of his greatcoat. The barley must remain buried for now and kept as a last resort, as its location next to the barn was easily visible day or night to anyone passing on the street.

From one of the bedrooms came the cry of a hungry child. Johann got to his feet, but the comforting murmur of Anna's voice reached him through the wall, and he sank back onto the cot. He was wracked with weariness, but sleep did not come easily these days, and he preferred to wait until he was overcome before he surrendered. It was the pain of chronic hunger that kept him alert; that, and the need to think ahead, always ahead to tomorrow, and the next day, and the day after that.

The midnight gong sounded from the Orthodox chapel, and Johann remembered Kozenko. He dipped water from the bucket and put a few acorns in his pocket. Once outside, he set his cap and stood for a moment breathing deeply. It was cool, but there was no wind. High above him, a glorious field of stars danced in the heavens. *"Aus der Tiefe rufe ich, Herr, zu dir,"* he whispered. "Out of the depths, O Lord, I implore you. Do not let your people perish!" How often had he prayed this simple prayer, he wondered? For his own family he prayed it daily, certainly, but also for all who suffered in these dire straits. And now there was Kozenko.

"He has come to us," Anna had whispered in Johann's ear. "We cannot turn him away."

On the steps of the summer kitchen he put his ear to the door. He eased the latch and stepped inside. Kozenko lay on his back with one arm across his forehead. He was snoring softly and would likely not stir before morning. Johan put the water on a stool beside the bed and adjusted the blanket around the sleeping man's shoulders. He reached for the acorns, then thought better of it. They were hard and potent, and surfeit could kill a starving man. He would keep them for the morning when, after *pripps* and a spoonful of oatmeal, Kozenko would be better able to tolerate them.

Back outside, he could hear his livestock, hungry and restless in their stalls. He entered the barn from the side door. The horses Johann had brought back from Volhynia in the spring of '18 were greatly diminished. He passed between them in the dark, stroking their flanks and muttering apologies. The little hay he had cut on the *plaven* had been consumed by Christmas, and he had been forced to pull thatching from the roofs of the barn and outbuildings to feed the animals. Now that the snow was gone, he led them out each day to graze on the grasses that were beginning to appear, but it would take some time before they regained their strength. With hunger everywhere, and the herdsman dead, there could be no thought of exposing them in the community pasture.

Miraculously, all four of his horses had remained — precariously — in his possession. The *Komitee* had seen no advantage to removing them from the care of a competent horseman whose reputation as trainer and veterinarian was well known. They remained his — on condition that they be available for service to the community as need arose.

Of his herd of seven milk cows he was permitted to keep two, and that only because of his large household. One still yielded a pint of milk each day, but the other was entirely spent, and he intended to slaughter her soon. There would be no fat, but he would be allowed to keep half the meat, and the yearling heifer would take her place. He had bred the heifer with the neighbour's bull just before it, too, was taken, and as long as she was pregnant, he was allowed to keep her out of the count. In hopes of a healthy calf, he had supplemented her rations. When she calved, there would be more milk for the children, and under the terms of Lenin's New Economic Policy, he could sell the butter to the *Komsomol*.

It was past one o'clock when he re-entered the kitchen. The door caught on the floor, and Johann reminded himself that he ought to fix the sagging hinge. He swung the door back into place and carefully lowered the latch. The stove was dead, but rather than seek warmth beside Anna, he would rest on the kitchen cot. Perhaps he could sleep for a few hours. The cot creaked as he bent to remove his shoes. He stretched out and covered himself with the day blanket. It was Sunday morning, and he remembered that he and Anna had agreed to host a short prayer service at eleven. Few would attend, and old Teichroeb no longer had the wind for long sermons. Anna's voice was still weak, so the singing would be feeble, even if her mother and sisters joined in. *Perhaps*, he thought, as his mind drifted sleepwards, *perhaps I can offer to start the hymns.*

# 16. Collapse

Johann was away, and Anna sat alone in the kitchen, her elbows on the table and her head in her hands. The pages of a letter lay strewn on the table before her, but her eyes were closed, and the only sound in the room was her own breathing, punctuated with occasional heavy sighs. Another of those paralyzing headaches had bloomed suddenly while she was putting little Abram down for his morning nap. She would have liked to ask for a hot compress to wind around her head and neck, but the children were at school and she did not know where Johann was. Sometimes, when the throbbing struck, she leaned as far as she dared over the hot stove. That usually brought some relief, but the breakfast fire had died long ago, and until the agony subsided on its own, she would have to resign herself to waiting. So she pushed her chair back slightly, lowered her head to rest on her crossed arms — and waited.

It seemed that waiting had woven itself into the very fabric of her universe, dominating all other aspects of life during these difficult times. It was nearly twelve years since the beginning of the Great War, and for the first three, she had waited anxiously for Johann to come home. Three more years of fearful suspension as the various combatant armies of the civil war swung back and forth through the region like a lethal pendulum. Then three terrible years of drought and famine had scythed the steppe of its people, taking dozens in Sergejewka, hundreds in Fürstenland, and millions across the land. Finally, these last three years of backbreaking labour, trying to coax the recovery of the land, and heartbreak as all efforts proved futile. A year ago, Johann had finally agreed to register for emigration, and now it was a matter of more waiting and watching as families from Molotschna, Chortitza and Ignatievo filled the quotas and left for America while Fürstenland was repeatedly shunted to the bottom of the list.

Anna did her best to hide her despair, which she felt most keenly when she thought of the children. Jascha was already fifteen, Njuta seventeen. What was there for them to look forward to? How would they find work? How would they find wives and husbands? If the trajectory of the past decade was anything to go by, the final collapse of the village was imminent. With the factory shuttered and agriculture reduced to bare subsistence, Anna could envision only yawning years of poverty and privation.

It was a marvel, Anna thought, that Johann had remained at least outwardly optimistic. Whenever he sensed that spirits were down, he liked to end his table grace by quoting the prophet Samuel: *'hitherto hath the Lord helped us!'* As though the memory of past miseries were a forecast of better times to come. Before the children he betrayed no discouragement, cheering them on as well as he could and celebrating as each crisis subsided.

"We have come through!" he would say each time an immediate danger had passed.

Anna knew that, despite everything, Johann's whole heart and soul were invested in the land, and that the thought of emigration pained him sorely. She remembered seeing him walk out to the fields the first spring after they were married and sink to his knees in the warming soil. Unaware he was being watched, he had plunged his hands below the surface and pushed them forward until he lay flat on his face, revelling in the fragrance of the reviving earth. He had taken her to the garden and made her grasp the hoe to let her feel how the snap of even the smallest weed was transmitted up through the handle to the hand. Every morning he rose in the dark, and neighbours spoke of hearing him singing at the top of his lungs, long before sunrise, in the fields above the village. The prospect of abandoning the land, the recovering orchard and gardens, his beloved horses, and the barn and outbuildings he had constructed with his own hands, filled him with dread, and remained almost beyond his imaginings. Not once had Anna heard him acknowledge urgency in the matter of emigration. He had been in no hurry to register and had finally done so only at Anna's insistence just before the last drought broke.

Only recently, in the evenings after the children had gone to bed, and he and Anna were alone in the kitchen, had she heard him confess that things had indeed come to a pass and that he had no clear vision of a way forward. The New Economic Policy had brought some relief, but with Lenin gone, the NEP was under threat, and his successors were considering the full collectivization of agriculture. It was hard to imagine what that would mean for a settlement like Fürstenland. The few farmers still functioning knew how desperate the situation was. Though there had been modest rains, most of the fields were strangled with generations of mature weeds. Only a third of Johann's land was still clear enough for planting. The rest of it would require more labour than he could muster, even with the willing help of Jascha. Johann had told Anna how he had tackled a single thistle five feet high. After cutting it off at ground level, he had pursued the tap root, using his shovel to cut more and more deeply. Twelve inches down, its cross-sectional stub still winked at him like a malevolent yellow eye. That day he confided to her that it all seemed futile.

At the sound of whimpering in the next room, Anna roused herself. Her headache had abated marginally, and she had work to do. Helene was still sleeping, but Abram was restless. She brought him into the kitchen and gave him a rusk and a little milk. She helped him with his shoes and gave him a few playthings. The boy was almost four and would have to fend for himself.

She was passing through the kitchen on her way to the great room to pick up her needlework when a glance through the window brought her up short. From this vantage point, the factory wharf on the *konstje* was just visible between the factory and the old Janzen residence, and tied up alongside was a small river barge. A half dozen men were busy coiling the ropes with which the barge had been towed the several hundred metres up the *konstje* from the main channel of the Dniepr. On the other side of the *plaven*, a river freighter lay anchored midstream, waiting. As Anna watched, a second group of men emerged from the factory, dragging hoisting gear and heavy chains. From the barge they brought timbers, which they laid down to create a skid track on the steep slope between the factory and the dock. On the wharf they assembled an iron tripod from which they suspended a block and tackle. Then all the men reentered the factory and for a time no further movement was visible.

When Johann came in from stabling the horses an hour later, he found Anna still standing at the window. She heard him enter, and without turning, she beckoned to him and threw the curtains open. He rinsed his hands at the basin and ran them once or twice through his red hair. He flicked his hat to the hook on the wall and picked up Abram on his way to stand beside his wife.

By now the factory grounds were a hive of activity. The double doors of the engine house had been pried from their hinges and lay in the dirt. The steam boiler and firebox were already dismantled and on the dock, along with an assortment of pumps and water tanks. From the doors of the main building emerged teams of men struggling with lathes, drills and cutting tools. From the foundry they brought the iron smelting pots and casting moulds and stacked them at water's edge. Among the swarm of men, Johann recognized Rudenko, who had not been seen in the village since the factory closed. He appeared to be overseeing the operation, leaving little doubt as to who had arranged for the barge and who would profit from the sale of the equipment.

Anna spoke quietly, but her voice had the clarity of crystal waters.

*"Johann, wir müssen einfach fort von hier!* We must! We simply *must* get away!"

She drew the curtains together and pulled a chair from under the table. Johann, who had been leaning on the window ledge while they watched the proceedings, straightened and stretched his back and shoulders. It was not like Anna to speak in imperatives. He turned to her, and his lack of expression signalled neither agreement nor disagreement, only that he had not arrived, just yet, at so definitive a conclusion. She continued, and her strength and resolve startled Johann.

"We cannot go on like this. We cannot stay here any longer. You have done what you could, ten times as much as many others. But we too are going under now. The village is falling to pieces around us. The land has not recovered, and again people are starving!"

For a minute or two Johann did not reply. He had turned back to the window, and stood with his hands in his pockets, peering through the gap between the curtains. A crew was up on ladders now and had begun pulling up great sheets of metal roofing, throwing them to the ground where other men folded and stacked them beside the skid path. The shouts of the men mingled with the clash of metal and the shriek of resistant nails.

Anna's family had been heavily invested in the firm her grandfather had founded. Seeing the factory pulled down before her eyes felt like a severing of the warp and weft of her own life. Onkel Gerhard had been master of the foundry. Numerous cousins and in-laws worked in all departments of the firm. Anna's father had been the head miller. How often had he taken her hand and shown her the workings of the giant millstones driven by the great belt that came from the engine in the steam plant? She had watched with fascination as his assistants poured grain into the opening in the centre of the spinning runner stone and seen it emerge as fine flour in the circular trough below. Her grandfather had taken her through the foundry and assembly rooms of the factory, and her heart had swelled with pride as she touched her fingers to the *Janzen-Neufeld Ko.* nameplate on the shiny machines in the warehouse. What she saw this day through the clear glass of her own kitchen window filled her with the deepest dismay.

Although his late Onkel Kornelius had been co-owner of the firm, Johann had never worked in the factory. Raised as a tiller of the soil since his early years, he felt a mild disdain for wage labour and the servitude to others it implied. But he did not disparage his wife's sorrow at the closing of this final chapter in the half-century story of the family firm. He squeezed her shoulder as he pulled out another chair for himself, and for a time neither of them spoke.

Between them on the table lay the letter from Tante Anna to her brother Jakob. Johann had already left for the fields when Jakob's children maneuvered their father's wheelchair over the broken street so he could share the letter with Anna's family. Anna had read the letter aloud while they sat together in the morning sun. Jakob, already in an advanced stage of paralysis, had struggled to explain that this was only the third letter from his sister and the first since her arrival in Canada.

Now Anna took up the letter again. She tilted the pages to catch the light and began reading it for Johann. After the salutation and a blessing from the Psalms came a summary of Tante Anna's experiences since leaving Sergejewka in November of 1918; the month-long rail journey to the West, through the killing fields of Europe, to Kornwestheim near

Stuttgart; her perilous existence during the foment of revolution in Germany itself; her sons-in-law finding no meaningful work; Herman's several failed attempts to return to Sergejewka via Rumania and Odessa; the inadequacy of the German ration system and the hazards of black-marketeering; and the interminable wait for the documents that had finally cleared the way for emigration to Canada.

*"Yes, dear brother Jakob, we had a time of it,"* she wrote. *"This was not the Germany we had imagined. How honourable and decent were the soldiers that protected us in Sergejewka! But at home they joined in the chaos and violence. We could never feel safe on the streets or even in our building. The forces that have destroyed Russia are now also in Germany ... How often I have wept, longing to return to our beloved Sergejewka. Even now, sometimes the longing is so strong I can hardly bear it. Here in Canada we are not afraid, but the people are strange, and the land so flat and so cold. I long to walk the village street, dig in my beloved garden, sing with you all in the Sunday services, and visit you in your homes ... "*

*"Ach!"* Johann drew a sharp breath. "Has no one written to her? Does she really not know how little is left of the Sergejewka she imagines?"

He took the letter from Anna's hand and continued scanning for details.

*" ... in Kornwestheim I and the three youngest ... two tiny rooms ... landlady a malicious and vindictive old shrew ... there cannot be many like her in the world. Why, one night she begged me to pray with her for her soul's salvation, and the next day she raised my rent!"*

Johann could not suppress a grin, and Anna, too, winced at the irony. But then came news of sorrow and tragedy.

*" ... and now I must write of my dear, dear Lena ... when that scoundrel Eugen learned that our wealth was lost, he broke off the engagement ... Lena deeply despondent ... never well afterwards ... very ill on the ship ... treatment for a burst appendix in Halifax ... too late ... died in hospital four days later ... buried in Herbert, Saskatchewan ... Onkel Heinrich preached ... "*

Johann looked up at Anna. He knew she had loved her younger cousin, that she had tried to dissuade her from the affair with Eugen and had held the girl in her arms as she wept hopelessly in the early days of her love. He took up the letter and read the final pages.

*" ... Herman took us with him from Saskatchewan to Scottdale ... godless Änglisch town with dirty air, coke ovens, steel mills ... bought the Rundschau and moved the presses to Winnipeg ... work for us all in the printshop ... German language churches here, with ministers we know from Russia ... Mennonites finding good land ... generous settlement assistance ... reasons to be grateful ... "*

The letter ended with wishes for the well-being of her brother and his family, and greetings for friends still in the village. Johann reassembled the pages and folded them back into the envelope. "So," he said. "They imagine they have found the promised land."

Anna spoke more quietly now but with no less fervour than before.

"I am sure they will have their hardships, Johann. But I am ready. This life is no longer a Pharoah's dream. The lean years began ten years ago, and no fat years — nor sheaves, nor cows — have followed them. I have stopped imagining things will get better, and I greatly fear for our children. It's time, Johann. We must get away from this place! Surely you see it too?"

Johann nodded, but not without a hint of impatience.

"But my dear Anna, you know we are already on the list. What more can ... ?"

"*Ja ja*, it is a fine thing to be on a list! But the list grows longer and longer, and always Fürstenland drops to the bottom."

It was true. Mennonite delegations in Moscow and Petrograd had extracted a commitment for three thousand exit visas for this year. But when it became clear that this would mean the loss of many of the best agriculturalists in the region, the quota had been cut to seven hundred fifty. And Fürstenland, which had already sustained a near deathblow to its economy, could not afford any further losses and was summarily stricken from the zone of eligibility.

Anna pressed on.

"Onkel Gerhard got his papers in Molotschna, where he was born. That is already three years ago, and today he and his family are in Canada. Onkel Herman and Tante Katharina are already there as well. And your own sister has her permits after registering in Ignatievo. You could go to

Nepluyevka, where you were born, or to Berdjansk district, where your father's people lived, those are not excluded. Perhaps if you registered there."

"And if I did?" Johann felt his frustration rising. "Who will buy our farm? Anna, we have no money, and I cannot stomach the thought of carrying twenty years of travel debt on my shoulders in that land of ice and snow."

There was a sharp rap at the door, and Anna watched as Johann went to answer it. It was Valentin Kyrylenko. He saw Anna and nodded a greeting over Johann's shoulder. But then the two men stepped outside, and the door closed behind them.

"Johann, Johann," Anna whispered to herself. She was trembling. The interruption was most untimely, and she resented it. She busied herself preparing the noon meal while she wondered what business might have brought Kyrylenko to their door.

Valentin Kyrylenko's return to oversee the foundry after Gerhard Enns fled had been welcomed by the workers, but as the factory went into decline the casting schedule was reduced to two or three days a month, and he had made ever fewer appearances in Sergejewka. Since the factory had shut down altogether in 1923, Johann had not seen him at all.

"I heard what was happening," said Kyrylenko, "and I came to collect my things."

He waved a limp hand in the direction of the foundry.

"But you can see for yourself. I am too late."

He had been met at the gate by Rudenko, who denounced him as a capitalist collaborator and sent him packing. Now he and Johann stood watching as the last of the heavy equipment was muscled down the skid to the barge.

"So, this is how it ends," said Kyrylenko. He stood shaking his head and kicking randomly at pebbles in the street. "At one time, we were more than a hundred fifty men."

"Come, my friend," said Johann. He put his hand on the other man's shoulder and turned him away from the factory. Slowly, they walked the rutted street to where it met the trail leading down to the *konstje*. At the junction, Kyrylenko stopped, and Johann noted the man's hunched left shoulder and the difficulty he had raising his arm to light a cigarette.

"I guess you might have wished for a better physician."

Kyrylenko laughed. "Yvan. Come now," he protested. "I'm eternally grateful. You did the best you could. None of the other bumpkins would have known what to do. Ha! In all likelihood, they would have left me lying in the dirt."

They spoke of the risks of their journey to Volhynia in 1918 — the route through German-occupied territory, encounters with trigger-happy partisans in the forest, and Kyrylenko's collision with the wagonload of drunks. Johann wondered about the three younger men who had accompanied them.

"Did that rascal Stepan ever show up again?" he asked.

"The horse I sent back with him was in the stable when I got home," Kyrylenko replied. "But I never saw the lad himself."

"And I never saw my uncle's horse again," said Johann with a laugh. "But he was more than glad to keep the one Stepan failed to claim. It was far superior, and when Enns emigrated in '23, I bought it back."

"But Stepan himself?" said Kyrylenko. "No one knows. There is a rumour he was killed fighting with Makhno."

As they spoke, they had begun their return to the village. On both sides of the street, empty barns stood like skeletons, the thatch gone for fodder during the drought years and never replaced. The yards were abandoned and littered with mounds of debris, the houses pulled down, and the materials removed by factory workers for reconstruction elsewhere. In orchards decimated by the need for firewood, a few feeble attempts had been made at replanting, but it would be years before mulberries would again purple the lips of children under the summer sun.

They arrived back at Johann's gate, and Kyrylenko turned to face Johann.

"So this is how it is now." His arm swept the air to include the entire village. "What will you do?"

Johann did not answer. Sounds from inside the house had distracted him.

"Have you thought what you will do, Yvan?"

Still, Johann did not answer. The voices from the house were animated adult voices, and he recognized Anna's among them. He reached for the latch, and the gate swung open.

"I think I must go, Valentin. There is someone in the house with Anna."

Kyrylenko extended his hand. "May it go well with you, Yvan. God be with you."

"And with you, Valentin, my friend."

Kyrylenko turned to leave, and Johann strode up the path to the front door where Anna met him, her face flushed with excitement.

"Johann, where have you been? Leppke is here from Alexanderthal, and he has brought the agent. They have the list, and we are on it!"

# 17. Divestment

Travelling with the newly elected *Oberschulze* of Fürstenland were an agent of Immigration Canada, and Dr. Drury, chief medical inspector for the Canadian Pacific Railway. Their interpreter, a teacher from the *Zentralschule* in Chortitza, made the introductions, and after handshakes all around, the men sat down while Anna prepared tea.

Leppke explained that after numerous deferrals, the official documents had arrived authorizing Fürstenlanders to emigrate. The agent spoke of the quota set by the Soviet government, which could not under any circumstances be exceeded. As for Canada, he said, only those with firm intentions of farming would be admitted.

"Our cities, I'm afraid, are already teeming with the unemployed and, to be frank, not everyone is as welcoming to immigrants as you might hope. But there is land — good land for good farmers willing to settle in Canada's prairies." And he confirmed that the CPR had agreed to a generous program of travel advances.

"Finally," he said, "a critical matter. All families must have a clean bill of health at the point of origin before visas will be issued for admission to Canada. When the day comes Dr. Drury will be conducting the examinations."

The agent spoke formally, and he punctuated each point with sharp taps of his pencil on the tabletop as though it might aid in translation. When he had finished, he rolled the pencil aside until it rested alongside his sheaf of papers. He leaned back in his chair and turned to Dr. Drury.

The doctor, a soft-spoken and kindly man, explained the two-fold purpose of their visit: to update the list of emigration applicants and to conduct a preliminary medical survey. Trachoma was by far the biggest concern as it was highly contagious and could spread rapidly in congested trains and ships. Early diagnosis and timely treatment in the village could help avoid disappointment later. Émigrés in whom the condition had been overlooked before they left Russia had been quarantined in Germany or England, where some were still undergoing treatment a full two years later.

The doctor pushed his chair back from the table.

"We have made the rounds of the other five villages and found only two cases. The symptoms are easy to detect. And," he said, "I can already confirm that neither of you are infected."

He smiled at Anna's surprise.

"Once we've checked the list, Herr Neufeld can take us to see the adults. This afternoon we will examine the pupils in the school, and if all goes well, we hope to meet the boat in Lepetykha in the evening."

The agent pulled the Sergejewka file from a folder and pushed it across the table, rotating it so Johann and Leppke could see the names. The list dated back more than half a decade, and a number of names had already been struck. Johann ran his finger down the column titled *Head of Household*. Applicants were listed by date of application and one of the earliest entries was Anna's Onkel Gerhard, dated 1921. After his son's tragic murder, Gerhard had rushed to re-register his family in Halbstadt and had emigrated from there. Johann ran the pencil through his name. Other families had left for Siberia or the Kuban. Johann's brother Peter had applied early, but he was under forty, and would be disqualified by the current prohibition for men of military age. He and Neta would have to wait, as would Anna's sister Greta, whose husband was also on the list. Johann struck out the names of starvation victims; old Heinrich Braun and his two sons. Their widows and children had been repatriated to their ancestral villages in Chortitza or taken in by relatives in Ignatievo. They would have to apply from there. Of the few factory workers on the list who were still resident in the village, there was the younger Koslowsky, whose brother had fled eight years ago with the Germans. And Cornelius Wohlgemuth, the factory bookkeeper, who had tried to reach his Polish homeland but had twice been turned back at the border.

These two families would no doubt wish to go. Johann found his own signature near the bottom of the final page, alongside Anna's and the list of their children. He noted that even little Helene was on the list. He had indeed been very late in registering.

When he had finished he turned the pages back to the agent.

"Well, you see how it is," he said. "We are no longer a vast multitude."

Leppke interjected with a quick shake of his head. "Not in Sergejewka, perhaps, but there are almost a hundred families from the other villages. But I am confident the quota will accommodate us all."

The interpreter finished his translation, and Johann rose and reached for his coat.

"Let me take you to see the ones who are still here."

The prospect of imminent emigration, which had opened so suddenly, was transformative in every imaginable way. In an instant about-face, Johann turned from nurturing his land and livestock to planning the divestment of it all. The greatest urgency was finding a buyer for the farm. He hoped to sell the large village lot with its tidy gardens and outbuildings at a price that would allow the family to pay at least part of their travel costs and thereby reduce the load of debt with which they would make their new beginnings in Canada. The house was well built and clean, and Johann had kept the barn and outbuildings in good repair. The garden was cleared of weeds, and even the small orchard had been nursed back to a semblance of health and should begin to bear fruit by the next summer.

But tenure on the fields he had inherited from his father-in-law, which he had struggled against such great odds to maintain, was quite another matter. Technically, he did not own the land. Fürstenland had been founded as a *Pachtkolonie* under lease from the brother of the Tsar. With the collapse of the empire and the liquidation of the aristocracy, there was no one left to whom rent was owed. Nor had the redistribution of land in the first years of the revolution had any lasting effect since most of the plots were abandoned during the famine years, and their proprietors had either starved to death or fled to the cities. Johann had kept most of his land intact. But the handful of others still farming in the village simply planted where they could, on the best of the abandoned fields, and left the rest to the encroachment of the steppe. A buyer could be confident of the house and yard but would have no firm guarantees as to farmland.

Once again it was the pedlar Dachenblecher who brought the critical news — that a group of German-speaking Volhynians had disembarked in Lepetykha. Upon their return from wartime exile in Siberia, they had found their villages levelled, and the region partitioned between Poland and the Soviet Union. They had come back east to investigate rumours that a wave of emigrations to America had made land available in southern Ukraine. The majority of the group had left for ethnic German settlements nearer the Black Sea, but two young brothers and their wives remained in Lepetykha awaiting the birth of a child. Dachenblecher had their names, and if Johann wished, he would bring word to them.

"Yes, yes! Send them as soon as you can! Tell them I can hold back for a few days, but I must begin selling the cattle and horses. All the machines and other equipment must go also, and there are neighbours who will want some of it. But I will wait to hear from the Volhynians."

The courier returned the next day, and with him were the two Walter brothers, Klaus and Manfred. Johann met them at the door and brought them into the kitchen, where Anna had Helene on the hip and was preparing tea. The brothers removed their hats and introduced themselves but said little more until Johann had seated them at the table. When the cups were full, Johann began by enquiring about their circumstances.

The younger brother, Manfred, explained how, in the first months of the Great War they had been deported to the Urals 2,500 *verst* to the east. Deposited in a makeshift village of Bashkir nomads, who resented both their own forced settlement and the presence of strangers, they had spent the past decade wresting a meagre living from garden plots in summer and day labour in Orenburg during the winter. Their parents had remained in Volhynia and had perished when the civil war overwhelmed the region.

"We found their graves," Manfred said, "and we set a stone in their memory. But there is nothing left of the village."

The older brother continued, full of emotion.

"To take our wives there now, and to begin again in the ruins of that place ..."

His voice trailed off, and he looked away to the window to compose himself.

"If there is land available here in south Russia, we can perhaps start again. Was the Jew correct in saying that it might be possible to purchase this farm? With livestock and equipment intact?"

"That is so," Johann replied. "I have promised one cow to Anna's uncle Jakob, but the rest of the cattle and horses can go with the farm. I could sell them separately, and I think the plough and seeder as well. But I will need to begin very soon as we are to leave within the month."

Klaus waited until Anna had refilled the cups.

"And the land? How much land goes with the farm?"

"There are thirty dessiatines which we took over when Anna's father died in 1909. I have kept twelve of these clear, even during the drought years. The rest, I'm afraid, will cost you much labour before they can be planted again. If the rains are timely, you will find it to be good land. But land *ownership* today is confusing."

Johann spelled out the matter as well as he could, minimizing the risks and emphasizing the likelihood that small holdings like his would not be much affected by foreseeable changes in government policy.

Once again the cups were empty, and Johann noticed that the brothers had begun scanning the walls and ceiling of the kitchen and peering through the open doorway to the living room. He pushed back his chair.

"Let us show you what you have come to see."

He and Anna took the men through the living room, the three bedrooms, and the large cold room in the back. Johann lifted the trapdoor in the kitchen floor and led the way to the root cellar. Though the potato bin was still half full, most of the jars and crocks aligned on the shelves remained empty, awaiting the full recovery of the gardens. In the attic, garlic and a few onions lay drying on the floor, and from the rafters a ham hung suspended beyond the reach of rodents.

The brothers followed with their hands clasped behind their backs, nodding as Anna explained the layout of the house and Johann pointed out recent improvements and extolled the soundness of the original construction.

Back in the kitchen, Johann opened the door to the corridor that led to the barn. In the years since the famine his herd had increased to four cows, and under the ever-changing terms of the NEP, he was allowed to keep them and sell milk and butter. There were two calves in a corner pen and a brood sow freshly brought from Molotschna whose expected litter would help restore the stock he had lost to the swine flu. The horses had regained some of their former glory, and there were admiring murmurs from the brothers as they stroked the sleek flanks of Mishka, his favourite.

Striding through the village on their way to the fields, the brothers noted the derelict factory, its empty doorway gaping on the other side of the street. A pair of dogs had dug out a nest of rats, and several raced for cover as the men watched.

"This will all be cleared away soon, we hope," Johann said. "Industry will not return here, and everything of value has been removed."

Frost had nipped the sprouts of winter wheat in the first field they came to, but Johann dug around a few of the plants to reveal the root mass that would survive to produce the first crop next summer. A small, second field lay fallow, ploughed and harrowed in preparation for seeding in spring. Above the last field, like a grim reminder that all things must pass, loomed the largest of the ancient tombs. Johann could tell the brothers little about it except that the local peasants held certain superstitions regarding it.

"I pay no attention to such lore," he said, "but Jascha, my oldest son, spent much of one night on its slopes, and he has no wish to repeat the experience." He laughed. "Dachenblecher played a noble role in that story. Perhaps you can ask him when he takes you back to Lepetykha."


Beyond the Dniepr, the sun was poised for its final descent when Johann returned to the yard with his guests. He showed the brothers the field equipment stored behind the barn and took them back inside so they could assess the condition of the harness and saddles. Then they returned to the kitchen through the connecting passage.

The children had returned from school, and Anna had given them their supper and set them about their duties. She had kept the soup hot and there was bread, and for the visitors, a slice of ham. Small talk prevailed while the men ate. Klaus asked about shipping on the river, and Manfred wondered about relations with nearby peasant communities. The two Lepetykha villages intrigued them. Mala Lepetykha was little more than a hamlet, but in Velyka Lepetykha they had seen two banks and a legal office, and they were sure they had heard French spoken by some of the citizens. What was the range of services they could expect there?

Anna was aware, as she listened, of an awkwardness in the air, as no one had spoken about a price. She suspected, now that the Walters had seen the farm, Johann hoped for an offer he could counter. Likely, the brothers hoped for the same. From either side, this would not be a straightforward matter. The reintroduction of the gold standard after the hyperinflation of the post-war period had done nothing to dispel confusion about the actual value of things. Before his emigration in 1923, Onkel Herman had sold his small farm in Ignatievo for a hundred billion of the old rubles. It had recently been resold for eight thousand of the new. Johann reckoned his farm was worth no less, and he decided to make the first move.

"Well, gentlemen. You have seen everything. What do you say? I consider eight thousand a reasonable price for the farm with everything included. As I say, I can sell the animals and machinery separately, but that would hardly be to your advantage, and I would still need seven thousand for the rest."

The brothers leaned back in their chairs and glanced at each other. Then Manfred took the lead.

"When the war began, our parents expected to escape to Germany, and they transferred most of their money to the Deutsche Bank. We have applied to Frankfurt requesting the release of our parents' estate, and we were promised a prompt response. Perhaps there will be an answer when we return this evening."

The older brother broke in. "But, Herr Neufeld, I beg you to understand. Eight thousand is out of range for us, and not only because, as you have so honourably informed us, tenure on the land is not assured in the long term."

"Well, my friend," Johann countered, "as these years have taught us, nothing whatsoever is secure in the long term other than our continuing labours and the grace of God to bear them. Let me know what you hear from Germany. It may be they will tell you to go to Kherson or even Odessa where the international banks have branches. I cannot promise to turn away other buyers, but if you keep me informed of your intentions, I will not sell for another week."

The brothers nodded in agreement, and the three men were still shaking hands when Dachenblecher's knock interrupted the exchange. Anna gave him a place at the table and set a bowl of soup before him. He thanked her and ate silently while the men finished their business.

"*Zeyer gut Suppe, Frau Anna. Danken dir,*" the courier said when he had finished. He stood with the other men, and they left the house. Darkness had enfolded the village and the light of a waxing moon glittered on frost in the grasses. Once more, Johann shook hands with the brothers before they stepped into Dachenblecher's cart.


Johann watched until the cart turned into the woods at the end of the village. Then he entered the barn through the side door to check his livestock before he retired. Shadows cast by the lantern played on the walls as he progressed down the aisle. Mishka neighed as he approached her stall, and he reached into the hopper for the ration of oats he gave her each night. The cattle were chewing the cud and did not turn their heads as he passed. Before entering the passageway to the kitchen, he reached into the nesting box and fended off a flurry of beaks as he fumbled for the half dozen eggs he knew would be there. He put the eggs carefully in the pocket of his greatcoat and opened the door. He found a bowl and placed the eggs where Anna would find them in the morning. He laid his coat over the back of the big chair near the window. The silhouette of the ruined factory loomed like a verdict over the village. Behind it, the river, placid and timeless as the moon, flowed freely to the sea, oblivious to every human misery. For a long while, Johann stood motionless, reviewing his encounter with the Volhynians. He was hopeful but not optimistic as he gauged the likelihood of a sale.

"Yes, they are interested." His whisper hissed from wall to wall in the darkness. "Their eyes were everywhere, and it was plain to see that all was to their liking."

He knew the rest of their party were exploring the richer soils in the German colonies near Berislav, and if they found land there the brothers would surely be tempted to join them once the child was born. They seemed to be men of their word, and Johann was confident he would hear from them, whatever they decided. With the departure date only weeks away, Johann knew he was not in a position of strength. Despite his bold naming of a price a few hours earlier, he would be forced to accept almost any offer that came his way.

"They are aware of our predicament," he thought. "So many of us leaving, and buyers as rare as storks in a winter storm."

The first days after the visit from the agent, while Johann occupied himself with the divestment of the farm and its assets, Anna was overwhelmed in a confusion of panic and paralysis as she considered the myriad tasks that lay before her. In the evenings, after the children were in bed, she sat at the kitchen table writing dozens of letters; brief notes to friends in the *Jannedarpa*, longer ones to sisters and brothers scattered among the various villages of Molotschna and Ignatievo, and notices alerting Johann's aunt and uncle in Canada to expect details of their arrival date in Winnipeg.

For Johann's mother, a short note was sufficient. She lived in nearby Michaelsburg with her daughter, the famine widow of the younger Heinrich Braun, and there would be time to visit. Still in robust health at eighty, she had, from the outset, waved off all talk of emigration.

"I'm too old for yet another new beginning," she said each time Johann brought up the subject with her. "I have outlived two husbands, and they have marked the path I well know I soon must follow."

After three or four such discussions, Johann had stopped pressing the point.

But the letter to Anna's own mother, now back in Ignatievo, was a desperate, pleading document touched throughout with anticipatory grief. For she knew that as long as her brothers were subject to conscription, her mother would never agree to emigrate. Nevertheless, Anna tried.

*'Ach, meine liebe Mama!'* she wrote. *'Every day I weep as I try to imagine living beyond the reach of your loving presence. I simply cannot do it. I beg you! We have put you and the sisters on the list. We can pay for your documents. You must come with us. Let Jakob and Georg do their duty, and in a few years they will be free to follow. Mama, I simply implore you to do this!'*

She watched for Dachenblecher the next morning and asked him to post the letter directly to the packet boat in Lepetykha.

During the shrinking daylight hours, Anna and daughter Njuta prepared the indestructible double-baked rusks that would sustain them until they reached Riga, where the CPR would begin supplying meals. There were shoes to repair, clothing to mend, and a hundred decisions about what to take and what to leave. Until the mustering date there could be no rest, and Anna frequently found herself on the edge of collapse.

At night, sleep would not come, and sometimes the voice of the agent echoed in her mind. *A clean bill of health,* he had said. There had been so much illness in the family. Aside from her own bouts with typhus, malnutrition during the famine years had left the children vulnerable to every infection that came along, and most of them had suffered in one way or another. The Great Hunger had struck just as Njuta was entering adolescence, and since then she had hardly grown. And there was Jascha with his sensitive stomach. But Anna's deepest concern was for nine-year-old Peter. Aways fragile and very thin, he had fallen gravely ill last Christmas with an unidentified malady that left him feverish and listless. For weeks he was bedridden, and neither Doktor Esau, who suspected scarlet fever, nor the Jewish *Mediker* could disabuse her of the fear that Peterchen might not live. Only with the lengthening days of spring had he begun to show signs of recovery, and when school began in the fall he had begged to rejoin his classmates. He walked with difficulty and fell when he tried to run, but when his older brothers, and Herr Kasper himself, promised to keep watch over him, Anna had relented and allowed him to attend. Now, with emigration on the horizon, she kept him home in the afternoons for fear of overtaxing his powers before Dr. Drury could see him.

Anna was alone in the great room sorting family heirlooms. Needlework sprawled on the arms and back of a chair and over the sides of the heavy portmanteau that stood like an open casket in the middle of the floor; doilies, runners, tablecloths and linens, a thousand hours of embroidery flashing its colours in the narrow slant of sunlight entering from the south window. On the cabinet near the chimney lay the family Bible, and next to it, her father's hymnbook, his pocket watch and chain, and the large iron key to the flour mill of which he had been the master. The heavy wooden doors of the case stood open, revealing a few books and three or four serving platters Anna had accepted from her Tante Anna before she fled with the Germans.

A number of photographs lay scattered on the sofa. Anna bent to pick up the largest of these with its heavy black frame, and with the back of a bent finger she swept the dust from the glass. It was a family portrait with, just to the right of centre, the only image of her father she possessed — Papa, handsome and proud, with his dense, finely trimmed black beard; all the children staring straight at the camera, even little Greta in the front row. And herself, the oldest, leaning awkwardly into the group from the back. Only Agatha — little Ota — was missing. Anna raised the photo to the light and turned it over to find the photographer's stamp. She whispered the words on the label. *Familie Peter und Maria Enns: Weihnachten 1908.*

"Ah yes, and Ota was born a week later on New Year's Day. I was barely twenty. Six weeks later we were married, and before the next Christmas, both of our *papas* were gone."

Anna reached for a woollen shawl from the armchair, doubled it and smoothed it on the worktable. She centred the photograph and folded the shawl around it from all sides before placing it carefully inside the trunk.

"Mama, there is someone at the door." She turned to see Peter rubbing sleep from his eyes.

"*Ja*, Peterchen, who is it then?" The boy turned his palms upwards and shrugged a shoulder. Anna brushed past him into the kitchen. She wiped her hands at the washstand and glanced out of the window before opening the door. Klaus Walter stood on the threshold, hat in hand. Behind him, she saw his brother Manfred leading a pair of horses to the water trough. Two young women were seated in the carriage, and one was holding an infant to her breast.

"*Guten Tag*, Frau Neufeld. We have come to show our wives. You will allow us? And I hope we may find Herr Neufeld at home?"

Anna went with him to meet the women, and the group was still clustered near the carriage when Johann rode up on Mishka. In a single practiced motion, he slipped from the saddle, looped the reins over a post and turned to greet his guests.

"Aha! So you have returned after all. I was beginning to think evil thoughts!" But his laughter swept aside any hint of pique. "Come, let us go inside. It is cold for the baby."

It took only an hour to conclude the sale of the farm. Reports from further south had been discouraging, the brothers said. Their party of Volhynians had aggravated the suspicions of a local populace deeply unsettled by years of foreign presence.

"Maybe if we were not so many. It seems everywhere is difficult. And just now ..."

The younger brother gestured towards his newborn daughter.

"We cannot keep wandering about the countryside. And at all costs we do not want to separate. We are brothers, and our wives are sisters, and we think perhaps if we stay together we can make a life here."

If the news from their compatriots was disappointing for the Walters, their telegram from Frankfurt was devastating for Johann and Anna. Yes, the brothers reported, the German bank had approved the application and was forwarding funds through their branch in Nikopol. But it seemed the principal amount deposited twelve years ago by their parents had been smaller than expected, and its value had withered during the rampant inflation of the post-war period.

"Herr Neufeld." Klaus Walter hesitated. He had been looking down at the table while his brother spoke. Now he straightened in his chair and looked up to face Johann and Anna squarely.

"Herr und Frau Neufeld. Forgive me, but this is our situation. We have not quite four thousand rubles — three from Germany and the rest from our winter employment in Orenburg. That is really all we have, and it is all we can offer you."

He cleared his throat and waited. Johann made no reply, and the silence grew awkward. The infant began to whimper, and when Anna gestured for the mother to come with her to the other room, both women rose and left with her. Alone with the two brothers, Johann leaned forward, elbows on the table. He folded his hands together and raised them to his lips. His eyes found an empty space on the wall behind the men. Then they closed, and the brothers believed he was at prayer. For an endless minute, there was only the slow working of his pursed lips and the sound of breathing. Twice he nodded, as though affirming something grasped in consultation. Then, as Anna and the other women reentered the room, Johann rose abruptly and extended his hand. "Gentlemen. I accept. What must be must be. Though it is too little for me, for you, perhaps, it is already too much. Let this be your journey's end, and may you prosper."

The signing of documents would take place in Velyka Lepetykha, and the three men agreed to meet at the law office in the morning. The women reached for their coats and capes. Many, many thanks, but no, they would not stay for supper. Their town hosts expected them. Outside, the horses were restless. Jascha had seen to their needs and coupled them to the carriage. He passed his parents on his way back to the house, and with his hand on the door, he turned to see them still at the gate. Then he entered the house, and Anna and Johann were left alone. Their eyes followed the carriage to the edge of the village.

"So. Their journey ends here." There was a tremor in Anna's voice, and Johann took her hand in his.

"*Na ja*" was all he said. His voice was steady, but his heaving shoulders betrayed him.

# 18. The List

Aron Leppke was in a hurry. He slapped the reins to speed his tired beast, but he was already entering the village, and a few moments later his carriage halted at Johann and Anna's gate. It was the first of November, and a chill north wind signalled the early onset of winter. Leppke tied the reins to the gatepost and glanced first at the sky, then across the street and past the ruins of the factory complex. The vast valley of the Dniepr was curtained with dense clouds. *There will be snow before evening,* he thought.

The *Oberschulze* had decided not to emigrate. Renowned for his resilience and optimism, he saw better times ahead for Russia. He would stay to care for his ailing parents and apply his skills and energies to facilitating the exit of others. He found Johann in the barn with Onkel Jakob and his young son, whom Johann was instructing in the care and feeding of the heifer who would soon calve. Onkel Jakob observed from his wheelchair. By now even his facial muscles had begun to atrophy, and he struggled to greet Leppke, an old friend.

Leppke got directly to the point. "The dates are set," he said, "and there is little time. Those with independent means are to register in Alexanderthal three days from now, on the fourth of November. Then they will be free to leave on their own schedule by routes of their own choosing."

Anna had been listening from the passageway, and Johann beckoned for her to join them. She closed the door behind her. "And for us who have not the 'independent means' as you call it," she asked, "what is the plan?"

"Travellers on credit and those who are sponsored by relatives already in Canada do not have a choice. You must travel via Moscow to Latvia and from there to England. Dr. Drury will examine you and your children on the sixth or seventh. Before you see him, your belongings should be ready for transport to the harbour in Velyka Lepetykha."

While he spoke, he had been searching the sheaf of papers in his hand.

"Actually, for you it is the seventh, as you are near the bottom of the list. Arrive as early as you can in the morning. In Alexanderthal, Internal Affairs will activate your passports, and the Canadian rail agent will issue the travel passes you will need from Riga to your final destination in Canada. The fare as far as Riga is your responsibility."

Leppke returned his files to the satchel that hung from his shoulder.

"If all goes well, you can expect to cross on the *CPR Metagama,* which sails on the twenty-third. You must be in Southampton by the twentieth to allow time for paperwork and your final medical exam. There will be later ships, but you want neither the expense of a long delay in England nor the hazards of a winter crossing."

He passed Anna a sheet of paper with the significant dates and times, and took his leave. After the door closed, Anna stood with her hands pressed to her temples.

"*Ach, du liebe Zeit!*" Dark dismay coloured her voice. "A week? How can we possibly be ready? One week is what we have?"

"It will be alright, Anna." Johann moved to her side and placed his arm on hers. Twice more he repeated, "*Es wird schon gehen, es wird schon gehen.*"

Pitiful as the proceeds had been, the sale of the farm had removed a great burden from Johann's shoulders. They could clear a few small debts to neighbours and pay the fare to Riga. There would be something for his mother and for Anna's, and in Nikopol they would buy winter clothing for the children. Nevertheless, the truth was that Johann roiled with regret at leaving. Here in Sergejewka, after seven years of service, first in the *Forestei* and then in the military hospital, he had finally found firm ground. For seventeen years he and Anna had lived in this village on the great river, years of honest labour on soil and among people he loved. Despite seasons of dissolution and deep distress, he and Anna had prevailed and made a life together. Seven children had come to them from the hand of God, and — a rarity in Sergejewka — all had survived the desperate years of privation. If the *Oberschulze* was right, better times lay ahead. But the die had been cast. The farm was lost, and the future lay in an alien land. If for Anna the coming week was the crisis, for Johann it was the years beyond that appalled.

Exhaustion had beckoned Anna to an hour or two of sleep, but a whimper from Peterchen roused her, and sleep would not return. Since the collapse of the factory, the bell in the Orthodox chapel had fallen silent, and there was nothing else to mark the hours. Long before dawn, when she heard Johann leaving to tend the cattle, she rose and built up the fire in the stove. She filled the kettle and two large pots with water and moved them over the flames. She lifted the zinc tub from its hook on the wall and carried it to the privacy of the bedroom. When the water was warm, she bathed. She was still dressing when Johann returned from the barn for his own bath. When he was done, he removed half of the water from the tub and replenished it from the pots on the stove. The two smallest children protested the early waking, but Anna bathed them and dressed them as warmly as she could. Peter managed on his own, then Hans and Jascha. When the oldest boys were done, they emptied the tub outdoors and refilled it for their sisters.

Black night still lurked at the windows when the family met for a breakfast of bread and oatmeal. When Johann judged that the horses had finished their rations, he sent Jascha and Hans to bring out the ladder wagon. A few minutes later, the rest of the family followed. Anna clutched the leather *Beutel* containing their documents tightly to herself, and once seated in the wagon, she tucked it into her coat. There were rings around the moon and ice in the air, and the children cringed in their coats. Johann arranged heavy rugs over their laps before taking the reins.

The horses were keen, but Johann held them to a steady walk. They would tire early if he gave them their head, and the first water was hours away. The cart trail levelled at the top of the slope, and in the vast expanse of the open steppe, the first hues of dawn welcomed the travellers.

The silhouette of the largest *kurgan* loomed like a sentinel and, as always when he saw it, Jascha remembered that night — the terrible dream and the Jew who had found him and comforted him in his strange language, which Jascha had somehow understood, who had fed him and warmed him with his own coat and returned him to his mother in the middle of the night. Dachenblecher winked at him now whenever he brought the mail, for he too remembered, and there was a bond between him and the boy that words would have tarnished. Jascha had missed him during the years he had disappeared, when the synagogues were burned in Lepetykha and Nikopol and Kherson, and the uncles and aunts clicked their tongues and shook their heads and spoke in whispers in the great room on Sunday afternoons.

For a time, only the jangling of harness chain and the intermittent complaint of a dry axle disturbed the silence. Johann and Anna sat at the front of the wagon, and their low voices drifted back to the children. Njuta smiled indulgently at ten-year-old Mariechen, who was reviewing with her youngest brothers what was expected of them when they met Dr. Drury.

*'... must stand tall and straight ... look up at the doctor ... faces bright and smiling ... and if he asks, answer with a strong voice.'*

Njuta snugged an arm around Peter, who was already asleep. From time to time, Jascha leaned over to check on him.

"*Ach*, just let him sleep," said the sister. "He will be stronger for the doctor."

The sun breached the horizon and touched the stubble plain. The children raised their faces to the warmth and stood to stretch their limbs. They scanned the distance and strained for a first glimpse of the Niebuhr factory chimney which should soon be coming into view.

A small stream crossed their path a few *verst* out of Alexanderthal, and while the horses drank and the family rested, another party arrived from Sergejewka. Wohlgemuth, the career factory man who owned neither team nor wagon, had secured a ride for his family with the Koslowskys. His young son Albert clambered out and asked if he might ride with his schoolmate Peter. By the time the three families were ready to commence the final leg of the journey, the two boys were scrambling among the rocks on the creek bank, and for the first time in months, Anna felt the slightest ebbing of anxiety.

It was noon when the wagons left the cart path and entered the single street that divided Alexanderthal neatly in two. The other three villages, Rosenbach, Georgsthal and Olgafeld, were within easy walking distance, and the street was flowing with pedestrians. A few families were still arriving, but many had already been processed that morning and were hurrying home with stamped certificates and exit visas clutched in their hands.

Johann led the way to the *Oberschulze's* yard, where a makeshift registration centre had been set up in his wagon shed. One corner was curtained off with sheets and canvas tarps to create a cubicle for Dr. Drury. In the centre of the building, a few planks thrown across a pair of sawhorses served as the main desk. Johann recognized the agent of the Canadian Pacific Railway and the same interpreter who had accompanied him on his visit to Sergejewka. Leppke was there as well, overseeing the master roll and checking and rechecking the tally, which was steadily creeping up on the quota set by the government. At a separate table sat a functionary of the Secretariat of Internal Affairs, checking birth certificates and passports before issuing exit visas. Overseeing the entire procedure was a military *Komissar* and his assistant, both in uniform, who made it their business to fuss with details properly in the domain of others. Dr. Drury, in particular, became incensed at their repeated reminders that no one in doubtful health was to be cleared.

As each family appeared at Leppke's station, they were given a card with the family's name and a number corresponding to their place on the rolls. The *Oberschulze* seemed annoyed to see the Koslowskys and Wohlgemuths. "Your day was yesterday. What happened?" he asked.

Koslowsky ignored the tone of the query. "What does it matter, Aron? We confirmed our intentions when you saw us a week ago in Sergejewka. We were delayed. We are here."

Leppke consulted his list and wrote out two cards, passed them to the two men and, with a silent shake of the head, inserted them at the head of the queue. In less than an hour they had cleared all hurdles and were free to return home. The two couples came over to the bench where Johann and Anna were feeding their family.

"Still waiting?" Koslowsky's intended sympathy was obscured by his obvious elation at his own family's success. "They have just called seventy-four. What's yours?" He leaned over to see the card Johann held up for him.

"Eighty-one. You'll be another hour at least. What a muddle altogether!"

"Well," said Anna, "you at least are well out of it." She was cradling Helene, and Abram was squirming on Johann's knee. "I don't suppose we'll get home much before midnight," she said. "It will be a long day for the horses. And, of course, for the children."

During the exchange, Wohlgemuth had been rolling his sheaf of documents into a cylinder. He tied it with a rough cord, and now he raised it in a gesture of farewell on behalf of their group before tucking it into the deep inner pocket of his overcoat. They left to collect their children, and Anna and Johann resumed their waiting. For the third or fourth time, Anna asked to see the card with their number on it.

"It can't be long now," she whispered as she nuzzled the head of Abram, who had fallen asleep in the crook of her arm.

The flow of new arrivals had ceased, and the half dozen families still remaining mingled in small groups along the outer edges of the shed or stood outside absorbing what was left of the afternoon sun. Above the clamour of restless children and the buzz of conversation, the voice of the *Oberschulze* rang out at regular intervals.

" *... number 76, Dyck, Herman, Alexanderthal, six persons! ... number 77, Derksen, Georg, Michaelsburg, nine souls! ... number 78, Klassen, Franz, Olgafeld, five persons! ... "*

A sudden commotion at the desk drew Johann's attention, and he left Anna's side to investigate. The *Komissar* and his assistant were stooped over the desk on either side of the *Oberschulze*. Leppke was protesting something. He turned from the desk, and with the sweep of his arm he indicated the families left in the queue. The *Komissar* was adamant.

"No! Not a single one beyond the quota," he said. "Those are my orders! You go no further until we have checked your figures."

He took Leppke's chair and motioned for his assistant to sit beside him. Running his finger down the column that recorded family sizes, he barked out the numbers. The junior officer struggled to keep up, repeating each figure as he wrote it down. Five figures in a column, three columns in a row, two rows per page. Then the subtotals, columned on a separate page, at the bottom of which, at long last, the grand total appeared.

Leppke had moved well back from the desk and stood with his arms crossed, watching intently. All conversation ceased, and parents shushed their children, and for long minutes the voices of the *Komissar* and his assistant were the only sounds.

"How can this be, Aron?" Johann touched his sleeve. "We are still four families here."

The *Oberschulze* did not reply. He stood staring at the desk in the centre of the space, listening to the stream of figures. "I made sure of my numbers, Johann," he whispered. "There will be room for more."

"For everyone?"

The *Oberschulze* shifted nervously. "The list is somewhat changed, Johann. There have been many births, and perhaps not so many deaths since we started the list."

"Aron." Johann was not listening, and now his voice was coarse with gravity and desperation. "Aron! Aron! The farm, the house and barn, the cattle, my horses. We have sold it all. Everything! We have nothing. Aron, you *will* find a way."

At that moment, Leppke was called back to the desk. The *Komissar* was scrutinizing the single sheet with the final tally. He tapped it sharply with his forefinger without looking up.

"We are nearly there. Proceed."

He gave up the chair but stayed at Leppke's elbow. Leppke picked up the list and called out.

"79 Wieler, Aganetha, Georgsthal, widow and child, two persons."

The poor woman, overcome with relief after the ominous delay, stepped forward with her daughter in her arms and was directed to Dr. Drury's corner.

"Number 80, Suderman, Heinrich, Rosenbach, eleven … "

Instantly, the Komissar waved him off.

"No! Room for nine. No more!"

A cry burst from Katharina Suderman. She rushed to the desk and fell on her knees before the *Oberschulze* and the *Komissar*. Her husband and children crowded around her, and the little ones began to wail. The officer looked down at them and then at Leppke.

"Deal with this," he said, turning back to the desk. "Next. Who is next?"

Leppke ignored him. He looked over at the officer from Internal Affairs responsible for issuing exit permits. Under the eye of the *Komissar*, there would be no negotiating with him, and Leppke knew it. At another desk, the CPR agent looked on while his translator whispered his version of events in his ear. Leppke leaned over and helped Frau Suderman to her feet. Her husband was beside himself. Like so many others, he had sold everything. Leppke put his hand on his shoulder.

"Heinrich, this is hard. But calm yourself. We expect another quota next year, and you will be at the top of the list. You can count on our help. Come see me tomorrow. Today I can only say that I am sorry."

The *Komissar* growled obscenities at the delay. He reached over Leppke's shoulder and seized the document from his hand. In a gruesome mockery of German, he read the next entry.

"Number 81, Neufeld, Johann, Sergejewka, nine persons! And that will be all!"

He took his pen, drew a heavy double line below entry #81 on Leppke's list, crossed out all names below it, and inscribed his signature at the bottom of the page. He called the Internal Affairs officer to the desk as a witness and handed him the pen. He signed the officer's papers in turn, keeping a copy for himself. Gathering his documents, he clamped them together and stuffed them into his valise. He nodded to Dr. Drury and the CPR man, who were standing side by side, watching. Then he waved his assistant to the door, and without a word, he was gone.

## 19. Exodus

Dawn was still hours away when Johann shook Anna awake. He was reluctant to disturb her, but when a porter made a rare pass through the car a few minutes earlier Johann had pointed to Anna and mimed a severe headache. The porter beckoned for him to follow him to the next car where, from his personal supply, he gave him a half dozen tablets of Bayer Aspirin. He held up two fingers to prescribe the dose and handed him a glass of water. Drawing his watch from a pocket of his crisp CPR uniform, he showed Johann that it was three o'clock and traced an arc from III to VI to indicate the interval between doses. He was the first Black man Johann had ever seen. Johann nodded his comprehension.

"*Vielen Dank*," he said. His offer of a handshake startled the porter.

"Oh, you're most welcome, sir. I hope your wife feels better soon."

Anna took the pills and handed the water glass back to Johann. The pain had made her nauseous, and great luminous blooms pulsed behind her closed eyelids. She whispered that the bed was uncomfortable, so Johann helped her stand for a moment while he folded the wooden slats into day position. He picked up the layer of coats that had served as mattress and pillow, and laid them across the back of the seat. The *Canadian Colonist* coach was draughty, and Johann draped Anna's neck and shoulders with a scarf before stepping past her and settling himself next to the window. Anna sat with her head nearly in her lap, kneading her temples. Except for a few half-suppressed moans that escaped her now and then, she was silent. Johann closed his eyes and waited for the light of dawn. When he felt Anna stir, he offered to make up the bed again, but she shook her head.

"Let me sit for a while," she whispered. "How is Peterchen? Has he slept?"

"A little. I think he is sleeping now. Njuta is good with him. He takes the medicine from her and calls her *meine kleine Mama* again, as he did during your typhus."

Anna managed a weak smile and let her head sink against Johann's shoulder. After a few minutes, her breathing changed, and Johann saw her face relax in sleep.

Always during these fearsome visitations of what Doktor Esau had called *Migrem*, there was this throbbing agony about the temples, the maelstroms of light, the nausea. Sometimes she felt herself sliding towards unconsciousness, and she feared she might succumb to a full-blown seizure of the kind that had killed her father. But on this occasion, as the Aspirin took effect and the pain began to subside, she sank instead into the oblivion of deep sleep. Amorphous islands of colour floated in a sea of blackness before resolving into faces she thought she recognized. A ragged triangle of blue laughed in the raucous tones of the *Komissar* as it slid through her field of vision, followed by a spinning circle with her mother's face. The sister wives of the Volhynians emerged as static figures, surrounded by the furniture of her rooms in Sergejewka. A church bell chimed, and columns of bandits forded the Dniepr on horseback. Her grandfather preached in the cemetery while Onkel Jakob wept among the gravestones. And in the gardens on the *plaven*, the stern faces of friends in Sergejewka stared straight ahead, unsmiling.

Slowly, Anna became aware that she had been dreaming, that the pain was receding, and that while she slept, Johann had somehow eased her into fetal position on the bench. He had covered her with his coat, and she was warm. It was still dark, and she knew only that the largest lake in all the Americas was somewhere on the left and that *Manitobah* was still far away. On the seat facing hers she could hear Johann snoring softly, but she did not open her eyes. Njuta and Jascha would take care of Peter, also Abram and little Helene. The release from pain was exquisite, and she hoped she might sleep again. But her dreams had disturbed her, and now they triggered a vivid review of the traumatic events since registration day in Alexanderthal.

After the awful suspense while the *Komissar* and Leppke reconciled their lists, they had been the last, *the very last!* to make the roster. Relief, yes, but dark surges of guilt as well. The Sudermans. What must they feel? What would they do? Johann had approached them before he left to get the wagon, and they had not blamed him, but there had been little to say.

Peter had not fared well on the return journey. Dr. Drury had confirmed in him the late stages of recovery from scarlet fever, and it was his opinion that his kidney infection was related. It would not prevent him from travelling, he said, providing there was no relapse, and he had written out the names of medicines. By the time they got him to bed he was feverish and coughing. Anna had stayed at his side for much of the night. In the morning he complained of a pain in his neck, which had not been there before.

They'd had a single day for final preparations and a last visit to the cemetery where so many uncles and aunts, cousins, parents and grandparents lay buried. In the evening, a round of the village for final good-byes before Johann's brother took them to Lepetykha for the short sail to Nikopol. There they bought clothing and Peter's medicine. Then a wretched seven-day journey north in a lurching cattle car shared with the Koslowskys and Wohlgemuths and several other families. There was no bedding on the sleeping pallets and only a small stove to repel the frost. The rusks they had brought with them were their primary food, sparsely supplemented with whatever could be found on station platforms.

On the morning of the third day, they had arrived at Moscow's Kursky Station and were ordered to leave the train for document inspection. Ninety families were corralled in a large hall where an official of the railway presented them with a rude shock. The visas of citizens wishing to leave the Soviet Union, she said, were subject to a surcharge. The fee was twenty rubles per ticket. Citizens opting to return, instead, to their place of origin were welcome to do so at no charge by exchanging their exit permits for return tickets. She pointed to the kiosks on one side of the hall where cashiers were waiting.

Anna recalled the buzz of dismay that reverberated in the great hall, and how Johann immediately strode to the nearest cashier and passed their papers through the slot in the glass. Of the children, only Njuta was old enough to require a separate visa. The younger ones travelled on their mother's, and Johann had his own. Anna heard the cashier announce the sum. Sixty rubles! A vast amount drawn on slender reserves. She watched Johann peel twenty-ruble notes from a thin roll and slap them down on the counter. He returned, receipt in hand, to find Anna with her arms around Aganetha Wieler. The widow — he recognized her as #79 from the queue in Alexanderthal — was standing with streaming eyes, her infant in her arms. She had six rubles and would have to go back if she could not find the rest. Anna took Johann aside.

"Can we do this, Johann?"

"Well, Anna." He paused for a moment. "Anna, we can, yes. But we will soon have to give up hope of beginning with something of our own in Canada. We too will have to beg and borrow." A smile wrinkled his face. "But yes, we can do this. After all, if number 79 had not taken two from 80, there would have been no 81."

He peeled off another twenty ruble note and pressed it into Anna's hand.

The next morning, shortly after the train left Moscow, Aganetha Wieler had come over to where Johann and Anna were sitting with their children. She was carrying a bulky wooden case which she placed carefully on the floor.

"My heart is filled with gratitude for your generosity towards me and my child," she said. "I want you to have this. It is the clock my husband had from his parents in Chortitza. It is why I brought it. But they are all gone now, and for me, it speaks mostly of sorrow and loss."

Johann bent to remove the lid of the case. It was a fine timepiece with an immaculate floral motif. He could not be sure, but it was not unlike the fine *Kroegers* Onkel Kornelius and Tante Anna kept on prominent display in the factory office and in the dining hall and study of their residence.

"But Frau Wieler," he said, shaking his head. "How can we accept this from you? Surely you know its value. Could you not sell this when you arrive in Canada?"

She raised a hand to ward off the protest. "It is I who must thank you. If you take it, I will know it is in kind hands."

With that, she returned to her sleeping child at the other end of the car.

Anna could just make out the heavy Roman numerals on the CPR clock at the end of the coach. It was still only six o'clock, and the first light filtering through the heavily rimed windows was cold and grey. Working with the edge of her comb, Anna cleared sufficient space for her to see that the train was passing through dense forest. Snow-laden branches of great pines, agitated by the blast of pressure created by the passage of the train, swept by the window like the brooms of giants.

The conductor entered the car to announce that the dining car was open and that the train would arrive in Fort William in two hours. Some of the children were awake, and Anna urged Johann to take them to claim a table. In a half hour or so she would wake the others and follow. But the intoxicating aroma of coffee had drifted in with the conductor, and when Johann insisted on her priority after the misery of her night, she did not resist.

Coffee! How she had craved it! It had vanished at the start of the Great War, and in the twelve years since, they had been forced to make do with that gall-bitter barley *pripps*. There had been good coffee on the German ship from Riga through the Kiel Canal, and Johann had offered her a cup. But her terror of ships, even on the gentle Dniepr, had always knotted her stomach and paralyzed all appetites except the keen desire for solid ground. Nor had she eaten anything during most of the Atlantic crossing. On the second day out of Liverpool, Anna had taken to her bed and stayed there, and coffee had been the furthest thing from her mind. The horrors of the storm that had raged for four days in the middle of the Atlantic were beyond description. Hardened crew members, including the captain, had sickened as the *Metagama* pitched and rolled helplessly between gigantic sea swells. At the peak of the storm, all communication was lost when the radio mast on the foredeck was taken by a rogue wave. By the time the ship arrived several days late in Saint John harbour, the papers had reported her missing and presumed lost with all fourteen hundred souls aboard. No, there had been no thought of coffee!

Johann arrived in the dining car with the two youngest children just as the sun rose on a majestic landscape. The train had left the forest and was skirting the edge of the lake. The children stood at the windows, taking in the scene. Beyond a mile-wide apron of shore ice, open water glistened like a field of tinted diamonds. As the track bent southward on its final approach to Fort William, the silhouette of a distant island lay on the horizon like a giant in repose.

Johann seated himself and found spaces for the little ones. "Well! How is the *Kaffee* on this train of the *Tzee Pee Yarrr*?" His deliberate mangling of the abbreviation amused the children. But then he turned to Anna and lowered his voice. He had left Peter with Njuta. It had been hard to wake the boy, he said. He seemed confused, and the stiffness in his neck had grown worse.

"You remember Dr. Drury was worried about a relapse," Anna said.

"Yes, of course I remember, but this is something new. Do you have any of the pills left? It might help him sleep for a few more hours."

While she and Johann were speaking, the train had begun its deceleration, and the shriek of a whistle startled Anna as she rose from the table with a glass of water for the boy. She would find the Aspirin and relieve Njuta, who would surely be longing for breakfast by now.


The stop in Fort William was just long enough to take on coal and water, and by midmorning the final leg of the journey had begun. Smoke and steam plumed in a windless sky as the train left the station and reentered the vast boreal wilderness of forest, rock and muskeg. Threading narrow channels blasted through granite cliffs, curling around countless lakes, slowing as it crossed wooden trestles over frozen rivers, the train advanced steadily westwards. Not once in a hundred miles was there a town or village. Only the occasional trapper's cabin or the odd railway crew leaning on picks and shovels and waving at the faces in the windows. Not since she was fifteen and on her way to Siberia with her parents had Anna seen wild emptiness such as this. To Johann, who had never left the steppes, it was unsettling.

"The famous *kanadische* wheat fields, where are they? The cows and gardens?" He shook his head vigorously and growled in mock despair. "We have taken the wrong train!"

A whistle stop at Rat Portage took on a dozen men homeward bound after a month's labour on the track. A few hours later, deciduous trees began to show among the pines, and gradually the forest thinned until, without warning, it dropped away entirely. The track stretched out on the open prairie, and soon the glimmer of city lights appeared in the dusk with their promise of refuge, rest and healing.

# 20. Thanksgiving Sunday 1931

I t was the seventh of October, Thanksgiving Sunday. For the fledgling congregation of the *Brüdergemeinde* of Niverville, *Erntedankfest* was a whole day affair. Their own building was still a vague and distant dream, but the Lutherans of the area, served by an itinerant minister once each month, graciously allowed other groups the use of their tiny chapel on the remaining Sundays.

On this occasion, the invited speaker was Johann's Onkel Herman, who had emigrated with his family three years before his nephew. But the old *Ältester* had failed to arrive until just before noon, so the time allotted for his sermon had been filled, instead, with singing and congregational prayer. Afterwards, the families picnicked together under the willows that ringed the churchyard, exchanging local gossip and the latest news from loved ones who had remained in Russia. Children played on the grass and among the gravestones, and the older boys harassed gophers and field mice until their parents declared Sunday a day of rest, even for pests. As the lunch hour drew to a close, the adults stashed tablecloths and dishes in the wagons and buggies that had transported them to the church and gathered their children in preparation for the afternoon service. A few of the men and older boys, Johann, Jasch and Hans among them, pumped water for the horses before following the others into the crowded building.

A hot southerly had been blowing since early morning. The windows of the tiny church were wide open, and the door was propped against the wind. Johann was one of the last to enter, and he found a chair against the back wall. He saw that Anna had taken their two youngest with her to the front benches on the women's side. Peterchen was sitting next to his friend Albert, and the two older boys were with friends near a window.

When all were assembled, Gerhard Enns rose to announce the first hymn. Johann sang along, but his thoughts were on the singer, not the song. That Onkel Gerhard was able to sing at all, how could that be? And this particular hymn, so unusual for a Thanksgiving service. *Wehrlos und verlassen* — helpless and forsaken — words that could not fail to call up the memory of his oldest son, tortured and murdered in place of the father. Surely, grief still surged within him. Yet Onkel Gerhard's honeyed tenor, strong as ever, rose above the congregation like incense, lifting the spirit and bringing comfort to others who had suffered their own griefs and sorrows.

> *Wehrlos und verlassen sehnt sich*
> *Oft mein Herz nach stiller Ruh';*
> *Doch Du deckest mit dem Fittich*
> *Deiner Liebe sanft mich zu.*
>
> *Unter Deinem sanften Fittich*
> *Find ich Frieden, Trost und Ruh,*
> *Denn Du schirmest mich so freundlich*
> *Schützest mich und deckst mich zu.*

'*Friede, Trost und Ruh,*' thought Johann. "There are not many here old enough to recall seasons of *peace, comfort and calm* in the old country."

When the hymn ended, Cornelius Wolgemuth mounted the podium to read scripture and lead the congregational prayers. He could be long-winded, and it was likely that on this festive occasion, he would supplement the reading with commentary of his own. Johann closed his hymnbook and scanned the assembly.

Tante Anna was sitting next to *his* Anna. She had written to say she would come for the weekend to join in the celebrations, and Johann had met her at the station on Friday night. On the way to the farm, their conversation had been light-hearted. She appeared to have forgotten the rancour that had flared between them in 1918 when, after the takeover of the factory, he had pleaded with her to listen to the workers' demands and consider the vulnerability her wealth represented under the new circumstances. He recalled her fury, how she had accused him of collusion with the Bolsheviks and of conspiring to bring her whole house down upon her head! Now she spoke mostly of her children, of pleasant work in the offices of her son-in-law Herman's *Rundschau,* of doings in the Winnipeg North End Church and, almost fawningly, of the prospect of fresh bacon and sausages, "if only, my dear Johann, you would be so kind as to fatten one or two of your many piglets for me over the winter." The letters she wrote from Winnipeg were always more sombre, describing the struggles of adjustment to city life and, most poignantly, her enduring grief over the loss of her daughter Lena, who had died before she had properly set foot on Canadian soil. Johann looked across at Tante Anna while Wohlgemuth finished with a resounding *'Hitherto hath the Lord helped us!'* He saw her nod her head in affirmation, but her shoulders sagged.

By now, the building was insufferably hot, and by the time Onkel Herman rose to deliver the sermon, children were squirming on the hard benches while women fanned their faces and men surreptitiously loosened their ties and the top buttons of their shirts.

The elder began by apologizing for missing the morning service. He and Katharina had set out from Winkler early enough, chauffeured by their son Ka Ha in a borrowed car. But problems at the ferry crossing in the French village, and confusion thereafter on the roads, had delayed their arrival until lunch — for which, he quipped, they had fortuitously arrived on time! And for which, on behalf of his wife and his son, he heartily thanked the congregation. As penance for his tardiness, he promised to limit himself to just the one sermon he had prepared for the afternoon and leave the other for another time. It was a rare attempt at humour for the aging preacher.

As his uncle spoke, Johann listened carefully, recalling the numerous times he had heard him in Sergejewka. His sermons were always dogmatic, sometimes fierce, and his diatribes against industrial wealth had given offence to his youngest brother Kornelius. Theologically, he left little room for difference, which had made even his dealings with the conciliatory Allianz movement difficult. Johann had recently learned how deeply hurt Onkel Herman had been when leading members of his own *Brüdergemeinde* in Ignatievo had finally let him know that he overestimated their appreciation of him.

But today, as his uncle spoke of grace and deliverance, of blessing and gratitude, it seemed to Johann that he was hearing a kinder, more humble man. He still cautioned against modernity and worldly compromises, but he did so, not with the severity of a prophet of doom but as a troubled visionary who sensed that he could not forestall the future. Absent were the invectives against intermarriage with the *Kirchliche*, against alcohol and tobacco, and against *Abende* — the 'evenings' of music and drama which he blamed for the falling away of youth from church life in Russia, and whose popularity among Mennonites had only increased in Canada. Instead, he spoke simply and passionately of the love and grace of God and of the single commandment of Christ to love one another and their neighbours. He closed with a fervent prayer of thanksgiving for the bounty of fields and gardens, and for the flourishing of this tiny congregation — "a tendril," he called it, "transplanted at last, in the soil of this new land, after so many seasons of travail and sorrow in the old." After the final hymn, the congregation stood for the benediction, and the festival of thanksgiving ended.

After the service, most of the former Sergejewka villagers came to the farm for *Faspa*. The uncles wanted a tour, and they admired what they saw. Onkel Herman walked slightly bent, with hands clasped behind his back, his pointed beard bobbing as he nodded emphatically now and then at evidence of industry and skill.

"If farmers in our Winkler district are generally more prosperous," he declared, "they would be hard-pressed to find poultry and horseflesh superior to yours. Just be very sure, Johann, that you have enough land and cattle for your children. Keep the boys close. You don't want them straying to the city where so many of our people are already adrift."

The Wohlgemuths and Koslowskys had cows to milk and did not stay after the meal. When only immediate family remained, letters from Russia were brought out to be read aloud. In Sergejewka, Tante Anna's brother Jakob had collapsed entirely. No longer able to speak or use the wheelchair, he was confined to his bed. The Walter brothers had abandoned the farm and left for the mines in Donetsk. Of the factory nothing remained. Even the stone fence and chimney had been pulled down, and the bricks carted off for repurposing elsewhere. Thistles and badger holes covered the ground where the complex had stood.

*'Just be grateful you are well out of this!'* wrote Jakob's wife, Maria. *'If we could meet in person, there would be so much more that I would tell you that I cannot write. But perhaps I need not spell it out.'*

Johann's sister-in-law Neta was more explicit, though still cautious enough to have circumvented the censor. Twice after Peter's release from prison, they had travelled to Moscow and were refused exit visas. The second time, they were singled out from the rest of their group and placed on a train to Bakhmut. They had made their way to one of the villages in nearby Ignatievo, where they were living in a single room. Their resources were exhausted, and with winter on the way, there was no fuel and very little food. The letter was scratched in pencil on flyleaves torn from Neta's hymnbook. She apologized for the desecration, but it was the only paper she could find.

*'We still don't know why Peter was arrested,'* she wrote. *'They accuse him of being an agitator, for what they do not say, perhaps for emigration. He is afraid to say much of anything about his treatment in prison. He is very weak and quiet, and he has difficulty with his hands. Perhaps you are unable to imagine things worse than the famine of 1921-22, but to us such things are now abundantly revealed. Then, we still had our houses. Now, we cannot have a house if we don't work. But Peter cannot work without a permit, and because he was a convict they will not give him one. And without a work permit, also no ration card. The NEP is abolished and everywhere there is talk of Kollektive. In Sergejewka there is no longer much of anything to 'kollekt,' so perhaps we can go back there. They might let us keep a cow and we could buy a little flour.'*

After the guests had left, Johann went to help finish the milking, and as always, he was the last to leave the barn. As he loved to do at the end of the day, he stood alone in the centre of the yard. The wind had expired, and the air had cooled abruptly after the sun went down. The silence was deep, and he could hear the croak of frogs in the slough a quarter mile away. Between him and the last sliver of a harvest moon, stood a stand of willows silhouetted against the western sky. Above him, the splash of the Milky Way lay across the vastness of the heavens. Of the few correspondences between life on this farm and Johann's memories of Sergejewka, the night sky was among the most poignant. How often he had stood on

the banks of the *konstje* at night after the labours of the day and watched
the reflections of the moon and stars wrinkling the waters.

"*Die Himmel erszählen,*" he murmured, recalling the psalm his uncle had
quoted in his sermon. "Yes, indeed. The heavens declare the glory of God,
and the firmament sheweth his handiwork." He relaxed his shoulders and
released a deep breath.

The porch door slammed, and Johann turned to see the two oldest boys
bounding down the steps and through the garden to the edge of the
nearest field. Jasch was carrying the rifle. There were fat Canada geese
roosting on the slough after gleaning fallen grain all day in the harvested
fields. "They are always welcome on the dinner table," thought Johann.
"But they won't be an easy target in this light."

Anna had followed the boys into the night air, tut-tutting about hunting
on the Lord's day. She stood on the stoop drying her hands, and when she
saw Johann in the yard, she draped the towel over the railing and came to
where he was standing. Her tentative laugh was a probe of his mood.
"Nah, Johann, what are you doing out here alone in the dark?"

"It's Thanksgiving, Anna. I'm counting my blessings."

"And they are ... ?"

"They are many, Anna," he said. In the dark, she could not see that he was
smiling. "But I have not finished counting."

It was a sign that he wished to be alone. She squeezed his arm and went
back to the house.

Johann sat down on one of the boulders encircling the flower bed. He felt
strangely buoyant, struck by a sudden persuasion that the trials and
sorrows of this life, severe though they might be, were not more true than
the immeasurable blessings of the Lord — the beauty of the earth, the
joys of family, the gratification of honest work, and the gift of community. He felt embraced by Providence, as though, despite the immensity
and timelessness of the universe, he could not ultimately be lost in it. It
was in this frame of mind that he surveyed the past and looked to the
future.

He remembered the day almost five years ago when he and his family had
first set eyes on this land. The decades of accumulated filth; the fallen

sheds; the barn roof leaking like a sieve, and sagging to meet the mountains of manure inside; the untended fields; the house unpainted in fifty
years of occupancy; the unspeakable privy. All that and much besides had
been put right in the years since. His family had regained its health and
strength. Peterchen's doctor had described his illness as 'a very close
affair.' His recovery was ongoing, but he was gaining weight and colour.
Anna still suffered from headaches, but they were reduced in intensity
and frequency. The Russian hunger of the 1920s was a distant memory,
and both *Butter und Wurst* were now in abundant supply. '*We have
indeed come through,*' he thought to himself.

He had no doubt there would be more hardship. There was the burden
of debt. Two-thirds of the family's *Reiseschuld,* more than $600, was
still owing to the CPR, and the Mennonite Board of Colonization,
which had guaranteed the loan, was growing impatient. There was also
the mortgage, more onerous now that grain prices had crashed. But
each year he and his sons wrested a few more acres from the willow
bogs, and the land was good. The new Marquis wheat he had tried for
the first time this year had proved rust-resistant, and had yielded
almost twice as much as the older Red Fife. His herd had grown to
fifteen milk cows and forty beef cattle. There was still too little money,
but tax credits were promised in exchange for labour on drainage
projects and upgrades to the high road, which were due to begin in
spring.

It was true that, in many respects, Johann still felt like a stranger in the
land. His nearest neighbours had been unfailingly generous in their
assistance, but they were either third-generation English settlers or
*Kanadier* Mennonites whose ways he did not always understand. Trips to
town still ended in embarrassments of language. In Winnipeg, the reply
to his garbled enquiry into the price of Christmas candy confused him.
Instead of "You pay per bag," he had heard "You paper bag!" *Surely some
vile idiom of the Änglische,* he thought, and walked out without making a
purchase.

On his way to Niverville in January, he had knocked at the door of the
elderly Muirs to ask if they needed anything. They asked for the mail, and
he brought them a hundred-pound bag of flour, *Mehl* for more bread
than the elderly couple would bake in a year. The old man had stared
uncomprehendingly at the gigantic sack, prodding it once or twice with
his cane. Then he took the receipt from Johann's hand and hobbled into

the bedroom. He brought out the $4.70 owing and handed it to Johann. At the door, he touched his sleeve and winked at him.

"Next time, Mr. Neufeld, the mail will be at the post office."

Despite the difficulties of adjustment, Johann could not deny that his nostalgia for the old country had dissipated. No longer did he dream longingly of Sergejewka. Instead, he was troubled by night terrors triggered by repressed trauma of war and famine. Sometimes he lay awake wondering what had become of Kozenko, who had stayed with the family for more than a year after Johann discovered him starving in the cattle pen and who had stood weeping in the street as the family left the village for the last time.

And Dachenblecher, the diminutive courier who had become a friend after his rescue of Jascha that night on the slopes of the *kurgan*. Three times, Dachenblecher had fled the pogroms during the wars. He had always returned, even after his house in Lepetykha had been torched during Easter week. Each time, he had been more despondent and wary. Now, with the Fürstenland villages virtually empty, most of his trade would have evaporated. Where was he now? Jascha said he always thought of him whenever another Chaim, the even shorter Chaim Zack, visited the farm with his wares. He sometimes stayed the night, and never failed to leave a gift.

Johann thought, too, about Kyrylenko, his fellow traveller on the journey to Volhynia. He had last seen him the day Rudenko and his gang pillaged the factory. He had his small farm, but he was getting old, and his shoulder had never healed properly. He must be struggling by now.

Always foremost in Johann's mind were the families he and Anna had left behind; their mothers, both twice widowed, lived in poverty with daughters in Sergejewka and Ignatievo. Both had refused to leave while their sons were in the army. And now it was too late. The exodus of November 1926 had been the very last permitted by the Soviet government. Johann's two nephews had arrived recently, but they were neither émigrés nor exiles; they were escapees who had exploited cracks in the wall and somehow found their way through Poland, Germany, and the Netherlands to Canada. The letter from his brother Peter and his wife suggested that sponsorships initiated from Canada might still be honoured by the Soviets, and Johann promised himself that he would look into it the next time he went to the city.

His thoughts were interrupted by the snap of a distant rifle shot. Then, a brief silence, and a second shot, followed by whoops of success. Johann rose to his feet and made his way to the summer kitchen. He lit the kerosene lamp and cleared the table. Tomorrow was Thanksgiving Monday, a holiday in Canada, and there would be roast goose for dinner. The whole family would be home, and more than likely, the young Peters fellow would come to see Njuta.

The boys saw his light and came bursting through the door of the summer kitchen, each with a huge bird slung over his shoulder.

"Pa! Two bullets, two geese!" cried Hans. It was his first success with the rifle.

"And? What now? One is more than enough, and the other will not keep!" His mock scolding amused the boys, who could not contain their excitement.

Johann helped them gut and dress the birds, and as they worked, he thought once more about the bounty of the land and the kindness of strangers. He thought of the elderly Muirs a half mile away, alone, their children and grandchildren far away in distant cities in the East. They, too, were separated from their loved ones. Perhaps, he thought, he could take one of these birds to the Muirs in the morning. Early enough to give them time to prepare it for their own Thanksgiving dinner. *Yes*, he thought, *this is something I could do. I will speak to Anna. Perhaps she will come too, and we can visit a little.*

# Afterword

From Zaporizhzhia, route M18 follows the left bank of the Dniepr, south through villages and small towns sprawled across predominantly agricultural lands. The road is in pitiful condition, and our driver grimaces at the imagined damage to his vehicle as he weaves among the gaps in the pavement.

After an hour, we leave the main road and begin arcing around the great bend in the river, skirting the vast reservoir created by the hydroelectric dam downstream at Kakhovka. On our right, the cooling towers of the Enerhodar Atomic Energy Plant are silhouetted against the sky, and beyond them, ten kilometres away on the opposite shore, smoke rises from the stacks of Nikopol's steel mills. Moments later, we pass a road sign for Michaylovka, formerly Michaelsburg, the administrative centre of the Fürstenland settlement. When the first of the Scythian *kurgans* appears between us and the river we know we are near our destination.

There is no longer an entry point from the north so we continue to Mala (Little) Lepetykha. Doubling back along a single gravelled lane we cross a deep ravine before passing briefly through a scrub forest of stunted trees and brambles. Emerging from the woods we see that we are well below the level of the steppe, but still some twenty metres above the Dniepr. Before us lies a broad terrace, the site of village #6, Sergejewka.

My brother Pete and I have left our tour group in Zaporizhzhia and come with our two daughters to find the place where Anna and Johann lived and raised their family. They were our grandparents, and Peter, our father, was their fifth child. He never expressed any interest in returning here. But his older brother Hans visited in the 1980s, and among the surviving households he could still find an elderly Ukrainian man for whom 'Schwitke' and his beautiful horses were childhood memories. Some years later the youngest brother Abram also visited with his oldest son and grandson. The village well and the foundation of the factory chimney were still there, and several old couples lived in the last hovel-like residences.

In the summer of 2018 we find only one farmyard. It has a relatively modern house and is located well away from the original village site. Our guide has been here once before, but that was twenty years ago, and she has difficulty orienting her map relative to the site. It is clear that she remembers nothing. She speaks no English and struggles to apologize with a few words in German. Bemused by her own embarrassment, she points out features already obvious: the plateau where the village stood, and the great river below. Our own research is more helpful, and we show her where a cemetery is marked on the village sketch we have brought with us. She takes the sketch back to the farmhouse and gets directions.

We find a faint trail that leads upwards and through a stand of small trees. In a few minutes we reach the cemetery and are surprised to find flowers on a fresh grave inside a picketed enclosure. The grounds are not other-wise maintained, and we find only four gravestones which the wind has combed over with generations of dead grasses. The stones are heavily eroded, and cannot give us the names of the souls they were meant to commemorate. It is a strange feeling to be standing in this silence on the anonymous graves of our ancestors.

We return to the road and cross to the other side. Tour organizers have warned us: 'There is nothing that remains of the Mennonite presence in Fürstenland.' Though we were not dissuaded, it was right of them to issue the warning. Where the village stood there is only a field of coarse hay, hemmed by dense grasses and weeds. Not a single building remains, no sign of cart trails or walking paths, or of the boundaries of the thirty-odd village lots laid out by the surveyors a century and a half ago, unless the few scattered clumps of hollyhocks are a clue. Even the main village street has been obliterated, and replaced, higher up the slope, with the lane that led us to this place.

While our daughters go to the river, my brother and I search for the well and the chimney base. We make our way across the hayfield and into the brambles on the other side. Russian thistle stands proud above the grasses, and we are reminded of our father's childhood memory of harvesting its dry seedpods to supplement scarce flour during the famines of the 1920s.

The day is bright and windless. There are no birds, and the only sound is that of flying insects. We look up into an immense blue sky, feathered with cirrus clouds, and we fail to see the nests of honey bees low on the stems of tumbleweeds, until we step into them. We are stung, and we flee back into the hay field. Pete takes a telephoto of a small mound in the distance, and we conclude that it must be the base of the factory chimney. But it is very hot and our stings are painful, so we do not go there. Instead, we return to the road, where our driver is showing signs of impatience.

Our youngest sister has sent with us a wooden ornament our father built in his workshop a few years before he died. It has a stamp with his name, and we have added 'Sergejewka' and his birth and death dates. There is a stunted tree beside the road, and Tobia and Carissa tie the artifact into one of its lower branches. It is small and fragile, and we notice that one or two of the glue joints have given way. It is likely that the wind and rain will soon claim it, and that no one will ever find it here. But for us it is a poignant moment.

Today the east bank of the Dniepr, from the nuclear power plant at Enerhodar to the Black Sea, is under military siege. The waters at Sergejewka have fallen some ten metres since the destruction of the dam at Kakhovka in June of 2022. The mighty Dniepr has retreated to its ancient channel, leaving its vast valley nearly dry, and exposing the plaven where Sergejewka's gardens once flourished. It may be that the little konstje flows again, and that over time it will purge itself of the detritus that has settled there in the years of its submersion. We cannot know. For us, what will remain in memory is the eloquent emptiness of the place where our own story is so deeply rooted.

J. Janzen & K. Neufeld Ko. ------------

**Jakob Janzen**
(1845-1917)

| Maria | 'Tante' Anna | Jakob |
|---|---|---|
| m. | m. | m. |
| Peter Enns | **Kornelius A. Neufeld** | Maria Redekopp |
| | (d. 1917) | |

Katharina
m.
**C. Wohlgemuth**

| Maria | Anna ('Annika') |
|---|---|
| m. | m. |

**Johan Koslowsky**    **Herman H. Neufeld** ('Ha Ha')
(brother of
Kornelius H. Neufeld,
'Ka Ha')

Anna
m.
Johann Neufeld

| Anna (Njuta) | Jasch(a) | Johann (Hans) | Mary | Peter |
|---|---|---|---|---|

**Bold print** = factory personnel

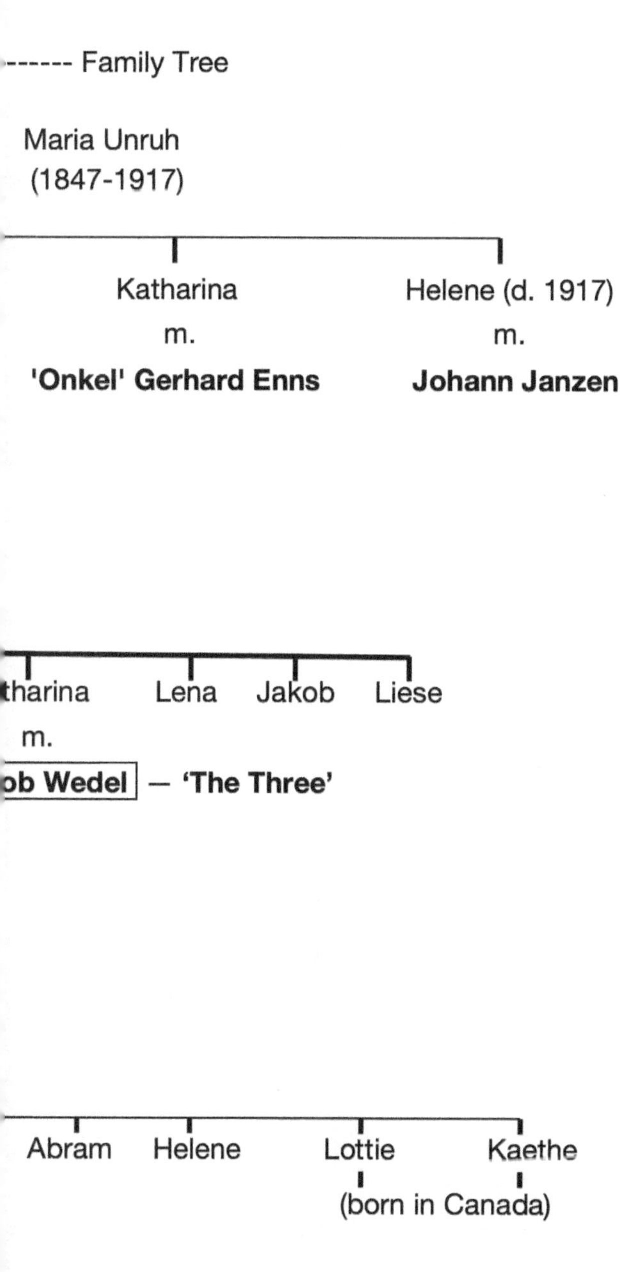
------ Family Tree

Maria Unruh
(1847-1917)

Katharina
m.
'Onkel' Gerhard Enns

Helene (d. 1917)
m.
Johann Janzen

tharina    Lena    Jakob    Liese
m.
ob Wedel — 'The Three'

Abram    Helene    Lottie    Kaethe
(born in Canada)

# Glossary

Aleksandrovsk – Zaporozhia (Russian) Zaporizhzhia (Ukrainian) city across the river from the Chortitza Mennonite colony

alles oder nix – all or nothing

Ältester – church elder

Beutel – purse, bag

Brüdergemeinde – Mennonite Brethren Church

Central Powers – Germany and its WWI allies, Austria-Hungary, Bulgaria and the Ottoman Empire

Chutor – rural estate

Dessiatine – unit of land area equal to 2.7 acres / 1.1 hectares

Dnipro – city to the north of Chortitza, formerly Ekaterinoslav

Du liebe Zeit, was denkst du – (idiomatic) for goodness sake! what can you be thinking?

Erntedankfest – Thanksgiving Day

Erweckung – spiritual revival

Faspa – (Low German) an afternoon lunch

Forestei – Russian forestry service, to which Mennonite men were assigned as an alternative to military service

Fritzi – derivative of 'Friedrich' the German Kaiser, but used as a derisive Russian term for the Germans during World War I

Fürst – duke

Gemeinde – 1. secular citizenry; 2. religious congregation

Grossfürst – grand duke

Jannedarpa – (Low German) 'the other villages' also referred to as 'the Alexanderthal villages' of the Fuerstenland colony

Judenplan — program of Jewish agricultural settlements with Mennonite farmers as mentors

Kanadier – Mennonites of the 1870s emigration to Canada

Kirchliche – the main body of Mennonites who worshipped in *Kirchen* (church buildings), as distinct from Mennonite Brethren *(Brüdergemeinde)* who initially met in their homes.

Knechte – male servants, farm labourers

Konstje – Russian word (pronounced *konst-ye*) small secondary channel of the Dniepr that cuts through Sergejewka

Kroeger – Mennonite clock manufacturer in Chortitza; clock made in the Kroeger factory

Kurgan – tumulus tomb of 4th century BCE Sythians

Landlose – landless citizens

Lebensgeschichte – memoir, autobiography

Mädchenschule – girls' school

Na? Was denn? – Well? What?

Oberschulze – regional superintendent

Oberleutnant – First Lieutenant

Old Colony – Chortitza, the original Mennonite settlement near Alexandrovsk

Pachtkolonie – colony on leased land

Plattdeutsch – Low German vernacular of the Russian Mennonites

Plaven – island in a flood plain subject to seasonal inundation

Pripps – a coffee substitute brewed with roasted barley

Regenbogen – rainbow

Reiseschuld – debt incurred by emigrants for travel via CPR ships and trains, underwritten by the Canadian Mennonite Board of Colonization

Rundschau – observer; *Die Mennonitische Rundschau* was an international German language periodical published in North America from 1880-2007

Schulze – village superintendent, mayor

Semlin – dugout dwelling with sod roof

Sich – (pronounced *sitch*) Cossack stronghold

Strassendorf – farming village aligned along a single street

Tu was – do something

Versammlung – meeting, religious service

Versammlungshaus – meetinghouse, the term the Mennonite Brethren used for their places of worship; as distinct from the 'churches' of the Kirchliche

Verst – unit of distance equal to 1.1 kilometres, 0.66 miles

Volksdeutsche – ethnic Germans

Vorwort – foreword

Wiedertäufer – the Anabaptists, who rejected infant baptism and were rebaptized as adults

Zemstvo – units of local self-government set up as part of the reforms of 1861

Zentralschule – central school, secondary school

Zuschläger – hammermen, blacksmith's assistants

# Author's Note

*Every Season Under Heaven* is a work of historical fiction. The names of principal characters are those of real people who lived in Sergejewka between its founding in the 1860s and its final collapse in about 1930. Key events in each chapter are documented in the journals of Anna Janzen Neufeld, in memoirs of members of her extended family, and in transcriptions of interviews with Anna Enns Neufeld and her children. Details relating to the origins of the Mennonite Brethren movement are taken from a letter of Jakob Janzen to P. M. Friesen, and from Friesen's *The Mennonite Brotherhood in Russia*.

I am grateful to Jonathan Seiling and his team at *Gelassenheit Publications,* and to the many friends who have supported and encouraged this project. Jon Isaak was unfailingly helpful in accessing archival materials at the Centre for Mennonite Brethren Studies in Winnipeg. David Elias and David Bergen read early chapters and offered valuable suggestions. John Whiteway read complete early drafts of the manuscript and would not let me rest. Joan Thomas and Leonard Friesen read a late draft, and their generous advice helped to clarify the text and to shorten it. Thanks, also, to Matt Broeska for technical assistance in the preparation of the maps. My deepest gratitude to my life partner, Dorothy, for her multi-faceted support during the years this project was on the boil.

Finally, this book could not exist without the labours of Peter Neudorf who, over a nine year period, deciphered and translated 70 letters of Kornelius Neufeld, and the 700-page journal of Anna Janzen Neufeld. Thank-you Peter!

Harold Neufeld is a retired educator, raised in rural Manitoba, whose childhood interest in the Russian Mennonite story was piqued, but never satisfied, by family lore.

His earlier book, *Rückblick: A Glance Backward* traces his family's origins in five different colonies in Ukraine and Russia, and explores the historic reasons for the emigrations of the 1870s and the 1920s.

He lives in Winnipeg and divides his days between the joys of grandparenthood, gardening, historical research, and the building of wooden artifacts, including several clocks.